I've been teaching in the UCLA Extension *Writers Program* for more than 30 years, and once in a while, I ask myself why. The money is lousy, and the Mothership treats us like crap — just last year, they took away our parking permits -- and then I reread the stories in a collection like *Crooked Out of Compton* and remember, *oh yeah, it's because you get to meet and teach writers like Ron Dowell.*

Ron's first class with me was in Fall 2015, and I wasn't easy on him. The talent was there, but so were some bad habits. Ron got called out a lot that year and the next. But he always listened, and he worked his ass off.

I was once a sportswriter, and my favorite sport to cover was track and field. If you watch the progress of a high school pole vaulter, they tend to plateau: 11 feet 6 inches, 11'7", 11'5", 11'8", 11'7", 11'5", and then suddenly they crack 13 feet. The body gradually learns what it needs to do to reach the next level. It's the same for writers. Depending on where you think vision lies, the mind or the brain is like a muscle. Writers train, they do the work, and then they make a leap. I can still remember the leap Ron made.

The story, the first time I saw it, in 2015, was called "Cover," a later draft was "Running for Safety," and the final draft was titled "Bruised." This final draft – the story you'll read in this collection – is the leap I discuss. The narrator is named Trina; her mother, Tamara, is dead, shot by her druggie husband, Marcus. Trina desperately tries to find her brother, Tyquan, lost in foster care. She finds out where he lives and guesses where he might go to school. The excerpt that follows is the hard-won voice, shaped by hard work, rewrite after rewrite, to perfect pitch. This is long, even though I've made some cuts. Stay with it.:

King Elementary School hugs itself with red brick and high wrought-iron bars, like a prison, in contrast to the Watts Towers' spires seen across the tracks less than two blocks away. An empty police car straddles the curb, and the uniformed officer peers out from the bars at the crowd of Black and Latina care-persons awaiting their charges.

The bell rings, gates burst open, and kids flood past me like raging water. The flood turns to a trickle, and the school police close one of two exits. I checked my watch. Is King the right school?

He's last, but Tyquan bounces away toward me, wearing a red hoodie. He's much taller now, but the hitch in his run is a dead giveaway. There was never anything physically wrong with Tyquan. I believe he imitated Marcus's swag, the slight delay and twist in his hip, the way he'd hitch his shoulder, causing his right arm to rise and move forward, graceful, like someone in control, cool even under pressure. Looking back, I think motherfuckin' Marcus was just crazy. My insides vibrate.

Crouched behind a palm tree, I await the right moment and leap into his path, "TYQUAN." My skin tingles. He ducks and covers his head as if under attack. His backpack thumps the grass. Eyes full, he double-takes.

"Trina?" he gasps, then jumps at my outstretched arms. His face blurs through my tears.

We face each other and sit cross-legged, knees touching. He looks like Marcus but has our mother's smile, and, for a moment, it's as if we're picnicking again at the Watts Towers, me wiping his butt after I happy dance.

"Are you hungry, li'l brother?"

Pop, pop, pop, gunshots sound nearby. I'm easily startled, and Mama's holey face worms into my mind. The small entry wound on Marcus' forehead was like a black asterisk. Tyquan jerks his paper-bag-brown face— he's a shade lighter than I am—and we jump up. That's when I notice a black welt below his eye. Police sirens wail past the corner. My shoulders tighten.

"That bruise—did you fight today?" He recoils when I brush the eye bruise with my thumb. His black-and-blue mark is not unlike those covering Mama's face, neck, and shoulders, her bleeding knuckles. Such injuries were clear signs that someone had enacted niggashit.

We're poised to run opposite the gunshots when a kid taller than Tyquan bully bumps between us, a red bandana tied to his bony arm. He holds up black school uniform pants hung halfway down his ass; butt crack exposed. He couldn't run from bullets or anything else if his life depended on it, but he had an attitude.

"Whaddup." He nods. "I got chronic." Tyquan ignores him. The kid struts a few yards to another curbside death memorial, a clump of candles surrounding a red baseball cap. A brown stuffed teddy bear and a sympathy card fastened to a makeshift cross read, RIP Li'l Renzo. Real G.

"Are you in a clique?" I ask Tyquan.

"Naw." He shrugs. "Everybody wears red."

"Gangsters wear much red—I'm just sayin'." My neighborhood wears blue colors. It's dumb since peach is my favorite color, more niggashit, as Mama would say, fighting over stuff we don't own, so we all wear colors of our neighborhoods even if we don't bang, which most don't. We feel safe in numbers, though, almost like family.

It's taken me far too long to find Tyquan. My chest tightens, and I hug him again.

The wiry kid passes again, slowly, and holds his pants. He frowns at Tyquan. "Whaddup, my nigga—I got sticky icky buds?"

Oh, shit. Those are fighting words in our house. Mama insisted we were never niggers or niggas, which means we struggled often.

"Back up before I bomb on your ass," I say. Chest to chest, I shove the kid into the dirt. "Bompton in the house." I bluff a gang name from my hood, a gang to which I don't belong.

The bony kid tries to stand. Tyquan kicks and leaves a single sneaker print on the boy's butt. It's two against one. The boy scowls, throws up Blood's finger signs, and hunkers away. "I'll be back," he says, disappearing into a jacaranda thicket scattered along the train tracks, scented lavender leaves in full bloom. I spread my fingers and fan myself.

"Bring your mama," Tyquan shouts. "We'll kick her ass too."

"Let's get the fuck out of here," I say, and we race toward the Towers in silence.

******

That voice, Trina's voice, backed me up and sat me

down. She was real. She was undeniable. I could listen to her all day.

It's the reversal of the old folk saying: It takes a village to raise a child. Here was a child that could raise a village. Trina is the voice of *Crooked Out of Compton*. Trina and Tyquan led to Starkaña and her crew, 'Becca and them, and then outward in concentric circles, social workers, therapists, cops, crooks and college boys, whores and homeboys, moms and civil servants, politicians, gadflies, concerned citizens, nurses, sign-spinners, hopeless high-school heroes, killers, divas, drummasters, Rastafarians, bullshit poets, cannabis salespeople and their adversaries, car thieves and Harriet Tubman. The saints, sinners, geniuses, cowboys and vaqueros, lunatics, and odd gods that make up the world of Compton distilled by Ron Dowell.

What I respond to here is the obvious regard that Ron has for the place and the people. It is the same regard you find with John Steinbeck for *Cannery Row* or Gloria Naylor for *The Women of Brewster Place*; neighborhoods like Compton are not beloved by realtors but with heart, grit, and soul. *Crooked Out of Compton* speaks to that same flawed striving give-me-one-more-chance human forgiving sensibility. And if you've gotten this far, you really need to read the book.

— LOU MATHEWS

Crooked out of Compton is a phantasmagoria of fantasy, horror, and urban life centered around the iconic city. Dowell has an ear for street talk, which shows in his realistic characters in this collection of short stories. These tales reflect the community's concerns from the 1960s to the present.

— DR. MAXINE THOMPSON, CEO,
BLACK BUTTERFLY PRESS

CROOKED OUT OF COMPTON explores South L.A. in all of its grim yet vivid glory, populated by a community fighting to be seen and understood — and Ron Dowell does just that, depicting the inhabitants of South L.A. with powerful urgency and humanity. These are characters intent on remaking themselves one small step at a time despite the violence that pervades their worlds and the justice and social services systems far too broken to offer anything but heartache. An unforgettable collection that will indelibly imprint itself on your brain.

— COLETTE SARTOR, AUTHOR OF ONCE REMOVED, WINNER OF THE FLANNERY O'CONNOR AWARD FOR SHORT FICTION.

In "Crooked Out of Compton," Ron Dowell masterfully takes us on a journey to the Hub city of Compton, a rabbit hole adventure like no other. Once we land in this potholed, drug-infested war zone, we are hit with another world's sights, smells, and sounds. We are introduced to some unforgettable characters as we navigate a land peopled with rogue cops, uncaring politicians, crooked government officials, lost mental health workers, apathetic foster parents, crackheads, and gang members.

The sight of young love and sibling tenderness touches me. I get an adrenaline rush fleeing the cops but hold on to your seats – every chapter pulls you into another dimension. The landscape is familiar – dilapidated parks, crowded living spaces, irresponsible churches, and hospitals. It seems like a nightmare for Blacks and Hispanics trapped in this never land. This is a look at racism at its best. If Mr. Dowell sent us a special invite, it would undoubtedly read, "From Compton with love and squalor."

— PATRICIA FORTE, AUTHOR,
SCREENWRITER, AND INSTRUCTOR AT
A.C. BILBREW WRITERS' WORKSHOP

Ron Dowell is a brilliantly imaginative writer who does not hesitate to take chances. "Crooked Out of Compton" demonstrates that fact. The first story in the book of short stories is a KafKaesque work that begins in the Palm Lake Projects Circa 1962, Watts, Los Angeles—got that?

What follows is a blizzard of seventeen stories. None of them are "easy" to read; the nuances insist that we pay close attention to what's being said. Or simply hinted at. Ron Dowell's poetic use of different language styles, from nerdy ghettoese to international jargon, takes us 'way outside of the UNUSUAL.

For example: A first generation – surface reading of the stories might seem to indicate that the works are concerned only with besieged people being forced to self-medicate "by any means necessary." 'Til we delve into the motivations of those who are supplying the medication.

There's no getting around it; the brother is deep. When was the last time you've smelled the funk, the aroma of a person, place or thing? If a sensitive reader takes the time to feel into what they are reading, what the writer is really writing about – check out "Crooked" to experience how it's done.

— ODIE HAWKINS, "THE UNDERGROUND MASTER," HAS WRITTEN THIRTY-TWO NOVELS, SHORT STORY COLLECTIONS, ESSAYS, TELEVISION SCRIPTS, AND RADIO AND FILM SCRIPTS. HE WAS ONE OF THE ORIGINAL MEMBERS OF THE FAMED WATTS WRITERS WORKSHOP, ESTABLISHED BY BUDD SCHULBERG IN THE WAKE OF THE WATTS REBELLION IN 1965

Finding your voice among the cacophony of voices clamoring to be heard is a writer's puzzle. Ron L. Dowell has shut out the hissing white noise of other writers and found his voice. His pen crafts beautiful pages of gold, original stories gleaned from the essence of his experiences growing up in Compton. In his new book of short stories, "Crooked Out of Compton," he shares stories like *Professor Roach, Dump City,* and *The Niggalators.* Respectively, they warn of the consequences of loneliness, the properties of hope, and the fear of change. Ron has not forgotten where he hails from. He writes about the people polite society tries to forget.

— ANTHONY MARTINEZ-JOHNSON,
AUTHOR OF *PHEROMONES* AND MORE.

Cops and hustlers, streetwalkers, junkies, psych techs, and fathers; Ron Dowell's collection bristles with the multidimensional energy of its namesake—Compton, CA—Hub City, L.A. Chippy, resilient, and clear-eyed, Dowell's stories are an intersecting grid from Watts to Whittier, Crenshaw to Chino, Leimert Park to Lakewood, told as only an Old School OG Angeleno could.

— PETE HSU, AUTHOR OF *IF I WERE THE OCEAN, I'D CARRY YOU HOME*

In "Crooked Out of Compton," Ron Dowell's take on a perspective of daily life in South Central Los Angeles and Compton, CA, will take you on several intriguing adventures. It reminds some and will educate others about how families lived in Black culture in the early 1960's and beyond. Speckled with undeniable imagery, it is rich with relatable accounts of day-to-day existence.

— MARTHA PICKETT-PATTERSON, *CITY OF COMPTON MANAGER, RETIRED, COMPTON ELITE COMMUNICATORS TOASTMASTERS, DTM*

CROOKED OUT OF COMPTON

RON L. DOWELL

RUNNING WILD

Crooked Out Of Compton
Text copyright © 2024 Reserved by Ron L. Dowell
Edited by Resa Alboher
All rights reserved.

Published in North America, Australia, and Europe by RIZE.
Visit Running Wild Press at www.runningwildpress.com/rize, Educators,
librarians, book clubs (as well as the eternally curious), go to
www.runningwildpress.com/rize.

ISBN (pbk) 978-1-960018-62-5
ISBN (ebook) 978-1-960018-37-3

This book is dedicated to God, my parents, my ancestors, and the people in South Central Los Angeles and beyond who helped me make it this far.

CONTENTS

PROFESSOR ROACH

It occurred to him how simple everything would be if somebody came to help him. Two strong people—he had his father and the maid in mind.

Metamorphosis
Franz Kafka
Translated by David Wyllie

C ockroaches scurried across the ceiling and down the wall, disappearing into crevices and cracks like demigods. Jubilee Washington lay on his side, then turned onto his back, breathing fast. His lids were half-closed, and his eyes gyrated.

"Wake up, wake up, Jubi. She's coming," a voice whispered in his ear.

"What?" His eyes pulled open just as the cercus of a German cockroach disappeared over his bed sheets' edge.

"Out those beds, boys!" their stepmother Naomi shouted.

He and Willie shared one of two bedrooms, a shallow living room, and a roach-turd-sized storage closet removed from the kitchen of their Palm Lane Public Housing unit in 1962 Watts, Los Angeles.

Jubilee bolted up in bed as if hit by white dwarf-star dust, scooched palms across his ebony face, and scratched his lizardy, leathery neck rash. He pulled the lamp chain atop his milk crate bookcase, which leaned sideways, filled with encyclopedias and comics about scientists who transformed into superheroes.

Willie slept, and his unwashed feet protruded from beneath his bed cover. The lightbulb warmed him and illuminated a Maury Wills poster, number 30, sliding into second base decorating the wall above Jubilee's twin bed. Go, Maury, go!

"I've got to dress—get to work—somebody's got to bring home grits, or you don't eat," Naomi said. A blues record played from her countertop radio.

Naomi was as she was every morning: amber skin, blue Spoolies in hair she'd hot-ironed the night before, dressed in a faded yellowish slip with small green flowers and furry pink house shoes. She turned and returned to the kitchen, leaving the door open to the smell of frying bacon and cooked grits. Cigarette smoke clung to the air like wet paper sticks to the glass.

"Get the hell in here, now. Or go live with your dope-head mama—if you can find her." Naomi always yakked, reminding Jubilee how his birth mother vanished. Finally, Naomi muttered something he never understood about Daddy, their bedroom, and other women.

Yes, his family was unlike Beaver Cleaver's or Ozzie Nelson's on TV, but if his birth mother ever returned—

Always edgy, Jubilee wanted to blend into the background

unnoticed, invisible, like a sofa roach. If only he could disappear too or transform like comic heroes.

"Yes, Naomi," Jubilee said. "I'm dressed, waiting for Willie." He threw a ball of socks, hitting Willie in the face. "Get your tail up before she comes in swinging a belt."

A pregnant roach moved unruffled across the windowsill, the ootheca sticking from her back end: sixteen babies would hatch from the egg sac in a few weeks. He dared not settle back to sleep. Instead, he watched the mother roach as she disappeared into a window putty crack. Small, dark, and ever-present roaches ruled.

Willie glared at Jubilee, then snatched the covers over his head and coughed. "You don't tell me what to do," he said, voice muffled.

An argument with Willie would undoubtedly bring back Naomi swinging her favorite leather belt. The thick belt Daddy sometimes used to support his tool pouch. She'd turn passionate as a plantation overseer beating recaptured enslaved people. She rarely drew blood, but her lashes raised webs of purplish-black welts. Her first, second, and third belt licks would be for Jubilee, who stood in t-shirts and drawers between their beds. Willie never got whipped. Jubilee rubbed his neck rash and flung the pillow aside before making his bed.

Willie's sleep had been fitful. *Huh, huh*—Willie's shrill whistle and labored wheeze sounded as if his only air source was through a straw. The wheeze signaled his whereabouts, and an imminent asthma attack almost drowned out clattering cans, dishes, and blues radio music in the kitchen. He drooled and, habitually, felt around for an asthma inhaler on the sturdy nightstand between their beds onto which Jubilee's bookshelf leaned. Jubilee reached out to help. "I can do it myself—I ain't retarded." Eyes cold, Willie sucked the medicine and made odd noises.

Jubilee's chest tightened when Naomi reappeared and said, "Don't give me that *yes, Naomi* shit, Jubilee. Move it—you're just like your cheatin' daddy—humph! Handyman, my ass," she said. "What handyman plumbs all night?" There'd be breakfast for three, again. "Plumbing other women, I bet." Daddy spent many days away from home fixing electrical problems, carpentry, and nighttime drain cleaning. Or, at least, that's what he said between fights and arguments. Naomi's tone softened. "Willie—get up, honey. You wouldn't want to be tardy for school." Like Naomi, Willie's skin was fair. The other kids called him *high yellow,* unlike Jubilee's *coal-black.* He even called their stepmother *mama.* Maybe Jubilee should catch asthma.

She turned for the kitchen again. "I try to do what your dope-head mother didn't...." Naomi said, "my best...." Once more, she banged utensils and cans. "All I do, cleanin' rich folks' houses—them callin' me nigger," she groaned while shaking her head. "Lord, Lord. When I save enough, I'm gettin' the hell out of here."

"We're on our way right now, Naomi!" Jubilee said to the empty doorway. Would she take him or just Willie with her? His heart jumped up and down. What if he was light-skinned?

Dishes clattered. Something was different, and Jubilee seemed more aware of dripping water from her leaky sink faucet and a ghost flush from the toilet behind a closed bathroom door, which stalled his breath and disoriented him. Usually, his bedroom gave him cover, and he'd never noticed those creaky sounds.

"You ain't gonna be shit either, just like your daddy," Naomi said. Jubilee's skin tightened, and his mind and his body were numbed. Head throbbing, he ground his teeth from side to side. Beneath his breath, he said, "Go to hell." He breathed deeply. A handyman's belt would stripe his flesh if he said that aloud. Maybe he should call her step-mommy or, better yet, stepmother to mark that she wasn't his birth mother but a mother anyway. It'd been six years, and he was still unsure what to call her.

"Show me the damn school project before I leave," Naomi said from the kitchen. "Isn't it due?"

Jubilee's stomach fluttered. Yes, Step-mommy—Coming, Stepmother—I love you too, Step-mama. How would that sound? —Nah.

"Uh, yes, Naomi," Jubilee said. "Tomorrow. It's due tomorrow. I've started it."

"Have the belt ready for me when I get home if you don't," Naomi said. "At least try and graduate when your time comes."

His teacher had said to prepare a class report, a project from life sciences—a pet is okay. *Do no stories about comic book heroes, please.*

Pets weren't allowed in public housing, and his mind shut down when TV news showed the world beyond Palm Lane— Negroes were called niggers and beaten by white police and fed to their German Shepherds.

Despite housing rules, the baby turtle Daddy had bought him as a birthday gift managed to escape the small, uncovered plastic aquarium bowl. Weeks later, Jubilee could not teach a caged parrot to say "shit" before someone stole the bird when he placed it outdoors for air.

What was a ten-year-old supposed to do? A roach ambled across his yellow Pee-Chee folder, stopped, and stood erect on two hind legs, waving its feelers toward Jubilee. Hmmm. That's it—*roaches*. Whoa. He'd lived with them all his life and had studied them in the encyclopedia and school library. He'd report on what he knew.

* * *

That night, Naomi rubbed down Willie's chest with VapoRub, had him swallow a dollop, and dabbed a glob under and inside his nose. The scents of camphor and menthol helped charge Jubilee, and he stayed awake, putting the finishing touches on his Mona Lisa. Then, finally, he'd blot out thoughts about his birth mother.

Like Leonardo da Vinci, he made careful, deft tints and shades with strokes, barely resembling crayons and Testors model car paints. He used a white polish from Daddy's shoebox and a charcoal briquette to draw an American cockroach on poster board. Dark brown was for compound eyes and cercus sensors near its anus: purple metal flake for the roach labium bottom lip, fire truck red for the maxilla mouth, sky blue for the mandible organ for biting, beret green for the labrum top lip, and gummi yellow for its clypeus to show the faceplate. In front of which, he glued grits and bacon bits to illustrate what they ate since they liked starch, sugary foods, grease, and meats, items found in abundance among the cans in Naomi's kitchen. They chewed sideways, but he couldn't draw that.

He drew the insect in side view crouched on Naomi's countertop, the size of a bread loaf, alongside her plastic lime-green sugar canister beside her stove. Two antennae, to smell stuff, pointed up and forward at a sixty-degree angle from one another. His cockroach drawing had six hairy legs and eighteen knees for a fast getaway.

He'd make Naomi smile like when she left her bedroom after a night with Daddy and listening to the radio. Then, once finished, Jubilee slept only to awaken occasionally, admire his work, and float on the lightness in his chest.

* * *

In the morning's white light, Jubilee sat on his bed, scratching himself. Roaches, male and female, big and small, young and old, watched him. In a corner, two cockroaches scurried toward the baseboard crevice as wide as a nickel thick. The brown adult roach, no longer than a pinto bean, and the younger nymph, runty, bell-shaped, and black, stopped and seemed to look back toward Jubilee, at each other, and back at Jubilee. Their antennae waved wild like palm fronds in a storm before they turned and vanished. Jubilee, mouth dry, hands sweaty and fidgety, repeatedly clicked his middle fingernail and thumbnail and looked at Willie, who was still in bed.

Willie finally snapped up, grabbed a rubber flip-flop, and crashed it on a roach facing his inhaler on the nightstand. Did bugs have asthma, too?

Willie struck a second time with more force.

"ROACHES," he snorted. He crushed the brown skin and orange blood mess three times as if he could discourage other roaches, which no doubt watched before he flung the sandal to the cold floor tile.

Jubilee cringed, shook his aching head, and looked down. Something inside of him burned. His lungs pumped his rib cage with each blow. "KILLER" he shouted.

"UGH." Willie stretched the sound as only a third grader would and eased toe-jammed feet into his flip-flops beside his unmade bed. He pointed to the roach drawing atop Jubilee's bed cover, the bed that Jubilee had already made Cub Scout tight. "It's UGLY," Willie said. "It looks real—what's its name?"

"Ralph."

"How do you know it's a boy?"

"He looks just like you—he's got your head."

Willie blinked several times as if considering the possibility.

Roaches scrambled helter-skelter in a glass jar on the floor

7

next to Jubilee's bedpost. Willie pulled on a Goofy t-shirt, tilted his head to the side, and asked, "What's that?" He kneeled in close, whiffed a smell, and wrinkled his nose.

The day before, like a scientist, Jubilee constructed a simple trap. He attached a piece of paper with a rubber band around an empty jar for traction, spread Vaseline along the inside lip to prevent escape, and placed a few raisins inside to capture several different-sized roach subjects.

"It's a magic bubble," Jubilee said. "They'll live a month without food, but I feed them daily to keep them happy." He lifted the jar above his head to admire his work and brushed his finger across raised letters, *Smucker's Jam.* "That's roach stink you smell."

His research said roaches discharged nauseating secretions from their mouths, and their turds left a long-lasting smell where deposited. Naomi would be glad to know, pleased to have him help her with his roach information. He'd even included her kitchen in the background of Ralph's portrait. Maybe he'd ask if he could call her Step Mama.

Willie narrowed his eyes and curled his lips. He lunged for the magic bubble, and they wrestled. Willie kicked Jubilee's shin. Jubilee resisted an impulse to smash the jar onto Willie's head; his charges might injure themselves if he did, so he held the jar firmly out of his brother's reach. Instead, he kneed Willie's groin and called him nigga.

Willie held himself before grabbing a fistful of comic books and throwing them at Jubilee. "I ain't no nigger," he said. "I'ma tell Mama. Who do you think you are—Professor Roach?"

In the bathroom, Jubilee sprinkled water on his face, brushed his teeth, popped into a Dodger #19 Junior Gilliam t-shirt, and squeezed the magic bubble and poster tight under his arm in case Willie wanted to fight again. Even Willie agreed. Ralph looked realistic.

* * *

For some strange reason, the smell of grease caused Jubilee's mouth to water more than usual. The scent compelled him into the kitchen for breakfast Naomi always prepared before sending Daddy off to work, whether Daddy came home or not. This was a *not* morning.

"Here's my project," Jubilee said, looking up to Naomi standing over the stove, arms folded, smoking a cigarette. Always within easy reach, Daddy's belt sagged over the empty chair back.

He delicately placed the poster, with the jar on top, on the dining table, over service for three, hands tucked into his armpits and thumbs pointed up. Naomi turned from the stove burners to him and flinched. "OHHH, no, you didn't—you didn't do your project on filthy roaches—did you?" She shivered, dropped her chin to her chest, and leaned over the poster. She tapped her cigarette ash on the drawing, which Jubilee hastily wiped away.

"Owww!" he screamed, falling into the table when Naomi's leather belt lashed his back.

"Lawd, have mercy," she said between strikes. "Help me beat the devil out of this child."

Jubilee's body collapsed into itself, arms falling to his side. He sat at the table, swiped at tears, rolled the poster board around the jar, placed it near the front door, and returned to his seat.

He'd never liked Naomi's runny eggs, yet they sparked him up. He drooled as he rubbed his burning arms and back. "I should've known you'd mess up—you call that a school project?" Jubilee turned his body, and the chest aches returned to him when Willie killed the nightstand roach. Head down, eyes moist. His throat grew scratchy and thick. She kept squawking, "I'm gonna pray for you."

It was best he not niggle. For him to tell Naomi about his research or how roach infestation caused skin rash, asthma, diarrhea, and how roaches dropped disease-carrying organisms from their legs on food and utensils could mean another beating. All-purpose Pepto Bismol remedy was always on her kitchen shelf. He scratched at his neck rash. What would happen to him now?

"Huh, huh, huh—" Willie wheezed to the table, lethargic.

"Willie, you've got to be smarter than your black-ass brother—do a real project—a space rocket." She clasped his cheeks and kissed Willie's forehead. "Something you can get a real job with."

Jubilee's chest became unusually stiff. He pinched his lips tight to keep them from trembling and remained silent. Didn't everybody in Palm Lane have roaches? Haters.

Cockroaches hustled from unit to unit, faking their death, and never starved, regardless of how often Naomi swept crumbs and cleaned the apartment. They marched through another hole after Daddy plugged one of many gaps in brick-dust-splotched work shoes with dried paint around his nail cuticles.

A time before, Daddy smelled like oil when he showed Jubilee how to use the pump action tube attached to a canister. "Try not to breathe this stuff when you spray them. That's it, my little nigga, grip the tube tight," he had said, grinning as if to convey some secret knowledge. However, Jubilee could never hold his breath long enough, and the fumes made him retch and puke. Roaches were hard to kill; they had families Jubilee could see but could not touch. "Next, I'll talk to you about women," Daddy had told Jubilee.

Jubilee's chest seized, gripping it with his right hand, body bent over the table. An unusual throbbing headache formed in the back of his head, but it was time to get off to a school where, now, he didn't much want to go.

* * *

Jubilee's was the final presentation before the last bell. Mrs. Johnson, the teacher, sat in a rumpled sailor-type pink blouse off to the side of her classroom, leaving her wooden desk upfront for student displays like Dot's and most students presenting before him. Forty restless students sat front to back in five rows. Half of them lived in Palm Lane and had roaches like him; the other half lived in new single-family homes surrounding Palm Lane, which had no cockroaches they'd acknowledge. Dot wore black and white Oxford shoes from the new homes and reported on her pet German Shepherd, Rex, which made Jubilee shake and his stomach hard.

In his dirty button-down shirt and scruffy khakis Larry described the candiru as a crazy Amazon vampire catfish that sucked anything with blood.

Curtis talked about a man named Gregor Samsa, who had turned into a roach. He said, "who's to say that we as humans didn't evolve from roaches millions of years ago?" Jubilee's heart seemed to freeze, then pounded. The other students shrugged, narrowed their eyes, and gave blank looks. Jubilee's insides vibrated. "YES," he said while smoothing his clothing. Perhaps he and Curtis had more in common than lunchtime peanut butter and jelly sandwiches.

"Ha!" scoffed Dot. "Mrs. Johnson said life science—not a fiction report, stupid." Her classmates laughed. "—project's boy," she said.

Jubilee's skin crawled, and his eyelids gummed up. He offered Curtis a watery smile. What did they know? Dummies.

Curtis ambled, then sprinted into the comfort of Mrs. Johnson's hug, unable to complete his report. "Nice job, Curtis." He wept into her bosom. "Some of your classmates might not yet accept that they could have evolved from insects before apes."

Except for Curtis's, the reports were boring and dull, making Jubilee sleepy. He kept his head still and glanced sidelong at his classmates on his way to the front.

"Uh, uh, roaches have three life stages," Jubilee said. He taped the roach portrait to the chalkboard behind him.

"Oh no, not another roach story," Dot said derisively.

Larry screamed from the back row, "Show us a trick and change into a roach!" Classmates giggled and moved around in their seats.

Mrs. Johnson shushed them, her crooked alabaster pointer finger at her thin lips.

Jubilee stood before the classroom and looked at the ceiling to avoid eye contact with his classmates. "Egg, baby, and grownup—ah, like this one—they're ghost white when born but molt, turn brown in a few hours."

Jubilee pulled the magic bubble from a paper bag and placed it on the teacher's desk. The captive roaches ran around crazily. He swallowed a lump when students in the front row shifted in their seats.

"That's nasty," a classmate from the new homes said. "You can tell he lives in the projects." Class laughter. Those words and stinging welts from Naomi's earlier belt distracted him. Mrs. Johnson nodded encouragement. Jubilee wrung his hands and pushed on.

"Cockroaches like to live, ah, close to people—in their trash cans, bathrooms, televisions, and radios." A girl with lime-green barrettes in her hair sitting before him winced and moaned.

Jubilee leaned on his heels to emphasize words. "They eat what we eat and more, such as blood, excrement, spit—and even the fingernails and toenails of babies and sleeping or sick persons."

Some students buried their faces in their hands. The girl in front looked groggy, raised her hand, and said, "Can I go to the bathroom, Mrs. Johnson?" She was dismissed to the restroom.

"I've never seen roach's fight. They probably don't argue and fuss either," Jubilee said. He'd never seen it in his research but said, "Roaches respect each other."

"Good job, Jubilee," the teacher said to him. Jubilee swiped nervous tears pooling behind his eyelids and wobbled back to his seat.

"Roach boy," a kid from the new homes said.

"Professor Roach," Jubilee shot back at him. *Crack!* Unnerved, Jubilee dropped the magic bubble, which crashed onto the linoleum tile, and his subjects ran every which way. Half his classmates lit for the door or stood on their chairs as the dismissal bell rang.

* * *

That night Jubilee lay half-awake, watching his roommates crawl across the ceiling. He turned to his right side, closed his eyes, turned to the left side, then back again, his head and chest throbbing. Something inside him wanted to leap out. Jubilee blinked into the bleakness on his back as the roaches concluded their trek across the bedroom ceiling. Willie breathed better, coughing a little in his sleep. After preparing a dinner of the usual greasy meat, beans, collards, and dessert pie, Naomi snored. Her cigarette smoke lingered in the cramped apartment.

All seemed to go well as his sleepy eyes finally closed for good when a squeaky voice startled him.

"Hzzz, Jubilee, Jubi—*click*, wake up, wake up," the voice said into his right ear.

"I don't wanna get up right now." He turned his head to face the voice.

A roach scaled Jubilee's pillow; its mouth wide open. Jubilee wanted to flee but froze, rooted to the bed. Was this a Willie trick? Of course, but in his bed, Willie panted and drooled. Jubilee clasped his rib cage like he'd been stabbed from inside with a fingernail file and began to whimper like a sick puppy.

"Hzzz, *click, click*, yes, I'm Ralph, your old friend. Don't you remember me, Jubi?" said the roach.

His heartbeat pounded in his ears, and he became sensitive to the hardness of his cotton-filled pillow, cigarette smoke, Willie's wheeze, and the ghost flush. Jubilee grabbed the back of his head to staunch the pain. His head flinched away from and then back into the coffee-colored eyes of the visitor.

"*Click, click*. I warned you, Friend, when Naomi approached yesterday morning. I posed for your beautiful portrait—hzzz, such a lovely job you did, too. It's award-winning."

"Friend?" Jubilee's voice quickened. "What do you mean —*friend*?" He leaned in closer to evaluate the visitor's reddish-brown appearance. He swallowed hard, eyebrows lowered and pinched together. "Why are you on my bed?"

The roach stood erect on two of his six legs, crossed the other four, and sneered.

"*Click*, hee-hee, ha, ha, ha! Let me explain it to you."

When Ralph laughed, his two antennae feelers stood straight above his tiny head, labrum and labium lips moving side to side in one direction, exposing his maxilla, which moved opposite. He was no bigger than a pistachio nut. Willie stirred and repositioned his smelly feet, too knocked out by asthma medicine. Jubilee rolled his eyes, sat up, and shook his head. Nothing made any sense.

Ralph pointed to his right with two legs where four other roaches crouched, an adult and three nymphs. "Meet my wife, Tush." Jubilee nodded his head. Tush grinned and opened her mouth to offer him mushed-up bacon bits and excrement.

"These three beauties are our nymphs, Ticky, Tasha, and Tedra. Aren't they wonderful? Hzzz—and single," Ralph said.

His lower rib pinched. Jubilee clasped nodules on both sides of his rib cage. He shook his head, glanced around for answers, and frowned. "WILLIE," he said. Willie gulped for breath but didn't budge. Instead, Jubi pressed his fists into two nodes growing on the back of his head. "What's happening to me?" His mind raced, his body trembled, and sweat poured. Jubilee jumped from the bed, trying to push down the two rib nodules protruding from his body. The ache at the back of his head worsened. He crumpled back onto the bed; thoughts scrambled. He tried to squish down the head nodes, now matching the length of his rib nodules.

Ralph, animated, used broad gestures as if to describe the earth's vastness.

"*Click*, we were here before humans—you could say we're immortal," Ralph said. "Unconquerable—omnipotent."

Jubilee's head nodes outpaced the rib nodule's growth in length two-to-one. He sighted himself in the mirror on the closet door across from his bed. The rib nodules grew right before his widened eyes. They started to look like long hairs, but they were straight, unlike the coiled hair he was accustomed to. The chest nodules burst through his pajama t-shirt. The nightmare might end if he tried to sleep, but his pillow grew more substantial, and soon his feet, which once touched the footboard, reached only halfway down the mattress. He squeezed his eyes shut and called, "Mama," though no mother came.

"Don't worry. You'll have family everywhere, and we have many adventures ahead, such as the space mission I once took with Col. John Glenn—you do know of him, don't you? I crawled across his space helmet and said to him, 'This is a small step for roaches and a giant leap for all roach-kind!'"

Jubi pictured Ralph's family, wife, daughters, and the warmth between them he'd never known in his apartment. Naomi had never introduced him as anything other than *the boy*.

Jubilee's life had sucked—his missing mama, Naomi, Daddy, Willie, police, German Shepherds, the class report, oh, that report, like a bad dream, made his lungs constrict, the heart slow, breaths hard. His head nodes grew, and his body shrank. His entire torso contorted when Jubilee crossed two rib nodules and his two arms to challenge Ralph's story. Gravity pushed his head forward; he fell to the mattress onto his knees and groaned, "Ralph, help me."

His ribs quaked as if hit by Naomi's belt. The head nodes slowed, but the rib nodules grew. His eyes moistened; he sniffled, sobbed, and snotted a green and sticky nasal discharge. His shoulders trembled and curled; his spine bent over forward. He couldn't process his changing body and peed himself. The nymphs bustled and dry-washed their tarsus, maybe awaiting a cue from Ralph to attack the piss.

"Look at yourself, Jubi. Embrace power, my son. You'll have six hairy legs and eighteen knees and will scale the highest wall."

"What'll happen to me now?" Jubilee asked, unable to control his transformation.

"You'll be fine—you can do this, Jubi. You'll dive into

Neptune's depths and hold your breath underwater for forty minutes. You'll see fossils of our distant relatives."

The mirror threw back the change. Jubi's body had turned into a pale white skeleton shell the size of a cantaloupe; the two hairs grew and waved uncontrolled above his head, now a fraction of its original size and shaped like a triangle. The rib nodules matched the length of his arms, and each developed three knees. His legs resembled both. His throat became sore.

"These hurt—please, Lord," Jubi wailed. "I'll call Naomi *Mama*."

"Sure, sure. Naomi will be glad to hear that from you," Ralph said, fatherly and sarcastic.

"Not to worry, my son," Tush said. "I'll feed, guard, and keep you close to me as we Blattaria moms have done for millions of years."

Ralph leaned in, faceplate beaming. Isn't this what he always wanted?

"There now... it's inevitable, Jubi. We've watched you for months. You appreciated us when everyone else treated us like shit," Ralph said. "You took the time to know us, and we want to help your transcendence."

Jubilee's feelers flew up. He was now potato size and vanilla ice cream color.

"Tedra kissed Willie one night while he slept, sucked his drool. Ticky nibbled his toenails. Ten o'clock every night, we frolic," Ralph said. "Naomi owns the apartment by day—we own the night."

The size of a grape, Jubi flinched and made odd noises in his throat. "Hzzz, *click, click*, MAMA, I'm having a nightmare!" Jubi tried to awaken himself, but he wasn't asleep. Still, no one came. Instead, his new mouth moved from side to side. He controlled the two feelers and found he could smell food with them and sense danger from behind with his cercus ass sensor. Most important, he had an appetite for anything his feelers detected, like glue inside shoes, which caused his mouth to water.

POOF, he was eye to eye with Ralph, process complete, his color ecru, his exoskeleton not yet hard or deep brown.

Jubi's midgut rumbled. He dumped a load onto the bed and turned to smell it with his feelers. Tasha used her whole body to block off her sisters and devoured the turd. Jubi was a part of something bigger than he was, and he could get used to being a roach, or Blattaria, as Tush called them, which sounded less derogatory.

Jubi rolled over on his back and laughed until his sides hurt. He was the big brother and covered for Willie but always had an unshakable sense of something wrong. No one covered him. It'd been a long time since he laughed about anything.

He hurried across the rickety bookcase and the nightstand and wrapped his labium over a portion of Willie's toenail. He manipulated the food with his mandible and maxilla after biting into the protein-laden keratin, which tasted chalky and meaty. No longer trapped by human defect, he gulped, righted himself on a sheet fold, and flipped his antennae back.

He shimmied down the bedpost into the baseboard crevice and waited. Willie snatched the cover around his head, fisted sleep from his eyes, and reached for the inhaler.

"Outta those beds, boys!" Naomi shouted from the kitchen. Sooner or later, she'd appear but wouldn't recognize the new Jubilee.

Jubi squatted. He pointed his antennae toward Naomi banging dishes against the stove and the tiny dining table. Her radio blasted blues music. Soon she'd leave for work, unable to rise above her circumstances. Like Willie, she was fragile.

He'd pray for them.

JOB COLLATERAL LIES DEAD ON
COMPTON CREEK

The 10 p.m. shift begins Saturday when Cowboy lopes the growling Crown Victoria onto potholed Willow-brook Avenue. At 10:05 p.m., we stop four well-dressed Xicana millennials, the front plate missing. We drug-search their brand-new AMG Beamer. Lips flat, nostrils flaring, seated curbside, the women twist their asses, shivering, thighs tight together, knees bent, and the companions tug and pull their hems, their miniskirts absorbing motor oil. "Bastards," one says. Cowboy hands back her driver's license. "Have a beautiful night, ladies," he says. Their dirty skirts? "Collateral comes with the job, Buck," Cowboy says. "Always."

Did the Lancaster deputy who killed my dad seventeen years ago see him as collateral? He'd said he feared for his life in court, although my dad never hurt anyone and didn't even spank his four kids.

"My name's Brown." Heat flushes me. "Daniel Brown. I'm okay with Dan or DB."

"Really? Not Demetrius, Malik, or some African shit like that?"

19

I tread carefully; his evaluation could land me back into working jails or assigned to a cold, foggy post in Rolling Hills Estates, frost in Santa Clarita, or some other dull place. It's like that in the sheriff's department. Best to go along to get along; one person's bullshit opinion sticks to your career like Super Glue. "Okay, Danise," he says.

Scott "Cowboy" Farris is my training officer, my TO. He's tall and built like Tim Tebow when he won the Heisman. His shifting velvet-brown eyes sit grave. His face is taut and tan. Mousy hair leaps to attention on the crown of his head like a quill pig. A tat obscured under rolled sleeves shows when he taps pouty lips, his fingers curled, tapered. He has a prognathic jaw and commanding voice, and his sideburns challenge sheriff policy.

Since 2001 I've worked at Men's Central Jail, CJ, where deputies start careers in sparse sunlight, persistent plumbing leaks, lockdowns, and power outages, where 19,000 men jostle for 15,000 beds, where we corral bad guys at best from shift start to finish. After a while, all strangers look like inmates.

Like most deputies, I'd fought inmates at first, as a fish, new to jail environments, until a widely read jailhouse lawyer said, "Most of us are here pretrial—haven't been convicted. We aren't all assholes. We want respect. Isn't respect what we all want, brother?"

Brother? That's when it hit me like a Mike Tyson hook. Hey, I could be on the other side of jail cell bars, one misstep, inattentive parents, no bail money, or a bad break. The training academy made me suspicious of everyone not wearing olive green, especially the many ethnic groups populating Los Angeles County. The jailhouse lawyer had said, "Try walking in our shoes." He even resembled a first cousin of mine. Afterward, if I gave respect, respect usually came back.

After seven years in CJ, it's a moonless winter night, my

first with Cowboy. I'm grateful for field duty, which I wanted from the start. A chance to show that not all police are dirty and that even Black communities could trust them, despite history. I'd be the change, like Michael Jackson's "Man in the Mirror," maybe offset the LAPD-Rodney King effect. Maybe understand why Dad had to die.

I remember the book Jailhouse Lawyer mentioned, *Community-oriented Policing Styles, COPS,* I'd read about respect-based, community partnership problem-solving. Empathy.

Our black-and-white Crown Vic purrs along Long Beach Boulevard past mottled bark sycamore tree roots buckling sidewalks. Winter warblers sing perched on spindly branches. At Primo Plaza, a strip mall anchored by a coin laundry and a smoke shop, the wonton soup scent from Chinese takeout makes me hungry. We turn slowly onto Marcelle Street. Cowboy brakes. Grin wide. He mutes the dispatch audio and types a mobile digital transmission computer message to another patrol unit. The MDT is the best way to communicate among field units.

In the chill, a figure materializes from the shadowy alley behind the plaza and smacks green-goddess tight lips, "What the fuck you want this time, Cowboy?" she asks. She's rail-thin, wearing a dark brown skirt so short the bottom quarter of her butt shows. The dress matches her skin. She crosses her arms over a loud pink halter top, barely covering her nipples.

"A quick pop, honey," he says. "Buck's my new partner."

One hand on Cowboy's doorsill, the woman cranes her neck, glaring at me; strong perfume rushes the Vic. A salty, sweet taste forms on the back of my tongue. "Pop Buck too, sweetie."

Cowboy unzips his fly, creaks open the Vic door, throws two duty work boots to the asphalt, and props himself between the steering wheel and bucket seat back, his back to me. The woman kneels, spreads Cowboy's legs, and sucks his dick.

He twists his neck and hitches his head to me; his lips turn up at the corners in diminished light from the MDT keyboard and small dash-cam screen above the rearview. I offer a watery smile and turn away.

Moments later, he groans, and his body sags like a nut sack. The sex worker stands, runs a backhand across her mouth, again glares, and says, "You too?"

Hair lifts off the back of my neck. "No." Nothing's wrong here, just *job collateral*, I say to my mind. I try to slow my breathing. "Maybe next time."

She shrugs, "Might be no next time, Buck." Her high heels clip-clop into the lee of a darkened doorway.

Cowboy's eyes sparkle. He turns the Vic and heads back to Primo Plaza's parking lot, where we regard the latest sex trade victims, young girls, an ethnic rainbow, minimally clothed, shivering in shadows. Cowboy says *Bompton Pirus* pimp the girls. Compton thugs lost money when community drug habits shifted from crack cocaine to prescription drugs, synthetics, and medical marijuana.

Tupac Shakur's "Dear Mama" bass line thumps from a lowrider parked across tight parking lanes. A guy dressed in red gestures like a madman to a young girl outside the smoke shop window. *Bitch, do what I tell you,* he says. She lowers her head and turns for the corner. My eyes connect with Red Man; *Bompton Piru,* he mouths, hops in the low-rider, guns the engine, and bounces away to the burnt smell of hydraulic pumps.

"I've got two daughters—two angels." Cowboy pulls a tattered picture from his wallet and points to his wife, a furrowed-faced, sturdy woman with gypsum skin, an aquiline nose, and her ash-blonde hair styled in a flip. On each side of her in the Sears family photo sit two mop-headed, mysterious girls, early teens maybe. "That's a few years back. They grow up too fast." Then he says, "I do not pity guerilla pimps that prey on children." He reads an MDT message on the green computer screen. Cowboy scrolls down as clothes tumble inside a heavy-duty Laundromat dryer. "Scumbags abduct them." His face reddens. "They beat, tat them up like cattle brands, gang rape them if they run—"

"My son's twelve," I say, the same age as me when Dad died. I share custody with my ex. The COPS book said pimps are hard to prosecute since their victims rarely testify against them. "Good thing I don't have a daughter."

Cowboy rolls the Vic several meters and points. A lone waif wearing an oversized hoodie moves under the lighted entrance of an animal hospital.

"That's a young boy," he says.

The child, maybe twelve, dances like an apparition and lobs a hand at lines of creeping cars. His face was angelic, like what musty jail pimps often bragged about, their "ho's," their "work," the money they made, unlike child pornographers, who were usually mute about their exploitation: Megan's Law felons, recidivists. Unrecoverable. Hungry moments before, I lose my appetite.

"Let's eat, Buck."

* * *

At the El Pollo Loco drive-through, Cowboy ignores several unread MDT service calls flashing red and yellow. I fold two twenties, reach and offer to pay for our dinner, but he pushes back my hand. He's not wearing the required Class A brass nametag on his uniform shirt, so I squeeze the pin and remove mine. My thoughts freeze. Maybe anonymity is not the best way to let community people know me, but I go with the flow anyway.

"We don't pay, Buck," Cowboy says, grabs the grub, and hands me the warm plastic bag. "They feed us to keep us coming around their businesses—they feel safer. Not all, but most pop us. TGIF's free, Sizzler's half off."

We smell fresh grilled chicken spread over in the parking lot and kept piping atop the Vic hood; the engine's always running. "Those who don't pop us will wait if they call us. No pop, no cop." I shove the nametag and money into my olive-green pants pocket.

"How do you like the yard bird, my nigger," Cowboy says. "If you like chicken, you'll love Compton."

"Beats beans and biscuits like you Simi Valley Okies eat." I expected to be hazed, but damn, the N-word right off. Asshole had my personnel jacket for weeks and knew my name.

They'd never invited me to the party, but I'd seen deputies' gang up on jail inmates, especially dings, who have a mental health condition in CJ. Maybe he's a skinhead. I sweat and pull the collar on my new Kevlar armor vest. "Don't confuse me with your mother, Cowboy."

He laughs. "I'm just fuckin' with you, partner. We have to trust each other. I gotta know you have my back, dude."

"I gotcha, Cowboy."

Back in the Vic, more messages swell the MDT screen.

"Why'd you become a cop?"

He pushes away the swing-arm-mounted MDT, leans, and whispers, "Tell ya a secret—the Association for the Advancement of White People doesn't pay as much." He laughs. "Seriously. I want to help people here and drive the crooked out of Compton. Gangs and pimps terrorize them—hold neighborhoods back. Shiiit." He stretches the word. "I put bad guys away."

"With arrests?" Jalapeño sauce burns my mouth. I put stuff in the universe from the COPS book to see what comes back.

"Whatever," Cowboy says. "These people hate gangs as much as they hate us—maybe more so, but they call us—they don't call Bompton Pirus for help." He pulls the MDT back and types. "Conflict? —they call Gangbusters."

"How do you know you're helping them?"

"What? Come again."

"Do you ever ask them?"

He sighs. "It's police work, Buck." The Vic engine snarls like a leopard. "What are you, some radical? Probably believe community policing, get-to-know-the-community-we-work-for-them bullshit, eh, Danny?"

"Do you respect them?"

Cowboy touches the keyboard, the MDT screen, and the rearview mirror. He reaches for the radio but hesitates. "Well. What's respect got to do with anything? I'm a cop."

I go COPS on him. "Can we serve and not respect?"

"What the fuck, fish?" He blows short breaths, reminds me I'm new here, holds his palm to me, and snaps, "I'm no social worker—see your pastor if you need love. I take bad guys off the street. Whatever it takes to get bad guys off the road." His eyes turn cold, callous. "What's love got to do with it?"

Cowboy returns to the animal hospital and hands the hooded boy food.

"Thank you," the boy says. He stuffs his mouth like he hasn't eaten in days.

"I know a shelter when you're ready," Cowboy says—the boy nods.

I finger the nametag but leave it in my pocket.

* * *

A woman is moving out of her apartment and fears her ex-boyfriend will interfere. In the Vic, Cowboy white-knuckles the wheel with one hand; the other pushes MDT buttons, checking the bloated service calls list. Cowboy pokes another button; the address is four miles away. Then he clicks the zoom bar, zeros in on the East Compton location, turns on the Christmas tree lights, and the Vic growls.

We're about halfway when Cowboy says, "Do you see that?"

"See what?"

"His rear plate lamp is out. Call it in."

Eastbound on Rosecrans Avenue, he pulls over the guys four deep, limping in a sunflower-yellow four-door Pontiac Aztek. Like a klieg, Vic's spotlight lights up the car from behind.

"Back me up, Danny."

We exit the Vic. Cowboy approaches the driver's side, Beretta in hand. The driver's looking all around, especially behind him, eyes huge. I hang back, palm on the holster, just behind the rear passenger door, where I see two guys in the back seat and the front seat passenger's reflection in the side door mirror.

Cowboy orders them out. "Hands on heads," he tells them. He directs them toward the Vic, which beckons us to feed the backseat prisoner cage. "Put your hands on the hood." We kick apart their legs and pat them down. A rear-seat guy lifts his hands from the hood. Cowboy trembles and aims the Beretta at the guy's face. "On the hood, shithead," he says. Cowboy searches the Aztek. Fear is palpable.

I understand why he's called Cowboy. He makes the job more complicated with his hard-charging, take-no-prisoners style. I don't like him, but I will keep my mind open.

"Keep your hands on the hood," I say to the guy from the

front passenger seat. He's wearing a maroon Morehouse College t-shirt and nerdy glasses.

The guy's voice pitches high when he says to me, "Tom."

Oh, hell no, he didn't just call me *Uncle Tom.* "Asshole." Before I know it, I'm back into jail-deputy mode. I snatch the guy's collar, sling him to the asphalt like a sack of potatoes, and force my knee into his back. He pisses himself, the smell pungent. Cowboy slides over and draws down on the guy, and the guy starts bawling. His friends shake visibly but keep their hands pressed to the hood.

"They're clean, Danny."

I hoist the guy up and dust him off. He's crying like a baby fresh from the pussy, and looky-loos slow their cars. A woman on the corner looks like she's recording on her cell phone.

"Disrespectful son of a bitch," I say to the guy. Death is one perceived comment, one suspicious move away, for these guys. My mouth sours.

"Get out of here," Cowboy says to the driver. "Have your plate lamp fixed the next time I see you."

In the Vic, backlogged MDT messages are down to the *next page* prompt when Cowboy says, "That was good, Dan. Teach those mothers respect."

"Yeah." I checked and then rechecked the time.

"That's my boy. You're learning. Keep that shit up, and I'll set you up for a commendation, maybe a promotion, Danese."

* * *

The Vic siren roars across Compton to a highly illuminated, dingy green two-story apartment building. The book said that to build trust, police should stop occasionally, leave their vehicles, and engage residents as partners instead of adversaries.

We stop before a parked U-Haul, and two voices are arguing. A storage box holds open a metal security door of the upstairs unit. "La Granja," a narcocorrido tune popular among jail inmates, shakes windows downstairs. We smell weed smoke everywhere but can't pinpoint the source.

"I hate DV calls," Cowboy says. "People are crazy as shit, especially Mexicans. They drink too much Cerveza and then beat up their women."

"Yeah, domestic violence is a problem everywhere."

"Usually, I jail both parties. Let the courts sort shit," Cowboy says.

Glass breaks. "Don't yell at me," a woman's voice screams upstairs. Cowboy inventories his gun belt under the Vic's dome light, touching each piece. The Beretta, holstered—check. Two fifteen-round magazine cases—check. Double handcuff case and OC spray canister holder next to it—check. Knife case— check. Taser X2 holster clipped opposite the firearm—check. Sig Sauer P290RS ankle backup—check, and he loosens the telescoping Handler 12 device. He's Robocop prepared for World War III.

My gear is standard issue, Beretta, side handle baton, cuffs, Taser, and additional magazine case. "You take the woman, and I'll take the dude. Separate them," Cowboy says.

On the landing, a wisp of a woman runs past Cowboy. "Help me," she says. She slams into me, and we both tumble. I grab her camisole, and we bump down ten steps. She bounces right up. I swipe off biting red harvester ants, and sit holding my forehead, back aching.

A man covered in blood stumbles out of the unit. *"Chinga tu Madre."* He scowls. Cowboy's face turns ashen. I'm not sure if Cowboy understands he's been called a bitch, and it probably doesn't matter as he repeatedly strikes the man's head and body with the metal Handler until the guy collapses, writhing on concrete. Cowboy's voice is shrill. "Damn aliens." I reach the top of the stairs, and the man looks barely conscious. Cowboy pepper sprays him, Tasers him. He punches the man in the stomach with the cuffs before slapping them to his wrists behind his back.

"That's for bullying the little woman, shit-face," he says.

"Don't hurt him," the woman screams, runs up the stairs, pushes Cowboy aside, and tries to comfort the injured guy. "Sweetheart," she says. "I didn't mean to cut you." She presses his bloodied head against her bosom. "You know I hate when you yell," she says.

His face swells twice its size. He gurgles, "I'm sorry, baby." He weeps.

She reaches under the neck of the guy's t-shirt, pulls over his head bloody dog tags, and hurls them at Cowboy.

The Vic groans and I'm copying Cowboy's report word for word. Those two threaten officer safety. We drive him to the lock-up infirmary for resisting arrest and send her to women's jail for assaulting a peace officer.

"Don't mention the guy's a Marine vet, okay?" Cowboy says. A mist hugs the ground. "Have you ever seen shit like that? Motherfucker's blood all over me."

"No, never," I say. "The only thing close was CJ cell extractions."

A red warning light blinks on the MDT keyboard, signaling another service call. I haven't had much community engagement time so far.

* * *

The COPS book said our job is to assist and help the community identify their problems. As leaders, we should talk to people, see things through their eyes, and take the initiative to help solve concerns as they place them. Roger that.

We cruise a strip mall parking lot. Alley cats attracted to the odor of rotting seafood jump into a dumpster behind Matt's Fried Fish. A stray black pit bull-Lab mix barks at the base of the dumpster, cats unconcerned.

A slip of a man, dark brown, perhaps in his early to middle thirties, paces back and forth, screaming gibberish, palms pressed like a vise to his temples. He looks unhoused in a dirty orange t-shirt and blue jeans. Cowboy and I flank him and cut off his path. He's between a white Ford dually and us about twenty-five feet away.

One way for me to build trust is to talk respectfully to people. "Hey, do you have a problem, sir?" I say, hands on my gun belt. "The call said you might need help." He smells like he's dived Matt's dumpster.

The guy shakes his head. His jowls shimmy, lips purse, and he voices an odd sound. Cowboy flinches.

"Stop right there." Face pallid, fearful maybe, Cowboy unstraps his Beretta holster, left hand clutching his Taser. He hitches his head for me to move farther right. "We got a gorilla here, Danny," he says.

The man ignores us, seemingly occupied with his thoughts. A light fog covers our ankles. Cowboy's in his emotions and reminds me of my dad in some ways. Was the Lancaster deputy who killed Dad afraid? The guy walks backward as if normal. Many Blacks fear the police. Any Black man ignoring police presence must be deaf or crazy, even when one cop is Black and the other, like Cowboy. Sick shit. That's why I joined. Must change.

Ding continues mumbling nonsense. A few people inside 7-Eleven peer out the windows. Others rush away from where the three of us circle dance.

"Let me see your hands," Cowboy commands.

The man stops briefly in bright light from store windows

and lot lamps, tightens the circle where he walks, and puts his hands in his pockets.

He mumbles louder, "Fuck it. I don't care what they say. I'm never going back ever they can't do nothing to me, bastards I'll show them fuck with me a child of God called everything except my name, everything but no respect."

Crazy shit. With two hands, I grip my X2 and put laser sights on Ding's chest. "Shouldn't we call the mental docs, Cowboy? Psych Emergency Team?" When Dad had his spells, PET teams were regulars at our house. He'd go long periods without sleep, food, *fasting*, he called it, threaten to hurt Mama and us, but he never did.

Like Wyatt Earp did at Tombstone, Cowboy points both X2 Taser and Beretta. "Show your hands," he says.

In my command voice, "Show us your hands, SIR."

Ding puts weight on his right foot, slowly slides his hands from his pockets, and clasps them together. Something in them glints, and I fire the X2. He jiggles over—seconds later, BANG, Bang. Cowboy blasts him with Taser and Beretta. Ding stops and plops down like a lead weight. Legs bend awkwardly beneath him, and his old flip phone breaks against the pavement.

"What'd you shoot him for?" a woman screams. "That man is sick—can't you see?"

"It's Cowboy—no fuckin' wonder!" someone else yells. "How many you kill this week, biaatch?"

The guy lies still, bleeding from his torso. Cowboy kicks the flip phone away and combs the guy's empty pockets. "Suspect down," he says into the radio mike pinned to his lapel. "Send backup and paramedics."

Ding has no pulse, and we make little effort to revive him.

Adrenaline tingles through me. "Oh fuck—what happened, Cowboy? Why'd you use your firearm?"

31

"We can't trust them," someone says among the fast-forming crowd. "Fuck the police."

"Looked like he had a firearm," Cowboy says as he motions people back, and we control the area.

"Pig ass muthafuckas shot another Black man."

"Dude, he was ding all day," I say. "We didn't need to go lethal."

"I feared my life." His lips, his chin, tremble. "I can't take chances." He stares at the spreading blood pool. "Got a family to get back to." To Cowboy, the ding potentially blocked him from seeing his Sears photograph family, his long-faced wife, and blowsy daughters. "We'll huddle over the report—right?" he says. "Scumbags all look the same to me," Cowboy says.

"All what? Blacks, Cowboy—mentally ill? What?" My body tenses. "Fuck you."

"It was an accident, Dan." He lifts his hands and then lets them fall. "Should've let you handle that one."

Crowd tension is thick as ground fog.

I try de-escalating tensions try talking. "Come on, people," I say, just like the COP book says.

"Black cop just like the white cop—they don't give a damn about us." Bodies push against and stretch the yellow tape.

"*Lo van a dejar sangrar hasta morir*—we're gonna get your ass, Cowboy—*eso es suficiente.*"

Backup arrives before paramedics and forces the pissed-off crowd further back—white foam leaks from Ding's mouth.

Eventually, homicide detectives, the DA, and sheriff's oversight people arrive. Cowboy and I answered in tandem about how we feared for our lives, how we thought Ding had a weapon, and how he appeared normal to us.

What a fucking first night. Have I proven that not all cops are corrupt and untrustworthy?

We're assigned desk duty.

* * *

But first things first. The task force is in town: FBI, DEA, ATF. An army to suppress crime in tiny Compton. Their addition could be an opportunity to improve relationships, and I can help, but in the newspaper photo op, no community members are on the team. Home invasions plague Rancho Palos Verdes Estates, and Compton gangs are suspect. During the briefing, the captain had said to concentrate on Bompton Pirus, check parole and probation status, take names, and kick ass.

It's Friday, two hours after the sun dips below the horizon, the week after our desk duty after the police-involved shooting inquiry ends. In the news, Al Sharpton calls Ding's death murder.

Cowboy and I turn onto Wilmington Avenue, and I'm driving. A fog rolls under the high thumbnail moon. The Vic engine rumbles on a full tank.

"You need more familiarity with the streets," Cowboy says. "Just like *Driving Miss Daisy*."

"Hated it," I say.

He rolls up his sleeve and shows me a skull and revolver tattoo. Three green bullets fill half the chambers. "Reaper," he says. When I worked in jails, I'd heard about the rogue gang but doubted their existence. "Got three kills," he says. "Taking them off the streets, Dan."

We're patrolling east of a concrete box channel connecting downstream to Compton Creek. Cars are dense in driveways, hugging curbs. We'd cruised the trashy, smelly, well-known street gang area our first night, a place fatly populated.

A young guy, twenties maybe, eats Flamin' Hot Cheetos, drinks Mountain Dew, wears a red baseball cap, red t-shirt, red Converse All-Stars, and red calf-length Dickies, leaves a neighborhood market on Arbutus Street. Cowboy points. "Parolee." He directs me to stop. "Maybe the Palos Verdes shit," he says.

"Yeah, I saw the asshole at Primo Plaza—calling young girls *bitches*."

I screech a stop near the market. Red Man sprints north, then west into low fog up Poplar Street, under dim streetlights, past tiny shotgun-type residences. Cowboy pulls on his Beretta and touches each piece in his arsenal. "Call backup—stay with the Vic," he says before giving chase. "I'll catch the rabbit."

I screech into the radio and reverse the Vic. Cowboy pursues Red Man. They scramble past a rusted *Compton Creek Garden Nature Park* sign to the cul-de-sac in misty darkness over the pedestrian bridge and storm drain channel flowing to the Los Angeles River watershed. The waterway smells of runoff from horse stables and underground septic tanks. On the west bank is Compton Creek trail. On the east are sycamores, cattails, and a walking path embedded with bicycle and off-road motorcycle tire marks, next to houses bordered by dilapidated fences.

Gunshots explode as Banda music thumps inside clapboard houses along the west bank. Cowboy will probably add another tattoo bullet or two. I burn rubber to the cul-de-sac; the Vic engine wails like a mother leopard that's lost her cub. I grab my flashlight and hustle across the bridge toward gunfire, my soles crunching gravel and my heart pounding. My partner might've gotten one right.

My high-lumen flashlight is almost useless in ground fog. My insides quiver. An Aero Bureau copter arrives and illuminates barely visible shell casings to my left.

Thirty meters away, duty boots and two olive-green pant legs poke from holes cut into chain link, the trail leading to Arbutus Street.

Cowboy lies still, ambushed, blood pooling on decomposed

twigs in sage and bark debris clumps. I empty a full clip and an extra magazine in the direction of voices. I shoulder away tears and perform CPR on Cowboy's lifeless red-ant-covered body. When support arrives, I run to three bodies sprawled in the street. It's Red Man. A few feet away lay job collateral, a young Latina, maybe sixteen, and a baby.

* * *

Attendance and press coverage at Scott "Cowboy" Farris' funeral is massive, and formaldehyde smells faint as thousands squeeze into the large church. I wear a black memorial patch over my badge, nameplate intact. A bagpiper in a red, green, and white plaid kilt plays Taps, and his tasseled cap sways in the breeze. Slowly, five other pallbearers and I creep the flag-draped casket, flanked by hundreds of deputies, their hands raised in a crisp salute.

It's like a family member's death, or, for me, maybe Cowboy is a distant cousin. By design, we'd spent so much time chasing the box from one call to another or getting popped, except for hookers and gangsters, like working jails, we never knew the vast majority, good folks, hard workers, and everyday people in Compton. I'd done nothing to prove all cops aren't corrupt and untrustworthy.

Policing style is hard to change. Should I even expect policy ever will? The captain directed deputies to crack down harder after Cowboy's death.

Inside, the church overflows, the crowd hushed, handkerchiefs dabble eyes, and butts twist against the hardwood pews. Mrs. Farris's face is firm. Her vision focused straight ahead. A daughter with a spiked green Mohawk hairstyle and diamond nose stud bends to pick up the obituary her mother drops. The other daughter wears dark sunglasses and a black dress to her mother's left. She accepts the folded casket flag from the sheriff.

The family receives commendations, and from the pulpit, the pastor says how great a deputy Cowboy was, how he served the community, how he knew his tactics and reduced crime, and how he is a hero.

Outdoors, the sun glows hot as we hoist the casket into the hearse. I hug Cowboy's wife and daughters.

"He loved you," I say to them collectively. "You're all he talked about."

Tears cascade down Mrs. Farris' face like a waterfall. She takes a deep breath and says, "Scott liked you. He said you're his best trainee."

My thoughts scrambled to understand. I nod.

"He liked your policing style, and you're right to serve and respect people—walk in their shoes."

I rub my cuff across my Class A shirt nametag, Daniel Brown. Dad might have been proud of me.

The Compton community? Maybe not so much.

LELAND OTIS DUNWITTY
DISCOVERS MYSTEREE'S SECRET

Beat 'em down, beat 'em down —way down! Go Apaches! Woo!
Wooo!

Centennial High School Apache's War Cry

To soothe his butt pain, Otis Dunwitty sways on the hardwood bleachers in the musty gym. At the Friday afternoon pep rally, three girls rollick two rows above to his right.

"Wakombozis—beat 'em down, beat 'em down—waaay down!" Their clamor challenges his brain, a brain dulled by the Lilly Pharmaceutical Tuinal F40 sedative hypnotics he'd swallowed to block out Wendy's affair and subsequent rejection, to help him force upset from his mind. It was all over the grapevine. Last Saturday night, at LeRoi Sykes's off-to-Vietnam party, Wendy spent the evening in LeRoi's coat closet with a jock, doing everything Otis had hoped to do with her but hadn't.

Tournament time in Compton is when different neighbor-hoods around Centennial High suspend their rivalries long enough to aggravate opposing basketball teams. A cheerleader, bitch Wendy, sits along the sideline far below, all hugged up with the power forward, a Willis Reed wannabe.

Last Monday before Homeroom, he'd confronted her.

"You're always broke, Otis," she'd said to him, her light-skinned, long, shiny legs like fence pickets below her miniskirt. His arms crossed over the empty Pee-Chee folder; pressed chest tight. "Me and you, uh, it was just for one night." His neck muscles tightened. "Besides, I don't see me hanging out in housing projects with you and your family. You never leave the PJs." Hollowness settled from his lungs to his navel. "Our back-grounds don't jell—sorry."

Sorry? What a goddamned sad word. What's wrong with government housing anyway? "It's not all bad," he had said as if the declaration would somehow minimize the sting of her curb kick to his gut. He shook his head slowly. She had rubbed Otis away like a squished roach wiped off a shoe sole onto the rug; that rug, that mid-spring, 1969. What a shitty way to end his senior year.

Now she has Power Forward in a lip-lock, and her head, her face angles away from his, seeming to look toward Otis. Her eye winks. Power Forward stands, angles, points, and nods his head. What the fuck? He'd never met the Cyclops motherfucka. The vinegary aftertaste of Silver Satin Bitter Lemon wine he'd used to wash down Tuinals sours his mouth, his head fogged by the joint he'd smoked to lighten his load, Otis' buzz now threatened by the girls in back and Wendy and Power Forward below him. He hopes Wendy can see him from so far away when he mouths; *I still love you.*

He rests his feet on the bleacher, chin in palms, eyelids

gummy. No matter how high he is, he can't block the hushed sniggers and his sense of being watched by the three girls behind him. The girls whisper and huddle in a game as if they do not want the opposition to overhear the next play.

Otis manages a shitty smile.

"Hey, don't you go with Wendy?" The beige-skinned girl with frilly auburn curls grins. "You know—Wendy." She points to the picket-fence-legged girl below. "She's a Squawnette." The grapevine worked fast if these three strangers knew about Wendy's closet escapade. "She likes basketball players," she says.

Otis's head falls. He bows his shoulders and tries to disappear. Voice weak, he says, "No—not anymore." He runs a hand across his short flat-top hair parted on the side and glances around for an escape route. "We broke up," he says, tapping the bleacher seat.

"Awww—that's sad," says the tall girl with full lips like Nina Simone. "Makes sense, in any case. You don't look like much of a ballplayer." She gestures with her palms a few inches apart and says, "You're way too little." Then she points to his pants leg. "Where's the flood?" Otis's bell bottom pants cuffs are high above his scuzzy gym socks, as visible as the sparkling Watts Tower pinnacles next to the apartment, where his family squeezes. "You're too dark-skinned for Wendy." The two girls bend over and cackle like magpies.

He tucks his arms closer to his sides and gives a halfhearted chuckle to save some semblance of a face in the stuffy gym.

The third girl doesn't laugh with the other two and sits with her back to him. She turns and faces Otis.

Otis stares into her large brown eyes, which have vibrancy he's unfamiliar with, shocking his lethargy and speeding his slow pulse. She's not skinny and indeed not fat, skin flawless, two shades darker than a brown paper bag; a small gold scorpion dangles from her neck on a nylon cord. Her hair is black, cut into a choppy bob, shorter on one side than the other. Otis's heart bangs against his chest.

"You're probably better off," she says. She scrunches her pudgy nose. "Wendy's a slut." He's never heard a raspy voice like hers, a soft, low-pitched, sultry quality like Eartha Kitt's, sexy, penetrating the wall of drugs surrounding him. "Everybody knows about her." The corners of her mouth turn up. "Well, maybe not everybody," she says and winks.

His stomach flutters in late April's stickiness, which feels like June swoon, and a wet, toothy grin splits his face. Who. Is. She?

The drummer hits a snare drum on the gym floor, snatching Otis' attention away from the girl to the proud Apache portrait painted mid-court. Trumpets blast, and the Squawnettes dance to the pep rally theme: boom, boom, boom, the drummer pounds. YEAH, three thousand students push to their feet, squeal, cry, and yell. Wendy and the other cheerleaders bounce, their shoulders back, their feathered headdresses flipped behind them like long hair; they hoist scarlet pompoms into the hot air. The building rocks so much that an earthquake would go unnoticed. Otis can't hear the three girls anymore.

After the rally, the teachers release each section, the three girls before him. The raspy-voiced girl pulls her blue plaid pleated skirt down to her knees, her white socks clothe her calves, and then bounds down the steps with her friends.

He'll hustle to catch them.

When permitted, he stands and wobbles to the handrail, his eyes following the girls as the crowd carries them away like foam on Dockweiler Beach waves.

He reaches the last bleacher rung, squints to the exit, misses the step, and stumbles face-first onto the gym floor.

Several players, the lanky center, the point guard whose over-bite makes him resemble a gopher, and Wendy's power forward all rush over. The guy is about six-four and probably thinks he is Willis Reed since he wears jersey number 19. His thick arms heft Otis to his feet. Power Forward crouches. For a moment, they are face to face. The guy's breath smells like lunch meat. He isn't as big as Otis had thought, but with his hard-faced clones as a backup, he's more than Otis can handle alone. He swallows—or tries but cannot find one saliva drop. Power Forward turns Otis toward the exit, dusts him off, and gives him a playful kick in the seat of his jeans.

"Watch you don't hurt yourself, little project's fella," he says as his clones laugh.

Projects? What has Wendy told this fool? Before Otis left for school, his dad had finished a cup of coffee and was off to work, black lunch pail in hand, when he turned back to Otis, who scarfed down the Cream of Wheat breakfast Mama had made. "Come on down to the rail yard after school." Dad pressured him to get a job since he was finishing high school. "Maybe you can get work sweeping boxcars or get your apart-ment across the courtyard."

"Do I have to live here?" Otis had asked.

Dad looked back through the door screen and said, "Where else you gon go? South Gate? Lynwood? Everybody knows Negroes aren't welcome in those places."

Now, the Cyclops' power forward is in his face, telling him to get back to the projects. Otis opens and closes his fist; veins in his neck harden. He twists and swings a wild left hook into the air. His right cross also misses its mark as Power Forward quickly leans away. Then Otis's face wipes the gym floor again. *Owww*, he screams when Gopher Teeth delivers a kick to his kidney.

Power Forward lifts Otis by his sweater lapels, grip tight

near his throat. "You crazy?" He holds Otis on his tippy-toes like a marionette dangling from a string. "I took your woman." Otis manages to control a sudden urge to pee his pants, barely. "I'll slam dunk your ass, too," Power Forward says.

The words of the raspy-voiced girl come back to him. "Everybody knows about her," she had said. Otis exposes most of his buff-colored teeth and says, "Keep the skank. The clap clinic opens at nine o'clock." Why should he get into a scrum over someone who had sex in a closet at a party with Willis Reed?

Power Forward blinks first. Otis draws back a corner of his mouth. His nose touches the guy's ear when he slurs, "Fuck you."

"HUDDLE UP," the basketball coach bellows across the gym floor. Power Forward releases Otis, makes an about-face, and he and his teammates jog away.

"Your daddy's calling, asshole," Otis says to Power Forward's back. Otis is outmanned and impaired but not outmaneuvered.

The raspy-voiced girl and her friends have disappeared into the late afternoon swelter. He'll find her.

* * *

Otis lights a menthol cigarette outside the gym. He'd met Wendy at a waistline party when he awoke after two days of steady drinking and drugging. He should've known it wouldn't work when she opened her droopy eyes and said, "I thought you were Billy." She had her nerve to say he never leaves the PJs. Their romance was quick and shitty, but now a new girl attracted him. He cranes his neck for the girl in the blue pleated skirt, who vibed differently than Wendy. But where is she? For sure, she's not from the PJs, where he knows everybody. He has to find her and stumbles across campus in the direction he thinks they've taken, across the asphalt tennis court to the track area, where he trips over a starting block and crashes onto hard dirt.

He picks himself up and ambles south into unexplored territory. Off the campus, he passes homes with attached garages, newer cars in driveways, loud splashes of purple-blue blossoms fallen from umbrellas of shady jacaranda trees, carpeting streets, towering over fenceless lawns. More trees are on the block than in the hundreds of government units where he lives. Unlike the continuous din, fuss, and blues music he'd heard through thin public housing walls on the high school's north side, the area's quiet. These Negroes have money.

The location is Nutty Buddy territory, rivals in a much different neighborhood than his. He has never been much for cliques and tries to get along with everybody, even assholes like Power Forward. Acid tastes on the back of his tongue, but his legs keep moving.

When he recognizes Khayin, a Black History classmate, Otis stops and describes the raspy-voiced girl in the blue pleated skirt. The guy, a squat drug dealer with a temper known for overusing his product, wears black-rimmed glass frames without a lens, which makes him look studious and stupid at the same time.

"You sold me my first joint last year in the bathroom. That was some good shit," Otis says. He reaches to dap, but the guy keeps his hands at his sides. "Have you seen her?" Otis asks.

"If I did, I ain't telling you. Project's motherfucker. You here to cop or what?"

"Lookin' for the girl," Otis says, both palms up. "That's all."

Khayin rifles a knuckle off Otis's mouth. He falls backward onto his back, rolls, and swipe-kicks the drug pushers shin.

Khayin yelps like a hurt puppy and falls to one knee. He

turns and whistles. Otis sucks blood and draws in slow, steady breaths until doors from several nearby homes slam behind boys carrying ax handles, chains, and baseball bats.

"It's war—get his ass," the dealer shouts. "Fuck him up."

Typically, Otis runs like a tortoise, but with twelve guys in pursuit, he sprints over sidewalks, gutters, lawns, and purple-blue blossoms into the street back toward the high school, lungs about to burst from pack-a-day Kool menthols.

He races across Segundo Boulevard, which runs alongside the school, where cars honk. One swerved to avoid him and crashed into a fire hydrant. The water explodes skyward, drenching Otis. A swan hood ornament detaches and ricochets off his knee, spewing his blood, but he feels no pain. Thank God the fools chasing him stop and wave their fists.

Until now, to Otis, Nutty Buddy was a lame name, a bunch of punks with money who liked candy bars. "Don't bring your black ass back," one yells. "We're Nutty Buddy," he says.

Who needs Vietnam to get killed when it's easier to die in Compton over bullshit?

Nutty Buddy does not cross the boulevard into PJ territory. They are brighter than Otis in that way. They leave, and he drags his damaged knee and busted lip home to the Palm Lane government housing projects, acres of single-story two- and three-bedroom units. He's again anxious to see his dad, mother, two sisters, brother, many cousins, granny and great-granddad, and friends. He gulps breaths, wheezes, and presses both hands to his chest, keeping his heart in check.

Maybe the raspy-voiced girl doesn't live in Nutty Buddy's direction. He needs to know for sure.

* * *

Otis must find the girl with the raspy voice. Like an apparition, he roams the campus and carefully avoids Nutty's between classes. He discovers she's a junior recently transferred from St. Michael's Catholic school.

Once the last bell rings, he lingers near the north gate, waiting for her or her two friends to walk through. It's a long shot because he knows almost everyone from Palm Lane, where none of the girls compare to the raspy-voiced girl. These students wear red, his neighborhood's color.

On Tuesday before Homeroom, Otis lolls against the east gate with the kids in gold. He monitors the west gate at the bell, where kids dressed in a purple color stream through like grunion.

On Wednesday, he stands sentry at the south entrance, shielding his eyes from white morning light as blue colors pass him.

Wendy approaches hand in hand with Gopher Teeth. She regards Otis a few seconds before she rams her tongue down Gopher's throat. She'd never kissed Otis that way.

She lets Gopher catch his breath and contorts her leg around his. "How's PJs life?" she asks.

Otis's thoughts scramble, his drug buzz running low. Maybe it's the strain of isolation; he is cut off from whatever's just across a street, beyond a park, or railroad tracks because of clothing colors or something else imaginary and artificial, which maintains division and discord in his community. People like Wendy only add to his confusion, but he'll not let her suck him in again. It's time for him to let go. Otis's breath quivers when he says to Gopher Teeth, "Have you made your clap clinic appointment yet? They open at nine o'clock." He considers Wendy. "Slut," he says to her.

She flips Otis off with her middle and ring fingers, a double fuck you gesture, and guides Gopher Teeth onto the campus.

The next day, Otis again searches. He listens to conversations, hoping to hear her distinctive voice. Visions of him and her on prom night creep through his drug-induced numbness. Maybe he'll glimpse a pleated skirt and white knee-high socks.

He's at the exit gateway to Nutty Buddy territory when he runs into Khayin, the dealer who had chased him.

"What's happening, my man?" the guy asks as if nothing had happened before. Otis's jaw tightens. "Buy a couple of these F40s—I'll tell you where the girl hangs out."

Otis will pay him for such information alone; the barbiturates mean a jackpot. He'd rifled a telephone booth with a clothes hanger and cashed in Blue Chip stamp books stolen from his mama's stash to scrounge enough snacks and dope money. "Check the quad by the band room at lunch," Khayin says.

Khayin didn't lie. She sits alone under a canopy in the quad, sheltering her from bird shit. Seagulls squall overhead.

"I'm Otis Dunwitty. What's your name?"

"Mysteree," she says.

"Oh, it's a secret?"

She smiles and looks up from the picnic bench.

"Just is," she says. She sips a Coke. "It's not just for any and everybody to know."

"But I told you my name," he says. Getting her name proves difficult; getting her to the prom could suck. He looks away.

"I told you my name," her laughter raspy. "It's M-Y-S-T-E-R-E-E—Mysteree."

He digs his hands into his pockets. What an unusual name. Maybe it's African with a special meaning. Her voice pierces something deep inside his gut. Then her smile fades. She might anticipate a stupid question or a comment about her name, which doesn't come.

"Hmmm—Otis Dunwitty. There's something about you I can't figure out. I'll call you Duu," she says.

And so Duu it is.

*　*　*

Otis closes his eyes and savors his moments with Mysteree when they walk the block from school to her house, holding hands under the shade of trees and over the carpet of purple-blue flowers. The school's proximity keeps him from entering Nutty Buddy territory too deep. She strokes his arm. He hugs her every several steps, lost in her clean body scent and warm, fresh breath. She smiles at nothing and, unlike Wendy, laughs at his jokes. He carries her books, which hides the erection he gets whenever he's with her and keeps a hand in his pocket half the time they are apart. She likes to dance, work on crossword puzzles, solve arithmetic problems, and play Scrabble. They spread the game board on the front porch of her tract home. "I'm not gonna mess this up," he says aloud.

"Then you'd better learn to use a dictionary," Mysteree says. She grabs her side in raspy laughter when he spells love "l-u-v." "—unless you want to join your daddy at the rail yard," she says.

His voice weakens. "Sweeping boxcars is what I don't want to do." But what option has he with graduation so close?

Otis always loses their board games, but he pushes himself until his brain aches trying to win. Even when sober, he's no match for her. Mysteree's no Wendy, and he wants to keep things that way.

"Will you be my prom date?" he asks.

He thrusts his fist skyward and says, "YES," when she agrees to attend the prom. He'll rent a tuxedo, and her mom will drive them to the fancy hotel.

A tingling sweeps up the back of his neck and across his face.

They sit and let their legs touch.

"Mysteree's a good girl," her mom says when she joins them on the porch. She's dressed as if she's going somewhere important, perhaps a PTA meeting. "Mysteree's going to college to study dance—what about you, Duu?" Mysteree's mom fumbles around in her purse. "I may have left my keys inside Mysteree. Please check for me."

College? He's never considered more education, never known anyone who'd attended except maybe some of his teachers. Would his 1.3 GPA do? His saliva dries, and he swallows air.

"She needs someone like her." Voice tense, she seemed to choose her words carefully, "You know—someone with high aspirations, perseverance."

Otis bounces his knee on the porch step. "Yes, ma'am," he says. He vows to study harder and look into the local junior college even though school ends soon.

"Poverty is a nonstarter, not an option for us," Mysteree's mom says. "It's hard, Duu—I've been there. It's like being held captive like you're a prisoner. You're waiting for someone to find you. You hope you live long enough for someone to find you in time and help you out of captivity—do you understand, Duu? Government housing is government policy, Duu. No one comes to save you. We don't choose what situation we're born into, but we can choose our destiny once we see the truth. That's all, Otis. Are you up to the challenge?" She pulls the car keys from her purse and powers to her Volvo parked in the driveway.

To an extent, her words penetrate Otis's mind fog. She has expectations, an intelligent daughter, and won't settle for less.

It's that simple. His dad wants him to visit the rail yard, get a job, and a government apartment. He wants another Tuinal. His stomach drops to his groin, and he offers a distracted nod.

She winks at Otis, starts the car, and drives off as Mysteree returns without the car keys. Otis's eyes follow the car's license plate until it turns the corner out of his view.

"We need our song," Mysteree says to Otis. They choose The Dells' "Always Together" as their favorite tune, just like Lilly F40s, and cheap wine is another favorite of his. She doesn't use alcohol and other drugs, and she's not like Wendy and the few other girls he's been with who'll drink anything handed to them in a cup, can, or bottle. She doesn't seem to mind his habits, but she's heard about LSD and its mind-expanding effects and believes hallucinogens will make her smarter.

"I want to try acid, Otis," Mysteree says.

"Acid is hard to handle—the high too long, unpredictable," he says. He understands Mysteree's mother wants him to be more like Mysteree, not the opposite. He rubs her hands. "You should try marijuana first."

"NO." She squeezes his hand in hers. "It stinks. It makes you stupid."

He concedes her observation since he's done much stupid shit when high on weed. "It's too dangerous," he says.

She flings his hands away and says, "No more so than F40s and cheap wine. Khayin will get it for me if you can't."

Otis rocks in place on the porch, quite aware he's discovered a new world on the other side of high school, a better one, and must now decide what's worse—having to deal with Khayin, betray Mysteree's mom, or displease Mysteree?

He'll get her the LSD.

* * *

Saturday night, Otis uses his mom's rust-bucket '57 Chevy to date Mysteree. "We're going to a movie," he tells her, momentarily weighing the pros and cons of lying.

"Always Together" blasts from the door speakers at Burrell-MacDonald Park's darkened parking lot. Heartbeat, sluggish, Otis says, "Here, let's put this on your tongue." Mysteree bites her lip, leans in, and opens her mouth—Otis tears a sliver of a pink-stained newspaper in half. "I'll give you just a little," he says. Sly and his Family Stone sing *Stand* from the eight-track player screwed beneath the dash. His extremities go numb when he hears the part about still being you in the end. He swallows half of the acid. He and Mysteree tongue kiss and cuddle, his erection so hard it hurts. He fingers around in her moistness. Ten minutes later, rainbow colors emanate from the tiny green light on the tape player. Otis hears unfamiliar melodies and new instruments in songs he's heard hundreds of times.

The refrain from "Chain of Fools" repeatedly plays in his head like water drips from a leaky faucet. Mysteree's eyes grow wide, and her lips move, yet no sound leaves her mouth. Aretha Franklin repeats the title again and again. Mysteree looks like a fish gasping for water, drowning in air. Again, the *chain* refrain. Mysteree hurries to the opposite seat corner and reaches back as if trying to touch Otis but can't. Her skin seems to blacken like charcoal under the car's dome light. The bass thumps, and Aretha's backup singers chorus the song title. The gold scorpion amulet Mysteree wears crawls across her chest, and the nylon cord tightens around her neck. "Chain of Fools."

"Where are you, Otis? I'm scared."

She's too high, and the only way to bring her down is with F40 capsules. He holds her close and starts to kiss her to comfort her with his familiarity. "I've got you, baby," he says to her. The windshield fogs from their panting, the green pine tree deodorizer shakes below the rearview mirror, and the seat springs bounce under pressure from their grinds and kisses. "Chain of Fools" lyrics bounce around like cave bats and fade into the blackness.

Mysteree is hysterical as if she's just seen the Bouncing Ball Man serial killer.

* * *

Monday, Otis waits at Mysteree's Homeroom. She doesn't show. He hasn't talked to her since their date. After school, he calls, and she answers the telephone.

"Where have you been?" he asks her.

There's a long pause; her voice breaks. "I can't talk to you anymore, Duu."

"What?" She has a quirky sense of humor. "I just saw you Saturday."

"I know, but I can't see you again."

"You're joking—right?"

"No—they saw it."

"I don't—" For once, he's not high and tries to fit pieces together.

"My mama saw your stuff on my socks."

"Mysteree—what're you talking about?" He trembles inside. "That's not funny."

"Your ejaculation was on my clothes."

There's silence. Otis takes a while to process the discussion. Both are inexperienced at fucking, and excited, Otis had come prematurely before he could enter her, or so he surmised. Stoned, neither of them was in control.

"I didn't mean that to happen," he says.

"My dad saw the stains on my socks when I got home."

Otis's chest falls to his stomach.

"—After you walked me to the door."

He grabs a paper bag and hyperventilates. "I didn't notice anything," he says.

"They don't want me pregnant, said I acted funny when I got home," she says, "like I was in another world." Her voice trails over the phone line. "They said that I couldn't see you anymore."

Otis's heart seems to stop beating for several seconds. A sharp ache explodes in his temples.

"We can't go to the prom together," she says.

* * *

By summer, high school ends for Otis. July burns hot, and he seeks coolness under a lone eucalyptus in the government apartments. Its aromatic scent offers respite from blues music and constant chatter among his Palm Lane PJs neighbors.

He pulls her picture from his empty billfold and runs his finger over its surface to help him remember her soft face, hair, and voice. On the reverse, she'd written, *I'm sorry things turned out the way they did. I hope you will find someone to love so you can know true happiness. Don't forget me! Love Always. Mysteree.*

His days and nights will be cold. He shakes his head slowly; his mind dulls from the effect of Lilly F40 barbiturates, and the aftertaste of Silver Satin Bitter Lemon sours his mouth. He'd ventured beyond public housing to be with Mysteree, and she'd never pushed him about his drug use.

If only he could return to the other high school side, salvation in another neighborhood. He misses the block on the edge of Nutty Buddy territory, where canopies of trees drop purple-blue blossoms.

He sits, elbows in palms, alone, studying the junior college course catalog and admissions application for a while. The PJs? Government policy. They're not all bad.

Then he hoists himself up and heads to the rail yard.

LELAND OTIS DUNWITTY
ELEVATES

P ain shot from my soles to my brain when Booker kicked hard. "Otis—WAKE up." The floor tiles were cold and sticky. My eyes popped open to two sets of waving antennas. Roaches were eating dried vomit that had crusted on my face. The vomit wasn't mine.

That was the worst place I'd ever slept.

In another room, the record stuck on a verse from Steppenwolf's "The Pusher." *Goddamn, the pusher* [skip], *Goddamn the pusher* [skip], *Goddamn the pusher* [skip].

Booker's voice boomed, "Get your black ass up." His head cocked, maybe from the weight of his twelve-inch Afro. He was undoubtedly hungover from last night, still in the grasp of Lilly F-40 barbiturates, weed, sweet wine, and whatever mystery capsules we could push into our mouths at a West L.A. house party celebrating the dawn of a new decade, the '70s. Maybe he wanted a better picture of me tucked under a sagging base cabinet door.

My head hurt, and Booker's voice rattled my brain like jets at LAX when, as a small child, my family parked underneath them ahead of the runway for Saturday night recreation.

"What the fuck?" I said, reeking like a skid row wino. "You woke me from sweet dreams about Connie—asshole."

"Looked like a wet dream to me. Holding your crotch and moanin'," Booker said. He was twenty and fancied himself a great dancer. He threw one leg on the kitchen counter, touching his knee with his head, stretching his hamstring. "I've got to practice for the audition—let's get the fuck outta here."

I pushed to my knees, grabbed the counter, and pulled up the rest of me. Beams of morning's white sunlight punched through holes in the window shades over a kitchen sink full of rotten dishes spackled with rancid grease and empty bottles. I splashed lukewarm water from the faucet onto my face.

"You got bus fare?" Booker asked.

I felt outside my Levi's pockets for loose change. I had none, not even a wallet, but a small packet wrapped in a scrap of glassine. Inside were two mescaline buttons and three gold-colored pills some bug-eyed guy in thick-soled buskins had handed me the night before in exchange for my last two bucks. "Indians use mes, man—out in the fuckin' desert," he said. "They have visions of all kinds of shit." He'd guaranteed the ride of my life. "Your money back if I ever see you again." It wasn't a total loss.

"Let's hitchhike," I said.

My heart leaped through my ribs, but I was too young for a heart attack at nineteen. To mollify my raging headache, for breakfast, I stuffed my mouth with a reddish-brown mes button, two gold pills, and Cheetos and washed everything down with a corner left in a Night Train Express bottle on the countertop. I rewrapped the mes button, and the gold pill left.

The fluorescent orange liquid's vinegary bite stung my gullet, leaving a warm trail down my gut.

Booker wanted to rehearse before *Soul Train* dance audi-
tions later that evening. More importantly, I needed to get to
The Courts in Watts to cop drugs from my parking lot connection, kick back on Connie's sofa, and get some pussy. No
plan B.

* * *

We were at Jefferson and La Brea with our thumbs out. Some
long-haired white guy in a meadow-green 1969 Olds Ninety-
Eight convertible pulled over. Booker's lips, like Elvis', had a
permanent pucker. He turned pirouettes the length of the Olds
like Fred Astaire, then did a James Brown split outside the
door.

I rode shotgun. The driver was strange in thick Clark Kent
glasses; he folded up the bench seat armrest and said, "Let's all
sit in front." A clump of pine-scented air fresheners dangled
from the rearview mirror, the top was down, and the driver was
drunk. He held out a palm. "I'm Brad."

Brad stopped to piss behind the Liquor Bank on Crenshaw
Boulevard when the mescaline gave me permission, false
courage, and obscured vision. I slid into the driver's seat,
pushed the gas, and the car lurched forward, stopped, and
lurched twice before it rocketed. The open driver's side door
slammed against the jamb, and the guy, holding his dick, raised
his fist. Brad's face grew long like the Joker in a Batman comic.
He twisted up his mouth. "Black bastards!" he said.

Buskins guy was right; the mes had a kick. A few months
back, a friend had let me drive his '55 Chevy station wagon a
couple of times in the tiny Cressy Park parking lot. Now was
the time to put those lessons to use, back to The Courts Public
Housing Projects.

Behind the wheel, I had an unbridled sense of freedom and

an opportunity to see what was on the other side of the horizon. My body cells orgasmed, and, like a Ferris wheel, a thousand thoughts entered my brain simultaneously. I picked one. *School.*

The school had been no friend to me. I'd had hard times ever since the third grade. That's when musty Raylon Skewlet snatched my book report on Harriet Tubman, scribbled on his name, and passed it to Mrs. Fontenot. Tubman was a conductor on the Underground Railroad and my all-time favorite heroine. I had punched Raylon's mouth; we fought. "Leland Otis Dunwitty, you're nothing but trouble," Fontenot had said. "You're never going to finish school." She twisted my ear between her knuckles and sent me for swats with the principal's perforated oak paddle, which sucked my ass into holes at each strike. Afterward, Raylon transferred to Special Education, but it was a small consolation.

"Since when do you drive?" Booker said, his bloodshot eyes shielded somewhat by gold-framed Gandhi sunglasses. "You don't even have a license."

"You don't know everything, mothafucka," I said, puffed up. "I took lessons." The wind rushed through my short, tight 'fro. The leather-wrapped steering wheel maneuvered soft in one hand, and my skinny elbow rested on the doorsill. Warmth radiated through my body before a fluttery, rolling feeling roiled my stomach. I joined not only to the elements of nature but to the entire universe.

We rumbled down Vernon Avenue to the freeway entrance. In eight seconds, the two-ton Rocket V-8 Turbo Hydromatic glided onto the 110 South at sixty miles per hour, where we became part of the busy, noisy, aggressive freeway.

Booker said, "Do you realize we could just point the hood east and continue to the other side of Compton?" He extended his legs, feet floored under the brushed aluminum glove compartment, and his body bent at his hips; he lowered his torso toward his legs and held his ankles, stretching his hamstrings again. "I gotta stay loose. Wait 'til you see me on TV —on stage next to Don Cornelius." He made a swim dance move. "Do you want my autograph now? —it'll cost you later." Always a good dancer, at Cressy Park dance hops, he'd set the floor ablaze, and others would circle to watch him when he did the Break, the Watusi, and the Slauson Shuffle. Girls would throw their panties his way.

Mine were two left feet no matter how hard I practiced, but drugs fortified me like spinach did Popeye, gave me courage enough to muddle through the old Mashed Potatoes, the only dance I could halfway do and not feel embarrassed. My hook was straight front teeth, and I flashed them often. Connie, my muse, liked running her tongue across them. A few girls would say, *you have a cute smile,* or at least that's what I thought they meant.

"Kiss my ass, dude," I said. Fuck that, and I did not need Booker's autograph. Any day Texaco would call me in for gas station attendant work. Until then, I'd stay high. "Autograph? You can't even spell your name," I said to Booker.

The Olds, in my mind, was like sailing a ship. Empowered by the wind, overhead street signs, July sun, and a nose full of pine freshener, I navigated the Olds like Columbus did the *Santa Maria.*

On AM radio, our heads bounced to The Jackson 5's "I Want You Back." Tears rushed to my eyes. "Damn, that's a bad jam," I sang along. *"Every street you walk on//I leave tear stains on the ground."* I swiped my eyes, all choked up. "You hear Michael Jackson? —shit, man." Tears rained onto my red nylon dress shirt, oversized collars, and balloon sleeves.

Booker made a Jerk dance move. His 'fro blew wild in the wind.

The aftertaste of cheap wine clung to the back of my tongue. No doubt, my breath stank, which was a non-starter when it came to Connie. She was my go-to pussy, as dependable as the Caucasian life insurance salesman with white hair and a gray suit who collected premiums from The Courts customers with religious zeal every other Monday. "You got any Chiclets?" I said to Booker.

"It won't help," he said. He lay across the front seat on his back, pulled his knees to his chest, and lifted his legs straight up. "Your breath smells like dog shit—maybe you can sell my autographed pictures."

My jaw tightened. "Your mama liked it when she licked my teeth and sucked my tongue." The street dividing lines jumped onto the hood, moved, and wiggled in unison. They separated simultaneously before they stopped and formed two racing stripes.

I punched the accelerator.

* * *

We approached the sand-colored projects on Imperial Highway, a sea of two-story cinder block buildings. The Ferris wheel in my head stopped on a large blue sign with white letters I'd never noticed before:

Housing Authority
City of Los Angeles
The Courts
A place where new and fertile
social habits can crystallize.

Booker wedged himself into the soft corner on the edge of the Olds seat, his back against the door armrest, forearm resting over a headrest, lap belt unbuckled. "Psychedelic Shack" played through radio static; he turned slightly to raise the volume. He fine-tuned and bobbed his head. I reached above the radio, hit the antenna-up switch, and squinted from sunlight reflected off the glove compartment door, eyes still moist from "I Want You Back." SHIT. I braked hard, and the checkered front-end grill dove into the rear of a Coupe de Ville stopped before us.

"Owww," Booker bellowed. His body slammed the dashboard sideways, and my face smashed the steering wheel horn. I spit blood, Chiclets, and straight front teeth onto the goldenrod transmission hump. The horn screamed like a red fox in the L.A. Zoo. A middle-aged woman in collard-green hot pants spilled from the Coupe and shouted, "Whiplash—whiplash," held her neck, and lay down in the left turn lane into The Courts. Drivers from oncoming traffic stopped to assist her.

I spat gunk onto the instrument panel and said, "Let's go, Booker."

"I can't move," Booker moaned, groggy. "I can't feel my leg."

I staggered around the rear of the Olds, forced open the door, grabbed Booker's arm, and pulled. "FUCK," Booker agonized but managed to turn and hobble up on his left leg since the right one was bent away from his body at the calf. His eyes glazed over as if he'd just read text from math, his worst school subject.

"You go on, Otis—I can't make it—" Booker's barely conscious voice trailed away.

Booker was too heavy, and we were too high, but I wasn't too mescaline infected to forget the street code my dead uncle had taught me. My uncle's tired open-casket face came into view; his gravelly voice penetrated the vast empty areas of my mind: *Come back home with the ones you left with.*

"Hold up!" a tiny woman in a long denim dress shouted from housing projects curbside. She held up her palm like a stop sign, and the other hand raised her hem when she floated through heavy traffic toward us.

"I'm Harriet." A keloid from what looked like pink pigskin rose between her eyebrows. Tight gray curls squeezed from underneath her lavender headscarf. Her face was leathery like soft shoes, angelic, a sparkly black diamond which made even her keloid beautiful. She wore heavy-looking, terribly soiled, ankle-high un-tanned brogans, legs unshaven.

I picked another thought from the Ferris wheel in my brain. "Harriet Tubman—from third grade? I know *you*."

"Let me help you," she said. She lifted Booker's other arm around her shoulder. "We've got to stay ahead of the catchers," she said. "They must be on the way by now."

The woman looked to be all of ninety years but was as agile as a cat, and I whiffed a scent of pine freshener on her as we crossed the street into The Courts with Booker limp between us. "Can't let them take your freedom," she said.

Booker dangled between us past the chain link onto public housing project grounds, over sidewalk pathways crowded with groups of crapshooters and along dirt trails; he howled in pain like a South Carolina slave under the master's lash in Harriet's time.

"Keep going," the old woman shouted. "I hear the hoofbeats of patter-roller nags."

I'd fucked up. Booker broke up like Tinker Toy pieces. Why had we stolen the white guy's car? I took two breaths. Harriet vanished. Where'd she go? She reappeared seconds later. Why didn't I let Booker drive? My belly knotted up. For a moment, I squeezed my eyes shut and considered what Connie had told me from the Kama Sutra about emotional release and liberation: *An intelligent and knowing person, without becoming the slave of his passions, will obtain success in everything he may do.*

* * *

Harriet and I humped with Booker for what seemed like miles to the other side of The Courts, which, in reality, was only several hundred yards from the car crash to a closed-door unit #313, Connie's apartment. I cupped my hand over my mouth and shouted to the open second-story window, "Open the door, Connie." Harriet kicked the door. Booker whimpered, dazed.

"Can't let them take your freedom now," the old woman said and kicked again.

Door locks, latches, and chains clanged undone inside Connie's unit. Sirens wailed not far away and seemed closer before she scootched open the heavy metal door and stood in a pink nightgown with tiny pink flowers that kept flying open. She was barefoot, ready for me. Connie was average, no Dorothy Dandridge, but then who was? Short, maybe five-three, petite figure, medium waist, a good match for my thin frame. However, those lips were like Gladys Knight's. Her smooth dark brown skin and short, pressed hair smelled like the Dixie Peach she used to flatten her edges. When the Ferris wheel stopped, she looked better than I'd ever seen. Good God Almighty.

"What the fuck—?" she said and moved to turn off *Bonanza* on the muted TV screen when Hoss Cartwright shot at a rustler. "Your mouth looks like shit."

I felt for Harriet, but she'd disappeared. My foggy brain raced for an explanation. The springs screamed like hungry alley cats when Connie and I dragged Booker inside and dropped him on her rickety sleeper bed, the same sleeper where I'd received an advanced lesson in kissing when she pecked my ear, neck, lips, where she'd forced open my mouth with hers and sucked my tongue nearly out of my head. Not wanting to cum in my pants, I thrust my hips back and away from her slow, deliberate grinds.

Booker slumped. My Ferris wheel stopped on an *Ebony* magazine on the gray shag rug. On its cover, a collage of Black people inside an outline of the United States captioned, *Which Way, Black America?* Frankincense and Connie's sacrament, weed cut with oregano, attacked my nose, burned my eyes, and boosted my high slightly. A plaid paper tray of Church's Chicken wishbones and half-eaten coleslaw was on the sofa. Edwin Starr's "War" fought through two tinny speakers from a record player straddling brick and board shelves populated with cheap decorations and pictures of the two small children Connie made a home for.

I bent over, gasping when Harriet's vision reappeared, turned, and said, "Only the righteous shall enter the gates."

I was in no mood for Christian rigmarole; besides, I hadn't read the Bible recently and had long ago given up my gate key by doing most of the things the Lord hated, like when I lied, devised wicked schemes, and stirred up conflict in the community, all in service of drugs. Nor had I attended Baptist church recently. Exactly how long it'd been, I couldn't remember. I did know my latest drug run had been three months of constant scuffle and hustle, beg, borrow, or steal. It's what I did to maintain.

I snapped at Harriet, "My name's already in the book."

"What?" Connie said. "What the fuck you sayin'?"

I looked again, but Harriet was gone. I rolled my shoulders and said, "But, but—"

"But shit. You must try and focus." Connie's pitch rose a level. "How much shit you take today?"

Booker's breaths sounded shallow, and his eyes closed; he grabbed at his hip and groaned.

I stood with my hands in my pockets, head down.

Connie pulled delicately on her gown. "You'd better get your shit together—get Booker over to Killer Kane." Kane was the county hospital and the only emergency room for miles around. Maybe Connie had a clue about the seriousness of Booker's injury. She turned to her guests. "Do you have transportation?"

"No vehicle," I said. "It crashed."

The older woman reappeared, eyeballed me, raised her hem, and pointed at her brogans. "I have the best transportation," she said.

I shook my head from side to side and traced red, black, and green stripes along the lines of Connie's forehead, face, and hairline.

Connie rubbed her brow to ward off a headache and lit a Virginia Slim. She didn't want to draw attention to an ambulance, so she called a taxi for Booker.

It'd been a long morning, and my high was leveling off. I unwrapped the mescaline button and gold pill, swallowed them, and washed them down with blood from my bleeding mouth.

We dragged Booker out and hoisted him into the back seat of a bright blue and yellow Checker Cab parked curbside near Connie's place. The driver, a Mexican in a sleeveless Bolero jacket open to puffs of black hair on his chest, punched the meter buttons, and Connie pushed him five bucks.

I sat up front, strapped my lap belt, and peered over the headrest to Booker, whose forehead Harriet stroked on her lap. His eyes closed. She started to moan what sounded like an old Negro spiritual I'd heard in church. "The enslaved sing most when they are most unhappy," she said.

I reached something buried in the depths of third-grade memory and finished her line for her when the Ferris wheel stopped. "The songs of the enslaved represent the sorrows of his heart." The cab driver glanced into his rearview, turned his head backward, and then squished his eyebrows together.

Booker tried to raise his right leg, maybe to stretch his hamstring, but his whole body collapsed.

In Kane's emergency room, X-rays showed Booker's leg was broken; he had head and hip damage. He needed immediate surgery. Soon, Booker would use a wheelchair. A few hours later, I was at Booker's bedside when the anesthesia wore off in post-op. How was I to know the fucking Cadillac would stop in front of me?

"What happened, Otis? I remember 'Psychedelic Shack' playing on the radio, then...." Booker said.

"Oh, we had a little fender-bender—an accident, Booker."

Booker gripped the handrail tight. His knuckles turned white, and blood spots appeared through the bandage from the I V needle stuck in the back of his hand. "I can't feel my legs, my feet—my brain's jumping out of my skull."

"Oh—that. The doctor says you'll be fine," I said. "With some rehab, you'll be back in the *Soul Train* line in no time." I rubbed the back of my neck. "Tell 'em, Harriet—what the doctor said."

"Harriet? Who're you talking to, Otis?"

I surveyed the surgery recovery area, but no one was inside the curtains besides Booker.

"Harriet, dude. The older woman, her scarred face? She helped me carry you to Connie's place. She rode with us in the cab. Remember?"

"Probably the mescaline, Otis." Booker grimaced in post-op pain. "Get me to the audition."

I glanced around the recovery room again, tapped a fist against my swollen, snaggletooth lips, sweated, and nodded. Then Booker's face went blank before he fell asleep.

I stretched out on a mattress-less gurney next to Booker and closed my eyes, but they popped back open. Turpentine, alcohol, and other hospital shit stifled the air. Booker's I V bag is attached to a pole next to him. The morgue-like cold hospital air chilled me under gray fluorescent lights. The day was halfway over, and I'd gone from semi-sober to stupid, with no roundtrip ticket available, and had a train wreck.

The curtain spread, a lion's head changed to Harriet's face and waved at me, and then her image turned and disappeared like when the Night Train Express left Sobriety Station.

Intravenous pain solution weighed down Booker's snores. Shit knocked Booker's ass right out. Maybe I could get a hit, slide the needle out of Booker, and spike my vein. He wouldn't mind. *Naw*—I was too afraid of needles. Besides, I didn't want to become a junkie.

I'd made bad choices and wished the day had never happened. In my dream, the Ferris wheel slowed; *you'll kill or get killed, Otis,* Connie had said. I had to return to The Courts, where I could reload on drugs, to Connie, to her sofa bed.

* * *

I left Kane Hospital. At 120th Street northbound on Wilmington Avenue, I began to walk-hitch back to Connie's place. Thumb out, I trudged in the street in the sticky late-afternoon heat. Across the parking lot behind me was Lickety Lick Chicken, with the usual din of people packed inside. Sweat brought what was left of my high down quicker. Connie would fix me up in more ways than one. I'd look for more mes in The Courts.

From somewhere among a line of cars, music assailed my ears above the racket of engines: drums, bass, strings, then Marvin and Tammi, *Ain't No Mountain High Enough,* whose lyrics always seemed to lighten my load. I recognized the

"Tank," a boxy rust-bucket '55 Chevy station wagon, weaved and thumped the curb. Its top was dull white, the body a faded rose that might've been red at one time, hammered-out dents covered with gray primer, no front hubcaps. The engine wheezed like it had asthma.

Poochie Felder brought terrible news and constantly introduced himself with loud music. He had a record player attached to six towering speakers at his converted garage apartment, two of which doubled as Tank speakers controlled by his eight-track tape player.

Curbside, Poochie leaned across Lanky Lonnie; a grin showed his missing front tooth. Red-boned with sandy hair and a Quo Vadis haircut, he had green irises that seemed to float in ponds of pink. A good fist-fighter, he was once a can't-miss pro baseball prospect.

Lanky Lonnie rested a Raven 25 caliber between his legs. "W-what's happening?" he said. His short, low-maintenance hair hadn't decided whether an Afro or conk job suited him. He played community college hoops until he busted a knee. Even before the injured knee, one leg looked shorter than the other. Now, he limped more.

I dapped Lonnie, then did Poochie. A strange face glowered in the back seat, leaning out from the angel dust fog.

Poochie turned down the volume.

"My cousin Skillet from Shreveport." Poochie nodded toward the passenger, a smutty, stocky guy who could easily pass as retarded, a Raylon Skewlet type. He grunted and lifted his upper lip. Underneath it glowed a gold tooth cap. Right away, something was not quite right about Skillet. I pulled back a tad, so the Tank's window post was a barrier between us.

"I'm going to The Courts. Y'all headed that way?" I said. I cut an eye to Skillet.

"Naw," Poochie said. "The other way—Compton."

"What? The records hop at Cressy Park?"

Poochie only danced fair but quickly pulled girls with his green eyes even though his rap was so-so. He'd always get girls to lie with him between tower speakers and other junk in the Tank's bed.

"I'll tell you what," Poochie said, "I'll drop you off in The Courts if you help us with a little problem—well, maybe two little problems."

I hesitated. These guys had reputations, and I'd almost gone to jail with them before behind some failed purse-snatching caper, and there was Skillet; one of his eyes glared straight at me, and the other one gazed above my head. But the trek to Connie's place stretched long, plus these guys probably had drugs. "I'm in. What's up, Poochie?"

"Some Compton niggas jumped me last night and tried to take the Tank when I dropped the girl at her house."

"Oh, hell, nawl." I leaped into the back with Skillet and the angel dust cloud. "Tried to take the Tank?"

Under the dome light, Skillet put his scarred knuckles over a Bryco .380 automatic on the seat, grunted, hitched his head, and leaned forward to greet me. Chicken stuck between his teeth. His breath flamed an acrid odor of yard bird mixed with angel dust and who knew what else. "I don't like you," Skillet's coarse voice slurred, his crazy stare blank.

"The night's still young," I said—slow mothafucka.

"About ten motherfuckers tried to jack me up," Poochie said. He had to be exaggerating. "I busted the leader in his mouth, and when they ran to help him, I got away."

"They tried to take the Tank? Man, you got to be shittin' me." I held two fingers for the angel dust joint, but Skillet left me hanging.

"Naw. W-we gonna b-bust caps on nem," Lanky Lonnie said. "I know w-where they ass hang out."

"YEAH—kill 'em mothafuckas," Skillet said. His eyes blinked like hummingbird wings. He was funky, like he hadn't showered in days. I tried to consider everything all at once.

Poochie changed the eight-track tape and said, "We got two guns—the Raven has two bullets. Skillet's piece has three. We'll show their asses."

"T-two guns, five bullets. That's f-firepower," Lonnie said.

"What's the other problem, Poochie?"

"We need gas money, Otis."

"You got a clothes hanger?" Among the junk in the wagon bed, he did. I unfolded the wire at the twist, straightened it out, and bent it in half with a small loop at the end. "Stop at the next phone booth."

* * *

Connie's words *do not harm others* floated like stop signs into my brain in the telephone booth, but angel dust's contact made me drive through them. I forced the looped hanger into the twenty-five-cent slot and jiggled. Coins poured into the return cup like a Vegas slot machine.

Poochie gave the Texaco attendant three dollars and seventy-five cents for gas. The lazy-ass didn't wipe the windows or check the fluids and didn't ask if we wanted him to check tire air. The Chevy engine coughed toward Compton.

Skillet grinned and finally passed the dope over. I licked on the angel dust joint. Lanky Lonnie tossed me red devils and yellow pills over the seat, which I picked off the floor and dry-dropped without thinking twice. My heart raced like The Spirit of America over salt flats.

Poochie drove to 135th Street, Compton's west side, and parked in a residential area of small, well-kept bungalows with manicured lawns. His dim headlamps, dull streetlights, and the full moon in the swelter came as the only light.

He parked in the middle of the street, exited the Tank, and shouted, "I'm back, motherfuckers." He posed in the Tank's headlights, fighting position like Joe Frazier, shadowboxed, jabbed, and hooked the air. "Bring y'all's punk-asses out. I know you hear me." He blasted the eight-track James Brown's "Super Bad."

I grabbed a baseball bat from the Tank's bed. House doors to the north of us swung open, followed by voices, "Let's fuck them up." Then bullets hailed in our direction like news clips of Vietnam firefights I'd seen on TV.

Me and Lanky Lonnie jumped behind hedges, Poochie the Tank. Bullets ricocheted off the Tank; others whizzed by my head and cracked into stucco walls behind me or zipped off sidewalks.

Plumes of smoke rose in the distance where the enemy advanced, dodging behind trees, cars, and trash cans. I gulped down breaths to stay quiet. I was dizzy, and my legs were too weak to stand. I had good reason to consider Poochie awful news, but my need for dope overruled what little sense I had, caught in the middle of the OK Corral shootout. Worse, I had a thirty-three-ounce baseball bat and no gun. I was going to die.

A gopher scurried by, stopped, gawked at me, shook his head from side to side, and scuttled away. Harriet appeared on the gravel beside me behind the hedges. "Blood runs fastest from those whipped the longest," she said. I threw up a prayer but didn't expect an answer. What if I got killed? My heart nearly exploded in my chest. Poochie and Lonnie would go to my funeral, high no doubt, pour liquor libation on my grave, and continue their life of crime within the hour.

Lonnie fired back twice from the hedges. Poochie, next to the Tank, turned his body to shield himself. Skillet stood before the Tank like Charles Bronson, exaggerating his gait. "Fuck all y'all—I'm Superman." A shoulder hit knocked him back into the hood. "You can't hurt me." He regrouped and squeezed off three rounds before Poochie hoisted him into the Tank. Lonnie and I scrambled over; Poochie burned into a driveway and over a lawn, sideswiped a palm tree, and turned around. Bullets pinged off the Tank's body, shattering the driver's side-view mirror, and its engine whined away.

In the back seat, Skillet bawled like a child. "Mama, I'm dying!" Blood spotting his white t-shirt. That could have been me, all behind some bullshit. I shut down.

At Kane Hospital, we lied and said Skillet got ambushed at Cressy Park. His was a flesh wound.

I still shook when I returned to Booker's hospital room. Booker slept to the beep, beep of blood pressure and vital sign machines. An IV solution ran into the back of his hand. His face looked peaceful in a way I'd never seen before. Next to Don Cornelius, he probably saw himself on TV, doing the Jerk, cha-cha, or the Hop, camera up close on him. He'd make a spin move and then split; girls tossed panties his way.

Two yellow pills beckoned from a small paper cup beside Booker's bedside table. I didn't know what they were, but habit had me pick them up and bring the small cup to my mouth— where I paused. Nearly killed hanging with Poochie and Lanky Lonnie, the real possibility of injury or death jolted me. Connie had told me about moksha, self-knowledge, and liberation from an endless cycle of ignorance.

All I had to do was keep my mouth shut to liberate myself. Heartbeat in my ears, my fingers were sensitive to the feel of the cup and its odorless content. Harriet stamped her brogans and said, "There are two things you have a right to: liberty or death."

I'd given up freedom long ago but must take it back.

There was such glory over everything at that moment. The sun shone like gold through a hospital window, palm trees swaying in the distance, the Compton Courthouse clogging the skyline over the low-slung houses. The way my heart jumped, I could've had a heart attack or, worse, overdosed like a stupid fuck.

If the drugs didn't kill me, the shit I did while using them would. I balled the cup with pills inside and lobbed them onto the bedside table. Booker might need them. I'd follow up on the Texaco job application and apply at Shell.

Maybe, just maybe, I could get back to Connie's lovingness, her sofa. Reload on her wisdom.

Tomorrow.

I cut my gaze to Booker and covered my face with my hands. I lay on the clean, cool floor tiles to the scent of disinfectant. Harriet kneeled beside me and said sternly, "I freed hundreds of enslaved people. I could have freed thousands more if they knew they were enslaved."

I slept.

LELAND O. DUNWITTY'S SQUARE
CIRCLE EDUMACATION

The relation between experience and behavior is the stone the builders will reject at their peril.

R.D. Laing in *The Politics of Experience*

Taking tests always made my ear ache and my ass hurt. The 7 p.m. community college psychology exam was that night. To pay for couch space at my mom's apartment and make my car note, I needed to pass the exam to keep my first real job. But over the weekend, I'd partied and didn't study.

"To stay among edumacated people, we need edumacation, Leland," Tony said, ears close to his head and barely visible under his well-moisturized full Afro. He used familiar colloquialisms that morning in our office nook, a set aside in a county mental health clinic lunch kitchen in Watts, Los Angeles. Our decrepit oak desks pushed together, and Tony and I sat facing each other. "We *need* the D-gree," he said. Since everyone else at work did their own thing, surely, I could pore over a few pages of R.D. Laing's *The Politics of Experience* before the test.

I needed a drug boost.

But in the summer of 1971, something was different that day when I was cramming.

Hans Demmer, a wavy ginger-haired psychiatric tech, white showing around his dead-blue irises, scanned the foul-smelling community refrigerator and pointed to a wax paper-wrapped sandwich. A tiny guy, his job was to handle acting-out patients physically. "Yours?" he said to us. We shook our heads. He loosened the wrap, took a whiff, then two quick bites. He frowned and laid the sandwich on the Amana between grease-packed heating elements. "It's better at room temperature." Congested, he always hawked phlegm into a dark blue hand-kerchief that hung from his back jeans pocket. He shuffled to our desks.

"What you need today, Dunwitty?"

"Bennies," I said, "—to stay up."

Hans tossed me his damp hanky reeking of hashish bundled around something mushy the size of a golf ball. Inside the package, among a drugstore of different colors and sizes of pills, I picked amphetamines and took relaxed breaths. The white boy always had the best drugs.

He nodded to Tony, whose face tightened. "In your ass," he said to Hans. "Stick it up your ass." Then Tony regarded me.

"You can't be serious," he said. "It's the same old shit with you, brother. You'd better go help Menzimer."

My job was to advocate, understand mental health, and help bridge the Grand Canyon of trust between government services and the Watts community. For the first two hours as a Bootstrap paraprofessional resource person, I assisted Stu Menzimer with his Monday morning therapy group in my huarache sandals, cornrows, and yellow tie-dyed *Are You Expe-*

rienced t-shirt with the fisheye photo of Jimi Hendrix. A pair of eyes peered out from Jimi's psychedelic jacket.

In the conference room surrounded by small offices, storage, and restrooms, Menzimer was the schizophrenia *go-to*, and all the patients no one else wanted the boss assigned to him and whatever help he could scrounge. Staff members avoided his small group, but head-asshole Dr. Boyo, the psychiatrist in charge of the clinic, tasked me with him for some reason.

A detail-focused psychiatric social worker who gave me the heebie-jeebies, Menzimer straightened his dull gray bow tie. He told the patient dressed like Roy Rogers in his German lilt, "You say your wife implanted a listening device in your teeth?" Menz pulled the lapels of his faded brown woolen tweed in the group circle. His coat smelled like mothballs and had black elbow patches and shoulder ridges as he'd hung it on small wire coat hangers. He leaned forward in the chair, elbows sharp on his knees, gnarly fingers entwined. The man dressed as a cowboy nodded his head *yes*. Cowboy's image is reflected in Menzimer's Gandhi eyeglasses covering a sizable portion of his ruddy rodent face. "She knows what you'll do before you do it —correct?" Cowboy nodded *yes* again. "It sounds as if you believe she's spying on you." He nodded a third time. "How does that make you feel?"

After a long pause, Cowboy stared away from Menzimer and stamped his foot like a woodpecker striking tree bark. "Angry—I wanna scream."

Liza, a skinny woman in a red Oaxaca peasant blouse with blue embroidered flowers, fidgeted. Jackson stared through Coke bottle glasses at a carpet hole. The other three patients sat tautly.

"It's okay to feel anger," Menzimer said. "You can scream now, right here—this moment—you certainly can."

Cowboy's eyes blinked like strobe lights, and his shoulders slumped. "It's okay?"

Menzimer nodded assent.

Cowboy loosed a low-volume snivel. "Ahhhhhhhh."

Jackson weighed in. "Ahhhhhhhh."

"Aw, come on—you can do better," Menzimer encouraged Cowboy. "Think about your wife spying on you and let it out —let go."

"AHHHHHH—AHHHHHHHHH—"

Liza recoiled, and Jackson laughed nasally. My stomach rolled.

"Not bad, not bad," Menzimer said. "Try again. Imagine the implants turned on this time, and she's listening from another room—let her know you don't like it."

Gung-ho Cowboy braced himself on the armrest, slid to the seat edge, and bellowed, "AHHHHHHHHHHHH—AHHHH-HHHHHHHHH—AHHHHHHHHHHHHH." He paused only to catch his breath.

My heartbeat thrashed in my ears.

"Hooray—yay!" Five other patients cheered him. "AHHH-HHHHHHHHHHHHHH—AHHHHHHHHHHHHHHH," they said.

How could I study among dingbats? I flipped through Laing, looked for pictures, and found none.

"You're shaking your head, Lee." Menzimer's forehead angled back, his nose most forward. "Would you like to share something with us—scream, maybe?"

I put my palms up and leaned back away. "Nah—"

"Why are you rolling your eyes, Lee?" Cowboy said.

"They look a little red, you know," Liza said.

I didn't know. "Huh—ha, ha." I laughed edgily. "I'm here only for the job—stupid-assed Boyo made me come." I dismissed her with a gesture, jabbed the air to drive home my point, and hesitated. I'd forgotten what I was about to say.

I'd never get a damn thing read in Menzimer's group. He might run the nut group, but he was not running me. "What good is screaming?" I said. Two hours. Blown. Focus hard. "I don't need no shrinking."

Jackson snorted laughter again. "Really?" he said. "We all need help sometimes."

"Speaking of help, let me know if you need help with Laing," Menzimer said.

* * *

I munched cardboard Jack in the Box burgers in the empty lunchtime conference room. I managed a chapter between barbiturates to smooth my nerves and coffee and amphetamines to jack me through exam time later. If I failed, I'd lose my car and probably surf from Mom's couch to the drug house—what a goddamned choice. In practice, among highly degreed therapists, paraprofessional employees from Watts may have been like Martians. They weren't quite sure what to do with us, and *they* were strange to me, their high education, worldly ways, new cars, and, for many, their whiteness. My head and ears ached. The wall clock ticked, ticked, ticked to remind me that test time was nearer.

In-service. The unexpected happened in staff training after lunch every second Monday, like last month's *rebirthing workshop*. Hans had chosen to re-experience the struggle and break out of the birth canal represented by the other staff who circled him.

He tossed me his snotty drug hanky to hold for him. The shithead fell asleep, snored loudly during the session, and later claimed, "It was a cesarean birth."

In-service training was like that, a perfect place to ignore guest speakers and read Laing's text on psychosis.

I sat, Laing on the floor with crossed legs, forehead cupped in the web of my hand, and blended in with yellow-flowered wallpaper. Laing seemed to say people are interconnected. I read: *If we can begin to understand sanity and madness in existential social terms, we shall see the extent to which we all confront common problems and share common dilemmas.*

Outdoors at my red V-dub, I swigged vodka and chain-smoked menthols. I tried to recollect what little I had read: *Psychosis represents a transient mental state. It could be resolved with sensitive support and guidance and transformed into a deeper understanding of one's place on this planet.* Screaming? Maybe Menzimer tried to change his group.

Back in the conference room, Toussaint, the featured speaker with a square beard, broad face like a tiger, and shaved head, had arrived early. Tall, he wore tailored Levi's pants and jacket, a gray turtleneck sweater under a Navajo turquoise squash blossom necklace. Maybe to set up props in front of the blackboard, or more realistically, he wanted to assess what kind of nut cases he'd have to deal with before speaking about epidemic alcohol and other drug use.

He chatted with Dr. Boyo and peered at me over Boyo's shoulder. I couldn't make out their conversation.

"Excuse me," Dr. Boyo told Toussaint and left the room.

Toussaint hitched his chin up to me. I threw back my head to reciprocate. A Black man like me, his presence relaxed me and added to what the drugs were already doing. Indeed, he'd relate brother to brother, understand why I would shine him on and read during his presentation, and do my thing like everyone else.

He faded back into the conference room silence.

Determined the meeting would not start on time, two

dozen staff members meandered in. Tony dragged behind them to where I sat on a purple sofa pillow. We fist-bumped.

My heartbeat was sluggish; the wall clock showed 2 p.m., five hours to test time. Things were not looking good. I blew into my cupped hands, leaned over to Tony, and said, "Hey, brother, do I smell of vodka?" I chewed on Doublemint. Amphetamines helped drive me along the center divider with an edgy attitude. "Do I look high?"

"You look like yourself," Tony said.

"What a goddamn waste of time," I mumbled. Tony grabbed a gold pillow and sat to my left on the worn, greenish, low-pile commercial carpet, cross-legged like a school kid. "Look at this shit," I said. Menzimer and Hans ambled in. "Most of these assholes don't help nobody in Watts—all they do is WAIT. They wait in their offices for people to come in with problems. Who comes in? People in the worst shape. But they run to the bank every two weeks and cash checks," I said. "They make good money too." I leaned back against the greasy yellow wall. "Look at them."

"1 Corinthians 13: 4-7 says, 'Love is not jealous or boastful,'" Tony said. "We'll join the club when we get the BS—Bullshit D-gree."

"This damn test," I said. My jaw hurt from clenched teeth. "How'd these assholes do it?"

"If they did, you can," Tony said.

"I'll do a few chapters," I said.

Menzimer stopped inside the conference room entrance to demonstrate to Hans how patients dance the Thorazine Shuffle.

"They have a shuffling gait," he explained. He dragged his right foot on the inside of his shoe in slow, stiff movement. "See, I'm not bending my elbows—don't move joints."

"Frankenstein?" Hans said. "A zombie."

Tony yelled at him through my ears, "Just like you, ZOMBIE."

Hans flinched and wagged his finger at Tony. "Horrible," he said to Menzimer.

"Yep, yep," Menzimer said. "They might want to scream, throw a fit—" He exaggerated the shuffle walk for effect. "But they can't do anything except twitch and grimace. It's a powerful antipsychotic."

We flanked Toussaint, who had watched quietly, me between Tony and Menzimer.

We helped form the larger circle. Standard practice for mental health workers is ignoring the speaker, taking refuge in numbers, and asking many irrelevant questions. In circles was how we'd service patients, lunch, socialize, and meet, along the walls, a square circle, on all-sized pillows, psychedelic, pastel, furry, soft. A broken fluorescent inside the entry flickered, and the Timex wall clock below, now 2:20 p.m., ticked closer to exam time.

We made even the best lecturer scurry for cover by design, never to return. It'd be no different for Toussaint.

"I'll fire up incense," Hans said. A pack of Zig-Zags, an oversized DO NOT DUPLICATE medicine closet key, and a prescription bottle fell from his pocket when he reached for a lighter. "Hindu lavender's good for depression," Hans said. I was okay with it. He said the smell helped with anxiety, restlessness, and headache pain.

I might pass the exam by focusing on a few chapters. I rubbed my eyes, then dropped my head onto Laing's words: *Insanity is a perfectly rational adjustment to an insane world. The relation between experience and behavior is the stone the builders will reject at their peril.* Hmmm.

The custodian's vacuum thundered down the hall. The

A/C hadn't kicked on, and the humid conference room filled with lavender-scented smoke.

Toussaint uncrossed his arms and offered a bemused smirk but did not speak.

Dr. Boyo returned. "Lee," he boomed over the din of other voices. "GO—have the janitor turn that thing off until after in-service."

Tony and I were permanently assigned grunt work. Everybody bossed us. My lunchtime drug cocktail spoke for me, a flunky reasoning he's mistreated. "WHAT?" I said.

Tony elbowed my side. "Dude," he said. "Don't be stupid."

Built like a brick shithouse, Doctor Boyo had muscles in his forehead. At best, he could fire me or whip my ass, but Tony forced a spark of light into my clouded brain. I placed Laing on the floor, raised my fist, and got the last word, "Free Muhammad Ali," before I dispatched.

The vacuum sounded like an old car with a spent muffler in the hallway. I hit the shutoff button, which didn't work. The unit shook, and the noise increased. I followed the power cord through the hall to the right and around another corner of the rectangular building, past perimeter offices. The raggedy machine plugged behind the janitor's cart, which blocked a closed restroom door entrance.

"Les," I called out to the janitor.

"Uhm," he grunted through the closed door. I wobbled to pull the power, tripped over the cord, reached back, and grabbed the cart to break my fall. In slow motion, cleaning-liquid-soaked paper towels and soiled sanitary napkins rained down from a shelf tray onto my t-shirt. My heartbeat raced as Jimi and his band faded away, and bleach poured onto the floor. Les appeared and shut off the vacuum. He looked me over and pushed a gray custodian's shirt with his name stitched over the pocket my way.

Shit always happened to me, a cut here, a scrape there, accidents, a janitor's shirt with Les's name. Why? I had a sour, bitter tang in my throat and puked burger meat and vodka onto the floor. Les stink-eyed me again before picking up his mop.

In the conference room, I tried but could hardly refocus when high, worse under time pressure, and nearly impossible to concentrate on Laing around space cadets Menzimer and Hans.

Menzimer turned to me. "Hey, Les," a stupid grin made his face, "I mean, Lee—I can use your help in the group after inservice."

Hell, NO. I kept reading Laing. I'd never get anything read. I turned away and acted as if I hadn't heard Menzimer. Perhaps he'd ask Tony.

Menzimer leaned into Hans, who sat in a lotus position. "My patients did primal screams this morning," he said. "—they hung it out." He ringed his collar with an index finger and loosened his bow tie but did not remove his brown tweed jacket. "They seemed to feel better having done so."

"We heard them from the back of the building, Menz," Hans said. "Hell, I thought you were killing the bastards."

"No. No, we'd never—those moments are like new sparks of light precipitated into the outer darkness. Who are we to decide it's hopeless?"

"Yeah," Betty Yoshida chimed in from next to Hans. She sat on a silvery pillow, knees bent, heels under her butt. Betty, a psychiatric nurse, always optimistic, had tried to help me with psychology class. "Blah, blah, blah," I had said to Betty. But she had infiltrated and found a place deep within me, a scrap of vulnerability. "I'm only doing this for you," I told her, even though my job was at stake, not hers. She needed to stop nagging me about schoolwork. Hell, I was almost twenty. "How's the study going, Lee?" Betty asked.

I yawned, turned my back to Betty, and skated over a few Laing pages: *We live in a moment of history where change is so speeded up that we begin to see the present only when it is already disappearing.*

* * *

Forty-five minutes after the scheduled in-service start, the wall clock ticked like a time bomb set to explode. I'd struggled with a few more pages during the lull—fuckin' test. In the third grade, Raylon Skewlet had snatched my Harriet Tubman paper, scribbled on his name, and passed it to Mrs. Fontenot. I punched his mouth. We fought. "Leland Dunwitty, you're nothing but trouble—*F*," she'd said. "Your grade is F." She twisted my ear between her knuckles and sent me to the principal's office for swats with his ass-sucking, perforated oak paddle. Tests were never fun afterward.

Dr. Boyo ran a hand through his gray hair. "Will everyone please sit and quiet down?" The group kept talking. On Boyo's third attempt, the room quieted some. I marked my place in Laing with Zig Zag paper.

"Our guest counsels addicts and is known internationally for his knowledge of drug use and abuse. Welcome —Toussaint."

Lukewarm applause and grimaces from indifferent professionals who probably believed they knew all about the Artane, Mellaril, and valium for the Watts community stashed on their shelves. "The nerve of him," a psych nurse said, one among a recalcitrant corner group. "What the hell can *he* tell *us*?"

I put my mind to Laing and ran an index finger down the page until Hans interrupted. Wrists resting on his knees, he made no effort to whisper. "Did you get his last name?" he asked.

"Toussaint?" Menz whispered. "Toussaint Toussaint—same name twice, maybe?"

Hans threw back his head and flung away hair that had fallen over dilated pupils; voice loud, he said, "Is he wearing lip gloss?"

Menz leaned away from Hans, removed his glasses, wiped the lens, and returned them to his squinting face.

Toussaint, still standing, exchanged a knowing look with Boyo and looped his thumbs in his front pockets.

I considered Laing's text: *If I don't know, I don't know, I think I know. If I don't know, I know, I think I don't know.* Deep—had to be on the exam.

Toussaint faced the group and stepped forward enough so all staff members sat before him, silent, hands clasped at his silver belt buckle, a slight upward turn at his mouth corners. He peered over aviator glasses, then through them. Several workers rocked on pillows. Some bit their fingernails; others tapped empty notepads with pens, mugged silly grins, crossed then uncrossed legs and arms. Incense smoke clouds coalesced near the dirty cottage cheese ceiling. *Ticka, ticka, ticka,* the broken light flittered on and off. Again, I tried to read.

I raised Laing's book to eye level to create a barrier between Toussaint and me and read: *There is a great deal of pain in life, and perhaps the only pain that can be avoided is the pain that comes from trying to avoid pain.* Toussaint's tactic felt uncomfortable. He silenced discordant voices and riveted attention toward him.

Tony elbowed my side again, voice low. "Dude, he's looking right at you."

I snapped. "Fuck Toussaint." He would have to earn my respect—if he wanted it. "I need this damn job for my car note," I said aloud as the drugs told me to do. Sweat glued Les's shirt to my back. Better than anything Boyo had said, the room went silent. They probably expected Boyo to discipline me, but he grinned, a sneaky grin as if he knew something the rest of us didn't.

In a soft, almost delicate tone belying his physical presence, Toussaint spoke.

"What would you do if your patient arrived forty-five minutes late?" His glasses reflected the flickering fluorescent. Boyo smirked. "Habits have consequences, but since you are paying me to be here, it's okay to start late—however, I must share with you what I have learned working with drug-dependent people." Several mouths slackened, Tony's neck bent forward, and room temperature upped as the smoke grew denser. The air conditioner rumbled on as if cued, cooled the room a tad, and created a swirl of scented smoke.

"Someone here might benefit today." His pitch lowered, and volume rose. "But I won't start until I have everyone's attention."

All heads jerked to me. Toussaint, eyebrows angled up and down, was in control. I was too far from the door to run and couldn't slide behind Tony, who'd covered a grin with his hand. Doublemint lumped down my throat. My lunchtime buzz faded, and Laing thumped the floor.

Toussaint gaped at me. "You—Custodian Shirt. You look almost intelligent. Do you know what the most abused drug is in America today?"

I whimpered, "No—I don't."

"Same question for you." Thumb extended, fingers straight, Toussaint pointed to Hans.

Hans scratched the top of his head and slurred, "Nooosssir."

"Can either of you two tell us what illegal drug your service community uses the most?"

I shook my head from side to side. Hans frowned and shifted on his pillow.

"Can anyone here answer my questions?" There were blank stares. BOOM. The A/C shut off, incense smoke stilled, and the broken light blinked faster.

"If you work in Watts, in mental health, and can't answer those questions, you've failed the community—what good are you?" Toussaint seemed to bask in the silence. "Alcohol abuse and marijuana use are huge problems here and nationwide. Cannabis is what we call a *gateway* drug."

Tony threw up his right hand, stood, and did a spirit-filled dance as people do at church. "Hallelujah," he said. "Praise the Lord."

"U-S-of-A is a drug culture. I call it the United States of Addiction." Toussaint gestured toward Menzimer. "Designer drugs—prescription drugs, and what people do with them wreak havoc." His eyes blazed from me to Hans, and his tone was ominous. "Dope fiends," he said.

My stomach hardened and dropped to my groin. I faked a smile. I'd never heard drugs explained how Toussaint had and, until then, hadn't considered wine and malt liquor, which I first used at twelve drugs. Marijuana? —harmless—was what I believed even though I couldn't remember shit when smoking it. How could I pass an exam stoned?

The fluorescent over the door finally burned out, dimming the room. My nostrils stung. Others gasped from thick incense smoke. Hans started to tremble, leaned, and collapsed to the floor. His eyes rolled to the top and disappeared under his eyelids; his body stiffened and jerked violently. I bounced up. Dr. Boyo rushed over, raised Hans's head, and shouted, "Lee, get a cold towel." My feet felt planted in concrete. He turned Hans' head to the side gently, like a mother handles her newborn. Hans pissed his pants and passed out.

"It looks like a seizure—grand mal," Boyo said. He raised his voice. "Move your ass, Lee."

"OKAY," I said. Fuck.

I retraced my steps back in the hallway, around two corners to the restroom, which had no paper towels. I found the janitor's cart—Les was nowhere in sight—grabbed a clump of damp towels from the cart tray, wavered back, and handed them to Boyo, who carefully placed them under Hans' head.

After several moments Hans recovered, sat up with Boyo's help, and rubbed his right eye vigorously. His hair had turned blond where his head rested on the damp towels. Boyo raised his hands to his nose and did a double-take. "Bleach?" I rubbed the back of my neck. "Irrigate his eye in the kitchen—flush it with water. HURRY." His feet dangled between them as Tony and Betty hoisted Hans to the kitchen. "He should be okay," Dr. Boyo said, "if he didn't get too much bleach in his eye."

Toussaint spoke about tough love and reality and spent time describing the effects of PCP, LSD, pharmaceuticals, speed, hash, and on and on, some of which I'd used over the weekend instead of studying.

"Would you visit a medical doctor you know is under the influence?" Toussaint asked rhetorically. He pointed to his bald head. "Would you trust *your* well-being to someone who's not all there?"

Toussaint's celestial form seemed to levitate behind a fog of incense smoke floating through a long silence. For once, no one answered or asked a ridiculous question. His honesty and information penetrated my high. I felt naked, like the emperor with no clothes.

"Nicotine—yes, it's a drug—smoking causes emphysema, cancer," he said.

Alcohol and other drugs were weaved into the fabric of Watts, like ketchupy Jack in the Box hamburgers. Except for a few like Tony, everyone I hung out with smoked, swallowed, or injected something, especially on weekends, making impairment seem reasonable.

Toussaint squinted at me and said, "Show me your friends, and I'll tell you who you are." I leaned forward when his tone lowered. "We use our drug habits to paste over what we don't like about ourselves." He eyed the book on the floor in front of me. "It's like when Laing says, *what we think is less than what we know: what we know is less than what we love: what we love is so much less than what there is. We are so much less than what we are.*"

My limbs felt heavy.

He wrapped up at 4 p.m. sharp. "How can you love yourself when you don't know yourself?" Toussaint asked.

Three hours to test time. What should I do? *We are so much less than what we are.* My mouth went dry.

* * *

After in-service, incense smoke cleared, and clock hands moved faster. The exam looked like a lost cause. I was still shaken from Toussaint's talk and what little I'd read in Laing. However, I was more sensitive about those who were fragile, Menzimer's schizophrenia group.

Liza shuffled in. She dragged the inside of her right foot and homed in on my custodian shirt. "I thought you were Lee? You got more than one job?" she said. Menz's patients were unpredictable and often among the more intelligent patients we'd see.

"No, one only," I said, "—barely."

Menzimer said, "Let's talk about the book you've been reading all day, Lee." Cowboy rested his hat on the armrest as Jackson adjusted his thick glasses and laughed. My belly fluttered. "Did you know some remember Laing for his insight into the relational rather than genetic dimensions of schizophrenia, for his understanding that madness can be the inevitable expression of an existential impasse created by relation binds and familial collusions? Did you know, Lee?"

"Yes," I said. "I agree." I read for the next two hours, and we examined passages from R.D. Laing.

That night, I answered exam questions on a Scantron sheet and sweated while the professor rushed away to score them on a machine. Sleeping on my mother's couch always hurt my back, but I'd suck it up before returning to the drug house, which flooded my community with brain-numbing food.

The instructor hunkered in and handed back the test results. The scent of failure reached my nose into my skull and hurt my head. My heart pounded against my ribs.

At the upper right was a letter scribbled in red, C+, and a note: *Good job!* My breaths were bottled in my chest; my face couldn't contain my grin.

*   *   *

Six months later, Toussaint returned. A bronze plaque above the conference room doorway read *The Hans Demmer Memorial Conference Room – Dedicated 1971*. Five months earlier, Hans had suffered a massive stroke and was on life support for a few weeks before hospital doctors pulled the plug. I attended his open-casket funeral. He looked solemn in a suit, his wavy ginger and half-blond hair, and right eye patch where bleach blinded him. I told Tony how I hated parts of me I saw in Hans. Those despised parts of me held me in check for so long. I imagined those stains transferred to the rose I tossed and lowered into the dirt with him. "I want my edumacation—that Bullshit D-gree," I told him.

"If they can, you can."

Betty and Menzimer mixed with the other staff, mingling under bright ceiling lights in the middle of a newly carpeted conference floor. The dusty cottage cheese ceiling had been scraped and repainted with the walls of Hindu lavender. The A/C was upgraded, and a digital clock with red numerals replaced the analog Timex. Les whizzed by with a quiet vacuum. Incense burned.

I struggled with my sobriety but didn't give in.

Laing remained on my new desk, but his words burned in my brain: *Whether life is worth living depends on whether there is love in life.*

"And that," Toussaint explained, "starts with learning to love oneself."

That's what I told the Watts community.

THE NIGGALATORS

Despite repeated supervisor warnings, Tamara's late again. After a sick day, her fingers resist when she runs them through red-coral Slauson Swap Meet hair. She believes her extensions are one hundred percent virgin Brazilian hair, now lacking the soft, silky, natural touch of just three weeks ago. The hair feels more like horsehair or, worse, some silicone-coated synthetic. She palm-tamps where it's parted in the middle, hoping the flowing weave helps highlight her cheekbones and brightens her dull moon-shaped face on the hottest recorded June day when Marcus, her estranged husband, calls to accuse her of fucking Fletch.

"I can't talk right now," Tamara says into her cell phone. She had kicked Marcus curbside weeks before and hadn't seen him, although he kept calling and cussing her. Reluctantly, she'd removed her wedding band and noticed her dark chocolate skin color hadn't yet returned to her ring finger. They'd been married the last two of her thirty-one years, and the rent was past due without his income.

"You owe me a little sumpin' sumpin' since you sucked

Fletch's dick," he says. His tone was flat and lifeless, like when he couldn't get his way, got drunk, and repeatedly threatened suicide. She's caught up in her feelings, signaling tears, reminding her how she now treads water in a lonely ocean.

The Niggalators rap music blares from his end:

> *I come up in the Downs, don't get much worse.*
> *I'm a dope gangster dressed for the hearse.*

Fifty feet away, her bug-eyed supervisor checks his watch and glares at her through his office door glass. Atop her stack of invoices, his typed note says her sick time is exhausted. Accordingly, her future paychecks will reflect less. At the bottom, he handwrites, *PS - your mistakes cost Vick's Pet Supply money, money, money.* She needs to concentrate and avoid errors. She whispers, "For the millionth time, Marcus, I didn't cheat." A salty-sweet taste sours the base of her tongue, and her shoulders curl over her chest.

She turns away, trying to keep the other clerks from realizing her upset, especially Keisha, whose ropy hair dances off her neck whenever she hears Marcus's name. Tamara glances over her shoulder at her and other coworkers, who watch her curiously.

"Marcus?" Keisha mouths, but Tamara pretends she doesn't understand.

"You're my husband," she says to Marcus, "—and Tyquan's daddy." She red stamps several invoices *Delinquent.* "I chose you, not Fletch. But things are different after what you did." She looks again and restamps invoices black, with today's date: *Paid June 18, 2009.*

Since Tamara met him, Keisha kept telling her he was cynical and selfish. "That stuttering motherfucker is lower than rat shit," she said.

"Aww, c-come on. Baby. I'm c-cool," he says, crazy rhymes playing in the background. He stutters most when he's sprung; she over-talks him or says something he doesn't like. "I ain't mad at you. Let's hang out, and I won't c-c-call your job no more. Otherwise, I'm coming to you."

"Is that him?" Keisha grumbles over Tamara's shoulder.

When she turns, Keisha's hovering over Tamara's table desk, hands gripping her hourglass waist, pale peach skin color, making her look like an Egyptian queen. Keisha hates Marcus as much as he hates her and would try throwing him out if he came to their job, making a disastrous scene and probably causing Bug Eye to fire them both.

Tamara pressed her pointer finger to her lips, silencing her, knowing Marcus would explode if he knew Keisha was listening.

Maybe she could still change him, and perhaps she'd better go to him, possibly talking him into helping himself, perhaps extracting some small apology. Tears usually follow the thickness in her throat, which she won't shed in Keisha's sight.

Tamara tells Marcus in a low voice, "I'll meet you in twenty minutes at Angeles Abbey." Distracted, she stamps several invoices as *Delinquent*. "I only have a half-hour lunch break."

"I'll be there," he says. *The Niggalators* music booms as if he's placed his phone near car speakers:

Like ripples in the pool, it's not free will
My woman's like a tool. Slap the ho still.

She shuts her cell phone and stuffs it into her Michael Kors clutch, heavily weighted with Laundromat quarters, next to the balled-up eviction notice. She sighs and tries not to look at Keisha.

Keisha squishes her plucked eyebrows and says, "Please tell me you're not gonna see his runty ass."

Tamara checks for car keys and straightens her desk. "I won't be long— promise."

"Dammit, Tamara, what's it going to take? Him hitting you fifty times in front of the kids? What about his restraining order? The TRO?"

The drama at Gonzales Park rushes back, choking her brain like Hurricane Katrina floodwaters filling the bowl called New Orleans.

WHACK. *"Owww!"* a punch and Tamara's head had lurched forward, the strike rattling her brain. Two more face punches dazed her. Before that moment at Gonzales Park, Marcus screamed and argued, grabbed her throat, shook her like an Etch a Sketch, and even gut-punched her a few times, where he wouldn't leave marks, causing her to miss work. But he'd never struck her in front of the kids. Trina, nine, and Tyquan, two, had trembled, their eyes wide in witness, faces terrified as if they heard an echo, his knuckle meeting her cheekbone. Whale-eyed London, their energetic steel-gray animal shelter mutt Tamara rescued, yelped, and cowered.

"You deserve more," Keisha says.

Keisha has a point. Even before the last straw, Marcus had little motivation to do anything, especially legit work or clean their smoke-filled apartment, when he struck her. He'd committed petty crimes and said, "Selling weed *is* my job," which got him jailed. "I got felonies to show for it." Still, his *twos and few* helped keep the roof over their heads in the 2009 Recession.

Keisha takes a breath and drops her hands, voice edging softer; she says, "You must look out for yourself. Get yourself a fine, smart Black man. Maybe a Mexican. Even a white man who's good to you will do. It's never too late to do something good for you."

"I have his child, Keish. And he's a better daddy than Fletch ever was to Trina." Marcus, whom she genuinely once loved, had *je ne sais quoi* and could make her nipples hard just smelling him when whatever he smoked hadn't seeped through his pores or when he lightly brushed her thighs. Those times, her body radiated heat, like when she turned on the shower and waited for the proper water temperature. When the water got hot, the experience was pleasant. A much older man, Fletch, came before him and was an occasional fireplace log who paid child support.

Tamara slings her leather clutch strap over her shoulder, grimacing when the laundry coins sting her middle back. "I ain't got time to worry about doin' something good for me. I gotta at least try to work this out with Marcus."

Hurrying to meet Marcus, she glances at the wall clock, Bug Eye leaning from his office doorway, looking; Keisha's calling from behind, "Tamara, wait!"

But Tamara's already out the door.

Tamara stops her Grand Prix in a nook of Angelus Abbey Mausoleum in Compton. She and Marcus often cuddled there in the dusky stillness, knowing the dead would speak no ill of them. Sometimes, a gesticulating Oscar, the grounds attendant, limped up, yelling, and ran them away. Oscar reminded them that a mausoleum, resembling the Taj Mahal in some eyes, is a resting place for the dead and not a motel. Having done her encyclopedia app homework, Tamara knows the florally engraved brick resembles the North African Moors design. The back of her neck is Goosebumps.

Gravel-covered graves with swaths of dry tussock, missing headstones, wilted flower sprays, and tired balloons stretch before Tamara, juxtaposed by Angelus Abbey's enduring beauty. One cracked tombstone is inscribed, *Dad, always loved, never forgotten, forever lost.* Tamara muses whether the dead feared death in life. Are they genuinely remembered, like when Mesoamericans celebrate Día de Los Muertos? Besides her children and maybe Keisha, who would celebrate her life when she dies? Indeed, the dead don't read headstones. Or do they?

Her belly knots. Will Marcus finally admit he has mental problems and needs help? Rehab maybe? She'd be there for him. Perhaps they'd find a way back together if he'll take responsibility for what he's done to her.

She slides into Marcus's beat-up yellow Saturn *to talk.* The air is hot, and he reeks liquor, likely from the Ciroc vodka bottle planted between his legs, his one-sided smile gripping a cigarillo stuffed with who knows what.

"What's that smell?" she asks. Marcus' eyelids are half-closed over far-set cranberry eyes. He inhales and throws back his large, round, tightly corn-rowed head, which seems to bobble on his bull neck.

"Spice," he says. "I'm cutting back on bud." He coughs chest-deep. "Told you I could stop."

"That shit's crazy-making." She draws slow, steady breaths and slams her clutch, denting the glove box. "You already have enough problems."

He won't look at her and turns up the music. The drumbeat, low-pitched bass, and Niggalators music booming from the CD player jar her.

Finally, he turns down the volume.

"It's Fletch's fault," he says. His flat nose is like a button sewn onto greasy cocoa skin. "Muthafucka, all in my business."

"What? I thought you were ready to apologize. Get serious," she says. She rummages her clutch, past rolls of quarters, pulls a handkerchief, and dabs her mascara tracks. "You lied."

"I only hit you *once* in front of th-them," Marcus says, his smile overly bright.

Tamara's stomach clenches. "Real men don't hit women ——that's just *niggashit*."

"I-I *am* a real man." He swigs Ciroc. "—I got a son."

"Any fool can make a baby." She snaps the clasp of her MK clutch. "You need help, Marcus—you need to man up."

Marcus flinches and stink-eyes Tamara. "B-b-baby, I don't need no psych," he says, his finger pads burnt from smoking anything passed to them. He fumbles over their family picture, which dangles from his rearview mirror. "I just want to get back with you— take care of my family—like I used to." His slight grin, she still finds cute. "My baby boy had just started walking, remember? We used to chill at the p-park."

The park. Gonzales Park is the last thing she wants to think about now. She rubs sweat from her middle forehead and scratches her dry scalp. Minutes before Marcus struck her, Fletch had texted her, wanting to take Trina to Watts Towers. "What's Methuselah muthafucka want?" Marcus had growled in a way she'd rarely heard before. "Old-ass nigga—tell that muthafucka I said to go drink some prune juice. I got a Mossberg for his broke-down ass." He snatched the phone from Tamara, returning the call to Fletch. "I'm going up in ya' if you call my woman again," he yelled. "Get your chin off my nuts, muthafucka." He slammed the phone shut. Marcus had always made ugly comments about Fletch but had never directly confronted him until then. Sure, they'd had good times, but now him knuckling her face is what she remembers most about the park.

In Marcus's rust bucket next to the abandoned cemetery,

her shoulders droop from the weight of a bootless marriage, good times fading away like the smoke from Marcus's joints.

"Aw, Tamara, you know me," Marcus says, staring down at his burnt fingers, again touching the photo from the rearview mirror. Exhaling a shallow sigh, he tries to sneak-kiss her.

Tamara recoils. "Getting back together isn't a good idea, Marcus," she says, swallowing hard. "All you do is hang with your boys and get twisted. Can you show me anything different? Anything?"

"You know n-nobody hires ex-cons. Can't you forget about the other shit?"

"I want out. We'll work out how you can see Tyquan." It's crucial for her that father and son stay connected despite Marcus's problems. Didn't Proverbs 17:6 say *the glory of children is their fathers?* For her, she'll spend more time with work; make fewer mistakes; get Bug Eye off her ass, and ask him for a raise. She'll take more pills to help her sleep nights.

Marcus wilts into the car seat, his mouth downturned, eyes red and streaming, and body funk escapes his dirty white oversized t-shirt. "Please, Tamara, d-don't leave me. I fucked up." His face puffy, fingernails overlong, he grasps the steering wheel tight. His forearm Black Panther tattoo pulsates with each squeeze.

In his way, he seems to admit his mistake. She needs to make sure. "When was the last time you washed your ass?" She shakes her head, exits the passenger seat, and slams the door. Unless he shows anything different in her mind, it's over. She leans into the open passenger window. "If I call five-O, you are goin' to jail," she says.

He exits, too. "Whatchu mean?" he screams. "I wanna be with you. You just gonna shade me?" Marcus huffs around the car and grabs and squeezes Tamara's neck.

Her bladder releases, spreading wet and warm pee across

the front of her skirt, snaking down her hose-less legs. "Don't do this." She tries to convince him to visit Kane Hospital for mental help. "There's a social worker we can speak to," she says.

"Think I'm crazy, uh, bitch—I learned to kill *stupid* mutha-fuckas in prison," he says, white foam sticking his mouth corners, his grip like a vise. "Got my D-gree on the prison yard."

She tries to calm him. Maybe he won't stutter if she lowers her voice. "If you stop now, we can work this through, Marcus."

"You still love me. I know you d-do. I know you're with that old nigga—w-why?"

"He's my baby's daddy."

He releases her, rubs his scraggly beard, and gazes from place to place. She believes she has gotten through to him by how he looks at her. His eyes are red and watery. She tests him. "You hurt me," she chokes.

He says nothing, leaving her on the empty abbey grounds hunched over and broken inside. She can't go back to work. Instead, she goes home. Once there, she turns off the phone, has Trina handle Tyquan and London, and showers for forty minutes. No way will she tell anyone what happened, espe-cially not Keisha. Tamara won't tell Keisha about a tiny spark of possibility, an ember of reconciliation, a smattering of remorse heard in Marcus' voice. She pulls at her tangled hair. She won't tell Keisha that without Marcus, she's thirsty.

She won't tell Keisha shit.

* * *

Tamara hopes to sneak to her desk, handle her duties, and slink home at the day's end. Maybe no one will notice her rattled expression, her turtleneck sweater in the summer heat hiding neck bruises. But Keisha waits next to Tamara's desk.

Tamara pretends not to notice Keisha's tapping toe and crossed arms.

"You look like shit," Keisha says. "What's with the hot-ass sweater?"

Tamara's mind freezes as other workers veer and peer. She pulls her sleeves. "I'm fine," she says, voice weak.

Several workers shuffle papers and lower their heads when Keisha glares back at them while turning Tamara into the corner next to her table desk.

"Talk to me, Tam."

Tamara's chest tightens like something is twisting her esophagus. Cupping her face, she tries not to whimper but can't help herself.

Keisha notices.

"What are those marks on your neck?"

It is then that Tamara tells Keisha about what happened the day before.

Keisha drapes her arm across Tamara's shoulder, encouraging her to share her fears that Tamara never thought she'd raise children, especially a son, alone. Her dreams seemed so realistic that Tamara could touch them. In dreams, she pictured Marcus walking Tyquan to school, helping him avoid a prison pipeline filled with Black men, and telling him how to handle inevitable police stops before admitting he doesn't know a safe way. Keisha listens; good listeners are too few in Tamara's life, except for her.

Bug Eye throws up his hands when Keisha barges into his office. She tells him they are going to the police station to report Marcus.

Behind the wheel of Tamara's car, Keisha says, "I hoped I was wrong when I called Marcus a watermelon head, pea brain muthafucka, Tam, but I saw lie-bumps on his tongue."

She punches the AC button to cool them from the muggy

outside heat. "He's always depressed, negative—the drugs—and listens to fucking rap about hurting people. I gave him a Public Enemy CD, but he's stupid, too jail-hardened to listen to it."

Inching along in congested traffic, Tamara turns away and then faces Keisha. "I know, Keish." She pushes the big button on the AC control, forcing more air. "He's gotten worse. He needs help—"

Keisha bites her lip and squints into the dirty windshield. "This ain't about him no more. You've got to save yourself."

"I hate getting five-O involved," Tamara says, reliving an image of the LAPD whipping Rodney King's ass, Rodney's face bloodied and swollen, imagining Marcus fighting back and getting killed. "No telling what police might do to him."

"I feel you, friend. But for me—his ass can burn."

A thousand tiny pins seem to prick Tamara's skin. "But—"

"But shit," Keisha says. "Do something good for you for a change."

How did she get here? Maybe she deserves to feel broken inside. She touches her neck wound and winces. This is about Marcus and his actions toward her and their family. About what she must do to solve the problem.

* * *

Tamara files her police report. Their next stop is the Pomona District Attorney's office, where Keisha waits in the lobby while Tamara meets Assistant DA Elizabeth V. Sturgeon, an ash-blond gimlet-eyed woman. Her blade-like nose, tapered translucent fingers tapping her desk with an expensive-looking pen. Her cubby-hole office smells like flowers though there are none visible.

"The police tell me they found handcuffs, duct tape in Mr. Thomas' trunk, and a gun concealed in the dashboard," Sturgeon says. "From what you've told me, Mrs. Thomas, I'll charge Marcus with false imprisonment—kidnapping and spouse abuse. He violated the TRO. As a felon possessing a gun, he violated his parole."

"Kidnapping?" Tamara's thoughts freeze, and she searches for answers. "What will happen to him?" she asks.

"With priors and two strikes, he's eligible for twenty-five years if convicted on these allegations."

Her vision blurs. "How will Tyquan see him?"

"Do the crime, do time. That's the way it goes, Mrs. Thomas."

"Will he stay in jail until he goes to prison?" she asks. She weighs the pros and cons. At least she might feel safe from Marcus' increasingly unpredictable behavior. On the other hand, she'll get no chance to work with him. If he's in jail, he can't get counseling, parenting classes, or anything to keep from returning to prison. This system doesn't give a fuck about what inmates leave behind. You're damned if you do, damned if you don't. "Can you protect me?"

"The sheriff won't release him from jail based on these charges. I can assure you," Sturgeon says. "Here." She offers Tamara a few papers and her fancy pen. "Fill out these. My office will notify you of his court date."

A wave of heat and cold slaps Tamara. For several moments she leaves Sturgeon hanging. Wrinkles form between the old woman's eyebrows. No matter what Marcus has done, he's still Tyquan's daddy. They'd always had their time in the park. He was once a good man. Tamara snatches the expensive pen and the papers and scribbles her name across them. "Will he get help with his problems?" She flings the pen and documents, which stop short of falling off the desk before Sturgeon.

Sturgeon looks up from the paperwork. "Excuse me?"

"His problems," Tamara repeats, jaw in pain from

clenching her teeth, reminding her of several missed dental appointments, Trina's need for teeth retainers, and how she must keep her job to pay for it all. "You know—stuttering, drugs —his reading problems. How can he stay out of jail if he doesn't have a chance outside?"

Shaking her head, Sturgeon mutters, "Sorry, Mrs. Thomas, that's not what we do here."

Tamara sags forward in her chair, one hand on the clutch lying heavy on her knees.

Sturgeon fiddles with her expensive pen as if trying to bend it between her thumb and forefinger. Tamara snaps, "All you can fucking do for him is lock him up? That's it?"

Sturgeon clears her throat and peers over her bifocals. "State prison offers vocational programs if he wants to learn something."

"He got hardened—said he'd learned how to kill in prison," Tamara says. "Of course, you wouldn't know what they learn in jail school— would you?"

Tipping back her head, Sturgeon juts her chin, "Are you okay, Mrs. Thomas?"

Tamara's round face masks her roiling belly heat. "I'm fine," she says while rocking in her chair. "Congratulations, another one enters your pipeline."

* * *

Friday, July 4th, weekend, Domestic Violence Notification Service sends a text message to Tamara's cell phone. Marcus is being released from jail *to get his affairs in order on his recognizance, OR.*

The café noise fades where she's reading an app on Islamic architecture. She grasps her soda cup. "OH, FUCK," she says while people watch. No one's notified her of the court hearing.

"What fucking *affairs?*" she says to baffled faces surrounding her. She slams the cell phone on the table, clasping her cup even tighter, splashing ice and Diet Coke onto her jeans.

She forces her weak legs to her car, barely noticing the people she passes. The electric doors lock once she's inside, the ignition fires, and the Grand Prix seemingly drives itself to the Pomona Police Station. The Grand Prix rumbles to the court when the officer can't find a restraining order in the system. The clerk says the judge will not revoke Marcus's OR without the defendant's presence or his public defender, who, like Sturgeon, is on vacation for Independence Day weekend.

While parked under a *Passenger Loading* sign, Tamara sits clutching papers, figuring she can salvage their relationship if she tries Marcus again. The TRO documents, like a prison, are no solution, teaching him methods and practices that only serve to harden and teach him murder.

* * *

Three days later, Marcus shuttles Tamara from Angeles Abbey to a Whittier hole-in-the-wall to *talk*. His car wobbles over every street surface cranny. Dashboard tattered from the police search, dented glove box missing entirely, they arrive at the shit-colored paint-peeling hovel of what passes as a motel. Stinking and looking like the next step up from a homeless tent, the ceiling fan rocks, one of three light bulbs lit. Daylight bleeds through a seam and cracks in faded opaque curtains. Every two minutes, bulky equipment from nearby factory clangs a dull bell-like sound through an open bathroom window. Tamara's heart thumps when Marcus hangs a *Do not disturb* sign on the outside doorknob. He removes his soiled t-shirt and pours himself a drink.

From the bedside, Marcus fires what smells like spice. "What y-you want to talk about?"

Tamara shifts herself in the rickety chair next to a small table. "Us," she says. "I think you should get some counseling. I'll go if you want."

Marcus inhales deeply and coughs. "Remember the park? How we used to fuck under the tree?"

They'd never fucked in Gonzales Park with kids present. "Wasn't me." A sudden coldness hits her core. "Must've been your other bitch," she says, only half in jest. "Angelus Abbey, yes. Park? No," she says.

Marcus covers his ears and rocks back and forth. "Was you," he mumbles, pressing his fist against his chest, rubbing as if to dislodge something painful. Humming The Niggalators, he pounces, wrestling Tamara unto the bed, zip-tying her left wrist to the metal headboard grill, her shrieks dying in the stale motel air. Her wrist swells, and she breaks her lime green press-on nail, trying to loosen the thick industrial zip-tie with her free hand.

Her clutch with her phone is within reach, but she doesn't dare. Who knows what Marcus will do if she does? Will anyone come if she screams? Will anyone even notice sounds other than headboards banging walls? *Thabump, thabump, thabump.* Maybe the maid will ignore Marcus' sign on the doorknob or take a nosy peek through the open curtain sliver to save her.

She's sure thin walls can't contain her voice, but one good scream could end her life as quickly as it could save her.

Marcus stops pacing and sits on the bed edge. A stench from years of alcohol and other drug use clings to his body, somewhere between a cornered skunk and rotting fish.

A hard grin splits his face. "Fletch can't help you," he says. Naked, he masturbates and holds the Glock in his left hand, eyes bloodshot and reeking; he keeps wiping sweat from his forehead while muttering. "Till death do us part—remember that shit?" Marcus rakes his palm across her face.

Tamara tastes blood inside her mouth yet feels no pain as he pours himself a motel tumbler of cognac, sitting the thick glass on the greasy nightstand before Crip-Walking into the bathroom where he rhymes, *The Niggalators*.

She tries to block his voice, tuning into the dull factory bell and the couple fucking next door, but the crazy Niggalator lyrics are loud.

He's in the bathroom when her phone rings Trina's ring-tone. Tamara must answer or risk not getting another chance.

She struggles to open her clutch and grasp the phone with her free hand. "I'm okay, baby girl," she says. Keisha is on the other end. Her lips tremble, and Tamara tries to sound calm. "He kidnapped me. Please take care of my kids."

"I'm calling the police. Where are you?"

Before Tamara can answer, Marcus stands in the bathroom doorway.

"I'm going home soon," she says to Keisha.

"Police?" Marcus yells. "Fuck the police. Y'all need two body bags tonight."

"It's not—I'm talking to Trina," she says. She swallows, but there's not much spit.

"Goddamnit." He dives, wrestles away the cell phone, and smashes it.

Tamara turns away, an empty pit in her stomach.

The constant clang continues outside the bathroom window like a muffled church bell. The musty room wraps her like plastic. He's never had much *savoir-faire,* and even his little grin she once found so cute is now a dismal relic.

Panting continues next door as the factory bell tolls. A

roach crosses the headboard. Tamara holds back a scream. If she doesn't anger him, maybe he'll let her go like before.

Marcus balances his elbow on the rickety chair armrest. He scratches his chin with the gun barrel, lowering it to suck his pipe, intensely, obstinately, contents popping and glowing in the dim light like a little sparkler, wild half-braided hair looking like Medusa. He's unhinged. "Whatcha gonna do now? All I gotta do is put the pillow over the Glock and then *pop*, sound just like popcorn." He smirks and barks, "Told you I got my crime *D*-gree—told you I wasn't going back to prison. *Woof, woof*. We gonna see God."

Nighttime quiets the hardscrabble city, except the factory noise rings louder. The ceiling fan rotates slower. *Thabump*. The couple next door fucks. His smothering stink, her studying Marcus sitting in the motel chair, probably planning on killing her if she yells, contemplating such possibility if she screams, wanting to step outside her body, foresee her situation, but can't.

Keisha always had her back. *It's never too late to do something good for you*, Keisha had said. Now is that time—

Marcus gloats. "Fucking D.A. thought she could put me under the jail—no way, not the big dog." He continues his rap song.

Marcus has made his choice, a fucked up one, her owning a seemingly limited choice to either prolong or end the madness, perhaps ending her habitual selection of wounded men, men unable to contextualize their greatness. Greatness, like the Moors, who designed Angelus Abbey.

His isn't the only choice, however. She can still do something good for herself. It's never too late.

Tamara's tied hand hangs, bleeding from the headboard. Body tense, she twists to face him. "Shut the fuck up, you no-rapping bitch—you're a dog all right; a sick one—God might forgive you—I will never," she says, her tone carefully controlled. "—Keisha was right—FUCK YOU."

"Wh-What?" Marcus leans his head back, the cognac glass to his lips.

Tamara laughs a seething but restrained laugh, snaps up the MK clutch, and hurls it. The glass tumbler explodes against his face. She howls an earsplitting wail.

Marcus rises. He pulls the broken glass from his face and eye, wobbles and aims.

Tamara will never know what happens to him or the kids. She will never know Sturgeon, returning from vacation, sought an arrest warrant for Marcus. She will never see the motel maid simultaneously peering through curtain cracks and spotting blood everywhere. She'll never know whether the Whittier PD determines the case to be domestic violence, murder-suicide, or both.

She will never know.

BRUISED

At sixteen, I'm new to Lost Souls Group Home in East Compton, my third stop in two years. They claim I need pills—I have trouble listening and following instructions and have attention deficiency. The psychiatrist said the other homes say I'm angry, resistant, ever ready to fight. Mad.

Besides Hattie Melrose, our adult live-in group home staff, almost everyone I know takes pills, drinks alcohol, or smokes something. Yeah, right, but the Adderall Dr. Woods prescribes combined with blunts and Olde English 800 Malt Liquor, eight-ball we call it, and the other drugs I've learned to like make me feel safe, like a Linus blanket, protected and sane. Dope is like air.

I deserve to feel safe and should not knuckle under bullshit. That's what Mama taught. Her heart-shaped lips and straight, bright teeth were hard to turn from, like Lauryn Hill's smile, even when she'd grind them. "It's just you two, Trina, and you must love Tyquan. Help him get through—*look at me*. Do you understand?" she'd say, her flowery scarf unable to hide bruises on her dark brown chin, neck, and shoulders. "That'll be your job, your responsibility," she said as if she could foretell something terrible.

Her words stuck to me like the cement Simon Rodia used to bond the Watts Towers without bolts, rivets, or welds. Watts Towers was our favorite place to visit. Then she emphasized, "Try to avoid *niggashit*, too, you hear?" She rubbed her wrists. "Just because the trap's set, you don't have to step on it."

That was before everything collapsed, and Mama was still alive when I thought the world was a safe place where someone would always take care of me. That was before Marcus, Tyquan's daddy, my son-of-a-bitch stepfather, murdered Mama and took his wretched life in a sleazy Whittier motel.

At Mama's funeral, the church pew strained my ass beside Dupree, the social worker. Tyquan sat to her left.

Throat scratchy, I studied the key lock on the closed pink casket and overheard Miss Dupree describe Mama's face as *riddled*. I imagined Mama's face potholed with deep, round holes, like a rock worn by loose, whirling stones.

A week later, Dupree made me attend Marcus's funeral. She said he had mental problems and depression as if to excuse his murderous *niggashit*. His open casket smelled like death, the small bullet hole to his forehead hardly visible. I hated him, but Mama was right. I must protect Tyquan.

However, Children's Services separated Tyquan and me and cast us astray in the shit-crazy world of county services, where I learned of all the county offices and their supposed mission.

I've searched for years, and no one will help me. *Talk to your director,* they'd say, but no one took the time to listen, permanently, *maybe later,* they'd say. Later tires me like an open cut, deep and aching.

Hattie's a good listener for an adult. She doesn't treat me as a pain in the ass, and I convince her to help me find where

Tyquan lives. She discovers he is staying near the Towers with a Watts woman named Starkaña Wilkerson. "At his age, he probably attends King Elementary," Hattie tells me. "Start there. You don't want to show up at Wilkerson's place unannounced."

What does Tyquan look like now? I have to know. I must find Tyquan, and nothing else matters. "That'll be your job, your responsibility," Mama said.

I will do something big like Rodia did with the Watts Towers.

* * *

The next day I skip Compton High School, push in earphones, and block out crap like the nasty bastard wearing a faded Lakers t-shirt sitting across the aisle on the crowded Metro Blue Line train. His hand thrusts, jerking himself, and his lips pull tight against his yellow teeth when he utters, "Hey, Nubian Queen."

Heads spin when I say, "Stop it, pervert," but nobody says or does anything. Harassment isn't right, and my muscles tense. It's like that. Sometimes people see shit and act as if nothing is happening, afraid to stop what they know is wrong.

He winks a droopy eye and says, "Yeah, I know. It's stupid, right?" Always on guard for danger, I cringe, turn away, and scrutinize the frenzied shapes and colors, sky-high spires, seashell-covered finials, and the Watts Towers' skeleton-like gazebo as we approach the platform.

Time would pass slowly when Mama, Tyquan, and I made our monthly trek to the Watts Towers. I noticed little things like when the bee's sucked nectar from small silvery-leaved flowers growing barely above the grass. The broad-leaved sycamores waved, and the yellow flowers on elderberry trees and Rodia's junk art made me happy dance. When Tyquan crapped himself shimmying the pavilion's center column, I was content to let him stink until Mama's stare. My chest tightened, and from habit, I cleaned his shitty butt.

Suppose Tyquan doesn't live with Starkaña Wilkerson or even in Watts? Clouds form, dulling Rodia's glass and scrap-metal-pocked fretwork assemblage. Suppose he's at another school, or worse, no school. I dry sweaty hands on my school uniform Dickies.

I'm almost numb to flower sprays, empty liquor bottles, and stuffed animal death memorials that rise in clusters along the Metro route before arriving at the 103rd/Watts Towers platform.

They buried Marcus in a plain box, but Mama's casket was her favorite pink color. Whenever I argued, her backhand found me, and when home, she'd have me pick an outdoor tree branch, a *switch* she called it, which she lashed across my naked legs.

Tyquan was two, and I was nine and almost her height when I finally rebelled. "But why's Tyquan my job? How's it on me to worry about *him*? I've changed his diapers since he was a baby—*he's* your kid."

"You smelling your piss?" Mama had said, glaring. Her tone, I understood. I whimpered into the backyard and pulled a switch that I thought might not sting. "You can do better, Trina." Those thoughts and words I can't seem to shake. Why'd God let her die?

* * *

My heart pounds between my lungs. King Elementary School hugs itself with red brick and high wrought-iron bars, like a prison, in contrast to the Watts Towers' spires seen across the tracks less than two blocks away. An empty police car straddles the curb, and the uniformed officer peers out from the bars at the crowd of Black and Latina care-persons awaiting their charges.

The bell rings, gates burst open, and kids flood past me like raging water. The flood turns to a trickle, and the school police close one of two exits. I check my watch. Is King the right school?

He's last, but Tyquan bounces away toward me, wearing a red hoodie. He's much taller now, but the hitch in his run is a dead giveaway. There was never anything physically wrong with Tyquan. I believe he imitated Marcus's swag, the slight delay and twist in his hip, the way he'd hitch his shoulder, causing his right arm to rise and move forward, graceful, like someone in control, cool even under pressure. Looking back, I think motherfuckin' Marcus was just crazy. My insides vibrate.

Crouched behind a palm tree, I await the right moment and leap into his path, "TYQUAN." My skin tingles. He ducks and covers his head as if under attack. His backpack thumps the grass. Eyes full, he double-takes.

"Trina?" he gasps, then jumps at my outstretched arms. His face blurs through my tears. Whoa, he's so frail and undersized, like starving Somaliland children on charity commercials, flies covering their bugged eyes. Why hadn't I found him sooner?

We face each other and sit cross-legged, knees touching. He looks like Marcus but has our mother's smile, and, for a moment, it's as if we're picnicking again at the Watts Towers, me wiping his butt after I happy dance. In short, we revisit what happened over the past several years—my throat scratchy.

"Are you hungry, li'l brother?"

Pop, pop, pop, gunshots sound nearby. I'm easily startled, and Mama's holey face worms into my mind. The small entry wound on Marcus' forehead was like a black asterisk. Tyquan jerks his paper-bag-brown face—he's a shade lighter than I am—and we jump up. That's when I notice a black welt below his eye. Police sirens wail past the corner. My shoulders tighten.

"That bruise—did you fight today?" He recoils when I brush the eye bruise with my thumb. His black-and-blue mark is not unlike those covering Mama's face, neck, and shoulders, her bleeding knuckles. Such injuries were clear signs that someone had enacted niggashit.

We're poised to run opposite the gunshots when a kid taller than Tyquan bully bumps between us, a red bandana tied to his bony arm. He holds up black school uniform pants hung halfway down his ass, butt crack exposed. He couldn't run from bullets or anything else if his life depended on it, but he had an attitude.

"Whaddup." He nods. "I got chronic." Tyquan ignores him. The kid struts a few yards to another curbside death memorial, a clump of candles surrounding a red baseball cap. A brown stuffed teddy bear and a sympathy card fastened to a makeshift cross read, *RIP Li'l Renzo. Real G.*

"Are you in a clique?" I ask Tyquan.

"Naw." He shrugs. "Everybody wears red."

"Gangsters wear much red—I'm just sayin'." My neighborhood wears blue colors. It's dumb since peach is my favorite color, more *niggashit,* as Mama would say, fighting over stuff we don't own, so we all wear colors of our neighborhoods even if we don't bang, which most don't. We feel safe in numbers, though, almost like family.

It's taken me far too long to find Tyquan. My chest tightens, and I hug him again. "What's your new home like?"

"Starkaña has friends over," he says. "They smell like smoke." He lowers his head.

"Smoke?"

"Yeah, they smoke pipes. Pops when they suck. The whole

house stinks." I cringe. "I bag empty liquor bottles, aluminum cans she recycles," he said.

Hmmm. "Sounds like crack cocaine—" My breath quickens. "—and eight-ball." Marcus often fouled the air, smoking menthol tobacco, blunts, crack, and whatever could maintain a spark. In his twisted mind, weed was medicine, and he saw no problem blowing smoke in our faces. He'd chug Olde English forties, nut up, punch our mother, and beat us for helping her. That was wrong, and I'll never let anyone beat up on me. FUCK THAT SHIT.

"Makes me sick—so I go to my bedroom, try n' sleep."

Sleep was always a problem. When Mama and Marcus would fuss and fight, and when he'd have over his *boys'* playing dominoes, Tyquan and I'd play video games. I still have sleep trouble. Now, I take Hattie's calming effect on my group home for granted. I feel my teeth grind.

The wiry kid passes again, slowly, and holds his pants. He frowns at Tyquan. "Whaddup, my nigga—I got sticky icky buds?"

Oh, shit. Those are fighting words in our house. Mama insisted we were never niggers or niggas, which means we struggled often.

"Back up before I bomb on your ass," I say. Chest to chest, I shove the kid into the dirt. "Bompton in the house." I bluff a gang name from my hood, a gang to which I don't belong.

The bony kid tries to stand. Tyquan kicks and leaves a single sneaker print on the boy's butt. It's two against one. The boy scowls, throws up *Blood's* finger signs, and hunkers away. "I'll be back," he says, disappearing into a jacaranda thicket scattered along the train tracks, scented lavender leaves in full bloom. I spread my fingers and fan myself.

"Bring your mama," Tyquan shouts. "We'll kick her ass too."

"Let's get the fuck out of here," I say, and we race toward the Towers in silence.

* * *

Once we reach the pavilion's lacy spider-like design, a headless cast-metal statue on its spire, I'm out of breath. I scan two small sculptures to the south from the pavilion's seating circle, the north wall's embedment—rows of corncobs, boots, and other shapes. Behind us are two interconnected sculptures. I fight off goosebumps sliding along my neck. We once ate greasy chicken beneath cloudless skies in the three main towers' shadows. White sunlight flashed through leaves, and our picnic blankets spread under the sharp eucalyptus smell near John Outterbridge Plaza, where men snored prone on the wrought-iron bench.

Sabato Rodia, an Italian immigrant, had checkered the Towers with small colored broken glass pieces, seashells, ceramic scraps, and found objects made with simple tile setter tools over thirty-four years. Tour guides reminded visitors of Rodia's motivating words: *I'm going to do something big*. Words I breathed deep like smog, which slowed me, triggering my asthma when I raced Tyquan over one hundred feet down 107th Street along the south wall, a wall embedded with the green 7-Up and blue Milk of Magnesia bottle parts and the discarded mosaic tile Rodia used.

"Tell me more about your foster home. Are you, too, on medication?"

"Ritalin. But Starkaña took it away and started selling it when I banged my head on the television. My brain said it didn't want to be in my body anymore."

"She doesn't put her hands on you, does she?"

Tyquan studies the Canton ware plate, shells, and ceramic scraps Rodia embedded into the column above our heads.

"Becca came yapping—snatched the cover—I bumped her chest by accident." After another long pause, Tyquan clutches his knuckles. His gaze locks on the heating register engraved on the gazebo floor. "She had a cigarette in her mouth. Their pit bull Buster was there, barking his head off beside my bed."

My stomach knots. "Who the fuck is Becca?" I lean forward. "And why is she in your bedroom?"

"Starkaña's homie. Then she burned my pee-pee and whipped me with a clothes hanger." His shoulders curl over his chest. "I thought about killing myself."

"Oh, hell naw." Pangs of fire gnaw inside me.

Gingerly, Tyquan peels back the sleeve of his hoodie. "Becca put my hand, my arm on the kitchen burner," he says. Scabbed-over burn marks form an X on his forearm. "I screamed, but Starkaña wouldn't help me." He juts his chin. "I'm good, though—didn't let the white girl see me cry. Starkaña's a black-ass bitch—just niggashit."

Mama once said white people took the worst part of themselves, invented niggers and niggas, flipped the script, and fed the scraps to Black people long ago, keeping the best of everything for themselves. People like Starkaña eat *niggerness* like they eat Popeyes fried chicken. *Like Judas Iscariot, they are traitors,* Mama told us when she taught history lessons and read Bible verses during our Watts Towers visits. *Know who you are,* she'd say.

My head drops. My brother's sturdy, but he's just a kid. Math isn't my favorite subject; I get by. I like history. History taught me how adults plus alcohol and other drugs plus children equal abuse. Abuse and neglect are the stories of my group home roommates. It's our story. I'd somehow forgotten history, given my eight-ball and blunt habits. A bitter taste forms in my throat. I long for our video-game-playing days.

I want revenge, but most of all, I want Tyquan safe. I could snatch him now—then what? I need the plan to save him before Starkaña kills him. Maybe I'll borrow a classmate's gun, do a run-by, and steal him away. Nonsense. I could hurt him by mistake or wound an innocent crackhead if there are such things, given the hell crackheads cause the community. Besides, I don't know how to shoot. I'm going to do something. I must do something, something big like the Watts Towers.

I give Tyquan my cell number and make him promise to call if anything else happens. I skulk to the Blue Line station, stuff weed into a Swisher Sweets cigar, and fire the blunt to get my head straight, but pot doesn't slow my racing heart nearly enough. He'll be with those twisted bitches another night. Hollowness sets my chest.

* * *

Back home in bed, I swig the eight-ball stashed in my backpack, wash down Adderall and Ritalin, scarf chili fries, toss one way, turn another, woozy, and watch the ceiling fan spin. If I close my eyes long enough, maybe I'll fall asleep, but they pop back open, and Mama's sweet pie face, shredded like mangled paper, turns long, hard-bitten. Her lips move a heartbeat before her words, *and you must love him, help him get through.* My body fights an urge to run outdoors. *Try to avoid niggashit, too,* she says.

Whaddup, nigga, whaddup, nigga, whaddup, nigga, the bony kid's words bounce between my ears. My mother once told us niggers and niggas are the same things, bucket crabs pulling each other, unable or unwilling to love or help one another rise. She had said to keep your body clean inside and out, bathe, wash your hands, don't drink too much alcohol or take harmful drugs. She joked about a *Deniggerlator*, a room with revolving doors to prevent drafts. And a machine, like an MRI, some of her people could pass through. Privileged beneficiaries would crowd the snaking lines, the white people who created niggers for the good ole U.S. of A. A *Deniggerlator* to recreate Americans like magic, cure hard-heart diseases, PTSS, and mental cancers so many needed. The inventor would make billions because some people repeat the pain several times, exorcising their *niggashit*.

Mama always laughed about the Deniggerlator. Maybe she wasn't joking. Something I can't touch lives inside my mother's wisdom, an extra weight I don't want. Can I avoid the traps—do better?

The rotating fan can't cool or stop me from thinking about Starkaña and how she allows Becca to abuse Tyquan.

I'll get Hattie's help again.

* * *

I sniff morning's fried bacon and coffee and follow Hattie's singing—*Through many dangers, toils, and snares, I have already come—'Tis Grace hath brought me safe thus far, And grace will lead me home.* She hovers over the stove. I'm in first and hug her waist.

Hattie gazes from her cup and smiles. She wears a purple headscarf and a white chef's jacket and has smooth brown-sugar skin.

Across the tiny table, I face her. "I saw Tyquan yesterday. I never would've found him without you. Thank you for getting his location."

"You're welcome, sweetie," Hattie says, honey-voiced. She blows her steaming coffee. "How is he?"

"Not good. My brother's foster mama is a crackhead bitch," I say, hoping Hattie will grab the keys, rush the door, start the van, peel rubber to Watts, and rescue Tyquan. Instead, she places her palms on the table as if she's having a manicure. "Starkaña and her people are hurting Tyquan—and I need your help again."

She squirms. "Tyquan's your brother and all, but maybe you should let go, Trina," she says. "Let the Children's Service Department handle Wilkerson."

"What do you mean to *let go*?" My voice rises. "My brother's in big trouble. Children's Service doesn't do shit but gets people killed." I pound the table, spill Hattie's coffee, and blindside her. "Group home staff ain't shit either." Immediately my knees weaken, having said such a fucked-up thing to someone like Hattie.

"You need to step back, little lady; chill out." Her eyes narrow. "Have you taken your medicine?" She pushes the coffee cup to the middle of the table and takes several deep breaths. Then, the furrows between her eyebrows disappear. "Hey, I understand. I was abused and lived in foster homes as a child, too. I even lost my two children to the system—from stupid shit I did." Her tone is sharp. "This job—my PO is helping me get them back."

Blah, blah, blah. Hattie's understanding, but I'm not hearing what she has to say. "I could kick Starkaña's ass." My hands burn hot, sliding atop my school uniform pants. "Will you call Children's Service and report Starkaña for me? They'll listen to you."

Hattie hesitates, but I can't change her mind. She shakes her head slowly. My eyelids get all gummy.

"No, Trina," she says. "I risked my job telling you where Tyquan lived. You even ditched school. And with your grades, you should double up on books, especially math." She collects the coffee cup, stands, steps to the sink, and turns her back. "I'm out, girlfriend."

BLAM. I slap and shove, and the table screeches. "Screw it. I'll figure it out myself." My head aches, my hand hurts, and a cold wave hits me.

I fuss to my bedroom, flick the ceiling fan high speed, lift the window, and push in a CD: a guy's rapping about drinking gin and smoking chronic. I fire a blunt, as the music suggests.

SHIT—Adderall, marijuana, Hattie's pissed and won't help me. It'll be my fault if Becca kills Tyquan. Sheesh, what drama. Maybe I need a clearer head to think things through, a plan to save Tyquan.

The ceiling fan turns round and round. The situation strains my brain way too much.

Maybe I can do better—dodge the niggashit trap. But how?

* * *

I'm lethargic; my mind is tormented like devils congregating in Baptist churches. *Get a grip*, I tell myself. I must get Tyquan nearer to me before it's too late. I have no rescue plan, not Hattie, and no armed kidnapping. What would Mama do? Simon Rodia?

Fuck it. I'll make the Children's Service do their job and investigate Starkaña and Becca.

I rake aside spare change and candy wrappers littering the greasy shared desk and flip *Hip Hop* magazine pages. The Children's Service hotline number delivers a recorded menu list, a droll voice sounding miles away. *Due to the high call volume, our wait time is thirty minutes. If you are calling to report a missing child, contact your local police department.*

Maybe we can live together in the same foster home. *If you wish to apply to become a foster parent, press one; to report suspected child abuse, stay on the line.*

The phone clicks and music-on-hold grates me an hour before another click.

"CSD, this is Gina speaking." She sounds friendly. Yes, I got this. "Please give me your name and tell me how can I help you today?"

"My name is Trina, Trina Thomas—that crackhead bitch Starkaña abuses my brother at her shack near the Watts Towers —you've heard of the Towers, the little dude who built them with stuff he found. She sells drugs to zombies and lives with bitch-Becca and their crazy dog, Buster—he has rabies, foaming at the mouth, always barking—"

"Okay, let's slow down a little, Trina. Are you at the house you're calling about?"

"No, ma'am."

She asks me the essentials: Tyquan's full name, our age, where I live, where he lives, annoying stuff that doesn't matter as much as wicked Watts witches torturing my little brother.

"Are you in temporary placement, a group home? What medications do you take?"

"A group home, ma'am," I say. A leaf blower whines and a mower engine rumbles outdoors. I hardly hear Gina as I pace, struggling to control my tone. "But this ain't about me. Starkaña and her friends hurt Tyquan, beat him with wire." I tell Gina about the stove burns and drug use. "They're killing him."

"Did you see any of these things occur?"

"No, ma'am, but he told me. I saw his black eye."

"When was that?"

"The day before yesterday. I went to his school—King Elementary in Watts—"

"What school do you attend when you go?"

"Compton High."

"Un-huh, please hold, Miss Thomas." Music-on-hold. Several minutes later, Gina returns. "Compton High School is several miles from King Elementary in another district. Shouldn't you have been in school?"

"Ahh... yes, ma'am—"

"You ditched? Schools don't get paid when you don't attend." Doubt hardens her voice. "So let me get this straight. You say you saw a bruise on your brother...."

I interrupt the bitch. "Yeah, but what about his burn scabs?"

Her tone sharpens. "—at his school in Watts when you should be in school, Compton High, correct?"

"Why do you keep asking me about me? Starkaña hurts Tyquan—go see yourself," I shout, lips pressing the cell phone. "Go right now." Begging makes my throat sore.

"Calm down, young lady. I want to help you here, but you must not raise your voice at me."

"How can I calm down when skanky Starkaña and her friends kill my brother?" My belly feels the heat. "What're you gonna do, wait till they murder him? Let me speak to your supervisor, bitch!"

"Hold, Miss Thomas." Stupid music on hold again rattles my ears. I slam the *Hip Hop* magazine to the floor.

"Hello, Miss Thomas. I'm supervisor Horace Jones." His tone is stern, like some of my teachers at school. "We looked into your allegations, and I shouldn't tell you confidential information, but I assure you—" I hear Jones swallow. "Our workers and their police team have visited Starkaña Wilkerson's home several times and found the environment satisfactory."

"Your workers are either blind or lying. Didn't they see Tyquan's bruises?"

"The children in the house showed no visible signs of abuse

and seemed to be adjusting well in the home—the complaints were unfounded."

If only I could reach through the phone and squeeze Jones's neck.

"Did you go to the right house? She is Starkaña, a scraggy bitch with missing teeth—a friend named Becca, a crazy dog named Buster."

"Sometimes, Miss Thomas," Jones says, "we have situations where siblings manipulate and scheme to reunite into the same household. That's what you sound like to us." Sickness in my stomach rises to my throat. "How did you find where Tyquan lived?"

"This is BULLSHIT," I say, my sweat-soaked shirt. "If you assholes won't help me, I'll fix it myself."

"Suit yourself. Know that we'll post a truant alert and notify your school district," Jones says. "Is there anything else we can help you with, Miss Thomas, before screening out your call?"

The leaf blower rumbles on the outside, and I nearly jump out of my skin. I curse Gina and Jones for their terrible service, niggashit, and slam the phone shut, my body tense. I fire the blunt, suck eight-ball, and lie back, watching the fan blades turn. The world seems to crumble around me, and I miss Mama even more. She told me not to expect fairness in this life and was right.

* * *

I'm still pretty fucked in a dream sleep when Tyquan calls sobbing.

"Becca hit me with a telephone book," Tyquan says. *Grrrrr*, Buster goes mad in the background. "She sicced Buster on me—said I stole her money—Buster bit my leg." I wobble and sit on the side of my bed. "Starkaña said she'd kill me if I told the school nurse."

Pull yourself together, girl. I have to if I'm to save Tyquan.

"Tomorrow morning, we're riding the Blue Line to the county office," he says, voice trailing, "to fill my prescription."

In county offices, some people go for niggashit, like Starkaña, when they run from office to office, hustling. They'll loud-talk and jack the overworked county workers and customers waiting for aid review. She'll front Tyquan and say she needs assistance and refill his Ritalin prescription for her to sell, standing one hundred on the niggashit trap. I press my palms together and pray.

"Can't you come and get me now?" he asks.

Woozy, my mind says maybe, but the body says no. "We'll see. Let's wrap you with a bow for now, okay?" What if I rode to Watts, grabbed my brother, and fled to safety? But where is such a place? We'd already be there if I had a clue.

"We'll meet there tomorrow." I strain for answers. "Act like you don't know me, okay?"

I watch the fan spin. I'll deniggerlate tonight: no medicine, weed, or alcohol for me in the morning. I have to do something —BIG.

* * *

Rain falls the next day, a rarity in summertime SoLA. Hattie smiles, serving me hot oatmeal, and sings,' *Twas grace that taught my heart to fear, and grace my fears relieved; How precious did that grace appear the hour I first believed.* Mama used to like that song that was played at her funeral.

"I couldn't get through to Children's Services, Trina." Hattie sits down to face me. "You do what you must for your brother," she says. "I would."

Outdoors, the drops cool my arms, and the sweet, musty smell of rain meets the hot concrete 103rd/Watts Towers Blue Line platform. My disguise, a Goldilocks wig, and dark Ray-Ban sunglasses borrowed from Hattie blend perfectly, making me look slightly older. I'm careful and must avoid bounty-hunting school police. I'll save my brother—snatch him away from Starkaña, cut her fucking throat—if she's not with Becca and Tyquan's not dead.

The canopy covering the platform protects riders from the warm rain. The bench underneath is already packed, so I mosey just beyond into the misting rain. A fluttery, empty feeling pits my stomach, the butcher knife handle in my waist-band pressing against me, concealed under my L.A. Sparks team jersey. The serrated steel blade is hungry for Starkaña's neck. I'll use the weapon if needed, but not because I have it. Mama had said that just because cars drive fast, don't operate them foolishly. I wait and wait. Could I have already missed them? A woman wearing a blue Metro Line uniform checks passenger tickets. My legs feel restless, and I sweat. She strolls by and down the platform.

My head jerks to a commotion at the platform base. Starkaña's dragging a limping Tyquan by his burned arm, casting him like a marionette.

Her hand cupped, she says, "Save Our Sons T's and camisoles for sale. I'm styling one." She wears tight fake designer jeans, a blinding pink camisole, and SOS scrawled across her tiny chest, flittering back and forth. She's like a scared bird, flip-flops, clack, clack. Each hoof beat, slapping hard against concrete. She stops and yelps, "You can buy the shirt off my back." She taps a card once on the transit access machine and whisks them past the turnstile. The combined stink of crack cocaine, beer, and weed hovers over her like a cloud when she passes and nudges away two women under the canopy.

I maneuver next to Starkaña. I lean behind her, using an index finger over my lips to silence Tyquan, who twists opposite her.

"What's up?" I say. Starkaña turns, and we lock eyes.

"Oh, feels sticky out, but I'm good," Starkaña says. She looks me over, and her dimly shaded eyes rest on my school Dickies. "Do I know you?"

I wipe sweaty hands on my pants and nod. Starkaña looks tinier than I'd imagined, even fragile. We're about the same height. Her eyes are red even through the tint; pupils dilated, lips blistered and cracked, having pressed hot pipes against them, skin pulled tight against her bony face, jowls sucked in resembling a walker on *The Walking Dead*. A *Killaz Life* tat stretches from her jaw to the base of her neck.

"You got anything to smoke?" she says. Suddenly, she turns and drags Tyquan past the STAY BEHIND THE YELLOW LINE strip to the platform edge, and my mouth falls open. She leans over a SUICIDE CRISIS LINE sign, shades her eyes, and gawks up the tracks toward downtown L.A. "We can hit a lick after I run to the county building."

She's a nervous rat, a bucket crab doing her part to keep Watts tormented. I must say something to this nut, but what? I must do something, but what? I can slit her throat and run, which might get me locked up in jail. Children's Services, police, and King Elementary are useless. Tyquan's in pain. What would Hattie do? Time seems to slow when Mama's advice slips from my lips. "You might try the Deniggerlator."

Instantly Starkaña's vacant expression turns furious. "What? Try what? You callin' me a nigga? Bitch, you don't know me."

I look away from her and study the spires on the Towers, the intricate fretwork at Starkaña's back.

"I'll throw your ass on them tracks," she says. "Nah mean?"

"My bad, miss—no disrespect." I show both palms.

Starkaña twists to Tyquan. "Nigga, tie your shoe," she says to him. His face flushes; both eyes are puffy and dark. He winces, but dirty gauze and duct tape covering his hand won't allow his fingers to flex. I slant away and feel for the knife handle. I picture my blade plunging, riddling her neck.

Starkaña squats. She pushes the strap of her fake Coach purse stuffed with shirts and ties Tyquan's shoe. "Don't let me find you poisoned Buster last night." She looms beneath the no-smoking sign, whips out a lighter and cigarette, fidgets, and lights a Newport. "He had his shots—was a good watchdog," she says, blowing smoke into Tyquan's face. "He was too quiet and hard as a brick this morning. I should've known something was up."

"I didn't," Tyquan says, his lips slightly smirking.

Starkaña deeply inhales nicotine, turns, and grins, baring rotted teeth. She puffs smoke in my face.

My eyes grow hot and wet, and I summon the softest voice I can muster.

"What happened to the boy's arm?"

"Oh, that. School accident—he's on the football team," Starkaña says. "The doctor said to give it some air. He'll be all right."

"Football—air?" I repeat, crowding Starkaña's personal space. She doesn't budge. "What about his black eyes?"

She whips purplish hair. "What's it to you, bitch? Huh? — All up in my business." She adjusts her camisole, an S covering her tiny tits, shoulders, and head, rolling from side to side. "Back off, biaatch, unless you want a scrum."

I shrug, lower my eyes onto Tyquan, and swallow. I'll grapple, maybe, *niggashit*, but not on her terms. Tyquan stares straight ahead in her grasp.

The train whines slowly and stops—passengers on the front board. Starkaña elbows people and cusses louder than ever to no one in particular. My legs are restless.

Mama's face again seizes my brain, Marcus's smoke, stupid fuck Becca and their idiot dog, and my weakness in math and drugs. For me, overcoming niggashit traps will be hard since many are challenging to recognize, having been set hundreds of years back to enslave us. But I will overcome it no matter how often I must enter the Deniggerlator. I'm gonna do something BIG.

Timing precisely, I grip the knife handle in my left hand and step ahead as Starkaña inches forward.

DON'T WORRY

B rrrrrrupt. Trella Tapia farts in short bursts like an AK47. "I was just here last night, ¡maldito sea!" she gasps. Brrrrrrupt.

Pressing her lips into a fine line, the horse-faced nurse looks Trella up and down and says, "Hmph. Ms. Tapia, again? Calm yourself." The nurse's blonde hair, big teeth, and equine features remind Trella of Mr. Ed. She sits between two other nurse effigies inside the booth behind Plexiglas.

However, Trella can't calm down. She hasn't pooped in days or maybe weeks. The ache feels unbearable this time, like tiny knives in her belly. Nothing helps, especially not the Advil she takes for everything from itchy feet to hot flashes or her regular cocktail of Kane Hospital prescription pills to numb out, Bud Extra to blast off, and Ecstasy to party, which she took earlier.

Trella leans her bloated body against Eliezer at the busy Kane Emergency Room entrance in South Central Los Angeles. Beyond the nurses' enclosure, the dark gray E.R. double swing doors leading to doctors squeak in and yawn out.

"Yeah, her job," Eliezer says, Horse Face stink eyeing him suspiciously. A digital clock behind the nurse's wall marks half before midnight military time, giving Trella time to see a doctor, fill her prescription, and still make her 10 a.m. job.

"They'll pay me minimum wage to dance—then I can pay my hospital bills," Trella says, hoping her debt promise might speed things up and get her through the double doors quicker to see doctors.

Maybe it's not an actual *job*; it's a demonstration for sign-spinning work with Libertine Tax Prep™.

From YouTube videos, she'd learned to krump to Usher's *Yeah!* Advil and amphetamines had helped her creaky forty-year-old joints, enabling her to wave her arms around, contorting her body into twisting spasmodic jerks and spinning on her head. She beat out several younger competitors and, with a backflip split, killed it. "I need something for pain," she says.

Trella whiffs the scent of hospital disinfectant, alcohol, and floor cleaner, her chest heavy recalling her Candy Striper days in her late teens and how Papi had died from sepsis in this very Kane E.R. Mamá would be proud of Trella's krumping job, but maybe not as much if she had become a nurse, their original plan. If Libertine's business increases, she could wind up legit, an independent contractor. Maybe pay her court fines, which might help lift the restraining order keeping her away from her son, Paco, Papi's namesake. However, in her early twenties, Trella dropped out of the community college nursing program after Mamá died instantly from an aneurysm weeks before Papi. Fuckin' sepsis—fucking aneurysm—fucking E.R. The job money will keep her buzzed if nothing else.

Trella slaps the glass. "I gotta get to my job," she says to Horse Face. *Be on time*, the Libertine Tax Prep™ person who hired her said. "Ohhhh," Trella groans. The stabbing pain is terrible. Even Horse Face will have to believe her and call for a gurney. Start an I V after mining her fleshy arm for a usable vein—a big job given the number of times they'd collapsed when she spiked speed—then whisk her through the swinging doors into the waiting hands of doctors who will cure her aching body in time to spin signs and put her life back on track.

Puke sours on the back of her tongue, gut rumbling like a runaway train, gingerly lifting her head to the three nurses pretending not to see her, them looking like Florence Nightingale clones even though Trella knows better.

Eliezer sweats in nighttime swelter, reeking of musk cologne, looking emaciated as if he's just run the Badwater Ultramarathon. Her top lip jumps when his sneakers squeak over Kane's pastel green linoleum, a floor scented by light vinegar, sparkling, invitingly shiny, sprouting rows of amber plastic chairs jammed with the groaning sick and injured.

With one hand, the twitchy woman wearing a loud pink camisole holds a bloody gauze over her eye and hawks' t-shirts. Other patients in the cramped Friday night E.R. avert their eyes away from Trella. She usually avoided the hospital on weekends since it seemed everyone from surrounding communities descended upon it for one reason or another. To Trella, the whole scene suggests she might be late for her new job.

The boxy room gyrates as Eliezer helps her check in. "Don't let me fall," she says. A fall could bruise her plump brown face on her first day, which wouldn't look good tomorrow.

He mops her face with a blue bandana already soaked with her sweat. "I'd never let my little butterball fall, mi Corazón," he says. He wipes his forehead with the rag before dabbing away sweat beads from her trembling upper lip.

Trella's MDMA-infected eyes linger on a janitor buffing the floor sliver between the nurse's booth and patient seats. He cordons off with orange cones and yellow caution tape. His gray and blue uniform pants sharply creased. Her back teeth rattle when the whir of his floor dryer raises the E.R. noise causing her to shout through a cluster of holes in the Plexiglas, "This is my third time here in two weeks, and that's your damn fault." Small children scream when playing hide-and-seek among listless adults seated facing the nurses. "I know what nurses are supposed to do," she says.

"Her new job starts in the morning." Eliezer's arm wraps around Trella's upper back, his musk cologne aggravating her headache, him pressing his lips, his well-worn, pockmarked face against the Plexiglas. "She needs to go first." He pinches and pulls on his standard uniform, a faded purple Lakers t-shirt.

"Yeah, I'm next," Trella says. She knows Horse Face from times when she's faked migraines for prescriptions. However, these last three times, her gut pain has been real. Still, the nurses have not let her see a doctor.

On the first visit a week ago, she tested positive for marijuana and traces of meth. Horse Face gave her a Valium script and sent Trella home. Yesterday, they assigned her to the holding room next to the double swing doors leading to the E.R. doctors, monitored by Mr. Ed, who discharged Trella with Tylenol and codeine before daybreak.

"¡APÚRATE! APÚRATE RAPIDA, MUJER!" Eliezer says. "Move your butts." His upper eyelids halfway cover his dark pupils.

Does he love drugs more than he loves her? Each time before, she had gobbled up the pills before he could ask for any, making him walk out in a huff, pissed off. He didn't stay with her before, so why should she share? Besides, she'd needed all the pills she could get. Even taking those hadn't dented the pain.

The Plexiglas shield reflects her well-traveled face, plucked-too-thin eyebrows, and the circles under her brown eyes inky on her copper skin. Her face resembles her mamá's when Mamá was much older than Trella is now, reminding her of past conversations they had. Mamá was a Guatemalan immigrant and expert dressmaker who handmade Trella's clothes when she was a little girl. Mamá weaved intricate corte with bright blue stripes and huipils embroidered with designs varying from suns and moons to birds and flowers, which other children pointed and laughed at. *You can be anything,* Mamá often said to Trella, *even a businesswoman or nurse.* Black braids dangling to her chest, her words slurring; even to her, Trella says, "I'll see a doctor or die here."

"Identification, please," Horse Face says, barely looking up.

"You already know me," Trella says.

Horse Face's lips flatten again.

Eliezer helps Trella unzip her butt pocket on her favorite pair of lavender Spandex. She pulls out an EBT food stamp I.D., an old community college payment receipt, a fraying social security card, her probation officer's business card, and an expired driver's license. *Invalid* is what the detention officer called her driver's license when she attempted to visit her daughter Ursulina at Eastlake Juvenile Hall a few weekends back. *Access denied.* "I suffered horrible nausea, constipation, and continuous vomiting for nine months. I'm only her mother, bitch," Trella said to the detention facility gatekeeper.

Ursulina had called recently, but Trella couldn't remember when or if she'd called her back. Trella flips her fuzzily photographed bus card under the banker's window. "I'm sick to my stomach," she says, her face pressing against Plexiglas. "When's my turn?" she asks, squeezing Elie's arm so hard he winces, her pain twice as bad as last night when boiled plant and herbal drinks failed.

"Yeah, when?" Eliezer says. "She needs drugs... I mean, a doctor right now."

Horse Face ignores him and examines Trella's bus card before looking back. "Our doctors see critical patients first. It looks to me like you can wait. Sit. I'll return your I.D. when we call you through."

"Don't worry, honey, I got you," Eliezer says. He holds her upright since it's standing room only in the E.R. "You're burning up, babe." Eliezer glowers at Horse Face, though Trella recognizes the sly look he gets when he's on the hustle. "Can't you give her a little something for pain?"

Horse Face scowls right back. "She has what we gave her last night and the time before."

Like that, Eliezer's bluster vanished. She couldn't help herself, the pain stinking bad. Moreover, none of it helped. Trella used up everything; she knows he knows.

"It didn't work," Trella tells the nurse, but Elie shushes her.

"Fuck this," he mumbles. He leans Trella against the booth, rifles through his pockets, and digs out a smudged OxyContin pill from God knows when. He pecks her lips with his. "Here, swallow." He puts the tablet in her mouth to his credit with two grimy fingers. "It'll keep your buzz."

Trella closes her eyes, takes a deep breath, and moans. The madness she calls life seems to spin downhill uncontrolled. Could the joints she smoked and the Vicodin she washed down with wine coolers in middle school have led to this? *Nah.* Maybe Eliezer loves her as much as he loves alcohol and other drugs. She feels the corners of her mouth turn up. Then her abdominal muscles contract and her retch forces the spicy taste of pepián de pollo to the back of her throat. "I'm gonna throw up," she says for all to hear, including the E.R. police.

The E.R. doors swing, patients trickle in, and some exit. If it weren't for the door cop, she'd bum rush through, but another night spent in the women's jail might make her late for work. Not smart.

* * *

Forever, Trella stands sandwiched between Eliezer and the nurse's booth. Fever fills her like boiling water. Horse Face sits securely behind the Plexiglas, chatting with the other nurses, shuffling papers, drinking coffee, and passing the time, the clock behind them reading 0239 hours, just hours away from Trella's life-changing work start.

Trella had once studied nursing but violated Nightingale's drug-use prohibition pledge and dropped out of Compton Community College. She knows she would've been a better nurse than Horse Face had she listened to Mamá and stayed in school. She sobs inside, not wanting the nurses and other patients to see.

Trella's skin feels itchier than usual. Her puffy face and runny eyeliner in the Plexiglas look like shit after spending time earlier to look presentable for her first day at Libertine Tax Prep™. Time spent washing and then blow-drying her hair straight, using a hair polisher to give it sheen. Gorilla booger gel to hold in place two cool braids and her bangs she teased and pushed back on top of her head, her looking almost as good as she had at her quinceañera twenty-five years ago. Mamá had told her in Spanish and Maya K'iche to always bathe regularly. What happened? What would Mamá think of her now?

"You gonna kick me down or keep shit all for yourself?" Eliezer says his eyes are bloodshot. Now is probably not the time for her to speak to Eliezer about how musk, his favorite cologne, makes her nauseous or his calling her *Mama* reminds her of her estranged children, her having birthed two babies by different men. Paco is in foster care, and her daughter Ursulina is in juvie for shoplifting. Eliezer's looking so jumpy, and he might leave her here. She can't be alone.

"Don't worry," she says. "I got you."

The admitting nurses loudly shuffle their forms and look past Trella, even though she knows they must see her pressed flat against their Plexiglas shield. After a while, one of them announces, "Edward Jones, Maricela Garcia, through the double doors," freeing seats near the check-in booth for which she and Eliezer race. Thank God. She can't stand another minute. In addition, she may get in quicker if they sit facing the nurses and sit up straight for them to see her and if she stares them down.

As soon as Trella sits, her stomach bucks and heaves. She upchucks unrecognizable bile, which can only be pollo, pepperoni pizza, and Pepto Bismol, and it's on the pristine floor, all over her toes, sandals, and her favorite pants.

The marbled floor design seems to move like beach waves. The stench is dangerous. She tries to sit herself up, pulling Eliezer's arm, but a dull abdominal ache forces her to bend over. Her tender abdomen belches and farts simultaneously, a stabbing pain worse than childbirth. Trella breathes heavier and frowns. "Fuckin' bitches won't help me," she shouts above the sickly voices in the E.R., who cautiously squeeze away from her.

An E.R. cop whose belly overhangs olive pants at his waist and whose beige uniform shirt stretches his buttonholes strides over from his post at the double doors. He leans over Trella. "You need to pipe down—show some respect—wait for your damn turn."

"Respect?"

"You've got a lotta nerve—respect—guarding poor people's emergency rooms." She tries to stand but can't. Instead, she motions for him to come closer, which he does, careful to avoid her vomit. She sucks air through her teeth, "*Tsk*—kiss my itchy butt—fake-ass cop."

The cop recoils, perhaps from Trella's stank breath, possibly from her comeback—maybe both. Fake Cop pops knuckles, backpedals, and looks daggers at her.

Warmth flushes through Trella but is short-lived when she starts to shiver. Teeth knocking loudly in her ears, the world goes blurry. She slumps onto Eliezer's lap, linoleum floor designs behaving weirdly, appearing as snakes, knives, and Satanic faces changing to soft, buoyant white pillow clouds. Lightheaded, she'd feel so much better stretched out on them. She's inside Middle Earth, the Ecstasy she took earlier, having kicked in, mixing with OxyContin before puking.

Her head thumps against his seat when Eliezer slides out of the chair, taking his warmth. She pushes herself up and watches him motion Horse Face to the check-in booth door. He steps before the gesticulating janitor, who argues with Horse Face about something. Eliezer's animated and talks with his hands, clasping them as if begging. Their exchange is muted under the steady buzz of the other sick and injured until the nurse's voice elevates.

"NO. Heavens no—you certainly aren't holding them for her." The muscles in her neck are taut. "She'll get no more until she sees the doctor."

It's an end-run around Trella. Does the stupid fuck think the nurse will give him drugs intended for her?

Boom! Eliezer kicks the booth's baseboard, riveting the attention of the E.R. police. Then he hurries and, as a bag of fruit is thrown onto a Food4Less checkout belt, lifts Trella's head back onto his lap.

"How ya feel, Mama?" Eliezer says, pupils huge. "Don't worry, Baby—I got you—I love, love, love you—"

He never says he loves her until he's high on something,

especially Ecstasy, the love pill. Still, she likes hearing him say it, so she puckers her lips, but he shies away.

"Lower than a rat's turd—muy inferma—Goddamn," Trella says. Time fades her high away somewhat. Stomach pain increases, and Eliezer? Let's say he falls short of her expectations. Is he the husband Mamá encouraged? With his Illustrated Man tattoos, Eliezer, from when he was a young *cholo* terrorizing la Raza, sniffing glue, burglarizing, stealing car batteries, stupid shit, incompetent to remove *CV155st* stamped on his forehead or *Weasel* inked across his jugular.

Had she obeyed Mamá, she would've run the other way. If she follows Mamá, she'll become a successful businessperson and twirl signs for Libertine Tax Prep™. If only she were here to ask.

Trella rests her head in his lap, focusing on whirling designs, images leaping from the floor, chimera krumping like the dance she'll do once she gets to her job, fraying braids, crinkling bangs, and all. She must get up, clean up, and make her sign-spinning debut. She needs to turn herself around.

* * *

Unable to will herself to stand, hours seem to pass, Trella's head lying fixed against the cold, unforgiving floor. When did she wind up on the floor anyway? It's 0330, and she still has time to pull shit together and make Libertine Tax Prep™. Her terrible life choices were a curse needing a cure, breath smelling like broken sewage, vomit sticking to her face and braids, feeling closer to death, and blackness, like dust covering roadkill lying curbside on Rosecrans Avenue. Eliezer paces, looking like the scarecrow in The Wizard of Oz.

Horse Face and her crew sit hard-faced behind the Plexiglas, her wiping down her workspace with Clorox Handi

Wipes, another occasionally smacking on potato chips. The third nurse sucks Coke, pointing, giving directions to the janitor who'd argued with Horse Face earlier. His military-like yet empathetic bearing pushes his mop bucket toward Trella, lying face-up on waxed linoleum, squinting into fluorescent ceiling lights, her energy waning.

"Excuse me," says the janitor. "I've got a job to do." He uses his mop to push a yellow bucket wringer on wheels—five burly stone-faced E.R. police watch, including the asshole posted at the swinging doors. Nauseous, Trella blinks. The janitor eyeballs her and then looks away. The clock inside the nurse's booth says 0415 hours, and her stomach has a weird, woozy feeling.

The janitor's mop absorbs the putrid junk food and blood mixture—not touching Trella but leaving a vomit nimbus around her. Kneeling, he adjusts his eyeglasses and tilts his head, finishing the job with a hand towel. She strains to focus on his uniform, his nameplate, *T. Neal.*

"They say you want drugs. Nurses are talking about you." T. Neal's hair is wooly, and his lined face ebony black, eyes sullen, probably from cleaning up turds, chemicals, and every-thing else people discard at Kane. Crouching beside her, he smells like pine with traces of vinegar.

"No, sir," Trella says, her voice a cut above a murmur. "Yes-terday, maybe—I need a doctor now."

T. Neal scrunches his face. "I'll c-call the administrator—he's a cousin. Tell him what's going on. Ignoring you ain't right —j-just hold on." He pushes up and hurries off.

Where's Eliezer's skinny ass?

Trella looks around the room from the relentless floor, other patients distancing themselves, staring. What are they saying? Maybe asking what Trella could have possibly done to deserve such fate. Someone whispers, "—maybe she has AIDS?" Trella closes her eyes again—not knowing for how long. Goosebumps slide along her neck momentarily when her Mamá's smiling image floats from the swinging doors adjacent to the nurse's booth. "Mamá," she says under her breath before gagging and vomiting.

Clack, clack, clack, the sound of snowshoe-sized flip-flops hit hard upon linoleum, and a full-throated voice snatches Trella's eyes open. With one hand, the sorrel-colored hard-lived woman in the pink camisole cups her pouty lips, still holding bloodstained gauze to her eye. She steps into Trella's fresh upchuck. SOS in blackletter emblazes across the front of her tank top.

"SOS—women tops and t-shirts for sale—Save Our Sons— five bucks each—SOS. I've got all colors—hand-painted." She bends toward Trella. "You look a mess, baby," she says. "Killer Kane Hospital won't help you?"

Trella's heart beats faster, like when she skin-pops speed. The woman pulls a cell phone from her purse and punches the screen with her thumb. Trella shifts her aching body. Where's Elie? He'd better have a good excuse or some bomb drugs to help her. Motherfucker.

"9 1 1? There's a woman on the Kane Hospital emergency room floor—yeah, right, in SoLA—South Central," the woman with the eye wound says. "Nurses walk by. They ignore her."

Trella's bowels loosen into Spandex; she smells the stink of shit. Her pants are ruined. She can't go to work this way.

"What do I want from you?" The woman's pitch rises. "I want you to *send* an ambulance to pick her off the damn floor, fool." She momentarily raises the patch from her eye, blood flowing down her face like red tears. "I know we're in the E.R., but these idiots aren't doing their jobs."

Over the loudspeaker, Horse Face announces, "Starkaña Wilkerson—through the double doors." A booth nurse arrives pushing a gurney, stopping beside the t-shirt woman, smoothing the sheet, gently cupping her hand over the woman's against the bloody gauze, the woman slapping shut her cell phone and saying to Trella, "I'll pray for you, honey. I'll hold an SOS shirt for you, too—five bucks. God bless you."

The nurse mindfully whisks the woman through the double doors.

Trella's sure to be next. She tries but can't move her legs.

"Ay Díos—I'm going to die. Will someone please help me?" Trella groans between dry heaves, her body crumpled.

As if he's sleepwalking, Eliezer reappears. Maybe he's found someone or something to help her. He sits, slapping his knees. "This is a goddamn hospital, but they keep dope locked up or in the pharmacy," he says.

What a bastard. The warmth of urine runs over feces stuck inside Trella's lavender pants onto the floor. Eliezer seems too preoccupied to notice.

Her limbs twitch, her top lip jumps, and the garish light overhead hurts her eyes.

Trella's gaze fixes onto a forest of legs tatted with varicose veins, swollen ankles, fake Air Jordan, crusty heels, and chipping nail polish. Bare feet shift about anxiously. A toddler drops a pacifier, picks it up, and continues to suck.

"If we wait long enough, they'll prescribe something," Eliezer says, eyes wide.

She rolls onto her back so she doesn't have to look at him.

"Drugs—that's all you care about."

"What? No way." Eliezer raises his palms. "You're my road dog, honey. Mi Corazón."

"Really? "I don't know you," she says. He's always twisted. She's done many things for him, like riding a larceny beef and doing his jail time, which got her probation. No wonder she lost Paco and Ursulina. The moisture is queasy in her Spandex pants, and her observation of Elie's intention signals that she has harmed her children.

Eliezer takes short, heavy breaths. His high is no doubt diminishing. "Hey, babe. I might have to roll up out of here in a few ticks." She sees the gap from his missing lower tooth when his lip moves, which she once thought was cute. "Got to handle my business, nah mean?"

"Is business about me or the drugs?" He holds out his hands as if weighing them in the air. "Musk stinks," she says.

What does she expect? He can't help her if she can't stand, and he needs to stay buzzed, or he'll disappear. She can't krump for Libertine Tax Prep™ if she can't stand.

There's a list of things she needs to do, like getting to that goddamn sign-spinning job by ten, calling back Ursulina, who never calls unless there's a problem, not that Trella was ever much help before. Like signing up for parenting classes, renewing her driver's license, re-enrolling in school, showing bitch Horse Face how to do fundamental nursing, making up for a skipped appointment with her probation officer, and a lie about why she missed. Like visiting her mother's grave since she can't remember whether she did so last Mother's Day.

She has to get up to re-braid her hair, clean her pants, and take a birdbath. She needs to start the day over.

Trella prays to her dead mother, "Mamá, me siento muy enferma." The double doors swoosh open. A woman in white scrubs reaches out to Trella, her stethoscope dangling around her neck, T. Neal bending behind her.

Mamá whispers, "Don't worry, Trella, I'm with you."

CROOKED OUT OF COMPTON

I choked on a cancerous cough and waited. The smell of grease in Popeyes roiled my stomach and made a puke rise in my throat. Lieutenant LeRoi Sykes, a retired cop, my nigga, knew how to help me find Trenese. As childhood friends, we had a history. He owed me.

Roi appeared at the Plexiglas doors just as I coughed for real, a fit that attacked my body and tore at my throat. He looked concerned, walked over to my table, and clapped a hand on my shoulder.

"That's one nasty cough," he said.

I forced myself to stop. "What's up, my brother?" I said, breathless from the fit.

He scanned the area, sifted through me, and smiled. "Tallent *Snotty Nose* Neal, still in Toughskins jeans."

I was not too fond of that nickname, but still, we man-hugged and shook hands, sixties Dap style. His grip was firm as if he'd done fingertip pushups before breakfast. I hadn't seen him since late 1974, at his Vietnam homecoming party forty-five years ago.

The nigga looked well-scrubbed, toothbrush mustache and a head shiny like Telly Savalas but brown. He slung a navy suede sports jacket over the booth and smoothed his striped button-down shirt collar with his thumb and forefinger. I glanced at my #7 Michael Vick jersey and repositioned my smudge-free white Adidas. My bus pass picture showed tight salt-and-pepper curls and gray face stubble from days when my shave razor felt heavy, like dead weight. Roi looked years younger than I did.

We exchanged decades of news: My wife, Ella, may her soul rest in peace, had worked part-time in a mortuary until she keeled over into an empty casket and died last year, 2008. It's funny that relatives and friends don't come around much since then. I told him that we rented in West Compton, about my estranged son, how I raised my granddaughter Trenese, and, because of DUIs, used the Metro to get to custodian work at Kane Public Hospital.

He'd been a good cop, or so I understood from what I'd read on the Internet. He sat ramrod straight, arms crossed, and told me he'd married a school principal, had three daughters, moved his family to Chino Hills, and lived well.

"Hate to— *cough*—cut you off," I spoke fast to Roi. "I'm, uh, proud of you—"

"What are we doing here, Snotty? What do you want?"

I pushed the uneaten chicken leg aside, the pain intensifying in my chest and throat. "My granddaughter disappeared," I said, fidgeting with the bus pass before jamming it back into my pants pocket filled with medication. "I last saw her two months ago—at Ramsaur Stadium. Dropped her off for Compton High's Homecoming cheer squad practice before the game. I should've known something was off. She usually changed into her uniform at home, the blue and white one with the Baby Tartar warrior mascot emblem, and...there was this guy—"

Roi licked his thick lips and interrupted. "I see where you're going, but I'm out of the game, dude," his expression suddenly closed and stoic, looking like a cop. "Had enough canteen culture—I keep the badge, the Beretta, but hung up my spurs when I retired."

I resisted the pain burning at the bottom of my throat. "You're my last hope. Motherfuckin' sheriff won't do shit. They think she just ran off to smoke crack and whore around. But that's not *my* girl." I wasn't the best daddy. I made mistakes with my son. I had told him *either a job, school or the Army*. He hocked his Purple Heart and chased OxyContin to Kentucky. I was going to raise my granddaughter the right way.

I checked my cell phone and sucked back tears welling behind my eyelids, not wanting Roi to notice.

"Uh-huh," Roi said, eyes half-lidded, yawning.

"Last I heard, she was in East Compton. I'm scared, man."

He rubbed at his mouth. "Sex workers stroll there."

"I know."

"Is she on the track?" he asked flatly. He stared blankly out of the window.

I needed leverage. "Remember how I rode the case when we stole baseballs from Thrifty Drug Store? *I* went to jail— didn't snitch you out, my nig—I mean, my brother."

Roi went utterly still. "We weren't good thieves," he stuttered, changing the subject. "What's with the cough?"

"Smoking." I coughed into my fist, clearing my throat, held up an unlit cigarette, and put a wad of napkins into my bulging pocket. "You started me on this shit—we were little niggas." We'd learned to smoke Kool menthols stolen from his mother.

Roi shifted in his seat. "I gave it up."

"Yeah. It's not cigarettes. It's stage 3 cancer. Lungs. I'm

taking a thousand damn pills." I fisted my chest to stem the pain.

Roi's voice cracked. "Are you sure?" He looked down and away.

"Ain't nothing a little bourbon whiskey won't handle. Who needs cannabis? I pill-rolled the cigarette. "We argued like always a few days before Trenese took off," I told Roi.

"Argued about what?"

My jaw tightened. "Over bullshit. Hairstyles, little shit like that." She'd asked for hair extensions. *No way*, I'd said to her at the time. Blonde hair weaves, tattoos, and body piercings were off-limits too. *It makes you look like a hoochie. Show your true beauty, not a Hollywood fake*, I'd said to Trenese.

Everybody else does—I can do nothing since Granny died—I hate you, she said before running to her room and slamming the door. Through the door, she said, *all you want me to do is schoolwork.* She was one hundred with that. What else did she need to do?

I dabbed my runny nose with a napkin and told Roi, "I don't like hot irons, burnt hair smell, so she wore Afro puffs which stuck above her head like Minnie Mouse ears." *You can stay with your no-good-ass mama—if you can find her*, I'd told Trenese.

Roi folded his arms over his stomach and said, "You know, sometimes teenage girls—

I cut him off. "Maybe Trenese was on the rag—I know how Ella used to get."

"What? That's some ignorant shit, Snotty," Roi said, raising his hand to his temple and shaking his head. "My girls relieved PMS symptoms with their lifestyle. It wasn't a big problem for us."

I glanced over my drugstore bifocals. A young girl's image reflected off Popeyes' countertop Plexiglas. Plexiglas protection separated people everywhere in Compton: liquor stores, city hall, and even the sheriff's station. If only I could have covered Trenese with it. My breaths grew loud and heavy. "She's pretty smart."

Roi propped a cheek on his fist and stared at me until I broke eye contact. I flipped the cell phone earpiece open and shut several times and swallowed grit in my throat.

"Okay, Homer Simpson, let's find Trenese," he said.

* * *

Roi's gut said we should start on the north end and roll south around Long Beach Boulevard. He drove a tricked-out candy apple red '63 Volkswagen Beetle like Herbie the Love Bug. It was so tiny that I imagined circus music playing when I squeezed my big ass inside. My knees hit the dash, and fastening the seat belt was a chore. It took a moment to accelerate even when Roi floored it.

"Guerrilla pimps abduct some girls," Roi said. His voice was matter-of-fact. "They promise them love."

"Speaking of gorillas, this guy came around before Trenese disappeared," I said. "And he was hanging around Ramsaur when I dropped her off. He might know something."

A week before she vanished, I'd opened the door to a guy whose crimson drawers flashed above gray Dickies belted halfway down his ass. Dark wraparound shades reflected my face underneath his red baseball cap over braided, shoulder-length hair. So many youngsters dressed like him these days, I didn't judge until he opened his mouth.

"What up, OG?" A hard grin split his face; his tone grated. "Where's Trenese?"

"For you, she's not here," I said, face tight. "Not yesterday, not today—*cough*—not ever."

"I'm up in it at the spot, know what uh mean?" He pointed two fingers and lowered his thumb like a pistol hammer at me. "Pow—tell her Rip in the cut."

My vision clouded. I shoulder faked, and young blood blinked. "You'd better back your ass up." I spat a lug of gunk next to his Jordans and said, "You should be embarrassed coming here. Get back, Satan!"

He turned, and I slammed the door.

Later, I boasted to Trenese about how I'd punked a thug.

Her sweet face turned sour; she slapped her hands to her cheeks and shook her head. "NO." Her voice was filthy and loud. "Peter is a math tutor and college freshman class president."

I grabbed the TV remote. "Peter? Pssh—bullshit—you can't believe that? He said his name was Rip. School hard-knocked his ass off-campus—get the pun?" I grinned.

She screamed, "Stop, Granddad!" Her tall-for-her-age frame shook.

I returned to *Sanford and Son* reruns. Julio and his goat had Fred cornered. "Rip—um, er, Peter's a gangbanger, at the very least, and too old to be around you, one eye half-closed—asshole never read a book in his life, not even Dr. Seuss—curse the devil."

She stomped upstairs and yelled, "I hope you die—you hypocrite."

She didn't speak to me for a whole week.

Roi shifted Beetle gears and explained street prostitution, how street pussy's the smallest yet most visible part of sex trafficking, how customers used the Web to locate whores, and how drug users shifted to prescription pills. Legalized marijuana replaced products street dealers sold to survive, yadda, which led street gangs to cannibalize young girls for money. Yadda yadda.

Pain stabbed my chest; Trenese's voice sounded in my head. *I hope you die.* I teared up, and Roi pulled over. In my mind, I saw her. "I'm sorry, Trenese. Forgive me—please." I trembled like a scared rabbit, and my lungs stuck.

Roi nudged my arm. "Hey, you're scaring me, Snot. Are you okay?"

"Uh-huh—medicine side effect. Sorry."

He whipped us back into traffic.

* * *

We exited the Bug and sucked exhaust fumes before Compton Fashion Center's indoor swap meet. The bustling sidewalk is polka-dotted black with trampled gum. On a bus bench, Roi whipped out his iPad mini. I covered my mouth and my nose. "Damn, this place is nasty. All these damn people—somebody had to see Trenese." My skin tightened. "Somebody knows where she is."

"Look here." His fingers glided across the keyboard like piano keys, loading a YouTube video of Kamilah Tang, an attractive former lead prostitute looking like Diahann Carroll at her self-assured best. *I'd lure young girls at my high school into street walking for Division in Compton pimping crew—D-I-C. I'd befriend and entice them by painting a glamorous picture, getting them on the track, working, and making money. Take their ID and cash, and cut off their families. In Vegas, we'd give a group of them free drugs, a D I C tattoo, and a taste of high life. Once they hooked, they ours.*

Roi logged off and looked me over. "Don't want to scare you —I'm just saying—I want to clarify the harm, the life-and-death struggle young girls face."

I'd not heard from Trenese in weeks, and what Tang said about cutting off families burned into my skull. Would Trenese even remember my number without her cell phone? I'd be pretty cut off if I lost my phone.

The grimy street bustled with scantily dressed girls who kept their heads down faces glued to cell phone screens, a lifeless imitation and robotic madness. Trenese always had her girlfriends over, and she'd go to their houses sometimes for sleepovers. I'd been okay with overnighters. But we'd never visited Las Vegas, yet Trenese had a Harrah's key fob. My insides iced.

Three women smoked cigarettes in a Jeep under a shady sycamore tree in front of All Souls MBC's iron security doors, a small white church directly across from the Fashion Center. One of them, fattish, with pearly skin and blonde cornrows, nodded her head, beckoning us.

Roi stood, walked over to his Beetle, tossed the iPad into the back seat, and leaned against the door. "You up for this, or should I do it?"

To my delight, Roi finally relinquished control, handing me a piece of the action, a chance to interrogate witnesses, suspects, whatever. I took quick breaths. "I got this." He fetched a shammy from the back seat and rubbed down his Beetle. I panted through what felt like tiny holes in my chest and turned to cross the street.

My stomach rolled like a six-four Chevy cruising Crenshaw Boulevard on Sunday. Before I could leave the curb, a girl about Trenese's age sashayed up and slipped a rail-thin leg in my path. Cherubic face, her purple weave one-sided, and a short brown skirt showed her butt, a poor man's Beyoncé. What did Trenese wear now?

She winked, grinned like a Cheshire cat, and brushed my hand with hers.

I waved her off and turned her down.

Her jingly voice turned severe. "If y'all don't want a date, what the fuck do you want?"

I shoved a picture of Trenese in Afro puffs at her. "I'm looking—*cough*— for my granddaughter. Have you seen her?"

She jerked. Her hair fanned when a fire truck screamed past. She glanced at the picture, her manner juvenile. "I don't know people out here."

My blood rose.

"Then why are you here spreading disease?"

"Getting paid—you old fuck."

Little bitch. I leaned in to backhand her.

With a crooked smile, Cherub Face said, "Nigga, you'd better lay your old ass down somewhere."

Car doors slammed. The trio of hard-looking women stormed across the street.

"You want your old ass beat?" said the blonde. "I'm one hundred with that."

Another looked dried, and a keloid scarred her cheek. She said scratchily, "I'll cut your balls off and stick 'em in your mouth." She popped a switchblade and thrust the tip up my nostrils. The greasy amber-skinned third woman stood back and didn't speak. The others surrounded me. I froze. A forward move could pierce my brain. If I bent backward, my blood would gush everywhere. "What you gotta say now, muthafucka?" said Switchblade. Her breath stank of a hundred sucked dicks and added insult to my injury.

They backed off when Roi flashed his cop badge. The cut inside my nose trickled blood when Switchblade withdrew her tool. I hoped Trenese hadn't met these bitches.

Cornrows turned to Roi. "Talk to your boy," she said. "Better find the little bitch before we do." She stalked off with Cherub Face and Switchblade.

Roi waited until they were across the street and turned to

me. "Check yourself, Tallent. Keep dogging these people, and we'll never find Trenese."

I kicked the ground. I couldn't help but see Trenese in every hooker, which scared the shit out of me and made me act crazy. I coughed into my fist.

But Roi was right. I had to back off. I forced a Popeyes napkin into my nostril to dam the blood flow. The hooker who'd quietly stayed out of the fray, obviously on a Jenny Crack diet, stepped forward. She wore a yellow sunflower camisole, her pupils like buttons.

"They wrong. Wrong," the crackhead said, voice girlish. "Bitches should have at least tried to help. We talked about getting out of the life, too—maybe setting up a shelter in the vacant building off the alley. They ain't ready yet. It ain't easy out here, especially for a new girl. Hard." Her movements jerked. She outstretched slender fingers. "Show me the picture. Picture."

A very light-skinned mulatto, she studied Trenese's photo. Her gold-colored necklace with cursive letters spelled *Esther*. At one time, she might've given Halle Berry a run.

"How long has she gone?" she asked. "Long?"

"Two months, twenty-three days exactly." Pain shot to my chest. Hands shook, and I dabbed my bloodied nose. "Today's her birthday." Trenese and I usually celebrated birthdays and most holidays. Before she took off, we'd revered Ella with an altar, her photo, and marigolds on the Day of the Dead. Would we reconnect before Christmas? How bad had I fucked up?

"Granddaddies don't usually look for children." I had a cough attack when exhaust fumes from a passing bus engulfed us. "Wish somebody had looked for me. Me." She focused on Trenese's picture. "Been in the game since I was eleven, nine long years. Long. Too long."

"Esther. Nice name," I said.

She sighed. "I could barely walk in heels tramping this goddammed track at first. Damn streets. Fucked twenty, thirty guys and some girls a day." She shook her head. "Couldn't keep the money. Can't. Street life is no joke—STD, pimps. Pimps." Her shoulders drooped. "I'd be better dead. DEAD." Her voice was flat and monotone, eyes were like a gravestone. "Wouldn't wish this shit on nobody." Her flowery perfume attacked my undamaged nostril. "On nobody. I'ma get out—off the track." I resisted an urge to hold her. She hit the speaker button when her cell phone rang.

"Bitch, I see you standin' around," said a man's voice that sounded familiar, but from where? "Make some money, or I'm up in ya. Get your yella ass back on the track."

"Gotta go—go." She pressed the mute button and cleared her throat. "Fool thinks we need his ass." She shut the flip phone. "Don't need that stupid mothafucka anymore—I'ma get rid of his bitch ass somehow. SOMEHOW."

Esther was not the kind of person to cross. Someone on the streets for nine years knew the ropes much more than the hookers I'd used on occasion.

"Young fool threatened to slice me up? Bullshit. BULL-SHIT." She seemed to study something, inhaled air through her nose, and pushed it through her mouth. "I saw this girl at the Hub Motel," she said. "A baby doll in a cheerleader dress works down there. She smart. SMART." She glided away like a runway model in high heels and didn't look back.

* * *

The best information yet about Trenese came from a hooker after nearly getting my ass kicked by women. I'd fucked a few whores when Ella was on her period, more since she passed when I couldn't sleep. Occasionally, I'd even brought one home. To me, I was discreet and quick. *She's an old friend*; I lied to Trenese if she happened to run into one of them.

Right before she disappeared, Trenese called me a hypocrite. She must've guessed the truth. I was stupid to bring a hooker home when I'd been so hard on my granddaughter. I tried to make sure she didn't turn into one. I had to find her, apologize, and make things right.

The Hub Motel was down the street. Roi said there'd been a significant sting operation there last month. The dull gray stucco motel was "C" shaped, one story, with a long, one-car driveway connected to Bowen on the east. The courtyard where we stood hid us from the street.

"If Trenese got sliced up," I said, my fist clenched, "I'm killing somebody."

Roi looked hard at me. "Don't act crazy again. Your temper is what almost got you stabbed back there."

We poked around in a sparse open room, which smelled of nuclear bleached-over piss and years of embedded smoke stank. A rock-firm queen-sized bed, a small table, a faded wilderness painting above a wood-product headboard, and two chairs in a corner completed the jungle habitat. Only pimps, whores, johns, and police would know about the Hub Motel hellhole. Had Trenese fallen this far? She'd be glad to get back home to her bed. My mouth went dry.

Roi entered the bathroom. I walked outside, lit the cigarette, and waited in the courtyard parking lot.

A black and white sheriff's cruiser braked in the narrow driveway.

"STOP THERE," someone yelled from inside the car.

Two deputies jumped out, hands on their holsters, their engine running. My legs weakened; a pain rushed through my chest.

"Show your hands—turn around and place them on the

hood," said one cop before he whirled me around, kicked my legs apart, frisked my ankles and groin, and massaged my balls.

"Owww!" I snatched my palms from the hot hood. "What the fuck—" The cop leaped on my back and choked my neck. "I can't breathe." My knee popped; legs buckled. When my eyes opened, I lay on my stomach, panting for air like underwater, hands cuffed so tight behind me that my fingers lost feeling. My neck hurt like hell. Bifocals bent across my face.

I took quick, whistled breaths. I shifted my body to breathe freer and craned a look at Gonzalez's uniform nameplate, the cop who'd grabbed me. He glowered over me: my Metro ID and the picture of Trenese in his hand.

"What'd I do?" My sweaty jersey mixed with motor oil.

Hansen, the other nameplate, squatted and moved cautiously, hands shaking, his gun barrel two feet from my face. A Viking image inked his tanned, muscled forearm.

I was tough but would be no match for these two, not prone, not at this stage in my life. My eye twitched. I strained to reach my knee, which pained me more than my chest and neck.

"What's your business here, Mr. Neal?" asked Gonzalez.

"Don't shoot me," I gasped, curled up on my side. "My granddaughter's missing."

He peered at the picture of Trenese. Then, Roi strolled from the motel room and scrunched up his face.

"He's with me." He nodded, saying something harsh to the deputies I couldn't make out. They must've recognized Roi, for when he reached to help me, the two cops backed off, re-holstered their guns, and quickly removed my handcuffs. Roi sat me up, his arm supporting my back. I squeezed my neck and clutched my knee with the other hand.

"We've had a lot of DIC trouble in the area," said Gonzalez. "They control drugs and sex trafficking."

Roi curled his lip, "Shit, does he look like a gangbanger to you?" I pressed my palms to my eyes. Roi had my back. "He's too old and raggedy to pimp." Both cops smirked. "Seen the girl or not?"

Gonzalez handed back the picture and my identification. "Can't say for sure—we always see them."

"Them?" I said. "What do you mean *them*?"

Hansen's Viking tattoo flexed when he placed both hands on his belt. "At least she's not the one sliced up by her pimp last week."

Thank God. I took their words as an indication that no harm had come to Trenese, which, for the moment, reduced my hatred of police and their usual activity in my community. Tears swelled beneath my eyelids. My knee throbbed when Roi helped me wobble to my feet.

"Cut her up and threw acid in her face," said Hansen. He climbed into the driver's side. "Good luck, sir."

"My ass," Roi said. "Use the gun because you have to, not because you have it—SHITHEADS. I'll speak to your captain later."

I tried to catch my breath, hunched over, hands on my knees, happy, for once, to have a cop on my side, one whose deeds did not start riots, to have Roi as my friend, even though he still called me Snotty Nose, which I didn't like. Roi was no *nigga*. If he wasn't, maybe none of us was.

However, where was Trenese?

* * *

I limped behind Roi to the motel's lobby. A buzzer let us into a cramped, seatless space. Rap music about drug use, fucking ho's, and killing people blared from a tinny ceiling speaker next to a dummy surveillance camera.

Someone moved ghostly on the other side of the smoky

Plexiglas window.

"Hwan-Yeong. Twenty-five dollars for one hour, forty dollars for two," said the shadowy female, her Korean accent muffled. "Are you together?"

My hand trembled when I slid the picture of Trenese into the banker's tray underneath Plexiglas.

"No want room—you look the picture," I said loud and slow in my best Far Eastern accent.

"Baby Doll, yes, she looks like Baby Doll," said the woman.

My body jolted. I adjusted my bifocals.

Roi slapped his badge against the Plexiglas and sounded officious. "When did you last see Baby Doll?"

"She was here, after the sting—with men."

"What did she say?"

"Nothing—she used to hang out with Rip n' Run—DIC. He michin, crazy motherfucker, slice girl quick."

Oh, God. Had this woman just described the asshole who came to my house? I had to stay calm if we would get the 4 1 1. Roi glowered into the Plexiglas as if he could see the woman on the other side.

"She kicks his ass to curb maybe—she's with a light-skin woman now."

"A partner?" Roi said. "Female pimp?"

After a long silence, the woman finally said, "When Rip comes, we call the ambulance for girl—bloody sheets." With two hands, she slid Trenese's picture back to me. "Baby Doll meets men herself, like an appointment."

Roi twists his body to face me. "She can't be setting up tricks herself at fourteen."

"Fifteen," I said. "My baby's smart. I told you that."

He leaned in and bent down to the Plexiglas opening. "Anything else you can tell us? Her partner?"

"No. Nothing else," the shadowy woman said, a tremble in

her voice before another silence. "I'm no snitch. Anybody asks, I deny. Kamsahamnida."

My worn face reflected in the smoky glass. "Trenese is my granddaughter," I said, but her answer was silence.

The door swung behind us when the woman called out. I caught the door and held it open. My knee pained as we turned to leave.

"Look 'round Jack Rabbit Liquor," she said. "Pimps and women all gather there."

* * *

Dusk descended on Long Beach Boulevard, making vision difficult as we crept along the street. Illumination came from dim streetlamps, whatever businesses dared stay open after dark, and a constellation of cell phones in which sex workers buried their faces. Once we crossed Alondra Boulevard, girls and a couple of boys solicited customers like an open-air market. Some girls looked Trenese's age, some younger.

"They're abused." Roi hit the lever on the dashboard to warm midwinter's air. "Children—but we throw them in jail anyway."

"I get it, Roi," I said, throat closing up. My battery ran low, my knee was swollen and stiff, and I had pain in the neck.

We drove quietly for a while. "You look like shit, Tallent. What's going on? I mean, besides cancer."

"It hurts, man." I caught myself grinding my teeth. "I might have forced Trenese into the streets."

The Beetle's heater worked too well, and the oily Vick jersey stuck to my body. Desolation had spawned boarded-up storefronts outside of the Beetle window. Maybe she was in good health, in one piece, after all. For that much, the deputies had been beneficial. Rip had a bad reputation. I'd fuck him up.

Ahead was Jack Rabbit Liquor. Behind the store was a ratty motel. Pimps and wannabe thugs milled around and clogged the entrance.

Roi parked in front and nodded toward the motel. "Pimps rent blocks of rooms to avoid a city ordinance against short-term room rentals."

The area reeked of marijuana, cheap liquor, and piss. Under the lighted Jack Rabbit Liquor blade sign, three pimps talked loud about their whores, or *ho's*, as they called them.

I glimpsed braids on one of them, a bright red cap. It was the fake college student, old Rip n' Run.

"That's the MF that came to my house." I scoured the Beetle for a weapon. He had to know something about Trenese. I could murder his ass right then and there, but I'd go to jail and still might not find her.

"Wait in the car," Roi said.

It took self-control to watch him leave the car and walk over to the shit pile while I stayed put.

It was chancy asking these guys. They looked stupider than stupid, unclean, and untidy in oversized t-shirts and Dickies. Their appearance diminished the pimp's profession. Old-school pimp Don "Magic" Juan probably cruised hell's streets in Satan's red Cadillac, cursing them. Only an impaired woman could fall under the spell of these pre-homeless fools. They'd never tell on themselves.

Earlier, Roi had explained the sex trade. Pimps were the hardest to arrest since johns rarely met them, and hookers protected them. Roi tried reasoning with three butt wipes. Fire in my belly, I leaned behind the window post and listened.

He handed the picture to the pimp with thick eyebrows and monkey ears, who must've been no taller than Mini-me. Rip n' Run stared into space the whole time, rock-faced.

"I've seen her before. I can't remember where," the tiny

pimp said in a deep Barry White baritone. "Is she from Compton?"

"She's a fine bitch—wish I did know her," said the big pimp with DIC tattooed on his forehead.

Rip n' Run settled back against the wall like he couldn't be bothered.

"Do I know you, nigga?" the midget asked Roi.

Roi shook his head *no*.

"You five-o?"

Rip n' Run interrupted. "Naw—we ain't seen her." He glanced over at me in the car. "Not yesterday, not today, never."

Liar.

"BULLSHIT—you son of a bitch," I yelled out the window. I struggled to unfasten the seat belt. I lunged from the car, buckled my injured knee, and tumbled to the sidewalk.

Rip and the big pimp ran. Rip held his pants like a toddler in a shitty diaper. Both had wobbled a hundred yards north on Long Beach Boulevard in a blink.

Mini-me took a wild swing at Roi and missed. Roi's left counter landed the tiny pimp's jaw; a right to the forehead hitched his short legs, and the left cross laid him on the grimy pavement.

I cursed, watched Rip escape, and smashed my fist against the sidewalk. "Fuck—fuck—fuck."

My throat ached. My heartbeat slowed somewhat. Anything could happen out there to any of the women, girls, and boys I'd seen that night. They were all somebody's child, sibling, and other.

I'd never give up, not on Trenese; I'd keep rolling. Rip n' Run must know something. Why else would he have run away? I'd find his ass.

* * *

Back in the Beetle, Roi chased after Rip n' Run. We'd rolled up and down with fucking leads, but still no Trenese. My chest pained, my head hurt, and my knee ached.

We continued to ride back and forth on Rip's dead-end trail while searching for Trenese until Roi touched my shoulder. "It's almost midnight. My friends are all cops, so I'm glad we reconnected. At least now we know whom to look for. Let's call it a night. Try again later."

He was right, as I didn't want to admit it. I felt worn, weak, and health impaired. We'd try another time.

Two silhouettes struggled under a faint streetlamp among the overgrown grass and litter. Closer, a man's braids flew wild as he flailed away over a woman. A belt buckle glinted as it thumped her body over and over. She flung a plastic stripper shoe, which hit him in the face. He grabbed his forehead. She snapped up the shoe, rolled onto her knees, and screamed, "I'm through!" Quickly, she stood and limped away.

Roi swung the Beetle such that his headlights illuminated her. She tripped off the curb and turned around to show her blood-streaked face. Deep copper curly hair reached the shoulder of a white and baby blue cheerleader uniform—now dirty and torn. Her mouth fell open.

"Granddad?" Trenese plucked at her stained sweater and touched the bruise on her cheek. "What the fuck are you doing here?"

She shuffled back and stumbled into the one sandal she still wore. I staggered from the car and reached to grab her.

A voice screeched in the darkness like worn-out car brake pads.

"Hey, motherfucker—hands off my bitch, or I'll bomb on your old ass." It was Rip n' Run, red cap, sagged pants, and all. I quickly faced him. Blood dripped from a hand clasped to his forehead. "D-I-C in the house," he said.

Trenese ducked behind me. Out of the car, Roi held something I couldn't make out. Rip n' Run sneered. He stepped toward me, hand in his waistband. I dragged my leg, shoulder faked, and like before, he flinched. I crouched into a fight position.

A left-right combination backed up Rip but didn't ground him. He kicked my knee, pain knifed through it, and I collapsed. Two kicks to my head dazed me. He whipped a knife blade across my outstretched hands.

A loud *pop* rattled me. I waited to feel piercing pain followed by moisture seeping from a hole in my torso, which never came.

Roi had slapped Rip in the temple. His bitch-ass screamed, hit the ground, and grabbed his head. Roi had fired his Beretta, but it was an old-school intimidation trick; fire and strike with the gun butt simultaneously. The fake-out always worked.

Roi spiked him with a Taser and hit the voltage switch. Rip jiggled on the asphalt shitted his pants, and wailed.

Back on my feet, I shouted, "Fuck you!" and doubled over in a coughing fit. Trenese pushed me aside. Barefooted, she smashed Rip's head with a stripper sandal over and over until Roi pulled her away.

"That's for kicking my granddad." Her gold tongue stud glistened in the dimness.

The ass-whipping was over by the time I stopped coughing. Should I tell her about my cancer? Rip's blood oozed into the curb gutter.

Rip had no Plexiglas protection, and he'd finally gone to school—old-school beatdown class. Roi called 911. An ambulance would probably take him to Kane Hospital and maybe the county jail surgery ward to remove the baseball hat and plastic fragments from Rip's brain.

Did I care? At last, I could see Trenese and touch her. She

looked older, face drawn in, skinnier, no longer the bounding little girl. Roi turned toward his Beetle as Trenese and I hugged and wept.

"We'll get through even if I have to take parenting or anger management classes," I said. Roi wiped down his bug and watched us from a distance. I apologized for being an asshole, begged forgiveness, told her how little I had understood about her, how I'd often treated women as thingamajigs, and how I'd been wrong. I said, "Happy birthday. There's something else I want to tell you, Trenese." My chest tightened, and my mouth went dry. I didn't want her to feel sorry for me. "I have cancer."

Trenese took two steps back and squeezed her eyes shut. "NO," she said and hugged me again. Trenese swiped the dust off, straightened her uniform, gathered her sandals, sat on the curb, and fitted them. I handed her a napkin, and she dabbed her face.

"Everything's going to be all right. We will get you some Afro puffs and get you back on track." I'd shield her like Plexiglas. "Lose those studs," I said.

She stood, shoulders back, chest out, regarding me. Then she smiled a sad, quiet smile.

"I'm fine, Granddad," she said. "I'm running late. I'll check on you. You take care now."

When I reached, she turned and walked toward an obscure figure who had breached the mist. A slender amber hand summoned her, and the two women clasped their bodies together.

"She'll be fine. FINE," Esther said.

"I'll see you soon, Grandad."

PLAY DADDY

Starkāna bounced a curled knuckle against her mouth when Bonnie Rice walked up from behind and touched her shoulder. She jumped and clenched the 2019 commencement program as a mother clasps a child's hand in a crowded swap meet. "Relax, sweetheart." She adjusted the Kinte cloth panel to hide Starkāna's *Killaz Life* neck tattoo. Starkāna's gown looked like a tent on her. "You'll be fine."

It was early summer in South Central L.A., SoLA, and at twenty-three, Starkāna Wilkerson never thought she'd walk the stage on graduation day. Yet she stood closer to that possibility, eye patch and black robe to match, unable to control the stomach flutter and sweat cascading her back like a waterfall.

She doodled sunflowers in the program margins and chattered within the cluster of graduates—all parolees and probationers like her, in a parking lot queue before the Imagine 2020 commencement exercise.

Few things had gone right in her life; she'd be glad when it was over. She glanced at her watch, closed her eyes, and lowered her head. Where was Mama?

Starkāna strained to look around Bonnie into the crowd of well-wishers. "Did you see my mother yet?" She'd invited her. What about Sunny? Indeed, her mom would bring Sunny, her grandchild, Starkāna's daughter.

Bonnie moved the gold tassel to the left side of Starkāna's black mortarboard cap, hair- pinned to short natural locks underneath. "No, honey, but let's give her a chance." She straightened shoulder pads and smoothed perspiration from Starkāna's forehead.

"She was supposed to be here already." Had she remembered to put the Forever stamp on the invitation she'd mailed to her mother? There had been many mailbox thefts lately in her mother's neighborhood. Had some fool stolen it? She arched her neck to look around Bonnie again and crumbled the drawing in her hand.

"She's never seen me graduate." Starkāna could not allow that to happen with Sunny. No. To do so would mean she'd end up like her mother, distant, as far away as Dockweiler Beach. And no matter what, she had to do better than that. Starkāna bowed her head. "She's missed every important moment in my life."

Bonnie cupped her wrinkled hands on Starkāna's dimpled cheeks. "But you still made it here, didn't you?" She stepped back from Starkāna. "Okay, big girl, everything's perfect."

A new silver cuspid crown showed under Starkāna's faint smile.

Heat wrapped her like a cocoon there in the parking lot. Every thought wilted in her brain except one. If time would only slow enough for her mother to make it, she would show her mother and everyone that she could be a good parent, better than her mother had been to her, like a mother she'd seen on TV.

The DJ played processional music, "A Love Supreme." She

hated it like the homeless detest snow. "A Love Supreme" was John Coltrane's classic jazz tune, her mother's favorite that helped her sleep. Surely, there must be some mistake. She didn't want to remember but to go somewhere quiet and think. Of all the tunes to play, why "A Love Supreme"? She hand-fanned her face and bosom. She closed her eyes and rubbed the middle of her forehead.

ii

Starkāna was seven when Play Daddy, one of her mother's dates, had begun calling her "Princess."

One night, he slinked into her bedroom and onto her twin bed, naked. When he pinched her ear between his aged lips, Old Spice cologne, gin, and cigarette smoke shot through her nose. She took short breaths and snatched her head away.

"*Shhhh*, your mama sent me to check on you, baby," Play Daddy whispered as he squeezed her tight from behind. The hair on his chest was like nappy doll hair, only rougher. His mustache tickled her neck like an errant housefly.

She lay on her side, knees curled up to her forearms glued to her chest, a ball. What was he doing in her bed? Should she scream? Instead, she gulped down the air and held her breath; she couldn't speak.

The music stopped.

Her mother called from the other room. "Marv?" He didn't answer. "MARVIN," she said a second time. She didn't look for him and began to snore. If Starkāna could count backward from one hundred, Mama might appear by magic and save her. One hundred, ninety-nine, ninety-eight...Her heartbeat thrashed in her ears.

"Relax, baby—I'mma makes you a woman tonight." He clasped both arms around her. A diamond from a pinky ring he wore glistened in the dimness. No. This felt wrong. She pushed and tried to wrangle free, but he was too strong.

He stiffened just below her butt, thrust forward and back several times, turned her over onto her back, raised her night-gown, fingered around and removed her panties, and was on top of her.

"No." She trembled. "Please."

The stench of his breath caused her to turn her head side-ways. His face was hard to see in the dark, even though she didn't want to see him. Her pulse surged, and her muscles tightened.

"Come to me, little child. Let the kingdom belong to you," he huffed. "Open your legs."

She cringed but obeyed. He thrust himself in her, and she jumped as if Play Daddy had pinched her from the inside. She put her hands over her eyes and cried. Where was Mama? She made up her mind never to have children.

Play Daddy would often visit her room after he moved into the household.

Later in the fourth grade, Starkāna tried to understand her homework. Her mother made her unlock the bedroom door and said, "I know you are not trying to lock me out——girl leave this door open." Starkāna sat on her bed. Mama smelled of musty gin. "How do you like your play daddy?"

She didn't. Starkāna began to rock back and forth. "He's okay——I don't like him in my room."

Mama stepped back. "Nawl, he all right—how can he be in your room when he's in mine?" She raised her voice. "We're thinking about getting married—"

"But Mama..." She held her elbows tight to her sides.

"But nothing." If Mama liked him so much, Starkāna would have to like him too. "You'd better not run him off."

A year later, Starkāna searched the audience for her mother

at her fifth-grade graduation. She'd managed to pass classes, somehow. But where was her mother? She never showed, and Starkāna refused to cross the stage unless her mother was there. Her neck hurt from looking back to the door.

Starkāna's heart shrank like the number of chips in a Doritos bag.

iii

"A Love Supreme" ended when the Imagine 2020 procession reached the center of a large activity room in the Libertine Tax Prep™ building. Mama was nowhere in sight. For sure, Play Daddy wouldn't be there. Maybe Mama blamed her for what happened to him. She stared down at her brand-new fire-red pedicure. She wore new shoes that would make her enemies visibly upset.

Metal folding chairs for graduates and guests faced the makeshift stage where Bonnie stood among officials. She gave a quick wave to Starkāna. Starkāna took her assigned seat and crossed her legs. What if they didn't call her name? What if her mama didn't show up again? Her foot shook up and down from the ankle.

With three chevron stripes on his uniform sleeve at the podium, Willie welcomed the audience and introduced Bonnie Rice and other dignitaries.

"Our students are amazing," he said. "They've worked hard and learned new skills to improve their lives. We started with fifty-four students, but these thirty-five are the last ones standing."

Huge Cheshire grins plastered the faces of fellow students, except Starkāna's lips formed a straight line. She turned to scan the crowd for Mama. Why would things be different now? She rarely had, if ever, come through for her. *You go on ahead, baby,*

I'll catch up with you, was her mama's favorite line. Like Wile E. Coyote chased the Road Runner, she never did.

Mama and Sunny once visited her at the Jackie Lacey Detention Center for Women. She fixed herself up as best she could for their visit.

Mama looked different.

"How's my favorite daughter?" Mama said through a speak-through in a Plexiglas barrier that separated inmates from visitors. Starkāna was an only child. A cloak of mustiness from hundreds of women housed in close quarters was thick on Starkāna's side.

Starkāna raised an eyebrow and clutched her chest. Mama's caramel face was fuller, her eyes clear, and she smiled often. Sunny squeezed in beside her grandmother, and they shared the metal stool. Colorful barrettes were attached to the ends of her braided hair. Her pretty skin was dark and smooth. Sunny was seven, the same age as Starkāna, when her Play Daddy troubles started. Did Mama have other dates? Another Play Daddy? Starkāna couldn't control her moan and plastered on an overly bright smile.

Sunny waved. Her brown eyes were wide and glowing. "Hi, mama," she said.

Mama told Starkāna how well Sunny did in school, how they'd spent time at museums, how Sunny was so artistic, and how it was about just the two of them.

"And Mama, I learned how to swim," Sunny said. Much time had passed between them. Starkāna had always wanted to learn to swim, but Mama never made time for her, and the local parks were too dangerous to navigate alone.

Mama and Sunny placed their hands against the Plexiglas. Starkāna fidgeted, hesitated, and did the same from the other side. Starkāna's heart hammered in her chest. "I'll see you when I'm out," she said, icy, unsure if she was speaking to one or both visitors.

Could Mama be a better grandmother than she was a mother? Nonetheless, she'd take over the job when she got out and do even better. But how? The jail environment had little to offer in that sense, as most of the talk was about the wrongs of men.

iv

Now Starkāna was on the cusp of finally succeeding at something on her own: graduation with a long overdue GED. Starkāna bounced a knee and eyed the entrance to her left. With what little spirituality she could muster, she prayed for Mama to show *with* Sunny.

In Imagine 2020, Starkāna had always been slow, a beat behind classmates, and struggled to understand things. The program was meant to habilitate criminals, to help them avoid more prison time, to give SoLA communities they preyed upon respite, and more importantly, to provide societies disconnected a living chance.

Sgt. Willie gestured with an open palm. "Starkāna Wilkerson has performed well in almost every area and deserves special recognition."

She dropped the pencil she'd doodled with and squeezed the commencement program. A flush of adrenaline tingled through her body. She hadn't seen this coming. Imagine 2020 was the hardest thing she had ever tried, the first she'd ever completed. She wouldn't have started if she knew it would be as tricky, the intense group and parenting sessions, hypnosis, yoga meditation, exorcism, one step forward and two back. She had to face her flaws, past crimes, and transgressions, her relationship with her daughter, Mama, Play Daddy, and most challenging of all, herself.

"We'll hang her sunflowers—a permanent display—to show others the possibilities," he told the audience.

That is okay for a one-eyed artist. She closed a teary eye and covered her mouth. Opening her good eye, she saw a knowing grin split Bonnie's dark-skinned, soft, round face. Starkána's classmates rose and applauded. Tingling swept up the back of her neck and across her face. She glanced to the entrance. No Mama. More tears.

Gladys sat beside her, still clapping like crazy. They'd gotten close during the program. Unlike friends Starkána had before, Gladys was brilliant and had been involved in embezzlement schemes, what she called white-collar stuff. She was good at numbers and always said things like *if you don't have a program, there's always someone around to give you one.*

"Girl, you're something else." Gladys hugged her. "I'm really happy for you—just keep working hard on yourself—and your sunflowers."

Starkána hugged her friend back, but she couldn't help wishing Mama was the one saying those words. Mama had never told her she was proud of her. Mama had never said much of anything nice. A mistake Starkána would not make with Sunny. Here she was, surrounded by new friends but not family. She slid down in the chair and pinched her lips tight to keep them from trembling.

She didn't want a hug from Carl Steele, who sat on her other side, even though he tried. An old criminal, he reminded her of what she imagined her real daddy, whom she had never known, was like. He was a crusty old fart, always flirting and soliciting sex on the side. And he reeked of Old Spice cologne, which she hated.

"Congratulations, Mama Africa," he whispered. His breath

caused her to lean away, doggie doo next to a tree. "I got a little something for you after we graduate." He slid his hand down across his pants zipper.

Before, she might have kicked his old ass. She'd fight anyone: boys, girls, teachers, police. It didn't matter. She was always touchy, a snake poised to strike. She took it in stride now. Besides, she liked his good-natured attention.

"Okay, Carl. That old shriveled-up thing?" She covered her mouth to hide a smile. "Be sure to bring your Christian wife along." She winked. "Ménage á Trois?" She looked past him to an empty doorway.

The commencement speaker, Nikki Giovanni, spoke about overcoming adversity, forgiveness, and better things to come. If only her mother were here to hear that part. It'd be great if her mama would walk in right now.

She shifted in her seat. Her mother had often been angry and had hurt her. She'd reach for the extension cord with the slightest perceived provocation and beat Starkāna so often that she'd no longer cry. Adversity was like a relative to Starkāna, a sister or close cousin.

A man entered with a woman that, at first, she thought was Mama. Starkāna sat up, the corners of her mouth turned up, but it wasn't her. Then, decades-old words surfaced. "You ain't shit and never will be," her mother had said between puffs of Newport menthol cigarettes. "Just like your daddy. Humph, he played that horn and shot up drugs."

She'd never back-talk Mama, but dyslexia and the fights with others landed her first in Special Education classes in elementary and later in thug training grounds, continuation schools. Now, her graduation tassel hung in her eye, and she stared down at the cuts and scars on her hands.

The world was alphabetized, and in that order, she sat as Sergeant Willie called classmates to receive their certificates.

W was always the last letter called. Glenda Adams, Celia Cruz, and Charlie Davis walked up the ramp, shook hands with Willie, and smiled for the photo. Starkăna rubbed her neck. Aside from a small circle of crime buddies, she collected while enslaved to drugs, like Becca and Omawaule, she'd never had many friends. Tears welled behind her eyelid. Her yellow nylon blouse stuck to her lower back. Those girls were her peeps. But her friendship with them had almost destroyed her.

v

Once at fourteen, Starkăna stood on the toilet seat of one of two doorless stalls the day before middle school graduation. She pulled three small paint spray cans from her backpack and made the white wall at the back of the commode her canvas, meticulously painting disc florets in shades of brown, small perfect flowers that cluster in spiral patterns within the head of sunflowers. She sprayed the little leaves and thick greenish stem onto the toilet flush mechanism. The seat shifted a little when she tiptoed to stroke bright yellow outer petals that attracted insects and had often held captive her gaze when in season. With just the right amount of shading, the sunflower was taller than her four-foot-eight-inch height. Perfect. Her lungs expanded full with deep, satisfying breaths.

A voice from behind startled Starkăna. "How'd you like to try a new flavor?" Becca said in the tiny bathroom, which began to fill with contact from the weed she smoked. She was with another girl. Becca was a squat, overweight white girl who seemed to roll when she walked. She wore thick blond corn-rows tight against her scalp, a dark red Pendleton shirt, blue jeans with razor-sharp creases, smacked gum, and blew bubbles through thin lips. She waddled a few steps to Starkana and held up the joint.

Starkāna was not lame. At least she didn't want to appear that way. She nodded slowly, lips parted, jaw jutted. "I'm down."

Becca put the burning part of the joint between the roof of her mouth and tongue and shotgunned smoke past Starkāna's pouty lips.

Starkāna's eyes widened. She stepped back but held the smoke in until she coughed. Next, Becca filled her cheeks with smoke, touched Starkāna's lips, and blew into her mouth. It was hard to tell if her buzz was from the chronic or Becca's lips.

"Skip graduation practice," Becca said. Starkāna hesitated. "You should roll with us—it'll be more fun." She lay hands on Starkāna's shoulders, pulled her close, backed her into the stall, and gave her a more prolonged smoke kiss. Omawaule, Becca's homie, peered past Becca into the stall. Omawaule was skinny and tall, a black-skinned Olive Oyl from a Popeye cartoon, her hair in rows of marble-sized Afro-puffs. She had a healed scar between her eyebrows that'd been stitched up. She squeezed in behind Starkāna. Would they jack her? All she had was a fingernail file in the out-of-reach backpack.

Starkāna's body stiffened, heartbeat raced. Three bodies pressed together, two warm breaths on her. Oooh! ——so tight ——Oooh! Becca kissed one cheek, then the other. Starkāna's mind said to leave, but her body did otherwise. She relaxed. "Besides, you can graduate high school——when it counts," Becca whispered.

Omawaule kissed Starkāna's shoulder and her neck. What if she did miss graduation? So the fuck what? Who gave a damn? Omawaule pressed against and groped her.

Starkāna's smile wavered. Did she want this?

Killaz Life was tattooed on Omawaule's forearm. In a high-pitched screeching voice, she said, "Let's party." Then she let loose with an odd laugh, a cross between a cackle and a squeal.

Anyone with any sense would have run away fast——but not Starkăna.

"Fuck the graduation—" Had she made the right choice?

To celebrate, Omawaule broke out a bottled wine cooler from her backpack. Starkăna snatched it away to open it with her teeth and chipped her cuspid. They shared its pineapple taste in the cramped stall.

The two girls took turns removing Starkana's few pieces of clothing: her stretch halter, baby doll skirt, thong, and flip-flops. Becca touched her body with hands and lips in places Starkăna didn't know existed as no one else had ever taken the time to do, especially Play Daddy.

Starkăna sat on the commode seat etched with graffiti as Becca affectionately placed Starkăna's leg over her left shoulder and orally sexed her. Omawaule stood behind, gently cupping Starkăna's developing breast, the painted sunflower to her back. In a fog of weed smoke, Starkăna buzzed from the wine cooler. She resisted as long as she could before her cold heart melted, her body quivered uncontrollably, and for the first time, she came.

A school bell rang, and student voices wailed outside. An adult voice shouted, "Bathroom check." Omawaule shrugged and screeched her odd laugh again, only louder in Starkăna's ear. Starkăna counted backward from one hundred. She reached for her clothes on the floor but bumped heads with Becca.

"Owww!" Starkăna grabbed her forehead. CRASH. Omawaule dropped the wine cooler. Cool liquid splashed Starkăna's feet. She shrieked but couldn't move as the three jiggled in the stall. She gazed at her bare feet at the shards of dark green glass and puddles of amber liquid on the cold tile floor. Her heart sank.

The three girls were suspended from school but managed

to get to a Brookside Park smoke-out in Pasadena that day and the next one on graduation day.

vi

At the Imagine 2020 graduation, Bonnie sat on stage with her legs crossed at the ankle and hands clasped on the lap of a flowered skirt that hit well below her knees. Sgt. Willie called Kwanza Knowles. She had one of those African-sounding names like Omawaule, Becca's crazy-ass ex-girlfriend. By the time she'd met them, she was already sexually active with plenty of pubescent boys. And Play Daddy, too. Of course. Always Play Daddy. *Nice little tits—I told you I'd make a woman out of you;* he'd remind her on his way back to Mama's room. Seven years and Mama never noticed what was going on. Or had she? Mama liked to call her stupid; perhaps it ran in the family, or maybe Mama still felt that way. She scraped a hand over her face. It was time for Starkāna to move on. She would try.

Sgt. Willie continued to call students to the stage. "David Ortiz, Jennifer Randle, Carl Steele..."

Carl brushed Starkāna's leg as he ambled up. "Oh, excuse me," he said when he bent over and squeezed Starkāna's knee, lingering momentarily.

She jerked away. "Bastard."

Carl sped up the ramp to the platform to receive his certificate. No Mama, but a man at the entrance resembled Play Daddy. Starkāna studied his profile. Close cut natural styled hair, pencil mustache, otherwise clean-shaven, tall and overweight, clothes a tight fit. He shot her a glance with intense brown eyes. Did Play Daddy have a twin, or was this his ghost? She squirmed in her chair.

vii

Starkāna, Becca, and Omawaule partied a lot until Starkāna's baby bump began to show.

"Who's the daddy?" Mama had asked.

"I don't know."

"You do know whom you were fucking—don't you?"

The baby daddy was Play Daddy. Besides, Mama had warned her not to run him off. She adjusted her top as if it chafed. "Huh—uhh." She tried to like him the best way she knew. This would be her secret.

Mama's eyes were coal red. "Stupid little bitch. It's too late for an abortion."

After Play Daddy moved out of their apartment, Sunny was born in February, and by March, Starkāna was in high school. One of several boys she'd had sex with and whom she pinned the baby on disavowed fatherhood and was never around. "Just one time, and I used a rubber. It can't be mine," he had said to her.

At first, Sunny was like having a baby doll, and Starkāna vowed to always be there for her, to keep her away from play daddies, to attend her graduations. But her mama had to take care of Sunny. Starkāna kept running with Becca and Omawaule, would sell drugs, run scams, and hustle to get money. They'd lure men into motels and rob them.

Play Daddy once called her and said he wanted to speak to her about something. Sex between them was less frequent after he moved out, but she knew the routine. She agreed to meet him. Besides, that might be a good time to tell him he was her baby's daddy and then watch him squirm.

There she sat on the 108 Motel queen bed. The room smelled of cheap disinfectant. She put the crack pipe, flip phone, and school ID in the nightstand drawer atop Gideon's bible and closed it. He must've wanted the usual bim-bam-thank-you-maám he'd been off and on with for years. But he walked in and stood.

Tone sharp, she said, "What's up, player?"

He cleared his throat. "I've stopped drinking—done some thinking since I moved out on your mama." His tone was lower, different than at any time before. He rested his chin on his palm and tapped an index finger against his cheek. He turned away to avoid eye contact and mumbled, "—maybe I was wrong."

"What?" Her mind wandered to tasks undone, loose ends that she needed to tie, and crack-induced la-dee-day stuff.

"I watched Joel Osteen preach on the television," he said. Play Daddy pinned his arms against his stomach. Starkāna had already taken off her bra and kicked off her sandals. He paced. "Osteen talked about righting wrongs—people we've hurt."

"Can we just get this over with?" Starkāna said. Naked, she lay back on the bed. He didn't undress as usual and had a pained expression. There was a long silence. His habit was to be all over her before she could undress; it would be over in three minutes. She drew her mouth into a straight line and bit her lip.

"I just want to apologize for what I did to you, Starkāna." He dropped his hands to his side. Her mind raced to understand what had just happened. "I need to get right with God." He had begun to sob. "Can you find it in your heart to forgive me?"

Her mouth opened, but nothing came out. Surely, there must be some mistake. The sonofabitch was fucking up her high. After a long pause, her voice quaked, "Me, forgive you?" She shook her head, and her thoughts froze. She clenched her fist and took care to control her tone. "Should Sunny forgive you too? What about Mama?"

"Sunny?"

"Your daughter, motherfucker."

BLAM. The door burst open. Becca was first in and hit Play Daddy across his chest with a metal softball bat. His knees buckled, and he crashed to the floor.

"This is payback, bitch." Becca pounded his shoulders, head, and outstretched hands with the bat.

Omawaule followed, pointing a small handgun, kicked him in the groin, and screamed, "Killaz Life." Blood gushed from his forehead and mouth. He grabbed the bat, wrestled it away from Becca, and tried to stand. They would hurt him and teach him a lesson not to fuck with little girls, but things happened so fast.

"Hold up," Starkāna shouted.

Play Daddy hollered, "Please stop."

Starkāna took a step towards him to shield him. He'd been beaten up plenty. It was time to end this.

Omawaule cackled loud enough to sober a drunk. BANG BANG, she fired twice. Play Daddy fell over the nightstand and collapsed onto the carpet. Blood seeped from the bullet wounds to his head. He lay motionless on his back, legs turned awkwardly underneath him, eyes opened as if he were looking up at Starkāna.

Becca grabbed his lifeless cheeks with one hand. "Get up, mothafucka." He didn't move. The planned ass-whipping had gone wrong.

"Stupid bitch. You killed my baby's daddy." Starkāna vomited onto the floor.

"Fuck it—let's go," Omawaule said. She rifled his pockets, snatched a gold cross and chain, and took his watch and diamond pinky ring.

Starkāna's heartbeat raced, and her skin tingled as she dressed fast. Like Starkāna, Sunny was now a bastard. How had it come to this?

They scrambled to the parking lot, hopped in Becca's white Alero, and burned rubber out of the driveway.

Later, they were caught. Starkãna had left her school ID in the drawer of the motel room nightstand.

Becca did juvenile prison time, and Omawaule tried as an adult, was sentenced to prison for the criminally insane. Starkãna received ninety days in juvenile detention, along with probation. After that, she was in and out of jail so much that it became like a regular vacation spot from the grit and grind of SoLA. She had graduated into a life of drug use and its companion, criminality. She attended jail school where successful graduation was to become a better criminal.

viii

Starkãna turned 21 in jail. Her mama continued to raise Sunny while Starkana had spent the last year incarcerated for abusing a foster son she'd adopted to hustle welfare money. The boy's sister punched out Starkãna's left eye in a scrum to free him from her.

Jail time had been rough, a constant barnacle in her ass. Her hair had gone primarily wild and unkempt to help ward off potential enemies in lockup. There were many, especially for diminutive inmates like her. There were fights and threats every day, but she was SoLA tough and clever enough to distract would-be adversaries with portraits she'd draw of them.

The day before her release, Starkãna met with her probation officer about options, like the Imagine 2020 program.

"Without it, you have a snowball's chance in hell of getting your daughter back," her PO said. "But if you complete the eighteen-month life skills program——graduate, get a certificate—we'll revisit the custody issue." The PO tossed the file onto the desk. "Your track record is poor. Personally——I don't think you can do it. For now, a halfway house is where you'll stay."

She looked a mess. Her skin was blotched. One area was light another was a shade darker, like dead areas on leaves. Pimples clustered on her forehead like cottage cheese from eating junk food with little to no exercise. What a fuck up. What an unfit mother. She gulped her thumping heart into place and wiped sweaty palms on her orange jail scrubs.

"Ain't nothing but a thang," she said. She didn't want to consider whether she'd have to revisit other dark places, such as Play Daddy. But she had to get the restraining order lifted to see her daughter.

ix

Sgt. Willie looked out to the crowd and smiled. "Starkāna Wilkerson," he announced. Again, her classmates woo-hooed and applauded her. "Go on, girl," Gladys said. Bonnie stood and shouted, "I love you," as Starkāna headed to the podium, knees weak. Imagine 2020 had been right for her, although it didn't start that way.

x

At first, Starkāna was sour and combative like a cornered cat.

"I don't need your help for nothing, pig," she said to Sergeant Willie, a deputy sheriff in charge of the Imagine 2020 program. Willie was far different from most deputies that formed gangs and routinely terrorized the community, just like the Bloods and Crips. "Me and my nigs got this." She mimicked confidence, knowing that her best dawgs, Becca and Omawaule, were still in jail. She'd never known love and mostly stayed to herself, a wallflower. She'd received few to no kind words from other people except those two. But Willie was persistent and confronted her about her attitude.

"If you're willing to do the work, you'll reap the benefits," Willie said. Pushed by him and her PO, Starkāna joined the Imagine 2020 program. She still had much fighting and distrust and would show up late, argue, and cuss.

"Don't sweat me," she said. She had plenty of explanations for her tardiness, like when she misplaced her bus pass, the halfway house van broke down, lost her keys, overslept, or, this or that, a new excuse each morning. But Starkāna observed as other program cohorts among the multiethnic group rapidly helped themselves once given a break. In group counseling, they were pressed to confront personal demons, explore their long-suppressed dreams, and pursue them. They learned to recognize vestiges of systemic racism and generational trauma from once being enslaved. They studied the Holocaust and WWII Japanese internment camps. They received opportunities that were, until their contact with Imagine 2020, unimaginable.

Sgt. Willie was passionate about his work and understood his charges.

"If there's anything we can do to help you arrive on time... if you can't, I'll have your PO violate you." A probation violation would have been a ticket to shoot a bullet: another year in county jail.

She feigned attention and nodded her head as he spoke.

"Uh-huh."

"You know, Starkāna——I've been in this game awhile. Like you, I was raised in SoLA," he said. "There's nothing new under the sun." He had a clean-shaven athletic build. "Tougher folks than you have graduated, become successful."

She curled her lip and smirked as he spoke. Then he introduced Starkăna to Bonnie Rice.

xi

Bonnie Rice had a tiny office upstairs at Libertine Tax Prep™ that was packed with pictures and Afro-centric stuff. Bonnie, a dainty, no-nonsense woman, had lived hard. There was a picture of Oprah Winfrey near the door and one of Nina Simone beside the window. Underneath Nina was a quote from Eleanor Roosevelt: *You must do the things you think you cannot do.* A framed picture of Malcolm X pointing his finger toward Starkăna seated on the other side of Bonnie's small wooden desk was on one of the few clear spots.

Starkăna motioned to the massive picture behind Bonnie's worn executive chair.

"Who's that? Ooga Booga?" Starkăna said with exaggerated casualness as she settled back in her chair. "Damn, she's ugly. Is that your grandmother?"

Bonnie flashed a bemused smile. "Harriet Tubman," she said. "She was a conductor on the Underground Railroad." Tubman's solemn eyes stared right back at Starkăna. "She's not my grandmother, but she could have been yours. Can you say for sure she wasn't?" Starkăna had no smart-alecky comeback. Bonnie held Starkăna's school transcripts in hand. "You missed high school graduation."

Starkăna scoped the Ashanti fertility figurine on the cluttered desk. She swallowed but could find no saliva. Something told her that Bonnie would not be played. "I didn't get the notice but partied with my girls anyway."

Bonnie looked over her glasses at Starkăna. "Show me your friends, and I'll tell you who you are."

Ouch. Starkăna screwed up her face. She'd never thought

much about her friend choices before. "Ain't nothing wrong with my friends," she said. "My peeps got my back." She pretended not to be uncomfortable.

"Where are they now?" Bonnie asked. Becca was still in jail for abusing Starkana's foster son, and Omawaule would never get out of prison for killing Play Daddy.

"Tsk," Starkăna sucked her chipped tooth and chewed her fingernails.

"Who are you, Starkăna?"

Starkăna jerked back. "You don't know me, woman." Her heartbeat was loud in her ears.

"The tests say you have some trouble reading."

Starkăna crossed her arms and pressed her lips flat. "I can read."

Bonnie searched around the desk and handed Starkăna a fourth-grade reader. "Read this to me," Bonnie said, pointing to a passage.

Starkăna rolled her eye and snatched at the book, but Bonnie pulled it back before she could grasp it. Starkăna winced, extended her hand, and focused on the Tubman picture.

Moments of silence passed before Bonnie handed her the reader. What kind of test was this? Starkăna's finger moved along the page in slow motion. The simple read was labored, and dots of sweat formed above her eye patch. Whom was she fooling? She swallowed again and again and slid down in the chair.

Bonnie dug in like spurs into a horse's ass. "You're in your early twenties. What jobs have you had?"

She'd never held a real job like a bagger at Ralph's Market, a Best Buy clerk, or even a sign twirler for Libertine Tax Prep™. "I recycle and sell things I paint on." She tried to make it sound important. She was good with the hustle. She'd recycle plastic, deal drugs, prostitute, run scams like taking on foster children temporarily even though she stayed in a rundown shack, hold artistic panhandler signs she'd drawn with charcoal briquettes over a Styrofoam cup at the freeway off-ramps, or sell small junk items that she'd paint sunflowers on, whatever for a dead president. She tossed back scarlet, shoulder length, fifty percent Indian hair that weaved unevenly into her own.

"Some of your artwork is good. Did you know Van Gogh painted sunflowers?" Bonnie asked.

Starkāna tugged at her ear. "Who?" Her mind searched for an answer. "Vango?"

"We can help you, Starkāna." Her emphatic but empathetic voice was wizened by her recovery from alcohol and other drugs that she freely disclosed. "It's your choice, dear."

Starkāna nodded with a tight expression. She would not commit to throwing it all in. No one had offered her help before other than Becca, but Bonnie had her attention.

"Can you take better care of yourself——give up drugs—— accept who you are?" Starkāna clutched her hand in her lap. "Are you willing to atone, seek forgiveness, and apologize to people you've hurt?" Starkāna glanced at Harriet Tubman, the clock, and the doorway. "Will you leave the unaffordable weaved hair behind——get your teeth fixed?"

What more could she lose? Maybe she'd get Sunny back.

"Maybe I—" Starkāna's voice trailed off, stomach churned.

"We'll work with you. We can teach you how to study and use a dictionary," Bonnie said. "I can show you how to handle misunderstood or wrongly understood words." Starkāna listened to her heartbeat. "When you get stuck, sketch, work it out with pen and pencil——we'll show you." Starkāna's posture stiffened. "Among other tools, we use Applied Scholastics."

"What does the word 'art' mean? A-R-T," Bonnie asked.

"Let's look it up." She reached back for and handed a dictionary to Starkāna.

"Humph."

"Take your time Starkāna," Bonnie said.

"'Pain—ting, potree, music r any activee n wich a persen makes or do someting dat is beautiful.'"

"Do you think that maybe your designs qualify?" Bonnie said. She retrieved the dictionary and laid it on a pile of papers. "It's okay for you to succeed, Starkāna." Starkāna smiled and swiped at a tear-soaked eye. "Who knows—you might even graduate. I'll still love you either way."

She gasped and clasped Bonnie's forearm. All that had been damned up in Starkāna was released right then and there. "Maybe I'll try it your way," she said.

xii

On the stage, Starkāna's name would be on the graduation certificate that Sgt. Willie was about to hand her. Bonnie high-fived her as she passed.

She wiped sweaty palms on her robe, put her shoulders back, and swallowed her fluttering heart into place, reached and gripped Willie's outstretched hand, and looked him dead in his eyes. Her mother had been wrong about her, and she forgave Becca and Omawaule, her mother, and Play Daddy. She had done many bad things but had to excuse herself to move forward.

A new life would not be easy. It would be easier to backslide, accept a drug-loaded pipe without thinking, hang with so called old friends, and visit old hangouts. Bonnie, Sgt. Willie, Gladys, and even Carl Steele would be there when she stumbled. She had to get Sunny first and keep things reasonable with Mama.

She took the graduation certificate, her name inscribed in bold calligraphy. A tight-lipped smile crossed her face.

Starkāna turned to pose for the photo, and that's when she saw them.

Two hands waved frantically above and behind the seated audience, and for a split second, Starkāna stopped breathing when she recognized them. Mama held Sunny's hand as the two of them pushed through the crowd that stood to applaud the graduates.

Starkāna thrust her fist into the air. She wobbled a little, then collected herself, stood tall, and glided with her chest out back to her seat as "A Love Supreme" began playing for the recessional march.

Her recessional march. She'd done it. She'd crossed the stage. She'd graduated.

DRUM CIRCLE

My West African djembe drum usually hooks people like angler's snag California steelhead in Compton Creek. Squeezing it between bent knees, I pound the goblet-shaped goatskin drumhead, *tap-tap-slap-tap-tap-slap-tap-tap-slap*. Hypnotic nine-beat jackhammer rhythms, finger taps, and hand slaps drive crows from trees, bounce off park structures, and talk to people like Lamba orators. But today, my first beat snares no one. Instead, we argue.

Four pissed-off drum circle performers surround me. Winfrey and a few other regulars don't play instruments but come to twirl, spin, and feel the vibration seizing our souls, feeding a collective spirit our four-hundred-year American sojourn hasn't yet killed. Despite the day job that has me dressing up like Lady Liberty in a turquoise ground-length smock and star-shaped tiara, whirling around and flipping signs at busy intersections for Libertine Tax Service™, our collective gives me a reason and purpose.

We're gathered here on a patch of Trella Tapia Park picnic area. Just as we have every Saturday morning for seven years in

Hub City, a South L.A. suburb with street potholes as big as craters like Baghdad after the bombs, a history of politicians jailed for graft. Water utility bills are so high that many of its one hundred thousand people shower once, maybe twice a week.

Everyone in my drum circle—artists like Joy, the shekere player; Jamaica, the dundun drummer; and Mysteree and Nneka, dancers and Compton natives—want out of Tapia Park. There are no outdoor restrooms and one operable water faucet near the ballpark. But until now, I've had good times here. I want to stay.

Usually, the gym with the restrooms is open for us to use, which we have, despite long lines. However, the gym has been mysteriously closed on Saturdays for the past month. *Budget cuts*, claims the lying park supervisor.

I'm Adofo, the Djembefola, a talking drum master. What good am I without the drum circle? It takes an ensemble to make the crowds smile, sing, clap, heads bob, and bodies sway.

Next to the birth of my daughter, drum circle Saturdays are the most important days of my life. Tap-tap-slap-tap-tap-slap-tap-tap-slap, I talk the drum with my hands, but again, no one dances. My throat hurts from begging the circle members and dumbass park supervisor Big Baller, a task I'm unsuited for, choosing the heartbeat instead and remaining in the background. As a kid, I bounced around different group homes and never wanted attachments and emotions that weakened me.

The concrete picnic tabletop kisses hard against my Type 2 sugar diabetic ass when Joy, an incense maker businesswoman, shakes her shekere. This cowrie shell-covered dried gourd sounds like maracas. *Rasp, rasp, rasp.*

"Leimert Park in SoLA is gentrifying," she says and then slaps the calabash against her palm in my face. "Leimert's kicking the homeless people out. Let's go there, Adofo."

"But we live in Compton, the Hub City." I was raised in Hub City and practically lived in Tapia Park. I've always thought our drum circle helps balance Hub City's *gangsta* reputation by making the park feel more inclusive, like a community. "It's miles away. Why should we leave now?"

"Why? You ask me *why*? Here's a bulletin for you—there're toilets—water faucets that work—" Close to my nose, she slaps the gourd harder. "I need water for my pressure pills."

I've got diabetic hunger and thirst, and I understand the strain. Joy's leashed to diuretics for blood pressure.

The vegan dancers complain of excess body toxin problems. "Let's move there," says Mysteree, the yoga teacher with an Egyptian ankh necklace and dreadlocks ponytail to the middle of her back. She takes several quick breaths, snaps her fingers rapidly, and cracks through my ear and out the other like an electric charge. My finger rims the neck of my tie-dyed dashiki. Sweat flows from my bald dome into the short Afro, which runs around my head, from one temple to the next.

They're right—all around us, the air whiffs of shit and piss. Spikes of sunlight force through clusters of jacarandas and coast live oak just west, near the closed gymnasium. Nearby, a Guatemalan mother uses her brocade shawl, with its horizontal and vertical yellow and navy stripes matching her wraparound corte, to shield her daughter, maybe three or four, whom she's teaching to crap while squatting in a clump of unshorn hedges.

Jamaica sits on the concrete picnic table bench, pounding a stick against the rawhide. *BOOM, BOOM, BOOM.* The drum is shaped like a small barrel attached to a shoulder strap at his side; its bass is so low-pitched and sounds so big my skin goosebumps. "Yeah, mon, me prostrate useta be pea-sized; now it's big as mango fruit," he says. "Rasklaat!" BPH stems his flow, taking him forever to release, even when he finds a private urination spot.

Nneka wears a bright orange kente cloth head wrap. A college sociology professor, she laughs with a cutting edge. "Hell, it's June 2016, and we're still begging Massa for a clean place to shit—a glass of water. It's unjust."

Winfrey sits cross-legged on gravel, lifts his head, and exhales a cloud of weed smoke. Once fearless and uncompromising, he was a 1960s Black Panther. Panthers knew how to protest and get shit done. "Punk-asses," he says. "All y'all." He offers a blunt, a Swisher Sweets cigar stuffed with marijuana, but I wave him off. "Get up—stand up for right." He sips from a Gatorade bottle filled with gin.

BOOM. Jamaica attacks his drum and faces Winfrey. "Tell we what ya know, mon?"

Winfrey sucks a long time on his blunt. "Niggers scared of revolution," he says, and a satisfied grin explodes across his craggy mug. "Back in the day, we didn't take no shit just like Shaka Zulu." He coughs and spits dark phlegm. "—got to be willing to die for something." He glares cranberry eyes at me. "You gonna stand up or lay down?"

For a moment, my brain stops working.

BOOM, BOOM, BOOM. "Yeah, mon," says Jamaica, again pounding his drum. "Like old Marcus Garvey."

Stomach hardening, I say, "Yeah! —Sweet Jesus! I got an idea!" Earlier, I'd passed fliers posted on the gym door for a one o'clock Town Hall meeting about three hours away. "Let's protest—" I say, "a *piss-in*, right here." I don't like confrontation, but I have to develop something fast to buy more time.

Winfrey can lead. *Tap-tap-slap-tap-tap-slap-tap-tap-slap.* Joy rattles her *shakere* and shakes her hips low.

Winfrey's eyes widen; he blows a smoke ring. "That's what I'm talkin' 'bout," he says.

Mysteree says, "Who do you think we are, Black Lives Matter?" She does salsa and steps into my chest.

Nneka picks up a eucalyptus tree branch, hammers on her clapper-less cowbell, and says, "I like it. Toilets matter—maybe we'll get a closer drinking faucet. Even a real restroom out of the city—eeeeeeeyah!" She dances an Africanized combination of old-school mashed potatoes and new-school Crip Walk, her invention. "One for men, one for women—one ungendered."

BOOM, BOOM, BOOM. Jamaica, not one for a long conversation, pounds his affirmation. Cell phones appear, and Tweets and Facebook calls go out for help. My heart rate doubles.

I'd gotten nowhere before with the park supervisor, even with a petition signed by our drum circle. He's a high school phenom known as "Big Baller," whose redbone skinny ass washed out of pro basketball Developmental League camp first week. He kept the number eight D League jersey, which he always wears.

"Hey, OG—I got you covered," Baller had said when he locked up the gym, rushed past me, and left much earlier than the 7 p.m. park closing time. He mumbled something about our drinking wine in the park. "More restrooms are on my to-do list, in my budget request. Shit takes time, maybe a year or two." His go-slow approach was okay before. I didn't want to ruffle feathers, but not now that the artists threatened to leave me. "You've got to be patient," he said.

Several stray dogs scamper across an empty parking lot a few hundred feet north of us. A mangy bulldog drops a load next to a dumpster overflowing with house remodeling scrap. They disappear into a vent opening underneath a shuttered baseball stadium, where they begin to bark and howl.

Winfrey should know what to do.

* * *

Winfrey is a Compton native who'd visited Jamaica and returned Rastafarian. He's short, with a broad chest and a large head. His eyes are small, his beard thin and sprinkled with gray, and he has a flat nose and black obsidian skin. He wears a red, gold, and green tam with long dreadlocks sewn onto the sweatband.

Grizzled, Winfrey likes to tell the story of how fellow Panthers kicked SWAT's ass back in the day. "I was in the 1969 shootout against LAPD's first SWAT team. Over on Forty-first and Central," he reminds anyone who'll listen between swigs from the Gatorade bottle. "They tried to creep on us, but we were ready—blasted their asses right out of the building," he says even to those who don't want to hear it before he offers a hit from his herb sacrament. Since our grammar school days, Winfrey's always good for a brawl. Besides, he says we agree that "Drum circles help build community."

The Town Hall meeting starts in a couple of hours. Calls for support over Twitter and Facebook swell our group to thirty, maybe forty people. The scent of eucalyptus, feces, and urine wafts on top of a breeze.

"We need signs," I say, pointing to the dumpster.

A gang-type guy wanders over as we head for the dumpster. He's well-tatted and wears a red ball cap sideways. He says he's *Blood*. His head continually swivels as if he's afraid. Winfrey forms a hand step to help him into the dumpster. The twins giggle. Jamaica, Blood, and I drag from the dumpster strips of baseboards, rusted nails, cardboard boxes, and near-empty spray paint cans at Winfrey's direction. I need to pee, hop in the dumpster, and cut loose.

We spread the dumpster booty over the parking lot asphalt and scrawl words onto the cardboard with paint cans and Blood's Sharpies. "WANTED: OUTDOOR RESTROOMS" and "NO PISS, NO PEACE." The Guatemalan mother takes

"Sin TOCADORES deberán utilizar casquillos," *use toilets, not bushes.* With rocks, we hammer signs to sticks. Jamaica and Blood haul the smelly alabaster toilet across the small parking lot in front of the gym entrance. It'll act as an executive chair, a rallying point to clarify our intentions.

A La Raza roach-coach rumbles up and offers free food to support our cause. We breathe in carne asada. I overeat on chorizo-filled tortillas. My blood sugar will spike from the starch, but the fares are free. Brrrph. My stomach grumbles. There'll be hell to pay later when it's time to shit.

I fill my water bottle at the faucet by the ballpark and pinch my nose to piss, blocking piles of shit in park nooks dropped by the dog pack and park goers. Flies hum in clusters over park crannies.

The chemicalized faucet water soothes my mouth; the diabetic itch makes me press my thighs tight against the drum stem. I'll play standing on restless legs.

By noon, the Town Hall is an hour away, gym doors open, and we scramble to rendezvous opposite the gym entrance. Naked jacarandas stand stark below the overcast sky. Eucalyptus seeds crunch under the feet. A growing crowd of drum circle devotees, families, weekend warriors, Garveyites, the homeless, and others answered the call. The performers from my drum circle came together for at least one more time.

Winfrey is beside me on the sidewalk, one foot on the toilet bowl rim.

"We're together in peace," he calls to the crowd. "Restrooms and drinking water are human rights."

Before the Town Hall starts, a school of locals, gadflies, politicians, the mayor, councilwoman, and bureaucrat minions' stream into the gym like horny grunions to a beach. Winfrey points to them.

"The pretty dark-skinned one—that's the councilwoman—

badass—like Hillary when she challenged Obama—thinks she's the shit, watch out for her." Her ankles squeeze over yellow designer sneakers.

The mayor looks ghostly, so light she could almost pass for white, and wears bleached hair, shaved on one side like actress Raven-Symoné.

I need to pee. Lines form for two restrooms inside the gym. A short window to use them before the meeting ends, and Big Baller locks up. Joy squints. Jamaica bounces a curled knuckle against his mouth.

* * *

"Are you sure that'll work?" I say to Winfrey as I drum.

Tap-tap-slap-tap-tap-slap-tap-tap-slap.

"Just talk the drum, Adofo," Winfrey says. "You don't know how to deal with these people like I do—you can't be a wimp."

The drum circle is too essential to let leave; it'd be my fault if that happened. "You've got this," I say. "Save the circle."

Winfrey's top lip draws up at one corner. "I'll do the talking," he says.

My fingers twitch. I nod. "Whatever—Huey," I say, as in Huey Newton. My mouth is dry. I swig park water from the bottle and pressure my bladder.

Winfrey turns to the protestors. "Before we start our momentous event," he says, voice gravelly, silver hair escaping underneath his knit cap. He scans faces. "Stay together—bureaucrats will try to divide us—they'll look for excuses to turn us down or form another committee to explore *their* options—keep shit status quo. Fuckin' Democrats!"

Jamaica looks like a fake African from an old Tarzan TV movie in a leopard-print loincloth. His chest closes on itself with several skin indentations and stitches from past surgeries.

He says he was once a pin cushion for prison shanks before discovering the healing power of drum circles. He helps Nneka chain her ankle to the *Welcome to Trella Tapia Park* sign, positioned under weeping ash trees several feet from the alabaster executive seat. "Hmph! I feel like the enslaved before Jim Crow," she says.

The breeze blends eucalyptus and disinfectant scents that drift across from the gym restrooms. The line snakes outdoors and includes Town Hall attendees and users who'd all eaten roach-coach breakfast. My stomach grumbles. I keep drumming. *Tap-tap-slap-tap-tap-slap-tap-tap-slap.*

"When I was a kid," Winfrey says to the crowd, now close to a hundred people, "Hub City used to be run by white folks—we had Boy Scouts, Little League—park toilets before they took their investments and ran after the Watts rebellion."

"Preach!" someone says. "Tell it like it is!"

"Don't get it twisted. I'm not saying we shouldn't fight dysfunction—the unearned advantage many white people have and identity politics that mindfucks bigots they refuse to own. We must redefine blackness on our terms, what it means to be brown—select competent leaders who value and respect us and hold them accountable—reject the lies that say we're lesser than and assign us to lower status."

"Burn, baby, burn," I say to Winfrey's Huey Newton speech. His call to action heightens my senses and energizes my hands. *Tap-tap-slap-tap-tap-slap-tap-tap-slap.* As he finishes each thought, *Tap-tap-slap-tap-tap-slap-tap-tap-slap.*

Winfrey is interrupted by buzzing sounds like hornets, and we duck. A desert-camouflaged, clover-shaped drone floats in the air; it's the size of a cornflake box, each leaf a propeller, a big sheriff's star in the middle.

Winfrey cowers and holds up his hand to create a shield.

The machine flies close enough to see the "Nikon" logo above the camera lens.

I face him. "Scared? Weed got you trippin'?" I ask.

"Drones carry C4 bombs, dude—remember MOVE in Philly? They killed women and children in eighty-five."

"It was a police helicopter, Win."

"Same difference, *Adofo*."

I expected him to throw a rock, moon it, or something. Instead, he sucks on the Gatorade bottle. Is he the guy who'd shot it out with SWAT?

Tap-tap-slap-tap-tap-slap-tap-tap-slap.

I stop drumming and angle away from the drone, but the damn thing follows me. I'd had a few run-ins with police before, Driving While Black, Sitting While Black, Breathing While Black, the usual stuff. I can't trust the Police—my belly knots like a pretzel. If I drink, I pee, and if I hold my piss, bladder troubles. I dance on tiptoes.

"We've got to get this done, man," I say to Winfrey, who looks like he just got bitch-slapped. "We gotta get someplace for us to pee. You okay?"

Before he responds, Joy bangs the beaded gourd. "Shoot the drone," she says.

The others chorus, "Shoot the drone—shoot the drone—shoot the drone—kill it!"

We clamor enough for Big Baller to leave the climate-controlled gymnasium office. He hustles outdoors. "HEY." His arms are stiff at his side, and cornrow hair strands jangle on his shoulders; he's a bull in a blue windbreaker with the city logo. "You people need permits to assemble," he says.

We are silent like a first-grade detention class—the drone hovers. Winfrey sits on his ass, although he's supposed to be our leader. I grab his elbow and get in his ear. "Say something, man."

Winfrey snatches away and cuts an eye to the crowd and Baller.

"You people?" he scoffs. "Doodley squat—if you'da moved that fast in camp, you'da made the basketball team." Fist-balled, he pushes his chin into Big Baller's chest. "We don't need no permit to gather in a public space, a public park."

Big Baller peers down at Winfrey. "We don't want y'all disrupting things," he says.

"We?" Winfrey's nostrils flare. "Who the fuck are *we*? All I see is *you*."

I flip off the drone, look into the Nikon, and mouth, "Fuck you!" *Tap-tap-slap-tap-tap-slap-tap-tap-slap.*

The other protesters cuss loudly.

The drone ascends, pauses, and barrel-rolls backward above willowy trees into the dreary sky. Winfrey swipes his brow as if relieved.

Perhaps to avoid violence, a few protesters leave; those remaining flank Winfrey. I crack my knuckles and roll up my sleeves.

Tap-tap-slap-tap-tap-slap-tap-tap-slap.

Joy and Jamaica blast Baller with sound.

Rasp, rasp, rasp. BOOM. BOOM. BOOM.

Mysteree clangs the cowbell and screams, "*Eeeeeyah!*"

Big Baller recoils. He looks startled. I cuss him again with a beat.

Tap-tap-slap-tap-tap-slap-tap-tap-slap.

Shaken, he hesitates and turns, "I'm callin' Po on you niggas." Baller vanishes back into the gymnasium, the only thing left in the park, relatively well maintained. It houses a meeting room and a few staff who rarely venture outside its walls.

Shit. First, the drone, then Big Baller. All we need now is

cops. The restroom lines twist away from the gym entry. I hold my balls.

* * *

It's one o'clock. The Town Hall starts; we circle outside the gym parking lot. What if we get arrested? I swallow hard. At least the jail will have toilets. Winfrey is right. Trella Tapia Park is not what it used to be when it was named Ezy E. Park. Before one politician decided, the politically correct thing was to change the name to a Central American one and placate the Latino population by calling it after a woman killed by Killer Kane, the local public hospital. She died from a perforated intestine, writhing on the emergency room floor like a fish flopping on the pier while nurses watched and did nothing. That same politician demolished Tapia's outdoor restrooms. He claimed that crimes were committed in them. The stupid fuck managed to criminalize shitting.

Big Baller distances himself from Winfrey and directs traffic. The restroom line hooks to the back of the gym next to the tennis courts with no nets. Even deodorizer chemicals aren't up to the stink challenge.

Tap-tap-slap-tap-tap-slap-tap-tap-slap.

"Our piss-in must work today—I can't wait," I tell Winfrey. I pull in my abdomen to keep from pissing my pants.

I breathe slowly, grip the djembe in one hand, and reposition the executive seat on the sidewalk. I want to piss on the mock toilet. But everyone will see me. Massed together, we march past the gym entrance for an impromptu drum circle.

Tap-tap-slap-tap-tap-slap-tap-tap-slap.

The dancers prance. Dreadlocked Mysteree screams, "Eeeeeeeeeeeyah." She feels my staccato beats and alternates the same arm and leg behind her several times. She swings her arms above her head and chicken scratches then stops, pushes off one foot, pivots off the other; pulsating hips hypnotize; arms cross above her head, and fingers snap behind her—bare feet on asphalt.

Protestors smile, sing, clap, heads bob, and bodies move around the small lot to the rasp of the gourd, boom of the drum, and the clang of a cowbell. *This*, the circle, is what we're trying to save.

Back in the executive seat, Winfrey sits with his sign. We circle repeatedly, and each time, we dance past the restroom line. I pause at the executive chair, which looks so enticing that I almost piss myself. Faces in the gym cue look hardened, so I don't break ranks and cut.

I squeeze my thighs tighter around the djembe, bend, nauseated; I suck up the pee urge. If I don't go soon, the back-load will squeeze off the urinary tract, which leads to a bladder infection. *Tap-tap-slap-tap-tap-slap-tap-tap-slap.*

Fuck it! The circle follows me into the gym, *tap-tap-slap-tap-tap-slap-tap-tap-slap,* past the line into the meeting room, up the aisle, *tap-tap-slap-tap-tap-slap-tap-tap-slap,* to the head table, where we stop. *Tap-tap-slap-tap-tap-slap-tap-tap-slap,* rasp, rasp, rasp, clanging cowbell, dancing. The Hillary wannabe cowers behind the mayor, who glares at Big Baller. He shrugs his shoulders and throws up his hands. Pulling her eyebrows close and down, she holds her thumb and pinky finger to her ear, mouthing for Big Baller to call the police. Some in the audience cheered us; a few stood and danced. *Tap-tap-slap-tap-tap-slap-tap-tap-slap.* I'll take one for the team as we parade back to the parking lot.

In the distance, police sirens wail until up screech three two-deputy patrol cars hook-sliding into the curb perpendicular to the gym in a fog of smoke and burnt rubber. Doors slam shut. Five uniforms surround a sergeant, who stands arms folded as locals, gadflies, and politicians continue to arrive at the Town Hall. My hands and feet tingle.

I don't trust the police, plus I'm on summary probation for disturbing the peace when I twirled the sign and drummed on a strip mall corner. Drumming worked for Matt's Fish Market, and business shot up, but the accountant next door didn't like the noise and put a restraining order on me.

Several protesters leave with hands jammed into their armpits, thinning our ranks. Some squirm faces ashen. Afraid deputies might shoot first and ask questions later.

"No good can come of this," I say loud enough for Winfrey to hear. I lock and load. My stomach squeezes.

Tap-tap-slap-tap-tap-slap-tap-tap-slap.

I call out, "What do we want?"

On cue, our group hoists signs up and down in waves of organized chaos and responds, "We want restrooms!"

"Bring them back—bring them back—bring them back."

Tap-tap-slap-tap-tap-slap-tap-tap-slap.

"What do we want?"

"A place to shit!"

"Bring them back—bring them back—bring them back."

Tap-tap-slap-tap-tap-slap-tap-tap-slap.

Nneka cups a hand to her mouth. "Don't want a tree for me. Don't want Black Code slavery," she says. She raises one leg like a dog would and pantomimes urination. Jamaica pretends to catch her piss with a Styrofoam cup.

The sergeant slides over and pulls Winfrey aside, the two animated like a silent movie.

Winfrey points his finger in the sergeant's face.

"Hell, we've met with Big Baller—sent letters—got on committees—nothing." Winfrey taps the sergeant's chest with his forefinger. Why did he do that?

The sergeant steps back, eyes Winfrey like he stole something, and unfastens his holster strap. Winfrey looks rattled. Is he having a flashback to the 1969 shootout? He was cleared of conspiracy but served prison time for a pipe bomb with his fingerprints.

My head feels light.

The sergeant turns to a female deputy who fidgets on her toes, knock-kneed, one hand on her Taser, the other on her abdomen. She's pee dancing. He then faces Winfrey and softens his tone. "Hey—I feel you—my deputies also need shitters on patrol. It's criminal to treat people like this," he scoffs. "—no goddamned toilets. Really?"

I see an opening. "You should sweep city hall—Rodney King 'em—put 'em all in jail."

"Put them in jail—put them in jail—put them in jail," the protesters chant.

Tap-tap-slap-tap-tap-slap-tap-tap-slap.

The councilwoman's boobs flop up and down when she lumbers out of the gym straight for Winfrey on the executive seat.

"You all must leave—now," she says, akimbo. "You're disruptive—got people inside asking us about park restrooms."

Winfrey grunts and weaves side to side on the toilet. "You've made people afraid to protest for their good, Madame Councilwoman."

"You need permits to protest. Did you get one?" She turns to the sergeant. "Please remove them from the park."

My body tenses. Confrontation is when police dealings with Black and Brown people typically go left.

Tap-tap-slap-tap-tap-slap-tap-tap-slap.

A few locals, gadflies, and others from the meeting crowd us. The female deputy separates herself, her hands on her knees and butt on the patrol car hood. My throat's dry.

I force myself to loosen my tight chest and, shoving Winfrey aside, speak truth to power.

"What do we want?"

"To. Pee. Now! —To. Pee. Now! —To. Pee. Now!"

"What do we want?"

"A clean place to shit!"

Tap-tap-slap-tap-tap-slap-tap-tap-slap.

Tap-tap-slap-tap-tap-slap-tap-tap-slap.

The councilwoman stamps her sneakers on the pavement and raises her voice to the sergeant. "Do something."

The sergeant shrugs. "It's peaceful, lawful." Arms crossed, he leans against the patrol car door. "Nothing we can do."

She pinches her lips together and stalks off.

Once again, we disrupt the meeting by playing instruments and dancing.

Town Hall ends, the mayor approaches, her Susan G. Komen ribbon pin sparkles and her bleached hair shines sharply against Tapia's dreariness.

We march toward the mock toilet Blood's sitting on, and seeing us approach, he pulls up his pants and skulks away.

"What exactly do you all want?" she says, pinching and pulling at a silk blouse stuck to her bosom. "We have restrooms in the gym."

Winfrey sighs, adding agitation to his slurred speech. "Yeah, it's always closed—and we ain't in the gym."

Flies circle Blood's banana-sized turd piled like chocolate Frosty Freeze in the waterless toilet; the mayor scrunches her face. "You've been drinking," she says.

With pants up, Winfrey plops onto the toilet, oblivious to the mayor's call-out and the turd. "Nowhere to shit," he says. "The fire department next door won't let us in."

In the most exegetical manner, I say to the mayor, "Drum circle musicians refuse to come to Tapia Park. Ancient people like me get sick, holding onto urine and feces. Do you know mothers train small daughters to squat in bushes?" I screw up my face. "It's cold and messy until they get the hang of it—they bring extra clothes." I nudge the sergeant. "Sheriffs are full of shit, too," I say, my elbow pressed into his side.

The sergeant's head bobbles in agreement. "Our *Know Your Purpose* youth mentees and mentor deputies need restrooms when the gym is closed. How can we teach kids to make good life decisions when they have to run off behind buildings to pee?" says the sergeant.

Tap-tap-slap-tap-tap-slap-tap-tap-slap.

The mayor glares at my djembe, skin bunched between her eyebrows.

"That's not in your budget," she says to the sergeant. "Your job is to arrest people—" She flashes me a cold smile. "A committee can address your problem; I'll include you all and put Big Baller on it immediately."

The sergeant raises his palms. "Hey. I try to respect the people we serve; that's all—" He backs off. "I can't understand why you don't."

"We got ideas," Winfrey sputters. He wobbles, glances at the restroom line, and shoves his hands into his pockets. "We'll form the committee." His voice is weak.

I take a deep breath. Big Baller? Oh, hell no! Winfrey loses his edge. Joy lowers her head, and Jamaica mouths *no*; the two dancers break eye contact. The Guatemalan mother slowly shakes her head, protest signs tilt, and the dog pack howls.

I'd been afraid of attachment, always in the background like dull wallpaper, but now, I find what I fear more is losing my drum circle family, our ensemble, our community, and our love for each other.

I'm tired and need to pee so badly. I can't see straight. I can't wait any longer. I shove Winfrey toward the mayor, unzip, and stream dark yellow piss into the tankless toilet onto the Frosty Freeze turd.

The sergeant is right that it is criminal not to have accessible public restrooms in Tapia Park as had been years before. It's easier to control a robot on Mars than to piss in private in Hub City's public park. But the drum circle must continue to bring peace, remind us of what we've lost, and bring spiritual energy, causing crowds to smile, sing, clap, heads to bob, and bodies to move.

The two o'clock ocean breeze sweeps leaves from the trees, a glint of warm white light sneaks between branches, and the eucalyptus scent overtakes shit smells for the moment. The trap inside the toilet fills; a brownish blob seeps from underneath the bowl onto the sidewalk.

"Ahhhhhhhhh." For me to finish takes a while.

The mayor steps back. She pulls up a silk collar and covers her mouth and nose. "Shame on you," she says.

I re-zip my pants and face the drum circle performers and regulars. "No toilets, no piss, no peace."

"EEEEEEEEEEEYAH," the dancers shout and dance; the cowbell clangs, *rasp, rasp, rasp,* BOOM, BOOM, BOOM.

Tap-tap-slap-tap-tap-slap-tap-tap-slap. Tap-tap-slap-tap-tap-slap-tap-tap-slap. Tap-tap-slap-tap-tap-slap-tap-tap-slap.

DUMP CITY

Juan Carlos Martinez sits high atop a newly bulldozed trash mountain in Dump City, Guatemala, shading his eyes from the muggy stench of summer. He hates work. He will violate custom, risk his family's well-being, and tell Mamá and Araceli once he descends. Until then, he uses a rusty screwdriver, pops the lid from the shoe glue tin, puts his hand in a plastic bag like a glove, pours rubbery, snot-colored content onto his hand, and turns the bag inside out. Damn bags. He must always find one without holes, unlike when he wants discretion and huffs paint thinner, for which toilet paper or rag will do. One hand squeezes the bag tight against his lip rash with the thumb and the forefinger, back bent somewhat, blowing like a balloon until it's as big as his seventeen-year-old head. His left-hand squeezes the bag toward his face, lungs expanding to their fullest, alucinógeno fumes going straight to his brain. He holds in the vapor until his eyes want to pop. He hammers the can shut with the screwdriver handle, keeping the glue from spoiling.

For a time, he feels no heat or discomfort and hardly notices

207

when clouds of smoke from underground fires leave the air heavy. Thousands of guajiro, trash pickers, move like ghosts in el basurero, the garbage dump; some jump on arriving dump trucks searching for food. Like Juan Carlos, many were born in el basurero.

Mamá had reminded him at sunrise, as her copper-brown face showed fatigue, wrinkles, and exasperation in her Spanish-speaking voice, "You're not making the weight, Juan Carlos. The cemetery people will dig up Papa and throw his bones in the basurero. We must pay twenty-five Quetzals every month to keep him. When she lost her job, your Tia Xochitl stopped sending us money from los Estado Unidos. You know this."

Juan Carlos sucks from the bag again. Xochitl was his favorite aunt, and things must have gone sour for her to stop sending money.

Drivers buzz around in their trucks like parasitic wasps outside the steel gates of the city dump; they wait for loot from guajiro like Juan Carlos and his family.

Nag, nag, nag. That's all Mamá does, and Juan Carlos has grown weary and doesn't want to collect plastic, metal, and old magazines from mounds of trash, selling the booty to recyclers based on weight.

Far below him, Araceli, his sickly thirteen-year-old sister, whose skin fits tight against her sucked-in face, tugs at an American Flyer wagon loaded with a full five-gallon water bottle she's filled from a fire hydrant. One wooden wheel is more significant than the others and causes the cart to squeak and lean. Pussyfoot is all she can do these days; they have no vehicle, and a doctor with medicines she needs lives in the lowlands on the other side of tall ash plumes from Fuego, Guatemala's most active volcano. The thought of lava fountaining causes his bladder to loosen.

She leaves the Flyer in direct sunlight at their lean-to door outside the basurero gates, even though he's asked her to park in the shade. The water sits halfway to boil until Juan moves the heavy bottle indoors. They have no running water, and the container will last several days before repeating after cooling. He feels a growing pressure to scavenge the dump for Araceli, his mamá, and himself.

Juan twists his neck, spying on Papa's gravesite in the cemetery perched above the dump. He draws from the bag again, helping kill his appetite for food, which is his sacrifice for Papa's grave, and offsets meal expenses and provisions in the dump. However, his sacrifice isn't enough, according to Mamá. She summoned Castaneda, the spiritual guide, to silence the volcano and help Juan make money or find direction.

Juan Carlos uses his lips and tongue, suctioning more glue vapor. A kettle of vultures tears at a dead rat halfway down the dump mound where he sits. The rat reassembles, grows as big as a mangy basurero dog, and plunges its teeth into a vulture's neck. His companions fly toward the graveyard above Juan's perch. He strains his neck, following them to where Papa stands on his headstone, shouting something toward him. Juan cups his ears to hear his papa's voice once again. *You can do better, my son. Go into real estate.*

Juan Carlos holds the inflated bag in a fist above his head. He defies the squalid basurero, which multiplies the misery of the guajiro below. Guajiro Juan's in no hurry to join. Juan inhales deeply from fume remnants; sweat soaks his grimy white Carlos Ruiz soccer jersey. He feels the corners of his lips turn up. "Ola, Papa—yes, we can."

* * *

That evening, Juan Carlos, Mamá, and Araceli hole up inside their unusually cold shack of corrugated metal and old tarpaulins within a warren of garbage-choked alleyways. Castaneda's dressed in his evening clothes, an ordinary white shirt with brilliantly colored Pantalones and a chaqueta. Juan Carlos has bandaged his hand, covering a fake injury sustained in the basurero on which he's sprinkled low-odor paint thinner. He'll sniff as needed from the grimy gauze and his jersey collar. The last time Juan Carlos saw him, Mamá invited Castaneda to say a few words to aid Papa's canoe journey to the Underworld.

Castaneda sits on an inverted bucket, a long machete in hand, and mumbles gibberish Juan Carlos can't quite make out. *Alberobello?* Maybe it's Maya Ki'che's language.

"Not enough to live the day," Mamá says as she sweeps around the wood crate in the middle of their one-room shanty, her bare feet crusted charcoal black. "I received Papa's eviction notice from the cemetery." Her huipil, colorful cross-striping, and angular designs are woven into the cloth and heavily soiled. A brocaded wraparound corte reaches her dirt-caked ankles. "If I pay the cemetery bill, we can't afford tortillas—what say you, Juan Carlos?"

"Um, uh—uh" is his best explanation.

"It concerns me your eyes always look bloodshot, mijo. You look more and more like resistoleros—sniffers. Have you no hope?"

"Nag, Mamá—that's all you do."

"Qué? Are you sassing me, Juan Carlos?" Posture stiff, broom in hand, she steps toward him. "I birthed you in el basurero, and I'll take you out here also."

Juan Carlos raises his bandaged hand to his collar, bends his head slightly, sniffs, and glances over to Araceli, curled into a ball and wasting away on a mat. She drags up her head and gazes at Juan Carlos. "I'm hungry, brother. I need medicine, but you bring snotty glue." She slumps back onto the floor mat, raising a dust cloud. "You insult me, dear brother."

Her words penetrate his fog partly. "Don't worry, Araceli, everything will work out."

Sloe-eyed, she drools onto the floor. Her lips fall in and out of sync with the sound of her words. "Help me, Juan Carlos."

Slowly, he processes Araceli's words. He glances sideways at Mamá and sniffs his collar and bandaged hand, which helps his body lessen the pain from family problems, basurero nails, splinters, and other sharps that pierce. He didn't want to think or feel anymore anyway.

"To help us, you must leave us, Juan Carlos. Castaneda will ask our Lord Maximon to help you," Mamá says. "He'll chant and pray to silence the volcanoes for your journey."

Juan Carlos makes odd noises in his throat. "No. I don't want to leave." He swipes the bandage under his nose, chest tightens. "I'll change, Mamá—I will."

"Upon your return, you will have answers, my boy. Things will get better. Maximon will guide your moccasins," she says. "Our survival depends on you. Have courage." She turns to Castaneda.

Castaneda rises on cue from the bucket on which he quietly sits. His quickness surprises Juan Carlos. Machete in hand, he wrestles to a corner shrine half surrounded by sandstone pebbles and waves the sharp blade furiously above his head. He chants to invoke the spirit of the Maya god Santiago Atitlan Maximon.

"Dandara—Alberobello—Cueta.

"Dandara—Alberobello—Cueta.

"Dandara—Alberobello—Cueta.

"Oh, Great God, Father Maximon, we ask you to protect Juan Carlos from witches, evil beings, and hot lava. Guide him to work—for money. He must fill the money gap left by Tia Xochitl." Castaneda points the machete at Juan Carlos, stabs the dirt, and prostrates himself before the deity, who wears a sand-colored cowboy hat. He crawls close to its carved ebony wooden face, removes the sacred Cuban cigar from its rigid lips, and places his right ear against it. He closes his eyes and nods as if receiving instruction from Maximon. "Gracias, gracias, Oh Mighty One."

Jesus! Juan Carlos wants to run out into the night. Instead, he raises his collar and sniffs fading thinner. The ceremony is way too complicated.

After several minutes with his ear pressed to the deity's wooden lips, Castaneda pinches up his face, then smooths out the colorful scarves around Maximon's rigid neck. He sits and slides on his butt, back and away. He faces Juan Carlos, who shivers in the cold. Three candles on the wooden crate illuminate the space next to a windup clock—the stink from rotting things is ever-present.

"He says you must seek Him to receive guidance that will clear you, find work for gravesite payment, medicine for Araceli, and protect and bring you back safely."

Juan Carlos stutters, "B... B... But where will I go?" So far, he was quivering in the evening's cold, but the direction of Castaneda's conversation heats him. "Maybe I'll leave next week?"

Castaneda raises his eyebrows and glances at the candles and then the clock. "Maximon says you must leave NOW— head west around the volcano toward the city." Castaneda winks at Mamá, who manages a sly grin. The scent of melting wax is stable. "Your answers will come to you once you find HIM." Castaneda points to the door flap.

"*Prisa*, Juan Carlos," says Araceli.

Juan Carlos's empty stomach feels rock hard; water forms behind his eyelids. Even though dead bodies turn up in the basurero quite frequently and drug gangs provide the only rule of law within its gates, he often imagines what dangers could exist beyond the boundary of Dump City. He seldom leaves Dump City, garbage truck drivers and recyclers being his primary contact with the outside world. A trucker rolls down his tinted window and glares at Juan Carlos occasionally. Less often, one will toss him a quetzal or two as payment for sweeping out his dumpster. And now he's getting kicked out into that world of complexity and madness.

Castaneda resumes his chant.

"Dandara—Alberobello—Cueta.

"Dandara—Alberobello—Cueta.

"Dandara—Alberobello—Cueta."

"But what meaning have your words, Castaneda?" Juan Carlos asks.

"Oh—those. Possible vacation spots I saw in National Geographic. I might visit—buy a parcel or two."

"You don't say?" In Juan Carlos' mind, the spiritual guide business must be good.

"Hold him safe, Mighty God Father," Castaneda says, placing his hand on Juan's shoulder. He lobs Juan Carlos an unopened can of sardines. No doubt scavenged from the dump. He raises his tone to a level that startles Juan Carlos. "Now, GO —FIND HIM. Know that Maximon has the power to shape change."

Juan Carlos rolls his eyes up to the rusty tin ceiling.

Mamá, a silent witness, suddenly breaks and sobs, and Araceli follows. Araceli forces herself to her feet, huddles with Mamá and Juan Carlos, and they weep. Castaneda drops to his knees, exhausted.

"GO," Castaneda says again, even more firmly.

"Dandara—Alberobello—Cueta.

"Dandara—Alberobello—Cueta.

"Dandara—Alberobello—Cueta."

Juan Carlos breathes faster, and there's a pain in the back

of his throat. He doesn't want to leave, but leave; he must. He'll seek the fate Maximon holds for him and his family.

He pockets a new glue tube and wears a red bandana, exiting the hut into the dark alley. He'll follow the trail around the volcano.

* * *

Juan's stomach growls to remind him of how he hasn't eaten. The night's incredibly dull and much blacker than he had experienced before, even when he scavenged without moonlight. He walks for a few hours until he reaches narrow, dimly lit streets, a place with big buildings like he's heard recyclers describe. No one is out at night, but he hears voices from inside buildings made of bricks, like bricks discarded in the basurero. A rat scurries by, and dogs tethered to stakes growl and bark at him. He squeezes the tube and, while spreading the glue into semicircles, massages the cloth holds it before his mouth with a closed fist, and sucks. He keys back the lid and drinks the juice before scarfing down four of the ten sardines. He inverts the glue tube cap and pierces the foil membrane. His heart pounds faster when he unties and lays his head bandana on the cobblestone walkway.

Juan Carlos happens upon a woman in a corte intricately woven with birds, clouds, and sun designs at daybreak. Her huipil has bright yellow and blue horizontal and vertical stripes. She balances a basket of avocados on her head, but several falls and Juan Carlos kicks them away.

Juan Carlos tells her about Dump City, his Papa's grave, Araceli's sickness, everything. "Can you tell me where to find Maximon, Donã?"

"Maximon may be closer than you think. But no, my job is

to procure avocados for my family, not to help lost boys find God."

Juan Carlos scrunches up his face and curses the woman. "Bitch."

Juan tramps through the small village into the rainforest, his clothes soaked from the heat and humidity and his mouth growing dry. He wrestles through dense, sun-blocking vegetation and jumps when monkeys whoop and roar in the trees.

He sees an older man in a small clearing, struggling to pick berries from bushes and off the ground. Juan squashes them with his soles.

"Where can I find Maximon, señor?" Again, Juan Carlos explains his dilemma, how he hates scavenging in the basurero, how he's always hungry, and how his mamá kicked him out. He sniffs the rag, but the fumes are faint, hardly enough to get a fly high. He's almost out of glue—his hand trembles.

"I do not discuss religion with lost boys. Besides, my job is to pick berries falling from the bush, take them home so I might eat later, and no, not to help young boys find God." The monkey howls grow louder, and Juan's head begins to hurt. Turkeys cloaked in iridescent bronze-green feathers scamper in the brush. He offers the man sardines as a bribe, but the older man waves him off.

Juan Carlos curses, "Old bastard."

Parrots feathered in brilliant blue and yellow squawk high in the trees. He is deep into the rainforest. Vapors are gone, and his glue tube is empty.

He eats half the remaining sardines, leaving him with three. His sweating becomes excessive even in the humid rain forest; his muscles cramp. He flashes back to Mamá, and Castaneda is sending him away, which causes him to grind his teeth. He fantasizes about Araceli dying on the floor mat and has difficulty seeing what's real before him when he comes upon a young woman about his age.

She appears to crack open nuts with rocks under a sign, which she stops and points to. "Chukox Aq'oom is my village. I, Izabella." She returns to work, and her two long black braids bounce with each blow to the nuts; her corte clings to her lithe body, soaked with sweat. Her name means *pledged to God*, and Juan Carlos believes he's in the right place with new knowledge.

He explains his quest, to which the girl instantly replies, "Yes, yes, I know where you can find Maximon."

Juan brightens, and he offers Izabella the last of his sardines. They sit on the ground, knees touching. "Eat." She shares some nuts that look like macadamia but reminds him of coffee beans upon closer inspection. "Drink." He shows his palms and shrugs. "It is atol, a corn drink with secret ingredients, Juan Carlos." She smiles, and so does he.

They talk for a long time; him about life in Dump City, the thousands and thousands of people living off the basurero, how they compete with vultures for food, and about glue to help curb his appetite. After all, that's all he knows.

She talks about life in the rainforest, howler monkeys, jaguars, and leaf-cutter ants. She knows a lot. She touches his leg, and Juan Carlos believes the girl is in love with him. His stomach flutters. He's hard.

He ducks away from a large butterfly with bright blue wings edged in black; shadows loom in the overgrowth. Another monkey howls, Juan's body shakes, and his heart beats faster. His mind sees Araceli curled up on the floor mat. He remembers why he's in the forest and clears his throat. "Dearest Izabella, tell me the location of Maximon."

Izabella goes silent for a long time. Has she been putting

him on? Maybe she's a witch, a shapeshifter like Castaneda had warned.

Nauseous, Juan Carlos stands, bends over, and grabs his stomach. He retches as if half his gut is ready to leave his body. Up come nuts floating in gray bile.

Izabella gives a quick shoulder shrug. "Your glue habit caused your body imbalance."

"What's the shit you gave me, witch? I'm dying!" Juan Carlos retches again but only emits greenish pus. He falls writhing in the dirt, the pain sharp like tiny knives.

"No, Juan Carlos. Your glue is the poison—herbs and seeds will help your body equalize itself. Devil mushroom prepares your mind for your journey home. It's what I do. I'm the curandera, the Person of Wisdom for my people."

His body purges stored glue to rebalance itself. He sits up and presses his palms into his eye sockets before standing in his moccasins.

Izabella shapeshifts into Castaneda. *"Dandara--Albero-bello—Cueta,"* she says in her female voice. She seems to float from the ground into standing in front of him. "Make-believe, Juan Carlos, my hand is a mirror."

In her palm, he sees a familiar reflection in broken mirror shards his mother and sister collected in the dump, his shoulder-length hair greased back with pomade he'd found. His wispy mustache, medium brown pitted skin, dark, sullen eyes, mouth rash, blistered lips, and off-white teeth.

His reflection in the girl's dirty hand is Maximon. The avocado woman was right. Maximon was all along closer to him than he'd thought. His mood boosts and his thoughts turn to a new situation, considering how he can best move forward. Juan Carlos's world now extends beyond the limits of Dump City. Inside, his body feels lighter, his mind somewhat brighter. He's seen the face of Maximon, his own.

The image of Castaneda changes back to Izabella. "To help yourself and your family, it is up to you to create the opportunity."

"But how? What should I do for money? Sell drugs in the basurero?"

Izabella touches her slender fingers to his forehead and flattens her lips before the corners turn up. "Have you thought about real estate?"

Juan opens his mouth, but nothing comes out at first. "Are you sure?"

"PSYCHE," Izabella whoops loudly while holding her side. "First, get a truck, Juan Carlos." She gives him plantains and a bag of cornmeal for his journey. "I'll pray for you."

Juan Carlos Martinez will try to get back home.

* * *

Juan Carlos is nearly out of the rainforest when he happens upon the berry picker. When he sees Juan Carlos, the older man struggles with several bags of berries and winces.

"I found God, señor."

"Humph," the old man sputters. Sweat rains off his face.

"Let me help your load." Juan Carlos throws bags over his shoulder and hoists one atop his head.

"God is great. I thank her daily for blessings, for sending me help like you, Juan Carlos."

They reach the older man's home, a shack with palm-leaved walls and a thatch roof. The older man is so grateful that he gives Juan Carlos a large bag of berries. "For your family," he says.

Juan Carlos travels onward, losing track of how often the morning star rises; he hardly notices the heat, the weight from plantains, cornmeal, and berries.

He happens across the avocado woman again, laboring with a basket on her head and the four bags she drags behind her. She sees him coming and turns away, but he catches up.

"I found God, Donã."

"Psshh." The woman sucks her teeth. Her huipil is drenched with sweat.

"You were right, Donã. Maximon was close to me. Let me help you with your load."

Juan Carlos balances two avocado bags on top of the berries and plantains and drags the other two with his cornmeal to the woman's tiny home.

"Thank you, my son. I'll pray for your safe journey home." She hands Juan Carlos two bags of avocados. "For your family," she says.

Juan Carlos walks all night, and at daybreak, he's once more in the small city with narrow streets, dim lamps, and brick buildings. He trades some avocados and berries for medicine and granulated antibiotics to mix with herbs, which Araceli will need.

Juan Carlos is on the trail leading around the volcano to his village by twilight. He feels more energetic, better than he has in some time. He can't recall a time he's felt better. Halfway around, the volcano spews dark gray clouds of smoke high; the earth rumbles below him but does not erupt. Juan Carlos answers Castaneda's prayers when he reaches their corrugated metal and old tarpaulin shack across the street from the basurero. He drops his booty of plantains, berries, avocados, cornmeal, and antibiotics inside the door flap.

Mamá sweeps around the wood crate placed in the middle of their hut. Castaneda prostrates himself in front of the deity. Candles flicker on the floor mat where he left Araceli. His eyes meet Mamá's.

"Dead." She drops her broom, stares at empty hands, and

walks toward Juan Carlos. "Waiting for three months was too long for her, Juan Carlos. Araceli's death meant less for food and more to pay for Papa's coffin. I buried them together, and the cost does not change."

Juan Carlos bites his lip and recalls the wooden wheel wagon, Araceli's out-of-sync words, and her telling him to hurry. He cups his mouth. Castaneda places a hand on his shoulder, but Juan Carlos jerks it away. Araceli can't be dead. Please, God.

Several days later, Juan Carlos sweats atop a newly formed basurero trash mountain, shades his eyes, and tries to focus on Papa and Araceli waving to him from their gravesite in the cemetery above him. Below him, thousands of guajiro mill about dancing in ghostly repetition. He sold avocados, berries, antibiotics, and plantains for a small truck parked at the base of his trash mound. He'll recycle and cut out the middleman.

Juan Carlos strains his neck and cups his ears. Araceli no longer looks sickly, and Papa seems strong once more. They chorus in unison from atop their shared headstone, *You can do better. Go into real estate.*

Real estate?

He sucks a deep fume-filled breath from snot-colored glue at the bottom of a plastic bag.

"Ola, Papa. Ola, Araceli—yes, we can."

WEED KILLERS

"Lies lies, and more lies they tell us about cannabis, marijuana, weed, ganja, chronic, or whatever the fuck your name for fake need. Some argue its medical value, assume everyone's sick, and want a botanical cure. Some monetize and substitute clear thinking with a foul, smoky fog, lying that art's created by subjugating our brain, a brain seeking something even more exhilarating, more potent than the last blunt, reefer, joint, laced with who knows what.

Chemical reactions create new toxins and synthetics to enliven stagnant body temples by some sham chemist who flunked out of ninth grade because he was always high or hungry, having learned in second-rate schools. That same hood-rat alchemist rearranges atoms, stretching the product further to survive in a jungle advantaged for the privileged. He's someone who doesn't realize how cards stack, the system rigged, how pharmaceutical and tobacco companies wait on the sidelines, knowing by day's end, with government help, they'll control the market, knowing then marijuana deals will become prescription-only.

Street merchants will again face jail, inextricably, inevitably, like the sea change following alcohol prohibition, controlled, taxed, and as legal as my itchy ass. Dope p-problems grow like bacteria when left unattended," I say, sometimes stuttering to Xochitl De León, the *Hue and Cry* newspaper reporter covering our protest.

"That's a pretty good speech," she says. It's her first assignment after La Opinión laid her off months ago. "I was unable to support my extended family back home," she says.

"I feel ya," I say. I smooth my coiled salt-and-pepper Bozo hair; my aching chest leans against Davis Middle School's security fence—cough—my lung cancer persists. Davis's cold bars are as black as I imagine Snoop Dogg's lungs, towering over me with an outward curve, terminating with triple-pointed spear tips. "I-I want bullshit to stop. One unemptied trash can mean the job's incomplete. Compton deserves better," I say as any good hospital janitor will.

I point to Rosecrans Avenue as we turn toward Queen Egypt, Chattom, and other protesters north on Matthiesen Street. An early spring pandemonium of thick, leathery, dark green oleander leaves with scented yellow flower clusters bursts through iron pickets. At the curbside lie clumps of tobacco, a crumpled, quivering 7-Eleven receipt, no doubt trashed by some weed-stoked zombie, sunlight glinting off a disposable lighter cap, and the metallic stripe on a grape-flavored Swisher Sweets cigarillo wrapper. "See how close paraphernalia is to the school?" I pick up the cigarillo wrapper before it blows into the schoolyard.

"What other reasons do you protest, Tallent?" Guatemalan, her face the color and shape of a marmalade plum, hair short, dark, and rough-dried, two yellow pencils stick like hairpins, forming a V, from her practical bun. Xochi wears no makeup. She looked fresh out of college and had probably partied high on drugs as college kids do. What the hell does she know?

"Truthfully, Agent Orange-tainted weed fucked me up in 'Nam. Back in the world, drugs retarded me. I hallucinated and failed a four-way stop sign. My road dog crashed through the windshield. I'd go back and change that if I could," I say, breathing hard, teeth grinding. "Nobody had told me shit. My son chased dope to the Midwest after my wife died. She helped save me." I hold back sobs. "I told him addiction's probably in his genes—in his DNA. I told him the truth nobody had told me. He went out anyway. Thank God Trenese, my grand-daughter turned her life around after a rough patch. She was always smart—smart enough to get off the streets. She's a school teacher now."

At first, it amused me when my two-year-old son sucked on my joint left smoldering in the ashtray. Twenty-eight years later, he's hooked on OxyContin somewhere in Kentucky, or dead for all I know. I wave off Xochi and swipe away tears before saying, "I've been clean and sober for years, though old habits and temptation never fully leave you." My body's numb and heavy before my muscles tighten. "My truth will spare other families the downside to marijuana's cachinnation like in Ecclesiastes 7:6, *For as the crackling of thorns under a pot, so is the fool's laughter: this also is vanity.* That's why, after a bout with cancer, I believe in total abstinence from alcohol and other drugs. That's my mission."

On Rosecrans, the sheriff's spy camera lens moves and whirrs atop a streetlight pole, watching from some remote loca-tion, sheriff's deputies monitoring us and all activity along the avenue. I'm looking over my shoulder, scanning the area for their swift, unwanted arrival. They'd said we needed a permit, but I don't believe we need government permission to protest. Besides, there's so much money involved with marijuana.

Whom can you trust? Still, in the back of my mind, deputies could break up our party at any time if we left the sidewalk, like when Alvarado Park May Day protesters overflowed onto city streets. LAPD had driven their motorcycles through the crowd using their batons and rubber bullets on people. My heart pounds against my rib cage. What if that happens today?

"We're weed protesters, rebels," says Chattom, his brown fist outstretched for the dap. A retired corrections officer from Puerto Rico, he was third runner-up to Ronnie Coleman in the Mr. Olympia contest. He wore a gold rope chain with a body-builder crucifix.

"No, we're *WEED KILLERS*," Queen Egypt says as we draw near. Her royal blue gele is knotted at her temple and covers her hair and ears, which leaves her periwinkle ankh earrings dangling.

Saturday morning traffic slows. A grassy median divides four east-west traffic lanes between two marijuana dispensaries. Some of a few dozen rebels roam into the street.

Drivers bump over potholes, avoiding inattentive rebels sneering down the block at a clutch of drunks perched on discarded furniture and wood crates, hunched in front of a 7-Eleven recently built beyond an empty lot next to a tiny shotgun house. Others put finishing touches on protest signs or point across to the line snaking around a cannabis storefront in an abandoned church. Several doors down from the old church, cars creep like pill bugs in and out of a 24/7 drive-through smoke shop.

From a rise on the median, Councilwoman Ethel "I Get the Last Word" Vickers' voice floats above murmuring rebels mingling under the sheriff's camera. "When we fight, we win," she says.

Why is she here? Conniving politicians usually come only to skin and grin before the camera to distract. A thick woman,

Vickers' skin is deep brown, hair gold. She's wearing a white summer dress and clutching a white purse that, when she speaks, crazily waves around as if she's going to throw it at you. Her stiletto heels clack against the street when she approaches, thrusting a sign at passing vehicles saying, *No Mas Drogas*. Vickers eyes Xochi's phone camera and says, "We should take a picture together, Tallent."

"Uh, no thanks." No way is she using me for her re-election campaign photo.

Dogs bark, rooster crows, and children play within the avenue's discombobulated zoning scheme. Occasionally, a car passes and honks in support of us rebels. Others slow, lower their dark-tinted windows, and shout, "FUCK Y'ALL. Go lay your asses down somewhere."

* * *

Not wanting to appear publicly stupid, I spell-check my THINK CLEAR! picket sign, paying particular care to exclamation point punctuation, wondering if I need it. Deciding on one instead of three will suffice before meeting up with antsy rebels. On the corner next to one of the clandestine storefronts, a faded sand-colored building projects from its wall a mural of pine trees set against an amber backdrop, suggesting a Garden of Eden or, at worst, a tranquil outdoor gathering spot, supposedly to capture the essence of the products made inside or perhaps to offset an otherwise depressing location. Thick steel plates cover one sliding door and three rectangular windows. A pale white side entry door behind a rickety wrought iron driveway gate is on one end.

Across Rosecrans looms cavernous Greater Love, a single-story dull gray converted church insidiously used to harvest and distribute weed. Carefully embedded in its stucco facing are three large white wooden crucifixion crosses, starkly reminiscent of Jesus' death and return to life, leaving me to wonder if He also smoked pot.

Weed Killers stink-eye Xochi, the media being, as a rule, Compton unfriendly. Writing about our potholed streets, calling us a *backwater*, and constantly reminding us that several corrupt governing officials went to prison. They report our *gang problem*, blah, blah, blah, and ignore that nearly all of us work hard to survive like everyone else. Whatever. We are made in America. Bastards.

Xochi presses her elbows into her side, which makes her look smaller, studies something on her cell phone, and says, "The majority of California's voters favored recreational marijuana use. Why do you think Compton residents voted against legalization?"

"It's dr-drug dealing," I say, "made legal, like p-prescription opiates. Superfly showed us how to snort cocaine. Shit got worse when Ronald Reagan dropped the crack bomb on us." My skin crawls. "Now, Trump spawned MAGA Republicans want to fuck everybody."

Trump. The rebels hoist their signs and erupt, "Fake president—Fake president—NOT MY PRESIDENT."

Vickers snarls and waves her purse like a symphony conductor, "Ten years ago, we passed an ordinance outlawing medical weed dispensaries." Facing Xochi, her back to me, she says, "We didn't want cannabis then, don't want cannabis now."

I shift from foot to foot as the number of rebels grows and blocks eastbound traffic, listening carefully for wailing sirens, picturing riot gear-clad deputies beating insurgents, them running away bloodied. My gut wiggles, swirling like Jell-O. Some Weed Killers give her a silent look, narrowing their eyes behind Vickers.

Vickers fails to mention how her tax-crazed, money-grub-bing fellow Democrats supported the recreational-use ballot measure, birthing cash-only, fly-by-night operations, spawning an infestation like cockroaches nesting willy-nilly throughout the city.

"First weed, next gentrification," I say. "We're pushing back. We're resisting."

Xochi jumps when rebels behind her shout, "No gentri-fuckation—No   gentrifuckation—NO GENTRIFUCKATION."

She white-knuckled her phone recorder and pushed it toward my mouth. "Some would say yours is a lost cause, Mr. Neal."

"I don't need to prove nothing to you," I say. I elbow around Vickers, throw a fist like John Carlos and Tommie Smith did at the 1968 Olympics, and say, "When we fight, we win."

Xochi frowns. The protesters raise their knuckles and chant, "When we fight, we win—When we fight, we win—When we fight. WE. WIN."

"I followed the crowd as a kid—I used to chug cheap wine, smoked cigarettes and marijuana by thirteen, and celebrated my fifteenth birthday high on LSD, downers, and weed on a rocket to nowhere," I tell her. "For some reason, fucked out of my mind felt right. My normal."

A craggy voice booms over the rebels parting the crowd, "Give thanks and praise to the Highest, Emperor Haile Selassie the First." Hearing Winfrey's false Jamaican accent tightens my chest. Why'd more bad news show now? "Lamb's bread is a sacrament for the use of man—a cool meditation, mon." Again, we listen as he gladly embellishes how he and fellow Panthers fought SWAT back in the day. "I was in the sixty-nine shootouts against LAPD's first SWAT team. We kicked their asses all over Forty-first and Central—fuck pigs," he says.

Yeah, yeah, yeah. Once uncompromising, he hated the police, and they hated him back. But when it comes to marijuana, all skin-folk aren't kinfolk.

"Sure, you helped us get porta-potties in public parks from the city, dude, but this fight ain't for you," I say. "Unless you're gonna put the weed away."

He was drunk and slurred, "Nah, mon. I and I never do dat. Ganga hurt nobody, mon. Whoa. You useta puff collie herb, Tallent Neal. Now you 'gainst it?" Reaching under his purple dashiki, he pulls, like a magician, a baggie full of buds, pushing his stash my way, testing me. As in times past, an old familiar taste of Zig-Zag gum Arabic returns to my mouth, the pungent smell and lung-irritating smoke. Baited, my shoulder twitches, and my hand trembles, but I check myself, refusing to revisit the self-centered, spaced-out asshole I was once and Winfrey is now. "What ya know, mon?" he says.

Winfrey doesn't appreciate the difficulty of my achievement, having replaced emptiness with purpose and confusion with intention. Still, I can recall how hard living on drugs can be, and I understand him. "That was years ago," I say. Heartbeat pounding in my ears, I do a little breath-of-fire Kundalini yoga, awakening spine energy and harnessing dangerous subtle impulses enticing me to bloody Winfrey's mouth, calming myself. "Now I'm clean and sober, my brother."

"Ghost yourself, fake-assed Rasta!" Chattom yells.

"Go fuck with LAPD," Queen Egypt says from the middle of the rebel crowd. "Go back to Jamaica."

Winfrey drags his palms down his legs and tries to face down the rebels.

"You can't even get a job," a rebel says. "Your stinky old piss'll test dirty."

The crowd closes in. Winfrey rocks slightly and raises his hand, warding them off.

"Bumbaklaat!" he says. Winfrey gazes at the churring spy camera. Then he flips it off, likely drawing the ire of controlling deputies, deputies who never liked Winfrey, deputies he always hated, deputies I hope will not appear now since they have an excuse. He holds the gesture as he squeezes through and away from the rebels, stops, and fires a spliff. "Rasklaat! Make we leave ya," he says, stumbling toward the new 7-Eleven.

Xochi scribbles onto a notepad and asks, "Is there any upside to marijuana cultivation and sale in Compton, Mr. Neal?"

"Hell, NO. It's a scheme by entrepreneurs and their political puppets to make money off poor people. They want to market it *Straight Out of Compton*.

"Fuck that," Chattom says.

I say, "If cannabis benefited Compton, we'd already be rich. Many people went to prison. It's a trick bag. Especially for Black people." I squeeze the THINK CLEAR! sign stick, hands hurting, palms turning red under pressure, picturing them around the neck of anyone responsible for us having to protest on Saturday morning.

Queen Egypt pushes out from the rebels, earrings glistening in the sun, her pinched face exposed, aggressively arguing, "Trick-bag is right. My husband's been in prison for ten years because of weed." She takes several quick breaths. "My son wants to open a dispensary one day." A big-eyed, skinny kid about thirteen, maybe fourteen, in a black wave cap, snatches his wrist away from her and, with his untied Vans, kicks at a breeze-blown cigarillo wrapper and traces sidewalk cracks. "Something's wrong with this picture," she says.

Crouching to the boy's eye level, I say, "Respect your mama." His name is Cory. "Do you smoke or vape?" The boy yawns, clearly bored. He's probably a Davis Middle School student, looking as if he's on the cusp of gangbanging, reminding me how I started smoking around his age and how no one ever told me shit about drugs, sex, nothing about life.

Xochi overlooks the boy and says, "But Mr. Neal, you seem to have turned out okay—kinda."

"With help, I turned away from drug dependence and from the thefts, robberies, c-crimes to support it—in and out of jail—police target practice." My arm twitches.

The boy mutters, "Whatever." Cory's daddy's doing prison time for what's no longer a crime.

"So, how'd you clean up, Mr. Neal?" Xochi says.

I threw the big-eyed boy a sidelong glance. Arms across his chest, he shrugs. "What do you know about running a business?" I say to him. "You do know dispensaries are businesses?"

His voice hardens. "Nothing. I don't know anything about business."

"Have you ever s-sold anything? Lemonade?"

"Chocolate turtles in the fourth grade," he says.

"H-how was it?"

"Kinda hard. Mom sold them for me."

"T-then you might have a clue. It's different because people believe they need weed. They'll come to you like moths to a flame. You could make much money off the weakness of others —if it's only about money."

"What else is it? I wanna come up like everybody else— wear bling, drive cars like Bonk Loc," he says, puffing out his chest.

Bonk Loc sells drugs on street corners and has supported his family by slinging chronic and who knows what else. He's street-smart but doesn't have enough business intelligence; he's one bust away from leaving his kids homeless, a guy who'd lace weed with chemicals and swear it's the bomb, dumb as a brick.

Cory looks down when I say, "What if you harm others? D-do you want to profit off the pain of people who look like you?" I picture my son and glance at Cory's mother. "Your mama raised you better. I can tell."

Cory squishes his big eyes together. "What else can I do?" he says.

I lightly touch Cory's shoulder and say, "Learn business if that's your interest. Learn capital access, marketing, and product development. Compton needs way more products than weed. The world's waiting just for you. Hell, you could build an exascale supercomputer capable of a quintillion calculation. You might have to look around, work hard, and grind. Weed? Yes, if you must. But not in Compton. It's illegal. L-love yourself FIRST. Then God, and then love others. You can make it if you try, Cory."

Cory nods slowly. Weed Killers don't miss the beat and say, "Love yourself—Love yourself—LOVE YOURSELF, FIRST."

"You can do better," I say. "We have always loved each other, Cory. We don't need drugs. Let the white boys have it."

Cory exhales and looks me in the eye; his gaze darts to Queen, whose eyes go dewy. She's cupping her face, weeping; several rebels sniffled. Of course, Vickers chimes in. "Don't worry about anything—instead, pray about everything," she says to Cory and hands his mama her business card. "Tell God your needs and remember to thank her for her answers," she tells him.

I turned Cory to face me. "Make the library and a dictionary app your new BFF. Educate yourself with the cell phone."

I return to Xochi. The rebels hold their signs and quietly lean in.

"Three marijuana felony strikes got Cory's daddy twenty-five years," I tell Xochi. "Decriminalization is good, but now my brothers camp around smoke shops instead of jail time." My fingers pill-roll. "I-I didn't need shit. I kicked cold turkey," I say, slightly taller, having voiced my accomplishment. "Everything will be all right if I do one day at a time—one day at a time," I say.

The protesters repeated, "One day at a time—One day at a time—ONE DAY AT A TIME."

"Holla!" Vickers says.

Several passing drivers honk their support. Another cusses us.

* * *

At first, rebels mill around the storefront mural with their hand-drawn signs. Some rebels place their signs along the wall under the painted pine trees. Some lean nonchalantly on their sign sticks as if they've forgotten their purpose. Others pose for cell phone photos and Internet uploading, complaining about how the city has only a Patria Coffee and one Starbucks, grumbling about the difficulty of staying caffeinated on Saturday morning.

Patiently Xochi's interviewing a gesticulating Chattom under the sheriff's camera until Queen Egypt, baring her teeth with Cory in tow, yells, "We didn't vote for this shit. Shut it down. Shut it *all down!*"

Grabbing their signs aggressively, marching past the mural, and approaching the side entry door, the Weed Killers spring alive, chorusing, "Shut it down—Shut it down—SHUT IT DOWN."

Behind the driveway gate, a security guard posts on trash-strewn, barren dirt. Guzman is on a fabric plate above where a pocket might have been on an authentic uniform shirt. He's styling knockoff Armani wraparound sunglasses, arms folded across his pudgy chest, sporting a blue polo shirt with black collar and epaulets, his potbelly hiding his belt. His upper arm has a patch like California's state bear. Only his looks more like

Yogi Bear. He hitches his head, smirks, and sits in the shade under a tree that grows just above the slanted roof; its spindly branches are weighted like Christmas ornaments with red Chinese globes the size of soccer balls.

Guzman jumps from his high chair, clutching a Taser attached to his belt, shuffling back when the rebels reach the gate, checking that the side door is locked, and fastening the gate latch to keep Weed Killers out.

Next to me, Chattom's muscled thighs and calves tested his cargo pants. Speaking to Xochi through his teeth while passing around a petition, petitioning to *Band the Box*, advocating ex-felons deserve jobs, juggling leaflets about Compton's unsolved homicides. "Read this. The list includes ones killed by PoPo, too. "Murder by the deputy is still murder," he says.

A wispy, androgynous white person walks behind the driveway gate wearing a dark gray baseball cap. A green caduceus is across the cap's crown, a short rod entwined by two snakes, topped by a pair of wings. "I'm Tosh," the person says, also in a lavender t-shirt, a sad lap dog surrounded by roses staring out.

The sharp odor of hydroponics shadows Tosh. Tosh's eyes aren't red like deadheads under the influence usually are, looking plausibly sober, pupils undilated. The scent is powerful but not unfamiliar, reminding me of the far weaker bunk weed I once copped years back. My chest runs gooey.

I declined Tosh's fist bump. Who is Tosh?

Weed Killers whisper. Some shake their heads disapprovingly, ogling Tosh, who's much too tiny to take on a hostile crowd, Tosh having, to them, just beamed down from outer space.

The moment is long and uncomfortable before Xochi asks, "What pronoun do you prefer?"

"They or them," Tosh says in a high, bubbly voice, reaching

for Chattom's petition. "It's my dispensary, and I don't understand your protest." Quickly reading and folding the appeal, Tosh stuffs it in their jeans pocket and carefully considers what to say next. "We care about customers and don't sell to children. We require identification—must be twenty-one," Tosh says.

Riled from their complacency, the protesters shout, "Get the fuck out of Compton. Get THE FUCK OUT NOW."

Xochi clicks on her cell phone recorder, and up goes my hand to quiet the rebels.

I point toward Davis Middle School, recalling the wind-blown cigarillo wrapper, steel fencing with pointed tips, and scented yellow flowers. "We've seen kids make beelines from school to your d-doors," I tell Tosh.

"We turn them away, and they cross the street," Tosh says.

Ever the interloper, with each word, Vickers casts and reels back her purse as if she's fishing. "We have enough problems and don't need you people bringing more drugs to Compton. I'll have the health department investigate you." She lowers her sign. "Do you assess the quality of your dope?"

"It's high quality, healthy." Tosh bounces on their toes. "We don't sell to people without a doctor's recommendation. Across the street, maybe they do."

I cut off Vickers and say, "You use p-pesticides on your products? Herbicides? Right?"

"No. Our growers don't use anything—maybe ladybugs," Tosh says. "It's organic."

"Sheesh," Chattom scoffs. He lisps, "¡la puta! Maybe we should eat the shit like goats," he says, hands to his throat, mimicking a gag reflex.

The rebels deride Tosh. "It's organic—It's organic—It's organic—LET'S EAT THE SHIT."

Xochi says, "Organic? Let's get this straight—your product

contains no myclobutanil or other pesticides?" She writes some-thing on her pad. "If you don't grow cannabis yourself, how do you know?"

"That's what they tell us," Tosh says.

"Psssh—whaaat? That stuff's a slow death—like antibiotics fed to cows and pigs in hamburgers and b-barbeque." My body temperature rises, and I taste bullshit. I go for the gut. "Th-that myclobutanil is like malathion p-pesticide and paraquat—systemic—stays in tissues for years."

Xochi stops writing and says, "Surely your suppliers certify against fungicides?"

"Well." Tosh crosses then uncrosses their arms. "—it's shipped from Seattle. I think it's sun-grown."

"Really?" Vickers says. Her purse juts back and forth in Tosh's face like a toilet plunger, causing Tosh to cross their eyes and lean back, the bag stopping just short of Tosh's sharp nose, giving Vickers the advantage. "You think it's sun-grown in rainy Seattle? I think you're full of shit. You think we're stupid—I think you're wrong and need to get your ratchet ass out of here. Think about that."

Weed Killers weigh in. "Ratchet ass—Ratchet ass—RATCHET ASS."

Refusing to allow Vickers the last word, I drop the large picket sign like a rapper drops his microphone, showing everyone she won't bogart my protest, and grinning slyly, I say, "Weed smoke causes cancer like tobacco. Do you warn them?"

Tosh fidgets and doesn't answer, their head spinning like Linda Blair's in *The Exorcist*.

Weed Killers huddle tight, shake the weakened gate, vocif-erously taunting Guzman, "Burn 'em down—" they repeat, "BURN 'EM DOWN."

Guzman grips the locked doorknob. Tosh squeezes their tiny frame between the gate and the rebels. The red globes on the spindly tree danced on a slight breeze like slanting rain. Chemical smells drift. The sheriff's camera focuses steadily, and a news helicopter rumbles overhead. I spit.

"We don't cause problems, and our customers mostly have medical issues," Tosh says.

Like my enlarged prostate, the crowd swells thanks to rebels' Tweets and Facebook posts, hundreds of people getting more challenging for me to control, primarily non-whites, which usually triggers a gang activity response from sheriff's deputies.

Pressed against the fence next to Tosh, a sweaty wooden guy with facial scars, quivering eyelids, ratty auburn hair, and rumpled clothes, around my son's age, appears to be about thirty. He separates strands on his head and, pointing to a stitched scalp gash, says to the rebels, "I need marijuana for seizures," his tongue coated silver. "I took shrapnel when our convoy hit a roadside IED in Afghanistan," he says, rubbing at the injury.

Vickers' purse was still at her side. "Thank you for your service," she says respectfully before her bag explodes into action, "but you'll have to find your medicine elsewhere—not in Compton," she says. *"It's illegal."*

The rebels weigh in. "Thank you—Thank you—Thank you —BUT NOT IN COMPTON."

Clenching his jaw, Gash Head tries but backs against the fence; there's no retreat, and the rebels don't budge. His arm jerks, eyes widen, and he jets from place to place. "It's in the box, soldier," he says, clearly agitated. He mutters under his breath, "They got the film. Get out, get out—holy shit. It's on the road. FUCK. Did you see that? It's on the road." He pulls at his clothing as if itching, trembling, clearly having an episode, plucking a cigarillo from a red package with a watermelon logo from his pocket, leaving me to wonder how good watermelon-flavored tobacco could possibly taste.

Gash whips out a fixed-blade survival knife. The crowd gasps and steps back when he slices along the glue seam, replacing tobacco with weed. His Zippo sparks the blunt, and he inhales smoke deeply, straightening his contorted face. He exhales infected butane smoke into my and Chattom's faces. Chattom reacts. *Whack!* He slaps the back of Gash's head and snatches the smoke from his lips, squishing the blunt into the sidewalk with his heel. "Shit stinks," he says. "Secondhand smoke kills."

"Awww, man," Gash Head says. Face flushing, he glances at his knife, elbows away from the rebels into the street, and bends, breathing hard, hands on his knees. Guzman's lips form a straight line, Tosh gawks, and Xochi's mouth makes an O.

What the f—? I breathe deep, turning to Tosh. "I don't care what your purpose is," I say, lifting the THINK! sign to my shoulder. "Mary J and cheap wine were my gateways to harder stuff, always searching for the higher high."

The crowd stops pushing and quiets.

"That's your experience. Everyone doesn't go there."

"How do you know? What do your customers mix with weed? Do they snort, shoot, or drink too? Do you even know?"

"Medicinal marijuana, especially the older ones," Tosh says.

Vickers interrupts, pointing her purse down the street to drunks congregated on crates outside 7-Eleven. "They're lost, twice defeated in the race," she says. "They waved the white flag, gave up on our struggle, gave up their Blackness for eye redness, to get their drunk on. It'll be the same with dispensaries."

Tosh's pitch rises. "People have rights. A choice to do what they want." Tosh glances at Vickers, Xochi, and Guzman and then looks away.

"And we have a right to feel safe. Where children can p-play, women can walk at night, and pass stores without hearing catcalls and bullshit from impaired morons. Drugs sabotage th-that right in our city. People high on drugs do stupid stuff, laugh at unfunny shit, run red lights, spin donuts for fun, and smoke in public spaces as if everybody wants to smell weed. PoPo uses our drug habits as an excuse to add to Chattom's murdered list. Freedom's not free."

Looking amused, Guzman smirks and leans one hand on his chair.

"Are you blaming all of those problems on marijuana?" Tosh asks.

"Yep. Th-that and all that comes with it—we gotta start somewhere."

"That's just old-fashioned reefer madness," Tosh says. "Prohibitionist!"

"Prohibitionist?" Xochi repeats.

Tosh's cheeks redden jaw sets. "That's right, and I reject your moral argument. Your unenlightened thinking does not move me. It's bullshit. Read my lips, 'we're not leaving.'"

My mouth sours. "We'll c-control what goes on within our city—just l-like any other c-community." My fingers pill roll again. "D-Drug problems affect us differently than in Beverly Hills, Palos Verdes Estates, or wh-wherever you come from— Republicans want to take our Obamacare. Then what? —we have no Betty Ford here. Just Say 'No' is crap." Edginess replaces my shoulder pain. "You suck the money out of Compton and leave us crimson-eyed in a fog, unable to think about how to do better." I slam the sign to the pavement, lean close, and picture my hands squeezed around Tosh's neck. "I'm keepin' it real."

"WORD," Queen Egypt says. "I'm one hundred with that."

Vickers' busies her purse. "You need a church to pastor, Tallent," she says. "Chill out."

My gut hardens, and I fire back, "And for a change, you should work for the people of Compton." I feel betrayed, but Vickers is right. If I assault Tosh, I'll look like a crazy Compton nigga and could end up in jail, which might create sympathy and help Tosh's business.

Xochi smiles. Her face softens, but her tone doesn't. "Do you remind your customers it's illegal to smoke marijuana in public? —not in parks, not on sidewalks," she asks Tosh.

"Not everyone gives a damn about other people," Tosh says, nodding their head to where Gash Head rocks back and forth on periphery command.

"I—"

Before I can finish, Vickers horns in.

"See," Vickers says, purse fully engaged, sign moving up then down. "How does Compton benefit from your dispensary? You bring outsiders who cop and hop: smoke shops, 7-Elevens, and weed dispensaries. Empty churches are what's left. The cost outweighs tax revenue."

"We do our part," Tosh says. "Just look across the street."

Groups more substantial than the number of Weed Killers stream through metal doors into the converted church. "They sell Green Hornet to little kids."

"What's that?" Xochi asks.

"Pure THC made like gummy bears," Tosh says, voice shaking. "Their Fifty-One-Fifty Bar is nothing but THC and sugar."

Vickers' nostrils flare. "Oh, HELL NAWL—it's genocide. Let's block the doors," she says.

Like politicians always do in Compton, Vickers tries to hijack the revolt, making empty, incompetent promises and treating elective offices like a lifetime job entitlement. She turns, heels clacking across the street, but the rebels don't follow her. "What should we do, Tallent?" Chattom says. I hesitate, my breath caught in my chest. Another rebel says, "Who's calling the shots?" I roll my neck and say, "CHARGE."

"Let's riot," a rebel says over loud voices.

"Ha! We need a Molotov." Queen Egypt laughs, sipping a red raspberry smoothie through a straw. "Turn this bitch into one big blunt," she says.

Chattom stops car traffic. We cross against the traffic light, belligerently waving our signs, shouting profanities, pissing off frustrated drivers, inviting sheriff intervention, and tossing smoothies that splash red against crosses on the repurposed church. "The blood of Jesus," a rebel shouts.

In front of the church, they explain how cannabidiol, which Tosh sells, has medical benefits. "CBD doesn't get you high like THC but curbs pain, acne, and PTSD," Tosh says.

Xochi turns away momentarily, tapping her cell phone against her lips. She says, "Um, PTSD? That's a clinical term for people experiencing trauma. Are you suggesting cannabis will help psychiatric disorders? If so, what do we need a psychiatrist for?"

"Yes."

"Excuse *me*. You make weed sound like the Emancipation Proclamation, the do-all end-all cure for everything." Belly knotting, I say to Tosh, "W-well, what about Post Traumatic Slave Syndrome? Does it heal PTSS, too? Cure multiple traumas over lifetimes, over generations?" Tosh wears a quizzical expression as if surprised to see that one coming, seemingly caught short, with no snappy comeback. I'll keep them on their heels and drop knowledge. "Many of us have been traumatized, past generations terrorized by slave patrollers, Klansman. Currently, by police, many are struggling against human-made barriers like racism and poor healthcare access, some even believing bullshit lies about themselves like the misfits who'd given Compton a bad reputation. Betrayed by incompetent and unethical leaders, scornfully tolerated, marginalized, and segregated, souls, getting crushed to the point of almost being unable by itself to recover, all gift-wrapped tight, suffocated in the American flag." Damn, I can use that in a poem.

Admittedly, marijuana reduced anxiety and made an other-ized existence somewhat tolerable even in my time. I couldn't study, do homework, or do job interviews but could *zone out*, scarf junk food, self-absorb on meaninglessness, and temporarily forget my circumstances. Pain shoots through my shoulder when I press my fist to my lips. Could a case be made for cancer patients and those in severe pain? I'd resisted using cannabis during my cancer struggle. If it were all that, Jamaicans would be the healthiest people in the world. They're not even the wealthiest. What about people with epilepsy like Gash Head? Winfrey's so-called *religious beliefs*? Bull. Maybe Tosh had a point, but why sell anything other than CBD? We can do better than staying high all the time. Can't we? I think total abstinence is best, though smokers choose dispensaries in Lynwood, the next city, or buy from Bonk Loc. We need more recovery spaces and a new endgame to devalue getting high. "PTSS? —a lot of us have that a-all right. But smoking dope to get sprung or twisted? FUCK NO," I say to Tosh. "Call me old-fashioned."

The customer line snaking around Greater Love vanishes when set upon by Weed Killers. The workers pack a Navigator with boxes and hurry away.

"One storefront down," Vickers says.

* * *

We're back across the street in front of Tosh's storefront. The pine mural looks less tranquil, red globes on the spindly tree bouncing helter-skelter, rebel numbers growing more abundant, boisterous, and almost riotous given their Greater Love accomplishment.

Xochi faces Tosh and says, "Assuming you are a legally organized, non-profit collective," She thrusts her recorder close to Tosh's thin lips. "Does your business have a state seller's permit?"

Tosh buries their face in their smartphone. "Yes. We do," Tosh says.

Weed Killers shake and rattle the gate that Guzman snorts and paces behind.

Knowing Compton does not issue permits, I ask Tosh, "Do you have a b-business license?" Next to me, Chattom punches his palm and observes. The lap dog's eyes on Tosh's t-shirt seem to droop.

CRASH. The gate slams on the sidewalk. Guzman, holding up both hands, backs away. Weed Killers reach for him. A voice shrills, "Yeah, muthafucka—what are you gonna do now?"

Guzman puts down his head and straightens his arm as Mickey Cureton did once on high school gridirons. *"No mas!"* He barrels over Queen Egypt and Cory. Eeeow! The kid screams as a child would when scraped face-first across the concrete. With Chattom and Cory in pursuit, Guzman rushes onto Rosecrans, wobbling east on the median toward Lynwood, having expectation and intention but no real chance of escape.

In confusion, Winfrey and Gash Head cower in the empty lot between the 7-Eleven and shotgun house next to Tosh's storefront. The smell of burnt rubber follows screeching tires. A black Escalade packed with dispensary supplies, equipment, and the scent of hydroponics tilts out of the driveway where Guzman had stood guard, Tosh behind the wheel.

"HIP, HIP, HOORAY." Smoothing back my coiled salt-and-pepper Bozo hair, I cheerlead. Ecstatic Weed Killers high-five and pose for Xochi's group photo and the surveillance camera, collectively knowing cannabis money is like a smoldering ember on a wood-shingled roof waiting for the right gust of wind. In the future, we'd need to remain vigilant and stay woke.

"Here's my headline," Xochi says, turning her notepad to me. "When They Fight, They Win: Compton Burns Weed Stores."

I point my pill-rolling fingers at the sheet of paper, basking in the word glow of our success, hoping we've created our narrative and made a difference. "That'll make a great t-shirt slogan. Maybe get Cory a business start. Why, Xochi?"

She says, "I've never used and wanted to know more about drugs after my nephew, Juan Carlos, killed himself in Guatemala. He overdosed in the basurero six months after his sister died." Her voice cracks. "A river of drugs flowed through our home to the U.S. We lived in Dump City when he started smoking marijuana, moved on to sniffing glue, and later crack cocaine. I requested this assignment."

My stomach squeezes.

A cluster of blue hydrangeas pokes through a crack in the concrete at the base of the streetlight. A sheriff's cruiser slows; its tires stir a Dutch Master chocolate flavor cigarillo wrapper from the asphalt that, from instinct, I reach to pick up.

Vickers forces her body between Xochi and me and says, "Two down, sixty more to go—where to next?" She pumps her purse and says, "We should take a picture together, Tallent."

LONGEST JOURNEY

My mother never liked to exercise before she received the pacemaker to spark her sluggish eighty-seven-year-old heart. She drove everywhere, even the corner mailbox, head barely visible above the dash of her ten-year-old silver Lexus. After the pacemaker operation, she complained to her doctor that she felt like a chicken with the pip during a routine checkup. He suggested she *move about, walk at a shopping mall, or hike around the block, something not too strenuous, Mrs. Woodson. Exercise some. Or die.*

She's the last living elder. Dad had died from hospital superbugs years back. My grandparents, uncles, and aunts were gone from hypertension, Type 2 sugar diabetes, or alcoholism. I'd look after mom, damn it, help kick-start her new lifestyle, keep her healthy and safe, alive longer.

"I clean house every week and push—" She breathed loudly. "Do you ever push Food4Less shopping carts?" she grumbled over the phone.

"No. I don't shop—"

Mom interrupted me. "You must climb over people, crawl

under shelves, bag your stuff. Even Brer Rabbit would have a hard time, and you know how tricky he is."

I snatched away the phone receiver when a laugh track from TV shows she'd been watching clobbered my eardrum.

Why was she so stubborn? "I'm always right about this stuff, Mom," I said in my kitchen, flipping through a *Men's Fitness* magazine, the low hum of my Ninja Nutri blender pulverizing vegan protein and organic veggies. Mom never listened or obeyed. "How can you not know?"

"Drugstore trips, the bank, washing clothes—more than enough exercise for me, Frederick."

Okay, Fred. Don't overreact. She's trying to bait you into giving up. Some people think I'm strange because I exercise a lot. My sergeant once asked me, *what will you do—die healthy?* That was right after she wrote me up for being late for work again. I pushed off the blender, popped a couple of high-potency vitamins, and bottomed up bitter lactose-free, sugar-free, and vegan homeopathic anti-anxiety remedies.

"I don't care what Doctor Quack says. I'm not changing. I'll slap taste from his mouth." She must've increased the TV volume or held the phone close to the source when the laugh track exploded through the earpiece. "Don't get yourself out of pocket now—you're sixty-five, but I'll still take my cane to your butt."

I pulled an ace from the deck. "Michelle Obama says everyone needs to get moving."

"Oh no, you didn't," she said, voice high-pitched. "Michelle's my girl—best first lady. Badass—right there with Eleanor Roosevelt."

We wrangled, and then she sighed. "Whatever, Frederick. As long as I don't miss my TV shows." She was suitable for the corner mailbox, about fifteen tiny, boxy homes up the block.

"It can't be too early in the morning—I need my rest, not

after dark in South L.A. I'm old, Frederick, and I don't feel safe —hell, between bad cops and thugs, I take my cane everywhere with me."

I worked as a parking enforcement officer with the LAPD. The arrangement left midday half-hour between *Jeopardy* and *Judge Judy* as the best option, fifteen minutes each way to the mailbox and back, enough lunch break for me to rush over in the company Prius with a half-hour to spare.

The next day was cloudless, warm, and crisp when I arrived in my lime-green jogging suit and yolk-yellow jogging shoes. Gangsters and cops often made mistakes, so I avoided red or blue gangbanger colors. It helps when others see you clearly when running through SoLA streets.

Her fading periwinkle shotgun corner house, built around World War II, faced north. My old bedroom window and the place seemed tinier than when I lived there. A shadow line advanced past the porch and flower garden over the yard toward the entry gate. Wind chimes held silent. I bounced ten jumping jacks and fork-latched her chain-linked fence gate behind me.

Inside, the scent of jasmine touched my nose during *Jeopardy*'s closing credits.

Mom's tight white curls showed beneath her red scarf. Black bifocals framed a face shaded in dark sand and hewn like soft leather. She grabbed her thick wool sweater and cane.

The cane's ebony hardwood was clearly defined throughout, two-toned wood grain shaft and derby handle shaped like an erect penis and passed to her down through generations. The pewter collar decorated with delicate carved flowers and foliage had a steel washer inside the purple rubber tip.

"I've never seen another one like it," she said.

"Neither have I." We made for the sidewalk.

Several Latina mothers huddled around a fruit cart on the corner outside the gate. In her huipil with colorful cross-striping and angular designs woven into the cloth, a woman blinked and said, "Ola, señora!" She touched her throat. "¿Dónde está tu auto?"

Mom flicked her gaze upward toward me. "Garage," she said.

"Are you going for a walk? ¿Para caminar?"

"Si. Estoy caminando a mi hijo."

Whatever she said, the women found it funny, and they slapped shoulders among themselves. They continued to speak about whatever mothers talked about after sending kids to school.

I spread my legs, squatted, placed my palms on the walkway, and did a few burpees to warm up. Mom paused for balance and grabbed the right hip. She fell and fractured her hip about four years back as if to align with the left ankle she broke seven years ago when she slipped on wet grass during the college graduation ceremony for my nephew. We'd ended in emergency surgery just before the commencement speech.

The assemblage cleared a path when Mom tapped a fence-post with her cane. She shaded her eyes and said, "I never noticed how far that mailbox is."

I barked an order. "Come on, Ma, just do it."

She took a deep breath. Camphor tree leaves covered the sidewalk, which buckled from roots. I walked a half step behind, hand on her elbow. She slowed at the sidewalk gradient, wavered but balanced on the cane. Sweat stuck the jogging suit to me, and my breaths accelerated.

"Hey, Pearlene." It was Miss Pumpkin, the nosy next-door neighbor's squawky voice. She wore a turquoise tunic drawn in at her thick waist over black leggings, hair a graying coiled mass framing her cocoa, moon-shaped face. "I never see you out front. That's a cute sweater—is something wrong with your car?"

"Nawl. Richard Simmons here—" she nodded, "thinks I need exercise."

Miss Pumpkin rolled her eyes. "Did you know Mr. Johnson passed?"

Mom stopped mid-stride on cracks at the sidewalk's ruptured peak that, to her, must've looked like Mount Everest. I held my breath and her triceps. "Oh, nawl—I saw him at Food4Less last week."

In my mind were images of her slipping on leaves. I slid between the two women and did neck rolls to stretch and refocus Mom. Miss Pumpkin folded her arms across her chest. I'd talk her down from the precipice. "Keep going, Mom," I said.

Mom pushed forward off the right foot, two or three steps, beyond the hump, through loose leaves. *Whew!* She scrunched her face, tapped her cane hard against the concrete, turned, and looked around me at Miss Pumpkin. Her pitch rose again. "At the checkout, I gave Johnson some coupons for toilet paper."

"He died on the bus stop bench—" Miss Pumpkin said. "Just closed his eyes and never reopened them."

"Five dollars for three rolls? No way should he pay that," Mom said.

"Only seventy-four, a young man, Pearlene. His kids are already fighting over his stuff."

"Full price for toilet paper?" She stroked her forearm in which hand she held the cane and furrowed her eyebrows as if to concentrate. "He'd been a fool to pay it."

"Had just gotten his hair cut, too," said the neighbor.

"Humph—they must think we're idiots. Pay that kind of

money just to wipe your ass. Might as well use paper money and flush that."

"Funeral's Saturday at Laurel Street MBC, Pearlene."

"Nawl."

"Yes, the viewing's at 10 a.m."

"Seventy-four, you sure? He looked okay to me."

"Ouch." She tapped my shin with her cane shaft.

"He was vegetarian, too."

"Mom—Mr. Johnson would've wanted you to keep walking."

"He's dead, and you're way too pushy."

"Have you seen Rufus?" Miss Pumpkin asked. "If you do, send him home. He can't afford no more trouble."

Maybe I was a little aggressive. But ten minutes had passed, and we weren't even past Miss Pumpkin's house. I'd need to shower, change, and return to work or face the sergeant's wrath.

We were in front of Mr. Johnson's small rectangular house a few homes later. A big U-Haul mover was backed across the lawn to the front door, its engine knocking, its exhaust releasing fumes burning our eyes. Sure enough, a couple of his children cursed and argued. A daughter, maybe forty-something, waved.

Mom's mouth turned downward. "Leave the toilet paper," she said. "Show some respect." The woman jumped when mom smashed her cane against the U-Haul hood. "He might need a wipe before he goes through the gates. I tell you as a good Christian."

The woman's head flinched back. She threw a box into the U-Haul, turned away, and fussed over a jewelry box with her brother.

A German Shepherd snuck up three more houses down and stuck her big head through the space between pickets of a wrought-iron fence. Bitch held one paw over the horizontal rail and growled like crazy at Mom before I could act. Mom stopped, leaned sideways, wobbled a bit, raised her cane high over her head, and brought the tip down on the shepherd's nose. She yelped and dashed into the backyard.

The sun was high, the air hot, typical July. My body weighed down like an anchor dropped into the sea. The exercise thing didn't seem like a good idea for Mom. What if she got hurt? My sergeant would surely tear into my ass if I were late again. I fell to the sidewalk and did twenty pushups. What else could happen?

* * *

Mom is the Great Depression resourceful. She clips store coupons and stuffs her garage full of staples for the next earthquake. She's mastered the art of recycling, removes "loomnum" foil from cooked food carefully, cleans and smooths it with a dish towel, and folds foil at postal worker speed. Grocery bags and plastic containers receive hoarder treatment, too.

Halfway to the mailbox, Harry, the Black face of L.A. homelessness, shuffled our way. "Top of the day to you, Mrs. Woodson—where's your car?" He threw me a sideways look. Gaunt and scraggly, his form blocked the sidewalk. Crack and weed stink seemed to ooze even from his sidewalk shadow. "Can you spare a quarter?" he said to her. "I'm not doing too great."

"Ass back, dude," I said to Harry. "Do we look like welfare to you?"

Mom looked unsteady, and Harry touched her shoulder to help stabilize her. "You owe me money," she said to him. "But as a real Christian, I'm going to forgive you. I've got empty bottles for you at home," she said to Harry. "Worth more than a quarter—you bag 'em—got cardboard, newspaper, and some metal scraps." His shoulders curled forward when she pushed her cane handle into his chest. "I want twenty percent, Harry."

Harry quirked an eyebrow and showed brown teeth. "I got yo back, Mrs. Woodson."

"Kick drugs, get in shape, dude," I told Harry. I faked a shoulder punch, and he flinched.

"Of course, you'll set my trash cans out on Thursday. Like a good Christian, if you don't, I will curb-kick you, Harry, after I cane-beat you like a runaway slave," Mom said. She flashed a tight grin. The scent of camphor leaves returned once Harry slunk away.

We were maybe fifty feet to the mailbox, and a coterie of young brothers was shooting dice on the sidewalk, bunched between a white picket fence and overflowing trash cans on the parkway, an unkempt patch of grass between the sidewalk and curb. They either didn't see us coming or decided to ignore us.

Their clique had more red colors than bloodshed in a Quentin Tarantino movie. "Whoop—seven-eleven got to get to heaven," one said. He crouched; a black wave cap squeezed his head. A forty-ounce Olde English 800 malt liquor bottle sweated on the pavement beside him.

"I got you faded," another said in dark blue Dickies, pants slung half down his ass, crimson drawers showing, and a red bandana hung from his back pocket.

Their group of six huddled tight, a couple on their knees I could barely see.

"Excuse us, young brothers," I said. They didn't budge, and their dice cracked against the concrete.

"You crapped out," said the guy with the red bandana.

Wave Cap had just lost his money. A beefy guy, he stood and twisted his body to face me. Twenty-something, razor-bumped blue-black face, his voice sounded like a tank rolling across gravel. His eyebrows squished together, eyelids cut in half his pupils, and ripples appeared in his jaw muscles. "You made me lose, OG," he said.

His top lip was upturned; his mouth was full of venom and bitterness. He was in my face, and the combined stench of tobacco, weed, and malt liquor reeked from his greasy pores. Fuck. I'd never known anyone in their right mind who could drink Olde English 800 and not go stupid.

"It's a chance, dude. How can I cause you to lose?" He believed in facts and knowledge that he didn't possess, superstitious. "You must've voted for Trump," I said, but I couldn't reach him. Carefully, I managed my voice and my tone to de-escalate drama.

"Nawl, OG, I want my money back—" he said, "from *you*."

Wise men say a good young man can beat a good older man. I was healthy. He was impaired. I clenched my fist.

"AHEM—" Mom cleared her throat. "That you, Rufus?" She looked down at a guy still on his knees. His back to us, he picked up loose change and turned.

"OH—what up, Mrs. Woodson—where's your Lexus?" He spun a fake gold bracelet that had discolored his amber wrist. Cigarette and weed smoke strangled the air.

"I'm out for a walk. Pumpkin's looking for you, young man." Mom pointed the purple cane tip at him. "You'd better see what she wants." Rufus nodded and waved his arm, and the others cleared space for us to continue. "Aren't you on parole? Don't go back to jail. I tell you as a Christian." A flush crept across his light-skinned cheeks. "Plus, I'll whip your ass with this cane like I used to spank you when you were bad."

His partners sniggered.

Rufus straightened his knees. "It's hard, Mrs. Woodson."

"Who told you living is easy?"

I released body tension when he pocketed the loose change and trotted home. We turned to continue our journey.

"NIGGERS," Wave Cap blurted. He scooped up the Olde English 800, which left a moist ring on the sidewalk, and offered me a taste. I waved him off. All I needed was to smell like malt liquor stank after being late to work. He took a slug. My mind searched for answers.

"Niggers voted for Trump—swamp niggers," he said. "I voted for Sanders." He pushed out his fist.

"Me too," I said. "In the primary." We bumped fists.

"Hillary here," Mom said. Wave Cap scratched his jaw. I stared at my palms as if they held answers. "We all lost," she said.

"It was Russians," he said.

"Chinese," I said.

"Yeah, Israelis," she said.

Mom and I reached the corner mailbox, and Judge Judy started in five minutes. I'd be late for work, and the sergeant would be pissed, overwhelmed with parking violators. Perhaps Mom would accept a new exercise routine, maybe not. I'd been pretty overprotective. There's a worldly saying that nursing the old is like nursing children. Mom was not yet a child again, nor were my dad, grandparents, aunts, and uncles.

They'd lived their lives as best they could, and when time and circumstance converged, like Mr. Johnson, life ended. Shit, it's God's plan. Other than comfort and unconditional love, I could give little else. I'd lower my blood pressure with less worry about her.

"Whew," Mom said, "let me rest a minute." She leaned on her cane, one hand on the hot dark blue mailbox.

Even in a wool sweater, she didn't sweat at high noon. This was all God's plan. I was where I needed to be.

"Maybe this wasn't the best idea, Mom," I said, mouth dry. "It took thirty minutes to reach the corner—you'll miss Judge Judy."

Mom squinted. "Oh, didn't I tell you?" She flashed dentures.

"Huh?" My thoughts froze. "Tell me what?"

"Reruns. They're showing Judge Judy reruns, Frederick—I've seen it before. Be a good Christian. Go, get my car."

She gave me the keys.

PREGNANCY TEST

When it came to Pearlene Woodson, his 88-year-old mother, Frederick, mostly did his best and cried the rest. "I misjudged the distance," Pearlene said from her over-sized wheelchair to the ER triage nurse dressed in ceil-blue scrubs. "That step was further than it used to be." Pearlene wore black plastic-framed bifocals that covered her brown, impish face like goggles. She didn't want to be there, but he couldn't take a chance, even if it meant arguing with his boss because he was late from lunch again. "All they do is make you wait, talk to you any old way. The doctor's gone before you can blink your eye," Pearlene had said before they left home, even though she could hardly bear the pain.

His mother's most recent fall happened two weeks ago. She let it slip after she nearly stumbled over her living room coffee table while he told her, again, about the shitty way his sergeant treated him at his parking enforcement job. "She's always in my ass about something," he said. "I need to be more *punctual*, she told me. Damn, I'm at work every day. What more does she want?"

Pearlene's white hair poked from beneath a checkered green-and-red headscarf. "Your daddy went into the hospital for his stroke. After a while, he came back to himself, up and talking. The next thing you know, they called and said he'd died from sepsis. What the hell is sepsis anyway? That's the way they do us. You go in but don't come out. Just another dead nigga from Watts," Pearlene said.

The nurse strapped a blood pressure cuff to Pearlene's arm. "Do you have any allergies to medicine?"

"Tylenol makes me woozy," Pearlene said and squint-eyed the monitor's systolic/diastolic pressure numbers. Her pulse rated one hundred eleven. Pearlene nodded her head toward Frederick. "He made me take some before we left."

Frederick pressed his lips flat in a false smile, disinfectant searing his nose. His eyes fell on a crinkled and soiled crepe on the exam table, and under the nurse's small desk, a waste container overflowed with dirty white tape and bloody gauze.

When Pearlene broke her hip several years ago, she required surgery, a hospital stay, recovery, painful PT, and lots of in-home care until she progressed from bedridden to a wheelchair, to the walker, to a cane, and back on her own two feet. He learned then to call 911 whenever an older adult falls. It was like watching a baby learn to walk. Pearlene took months of repair, the time he no longer had since Sergeant Asshole rode him like Frederick rode exercise bikes in spinning class. Republicans were forever trying to kill Obamacare, and where would she go if she needed long-term care? After arguing, he sped off to the St. Francis of Assisi ER. Frederick's tension was released when the triage nurse's screensaver flashed: *It's never wrong to do the right thing.*

"It's a good idea for the ER visit because old bones are brittle, fragile, and need viewing with an X-ray," the nurse said.

Pearlene gripped her upper thigh and tried to lean forward. "Shit, that hurts," she said. "Tylenol's not worth a damn thing."

"We'll get you over for X-rays," the triage nurse said. She removed the blood pressure cuff from Pearlene's arm, rubbed her shoulder, and gestured for the nurse assistant to bring a wheelchair.

"WORD—I'm dizzy. WHOA," Pearlene said, her face scrunched with pain.

"Do we need a pregnancy test?" the assistant said—tiny employee-of-the-month pins clustered on the NA's breast pocket. The pink Y-tube of her stethoscope dangled from her instrument pocket. People under gray fluorescents, writhing on gurneys like worms, flanked the ER corridor as she pushed his mother's squeaky wheelchair across scuffed floors through a tincture of iodine odor.

"Ha! It hurts when you make me laugh," Pearlene said, grabbing her hip. Despite the pain, sunshine rose on Pearlene's face as white light pierced popcorn clouds.

"I'm sixty-six," Frederick said. Despite his throat thickness, he was grateful that the nurse could coax humor and see his mother smile, given the situation and their mutual hospital apprehension and suspicions. "Too old for a little brother." Frederick was an only child and often wondered what having a sibling would be like. He was sure a brother or sister would have been preferable to a few cousins and friends. Frederick passed on marriage opportunities and had no children of his own. Pearlene and his job were all he had.

The nurse belly-laughed. "Would a baby sister work for you?" she said while wheeling Pearlene into space #13, the last unoccupied area, thick puce accordion curtains on two sides, a vital sign machine, exam gloves, cotton balls, and other medical stuff behind the headboard.

Space #13 offered a clear view of activity in the main

corridor and, of course, the unsettling monitor beeps, screams, and a mix of shit and alcohol redolent of urban emergency rooms.

Maybe he should call Sergeant Asshole and let her know about his situation. He used so many excuses before. His truths now seemed like a lie. He rubbed the cell phone screen with his thumb. He lost his train of thought when he saw a technician roll by with a woman on a gurney in four-point restraints, escorted by a deputy sheriff.

"I still gotta get shoes for two kids, vampire teeth, and a pumpkin," the woman said, lifting her torso somewhat, unable to move her limbs. Halloween was three days away.

Pearlene yelled, "Try the 99-Cent Store next to the Well of Good Wishes. It's at the Compton Artesia Blue Line station," she said.

A deputy said something about fifty-one-fifty into his lapel radio.

The woman struggled on the gurney against the constraints and said, "Calluses on your hands stay forever—they never go away."

"I'm praying for you, honey," Pearlene said. She turned her wheelchair toward the corridor, regarded the woman, and said softly, "You should try Jergens Lotion. Get it at the 99-Cent Store." Then, glaring at the deputies and technician, Pearlene said, "Free up her hands—loosen the straps."

"Calm down, Ma," Frederick said. "That's just the Tylenol you took talking."

While waiting for the X-ray tech, Frederick and Pearlene overheard an interview through the curtains. The voice sounded like a male nurse or another attendant. White walking shoes and twilight-blue scrub legs moved between the curtain wall and the tiled floor.

"We've told you before that your impaired liver probably

causes the edema from drinking so much alcohol, Mr. Irons."

Irons said, "I tried to stop—but it was too hard. Everybody in my family uses drugs. I caught my parent's mainlining horse in the kitchen when I was eight. My daddy stuck the needle in his neck. Yeah. I love to drink. I started with alcohol, tried marijuana—everything."

The voice said, "It might be right for them, Mr. Irons, but wrong for you."

Pearlene said, "My cousin Harold's heart twitched from drinking too much."

Beyond the curtain, there was a rasping sound like Velcro removed. The person interviewing the drunk said, "It takes less time to do things right than to explain why you did wrong."

"Yak, yak, yak," he said. "You sound like my ex."

Frederick checked his cell phone time. The situation did not look good. Sergeant Asshole would be pissed when he showed up late, reprimanding him in her log, threatening to transfer him to traffic control, where he'd stand in rush-hour intersections, directing crazy South L.A. drivers.

The attendant said to Irons, "Let's fight the flu." Irons groaned. "Have you had your flu shot?" he asked. Irons groaned again. "Roll up your sleeve."

Pearlene turned in her wheelchair, faced the curtain, and said, "Harold died from consumption. His brain just shut down."

Frederick's breathing grew heavier. He stepped into the corridor, squinted down the hall, and muttered, "Where's the X-ray guy?" Sergeant Asshole was probably asking herself the same question about him.

Pearlene scoffed at the curtain separating her from space #12. "He loves to drink?" she said. "I hope the fool doesn't drive."

Irons said, "HEY," and started coughing. Then, an ugly

gurgle and choking sound preceded a flurry of activity in space #12. *Code Sepsis* crackled through the PA system.

Whisked away, red-faced Irons bounced up and down, I V lines attached to his wrist.

Pearlene cupped her hands around her mouth. "CONSUMPTION," she said.

Seated on the doctor's stool, Frederick did toe raises and folded his arms across his body. What if she needed surgery? He winced at the whiff of antiseptic something-or-other. He glanced at the wall clock. He'd lose money if he didn't return to work or lose his job. He could lose Pearlene if he did. She moaned in agony and hummed, "Amazing Grace." She only sings hymns when she's gloomy and depressed.

"See?" Pearlene said. "What I tell you? They'll have us waiting here forever." She shook her head as if to clear cobwebs. "Never get out of this damn place," she said.

"Things could be worse, Ma." In her large eyeglasses, he regarded a dim reflection of his receded hairline, having watched it over the years gradually thin at his temples into an M shape, thinning on his crown. Eventually, the two areas met, forming a U shape like a horseshoe. Did the cornrows he'd styled as a young buck or perhaps his man-bun worn in his thirties cause him to lose his mane? He read somewhere that coconut milk might regrow hair. He'd lived long enough to see Black hairstyles come and go, from close and nappy to chemically straightened, to blown-out naturals, to Jheri curls, and back again, sometimes, somewhere in between along the way, versatile. He liked the manageability of an outdated semi-processed loop, even with its expense and maintenance requirements. Inevitably, styles would change again to a mohawk, shaved temples, or maybe just wild. Would he live to see the next hair fad? He imagined himself in the Slauson Avenue and Crenshaw Boulevard intersection directing traffic, Jheri-curl juice dripping onto his uniform shoulder; he'd look good. "You could've hit your head or something, Ma," he told Pearlene.

She sat stiffly in the wheelchair until a disturbance.

"They shot my baby!" a young woman's voice wailed through the ER corridor.

A little body, maybe a year old, give or take a month, lay surrounded by three paramedics, a bloodied towel under his tiny head. One paramedic covered the child's mouth and nose with the BVM, one squeezed the bag to deliver ventilation, and the third navigated the gurney in the same direction Irons and the restrained woman had gone.

Code Red, said the voice over the PA system.

A gaggle of young men wearing blue clothing followed the woman, shouting, cursing, and imploring stragglers to move. "Get the fuck outta the way," one said. "We know who did this," said another. The corridor, thick with Crip members, overwhelmed hospital security guards. Pearlene jumped to the *clack, clack, clack* of weapons loading. Nurses and attendants created a human barrier between gang members and the operating room at the end of the corridor. No one got in.

"Drive-by," Pearlene said. She closed her eyes and moaned as if to process all that had happened. "We'll probably camp here tonight—I hurt. I'm tired, Frederick—I need to lie down," she said.

Her eyes dulled, her voice a monotone.

Frederick helped his mother to stand. "Owww," she hollered. He unfurled a fresh piece, tore it, and smoothed out the crepe covering the exam table. Was it anywhere safer than a hospital emergency room? He removed her shoes, and she grimaced when he lifted her under her arms onto the table like a child. Unable to sit, she lay on her side. "Could I stand with a broken hip?" she asked Frederick. He shrugged and covered her with a backless examination gown. He tried to comfort her and told her about his meter maid job, how people double-park, block street sweepers, ignore No Parking signs during rush hour, and how his sergeant makes him do all of the crud work she doesn't like to do, such as ticketing elders who forgot their handicap placards. He didn't mention his obsession with physical fitness, how he was late to work mornings when jogging, and late from lunch when he visited the gym. "My sergeant's a real bitch."

"I could've written that book," she said. "Like *Ghost Summer: Stories*. Sounds like Abbie in *The Lake*. Now there's a real bitch, using her young boy students to fix her house in the Florida swamps. She turns into a fish, and then she eats them. You should read it." Her stare was empty, head resting on prayer palms, pressed together. "I've seen much abuse," she said. "It's like calluses on your hands, stays forever—never goes away."

Frederick was more of a television guy and never read his mother's suggestions. He preferred crime drama and legal stuff like *Better Call Saul*. "Yeah," he said. "Running through stop signs and red lights is the new sport—people do all kinds of stupid shit in cars these days," he said. Except for the noisy patient monitors, there was a moment of complete silence until Frederick pulled back the privacy curtain and stared into the empty corridor. "Shit. If I were a cop, I'd shoot half of 'em." His jaw and facial muscles tightened. "What's taking these people so long?" Sergeant Asshole was probably ticketing and posting the intersection by herself by now. Maybe he'd help her some, be more punctual.

Pearlene's eyes closed when she said, "Humph! I've seen them speeding and texting. Got my Jergens, though."

Teachers turning into fish? Jergens, when the hospital uses Nivea? Was mom showing signs of old age? "I have a deadline, Ma," Frederick told Pearlene.

"I do, too," she said. "With God. Who's yours with?"

He considered what she said. "Nobody, Ma," he said. "I'm staying here with you." Frederick rolled the stool he was sitting on to the foot of the exam table. He unwound it to top height and then laid his head down into folded arms, like a first-grader taking a nap at school. He closed his eyes but opened them when a platoon of SWAT deputies raced down the corridor for the operating room.

"We're en route to the OR," a deputy said into his lapel radio. "Put down your weapons," one of them shouted.

"Fuck the police," was the reply.

"Gang members— need backup," the SWAT deputy said.

Gunfire exploded like on news footage of Syrian battles. Stray bullets whizzed by, pinged metal medical equipment, and embedded into walls.

"Do you hear that?" Pearlene said. Frederick did not answer. He stood and bent over his mother to shield her. The shooting stopped as suddenly as it had started. There was a commotion near the operating room. Heavily tatted deputies hoisted several young men in handcuffs down the corridor by their collars.

Frederick's skin tightened, and words exploded from his throat. "Take their stupid asses to jail."

Pearlene's X-ray results arrived with an emergency room doctor four hours later. "Just a contusion," she said. "Give it a few days—return in a week." Then, the doctor vanished.

"Well, at least we know one thing," said the NA as she rolled Pearlene outdoors to a patient loading area.

Pearlene's eyebrows squished together. Frederick's stomach muscles tightened like when he did sit-ups.

"You're not pregnant," she said.

Frederick punched his cell phone buttons, deciding to order coconut milk online. He called Sergeant Asshole.

THE VEGAN WHOLE

As executive chef, I could make shoe soles taste like porcini-crusted tofu with shallot gravy, but my meat-free restaurant was on the line, and so was my life. Because I wanted so badly to bring some healthy eating to South Central Los Angeles' Death Alley, I'd risked borrowing the startup money from a thug like Jojo. My sugar-diabetic dad had died from cancer: his arteries were lard-clogged, and his colon spareribs impacted. He was what he ate, so I believed particular heart-friendly food would turn things around in SoLA.

Jojo's shrill voice on my phone made me picture dark rooms and broken bones. "You fucked me like a virgin, Rollie," he said. "My ass's still sore. You could've used some grease."

He'd called to tell me where to find Booger.

"We can work this out, Big Jo."

But he hung up. A day before, an emaciated woman with a black eye patch delivered me a stinky, decomposing crow inside a shoebox.

Maybe he'd just had Booger beat down. That had to have

been it, to scare us, make sure we'd keep working to make the restaurant successful so he could get his money back.

I sucked salty air in the car as I drove down where Speedway turns into Via Marina west of SoLA.

Booger was a crackhead who'd always disappear and do anything for money. He was my go-between, a flunky sous chef who'd learned his craft well as a jailhouse trusty despite his flaws. I'd met him as a sobriety advocate for Love Corner Alcoholic Drop-In Center on Vermont Avenue, in the middle of Death Alley, a food desert infested with street gangs, rogue cops, and sex trafficking. For a New York minute, he stopped using, cleaned up, and committed to helping others kick alcohol and other drugs blanketing the community. However, the SoLA safety nets were full of holes, and Booker fell through with a thud. A much better person when sober, I hoped he would once again make new friends if I kept him close.

Compton College classes made my eatery business plan bulletproof, but my Chase card maxed; Wells Fargo redlined the area, so Booger came up with an idea. "My boy Jojo'll hook you up, Rollie." Jojo had cash to launder to help me open my restaurant.

Bronze-skinned and lanky, Jojo smelled like a swap meet cologne when we sealed the deal at the marina. Booger stood grinning next to me as Jojo gripped my hand so hard it hurt. His hair extensions jumped in all directions under a Raiders cap fitted sideways.

"Aw, come on, Jo. Rollie's good." Booger said with a wink. "Do this, and I'll hook you up with my specialty, Mushroom-Bean Bourguignon. It'll unbraid your hair."

JoJo flinched and dragged his hands through his hair repeatedly. "Here's fiddy," he said crisply when he finally released my hand. "Don't waste it." "Shut the fuck up," he told Booger before he lent me fifty thousand at 50 percent interest plus an ownership stake to renovate a boarded-up Golden Bird Chicken shack nearby.

However, the people in Death Alley dug their graves with spoons. They would not give up starchy, processed, and greasy food even if their lives depended on it. Mine did.

On opening day, we released white doves and floated red, green, and black balloons with Vegan Whole printed on them into the muggy, smoggy summer sky.

Dressed in sand camouflage fatigues, an army veteran sat in a plastic chair and carried the sound of uncertainty and the stench of homelessness with him. Gently, he laid his Purple Heart on the table. "Got MREs?"

"No," I said. "Our food tastes better than military rations."

"Are you sure?"

"Here, I'll hook you up with our Cabbage Rolls with Wild Rice and Mushroom Stuffing."

He glanced at the savory-looking menu picture.

"Uh. Are you sure?"

"Yes, and thank you for your service."

In a lavender wide-brimmed Sunday hat, an old gray woman leaned over her walker, studied the counter menu, and pointed to the chef's special. "Is that pork?"

"Hmmm," she licked her lips, "—to God be the glory." She loved the wholesome meals made with protein-rich whole grains, beans, and fresh produce like our Roasty Soba Bowl with Miso Tahini.

The veteran guy and Sunday Hat Lady became regulars. Our only ones.

We had a plan. Maybe they could help us raise Jojo's money.

At the veteran guy's VFW post, Booger talked up the Vegan Whole, where he competed with blues music, domino games, and clinking liquor bottles. "I used to hit the pipe before breakfast," he told them. "Now I start with a heart-healthy vegan burrito."

I preached healthy eating at the older woman's Baptist church. "We don't need to gentrify to eat well," I said. As I spoke, the pastor napped, and half the congregation's heads dipped and snapped.

Up went the signs a month later: *Going out of business!*

When I parked and walked down the jetty as Jojo told me to, a bloated body lay face down in the water, arms outstretched, a gaping hole in what used to be a bald spot.

The corpse drifted near the jetty. I poked it closer with a moored paddleboard oar and slid the paddle under what remained of Booger's waxy, soapy face.

It was him, all right. My gizzards high jumped inside my belly.

I'd received Jojo's message. The payment was due. Now.

What Jojo did was a fucking shame. Even scum like Booger deserved better, a broken leg maybe, but to shatter what little brains he had as crab food?

Death Alley was nowhere to eat healthily, and Jojo would come for me. I'd relocate, Oakland maybe, the lands of KFCs and Popeyes, or head south, Atlanta or Fort Worth with their DQs and Waffle Houses, start another Vegan Whole.

Tears met at my chin. I used the oar at low tide, dialed 911, and pushed Booger out to sea.

I'd stop by the Vegan Whole, visit the kitchen with the old lady and veteran guy again, and hold a moment of silence for Booger on my way out of SoLA.

To avoid Jojo, I drove side streets, east on 92nd Place.

People lined Budlong Street. Up the block and around the corner onto Vermont Avenue, a crowd gathered at the Vegan Whole door. I bumped the curb and got out.

The sea of people parted for the older woman when she

tapped the pavement with a black cane. "Church family," she said. The veteran guy stood next to her, all scrubbed up. "My peeps," he said, pointing to a squad of armed, uniformed soldiers.

They both helped me in the kitchen. "Pass the olive oil—"

Fuck it. I wasn't going out like Booger.

Highly fragrant and savory cumin filled our tiny kitchen; warm clouds of white rose over the veggie steamer.

"Pass the pepper. Let's keep the food coming."

BABA NAM KEVELAM

(MY MOST BELOVED IS THE ONLY ONE)

U lan Mohammed's spit was thick, and his tongue was
swollen. He stuck his tongue tip into a decaying molar
and clutched his throbbing black face. He licked his parched
lips and shooed away the gaggle of dogs, rats, and other animals
skulking around his tent flap door, wanting to sniff his butt, a
worsening problem. Hampered by his aching right leg and
micro-surgically repaired hand that was shot during a scuffle
with thieves while napping on the embankment, him spending
two weeks in the hospital and losing four pints of blood through
his wounds, now focusing sleep-starved eyes on the empty
gourd he'd used to collect reclaimed water from a local golf
course, poking his nappy locks out from his tent, crooked
fingers partially shielding his eyes when mid-summers orange
sun glinted off shards of glass and empty food cans, scratching
at scabies in his armpits, and body lice on his groin, hesitating,
not wanting to face once more the gather of animals lolling
around his home, flashing red and white lights momentarily
hypnotizing him as a rad bot tinkered with X-ray and heart
monitor settings inside rear doors of their expandable Smart

Pod mobile emergency room, two humanoid medic bots bending at their waist, one crouching, another two kneeling on dirt, their composite hands pumping valiantly before they stop.

"He's gone, doctor," the medic bot relayed to an MD who watched remotely through its body cam, "mark it at 0639 hours, Tuesday, July 7, 2037," simultaneously informing the other service bots that were on the emergency response team with it, "—hyperthermia from exposure, sir."

Tyrone Harris, a camp newbie who had coughed and cried throughout the night, was dead.

Ulan slapped his tent flap door and lapped his tongue across his chapped thirty-nine-year-old lips while scraping his yellowing teeth with a chew stick, his world slowing.

He scanned shopping carts, personal belongings, and mostly black faces in skyscraper shadows in nearby shanties along the L.A. River embankment.

Had someone, anyone, cared, maybe Tyrone would've lived to old age, looking as he had to be in his late twenties, scraggly, emaciated, extremely vulnerable to the ravages of record-breaking heat, smoky wildfires, the concrete L.A. River bed itself just a trickle over the past ten years, too brackish for an occasional bath, good for nothing more than hundreds if not thousands of recreational vehicles, vans, and cars occupied by ethnic immigrants, the unemployed, and others displaced by some combination of gentrification, racialized housing policy, or artificial intelligence. People were dying daily as enslaved Africans did over the middle passage.

There must be something Ulan could do if he could survive long enough.

Ulan hummed *Nearer to Thee*, an old Sam Cooke gospel song as he always had when feeling helpless, carrying it with him, a tune his granny had taught him as a little boy when she told him about Job, a song about trouble being one thing entering everyone's life, the poor and even the rich sometimes have troubled minds. He'd always doubted the part about rich people with troubles.

Eyes gummy, nose runny, pulling at his sticky, dirty t-shirt, Ulan waddled a few feet to a gray shopping cart lying upside down in a litter pandemonium at the end of the dirt trail leading into the camp, its hexagon basket pattern upturned, dusty, violated, mice, a murder of crows, opossums are surrounding him looking expectant.

A city sanitation crew appeared at the top of the dirt trail led by a tech bot, a beige Stetson hat stretched across its metallic head, searching for dead bodies and what they said were abandoned tents and belongings scattered about atop the embankment overlooking the sea of vehicles on the riverbed. "Please move your belongings to the other side of the trail," the tech bot announced, causing many unsheltered people to rush while others looked confused.

Ulan stink-eyed the tech bot and counted the other team members; three Cyclops cop bots that road on levitation cycles had steel knuckles and holstered vintage magnum guns, five lumbering four-armed bipedal fetch bots with long-handled grippers, and two snail-paced automated caterpillar-tracked freight bot trucks used to haul away corpses and tons of stuff such as car tires, sleeping bags, and electronics, eighty percent of which had been dumped illegally, perhaps by haulers or merchants avoiding fees by using as landfills encampments of the unhoused. The back of Ulan's neck prickled each time bots communicated in a low-pitched moan like a dying animal.

He quickly gathered his propane-fueled hotplate and plastic bags filled with clothing, blankets, and well-worn Air Jordans. A cop bot trailed behind him, bird-dogging his every move as if he were a baby being potty-trained. The cop bot popped its steel knuckles, subtly challenging Ulan to move falsely. "Get out of my ass," Ulan said.

"Move it," growled the cop bot, caressing its vintage .357 magnum as if it were a toy.

Ulan pretended to ignore the cop bot, moving slowly so as not to give the cop bot reason to fear for itself, a reason Ulan knew could motivate the bot to shoot and ask questions later, him knowing that when it came to cop bots, there could be no guaranteed safe response to their bullshit.

A fetch bot used its grippers to snag a hypodermic needle from Tyrone's suitcase, confiscated knives, medications, and bagged clothing, some soiled by urine, feces, or other contaminants.

Ulan's tears flowed unrestrained. "I've been on the housing waiting list for years," he said, hoping to gain empathy from a machine even less forgiving than the government workers that sent it. "This will work out," Ulan said optimistically. His head began to hurt, a clear sign that his BP was up, as he moved his things just ahead of the sanitation team, hassled by the ornery cop bot. He uprighted the rickety shopping cart, wiping off its handle with his ragged shirt, filling it with his stuff, the pack of animals howling and growling at the cop bot. Limping, Ulan bumped it across the cop bot's foot to the other side of the dirt trail. The dickhead cop bot didn't even feel it.

Once the bots had rumbled past in a dust cloud, Ulan sat down among thick, leathery, dark green oleander leaves and yellow flowers that seemed to grieve at the end of each branch. "I'm not giving in, never giving up," he said to the broken shopping cart, laying his head on his arms, the animal pack, undeterred by the sanitation crew, eyeing his every move.

"Showyourite—but delivery drones and Uber Eats have made me obsolete," the cart seemed to whisper. No matter how hard he pressed his palms against his ears, Ulan couldn't unhear the cart when it said, "Maybe next time I'll return as a monarch butterfly."

A lump forming in his throat, Ulan wheeled the cart around to fend off hungry animals, a parliament of owls, a knot of frogs, his nervous stomach forcing him to squat and shit, the animals wildly competing for every poop morsel.

Ulan's thoughts turned to Sonora Hollingsworth. Thank God.

$$

Once, sometimes twice a week on evenings, Sonora Hollingsworth visited Ulan's encampment, passing from her packsack what she called *blessing bags*, one-gallon Ziplocs filled with small packs of cookies, fruit cups, water, and Slim Jim's. She fought through the ring of scavenger dogs, cats, pigeons, and rats outside of Ulan's tent, them compatibly and contentedly pecking or rolling in the desert soil, awaiting the reappearance of their main attraction, an opportunity to glimpse him, a chance to sniff his oily trousers, or even better, hoping he'd take a savory dump somewhere, anywhere, among the camp shanties on embanked swaths of tuft straddling the concrete river, enabling them to taste his poop pellets, which transformed them into blissful ninnies that happily ransacked local tent cities.

Ulan Mohammed looked forward to the times when he could gaze into Sonora's intense brown eyes, wishing he could kiss her prominent forehead and strawberry-shaped lips and speak with her about her day, her school psychologist job. He believed her heart banged, as did his, especially when he gave her small trinkets he'd found while foraging through dumpsters.

"I've called animal control, Mr. Mohammed," Sonora said,

in a blue dress with a turquoise paisley shawl, gold hoop earrings, and a pinkish-beige head scarf, kicking at a rat and causing her purple amulet to bounce into her sweaty cleavage, using a blessings bag to shoo away a dog smelling around Ulan's groin.

"Animals have always liked me," Ulan said, fanning himself with cardboard. "Now it seems out of control. I don't know what it is." He opened the blessings bag and devoured the Oreo cookies, which, although tasty as fuck, only added to his nausea and caused his teeth to ache. "They follow wherever I go and even eat my shit. That cat tried to lick my ass," he said, pointing to a hissing, feral cat.

Closing her eyes, which seemed to swell like a soaked kitchen sponge, Sonora bared her teeth back at the cat, her teeth looking like little picket fences, her eyes turning fire-coal red when she reopened them. "Sounds like a spell's been put on you," she said in a raspy voice. The cat hunched its back, screeched loudly, turned a full circle, and bolted away. "My gris-gris bag can help protect you from evil."

Ulan showed his palms. "Nah. I don't believe in that shit."

"It's not about whether you believe or not," she said. "You could need help at the crossroads."

"I don't think so." Ulan snorted quickly through his nose. "Just because you scare cats away—anybody can do that," he said, trembling and working hard to keep his voice light but wishing he had her power.

He'd met Sonora about a year ago and looked forward to it when she made her rounds through the encampment. She seemed to like him, too. She sometimes gave him an extra blessings bag, and he got a boner when her hand touched his. She even offered to drive him to a county dental office. But how could a beautiful and accomplished woman like she ever get with a pauper like him?

Ulan's knees buckled, and he nearly fainted when a shadow darkened the light from the west-setting sun.

A black air taxi, propeller pods upward, swirled dust onto the untidy lives below when it slowed and landed. The stray animals skulked away, and Sonora held down her skirt. Its vertical electric motors attached perpendicular to wing tips folded and disappeared into its carbon fiber body. Steel-grey scissor doors rotated. Ulan braced himself for another cop bot rousting.

Out buzzed a silvery metallic cockroach-shaped aerial drone. Next, a pair of tan alligator cowboy boots crunched denuded sandy soil.

"That's him," said the six-legged walnut-sized drone, in chirpy androgynous lip smacks. The jowly pink-faced boots guy stretched out his hand and pushed Ulan his business card. "I'm Rhinehard, PharmaBrothers, CEO," he said. "Our DNA samples traced the y-marker to you; your saliva, hair roots— even your arrest record, all match. We've studied the animals." Coolly, he didn't break a sweat as if he carried a personal air conditioner. "We'll pay you handsomely for it."

Ulan's thoughts froze. He considered Rhinehard's expensive suit, platinum Rolex watch, and perfect sparkling teeth underneath his sneer. "Pay me for what?" Rhinehard wasn't the police but was clearly among the one percent controlling them.

Rhinehard squeezed on greasy hand sanitizer. He washed his hands. "You're BM," he said. "Your feces, Mr. Mohammed."

"Oh snap—*my shit?*"

Sonora put her hand over her face and shook her head, "His doo doo?"

Ulan lifted his chin and tried to make sense of Rhinehard's proposition. He'd seen the old Punk'd videos where celebrities were made victims of pranks. Did this crusty white guy think he could game Ulan Mohammed, who'd resisted post-election funk that millions fell into nearly a generation before, them feeling beat down like Whipped Peter, all covered in welts and scars?

Ulan had held fast during the 2033 Recession when he lost his wife, home, and his coveted Walmart cart retrieval job, where coworkers called him the *cart-whisperer*. Earlier, the upturned shopping cart had mentioned being replaced by bots. Had Ulan's retrieval job also become obsolete? Still, he was unfazed by the warm, cunning, devilish emotional depression spreading around him. He cleared his throat and looked at Sonora's wrinkled brow and flushed amber skin.

He'd play along. "BAM. How much?"

"Maybe a price based on volume or weight," Rhinehard said. "I'm sure my people and your people can negotiate something mutually beneficial; he said matter-of-factly as if he made such deals routinely." Unlike most, Rhinehard didn't wheeze or breathe hard in the frowsy air but seemed to recoil from the stench of campsite piss and shit Ulan was used to.

Ulan's dry throat moistened somewhat when Rhinehard advanced thirty Bitcoin vouchers and whipped out a contract that, heartbeat racing, him being distracted by the odd offer and even odder offeror, Ulan signed without reading.

Was he about to finally come up?

$$$

A year later, Rhinehard had reassigned the wrinkly walnut-sized drone to Ulan. It flew about without human intervention, often rubbing its two front hands together like it had a tic. It could morph into holographic soma images like Mr. Olympia, Ms. Universe, or, as Alex considered itself, something non-binary with a range of body options.

"Where's that Bugatti driverless I asked for?" Ulan said.

Old-school rappers were prominent on the car and Champagne Carbon. Ulan would be, too, adjusting his ARGs, the augmented reality glasses he used to improve his sight and enhance the touch component on Alex XXV's holograms, and smoothing out the expensive suit he'd acquired a penchant for wearing à la Rhinehard. "I can't be late for Sonora—try again. Use voice recognition. Tell them I said to hurry the fuck up." Ulan rocked on a gold-plated toilet seat that warmed his butt and drifted into *How to Eat to Live,* a virtual e-zine about vegan diets.

"Hold your piss, my nigga," said Alex sounding chirpy like a constipated cricket. "I'm tracking it."

His expansive eightieth-floor condo office felt like jail despite its accouterments, piped-in white noise, air conditioning, cherry wood-topped desk, and his assistant, Alex.

Habits were hard to break, and, with one eye open, he often slept in the sleeping bag in the tent he'd erected on the balcony. He gazed from his semi-private toilet and bidet enclave to rooftop sky ports below him, westward to the L.A. River, and the south, the behemoth Compton Courthouse dominating that city's dusky skyline, all from a collaborative workspace occupied by him and nosy Alex. "While you're at it, get my Affixa™ allowance for this month."

Ulan swiped the e-zine to product advertisements. MacGillivray had developed *Gutpo,* bacteria formed from intestinal tracts of healthy people for patients showing flu symptoms, Chlamydia, or similar gut distress. *Skinnypoop* was feces from scraggy rats that helped takers lose weight. *ChemPee,* an older product that, when dissolved, turned urine into drinkable water and had made trillions for the T. Bone Picker's Group, which owned the patent during the past two decades of global warming-induced drought conditions. All were decent products with terrible side effects, like causing people to embrace conspiracy theories or walk backward, constipation, kidney stones, dizziness or fainting, and sometimes, death.

He swiped to a full-page ad showing a spry, shirtless, shoulder-length blonde, blue-eyed, white man. His scruffy beard reminded Ulan of old Jesus Christ pictures he'd seen in his granny's Baptist church. PharmaBrothers believed it more profitable to claim that their antidepressant came from the ass of a white guy standing in a sunshine nimbus. It was probably in the contract language that he'd failed to read.

BULLSHIT.

WHOOSH. Ulan flushed the toilet. The floor beneath him vibrated, electromechanical pulleys groaned, and toothed wheel gears grated like boisterous roisters. His business was sucked down to be processed into Affixa™, the most popular and powerful antidepressant ever invented.

Depressed, most everyone had turned to antipsychotics, hydroponic weed, opioids, and that old reliable booze. Not Ulan. He straightened himself, expanded his lungs to their fullest, and took deep, satisfying breaths. He coped better than most when things were difficult and found vitality when he suffered because—well, just because.

In his mind, there was nothing better than Affixa™. None of the other products compared to the efficacy of Affixa™, and he got paid well. He'd conquer the world—for a price.

Armani's pants bunched around his ankles. Ulan checked the time, scooched his butt on the gold seat, and swiped at the screen before him. He swallowed the bitter devil-red specially formulated PharmaBrothers pill that looked like a One-A-Day vitamin which rendered his doo doo stink-less and encouraged him to sit longer until his legs pinned and needled.

To monitor poop potency for quality control, Alex alighted on his upper thigh to synch with Ulan's Gastro-Homie tracker app. He inhaled profoundly but smelled only the sterility of his environment. It stood and dry-washed its hands. Ulan whisked it away and dumped a load that caused water to splash his ass.

"I'll drop the pill bottle on your desk with the poop bags," Alex said. Alex buzzed low to his left and said, "Did you sleep well, Ulan? Last night, I noticed that your REM sleep was that of an eighty-year-old." Ulan had just turned forty. "My electrooculography monitor detected that, as usual, you become sexually aroused, but your erection lasted considerably shorter. What did you dream about? Is there any way that I can assist you?"

Ulan's skin tingled.

Fuckin freak. The day before, Alex had morphed into a porn star's lifelike image that, combined with the touch effect from his ARGs, Ulan used to masturbate, which was better than a Polly Porno doll that he'd have to clean.

Ulan felt the corner of his mouth rise slightly. He rolled his shoulders and checked his ARG time. He didn't want to be late for lunch with Sonora Hollingsworth, the psychologist at Robert E. Lee, a middle school in High Desert that Ulan believed was for retards. She was a sweet beignet from Nawlin's, on direct bloodline from energy conjurer Madame Marie Laveau, the Voodoo Queen, she'd told him. Yeah, right. His ribs tightened slightly. But to hang out with Sonora, he'd fake belief.

Alex said, "You're approaching the fifteen-minute mark, Ulan." Sitting beyond fifteen minutes disrupted normal poop processes and caused his hemorrhoids to flare up and BP to spike dangerously close to apoplexy country. "It's nearing your monthly appointment. Should I schedule you for Maya's abdominal massage or a Panchakarma purge? —you haven't had a probiotic colonic in a while?"

"Panchakarma," Ulan said. "Panchakarma—my dosha is

Vata—uneven. I need to restore balance to my soul, my body," he said to Alex.

"Your diet analysis says that you lack sufficient fiber, Ulan," Alex said. "I suggest an uptake in lentils, black beans, and raspberries. You like raspberries, non-GMO, of course, or use fiber supplements."

"You're close but haven't reached singularity yet, Alex. I'll handle my diet until your kind's fake intelligence takes over. It's all in this e-zine."

After Ulan wiped his balls with it, Alex pecked around like a chicken on the blue towel Ulan had placed back on the rack. Alex buzzed around his head and said, "I saw a few useless pellets, Ulan—but enough smooth turds to keep." "You've just crapped out what could be a panacea for thousands, maybe millions of suffering souls, my nigga," Alex said as it alighted on Ulan's leg to examine Gastro-Homie readings.

Jaw muscles tight, Ulan checked his new fade haircut in the mirror. "I ain't your nigga. Scrotum face muthafucka. If I told you once, I told you a thousand times, DON'T CALL ME NIGGA."

No matter how far he'd come up, the N-word managed to follow him like assistance claim investigators barging into homes and poring over applicant toothbrushes and underwear. He backhanded Alex from his leg, slamming the pesky drone against the ceramic wall tile.

"Showyourite. But the great Tupac Shakur once said *A Nigger is a black man with a slavery chain around his neck. A Nigga is a black man with a gold chain on his neck.*"

Ulan ground his teeth, and his blood pressured upward. "A chain is a chain. My granny told me about the origin of nigger and how white people used it to degrade us and make themselves feel superior to us. She taught me how this country's wealth was built on our ancestor's backs. Look at me. I saw how a new generation of weed-smoking, pants-sagging, no-book reading, Hennessy-drinking *niggas* adapted the word trying to own it, redefine and disempower it, replacing *brother* with it. They'd never felt the fire hose water, saw bodies swinging by the neck from trees, the *white-only* signs, or walked on the other side of the street to let whites pass." Ulan's head might explode into a full-blown stroke. "Some made music money off being *niggas* fifty years ago and wanted credit for it. Some died trying. Imagine wanting the enslaver to credit you for some fictitious bullshit they invented to keep us in check. It's an *anti-word* that I don't use without apology." Ulan was exhausted pleading his case to an artificially intelligent drone that had been programmed by racists, even though people received help from the poop of a black man. Was that in the contract, too? "FUCK THE COP BOTS. That I agree with."

"The Bugatti is here," Alex said. "—do you have your gold chain? Don't forget your poop bags, my nigga."

The bags were for offsite poop collection, and Ulan hated using them, significantly when he'd lift grimy toilet seats, spread the bags over the bowl, shit in them, and tie them up like a slave with cotton picker's bags. They were heavy, and he had to carry them back. He should've read that contract before he signed it. Maybe he'd ask Rhinehard for a freight bot. "Don't forget the bear repellent, shithead," he said to Alex.

Ulan slid onto the bidet. *SWISH*. He motioned a maimed hand, and warm, recycled water splashed into his butt crack. *SWISH*. Again, he waved over the sensor twice more. Weightless, he imagined his face and neck flushed with color.

Ulan pulled his trousers halfway up his butt. He fastened his belt, which left his pants hanging below the elastic of his periwinkle drawers, a sign of his individuality and discontent. His upset stomach and the heaviness in his body were not about diet. Something about his new lifestyle disturbed him.

Since he'd come up, he'd never again visited desperate voices inside cardboard shanties at the boiling river camp, even though the vision of Tyrone Harris choking out his last breath constantly invaded his mind. His ascent from homelessness had been mind-boggling, and he recalled how his former makeshift homes eventually turned to garbage: abandoned tents, torn mattresses, used needles scattered about, a baby doll, a pile of yams, gas cans, marine batteries, and tons of detritus removed by hazard teams. There was hostile architecture like gapped awnings at bus stops and corporate buildings, curved benches sectioned off by "armrests," and even artificial foliage to keep people experiencing homelessness from finding shelter there, criminalized for trying to exist—shopping carts with anti-theft brakes. His overheated apartment reminded him of nights spent huddled in blanket scraps, the wind blowing through holes in his tent. Rain.

Last night's sleep was indeed difficult.

But lunchtime with Sonora was nearby. He clapped his hands, and the e-zine virtual screen vanished.

On his executive desk a few feet away, Ulan glanced at the pill bottle, the poop bags, bear repellent, and the only thing in his in-basket, the spiral-bound contract marked *CONFIDEN-TIAL*. He was sure that PharmaBrothers held the rights to his shit; by all indications, they also owned him.

He began to hum and sing words about being with others, stealing away alone, *Nearer to Thee* being his consolation song when trouble came.

That he benefitted from corporate-manufactured solutions to the blues wasn't enough. Something was missing.

$$$$

Ulan dusted off his suit, having fought off a gang of wild

animals with bear repellent before he met Sonora in the Vegan Whole vestibule for lunch. He hugged Sonora's sticky softness, and the glint of copper within her orgonite pendant caught his eye. A whiff of lavender nudged his nose. His lips passed near hers, him having looked forward to this moment since he left the river encampment, she pulling back, seeming preoccupied.

"They're SpED students, special education, not retards," Sonora said to Ulan at the eatery in Watts he'd chosen, his treat even though she'd told him she had her own money. "Some are mislabeled, considered slow, ADHD, autistic, or downright crazy." She told him that adult action had damaged most, or in some cases, their inaction. "For you to call them anything else is condescending and pretty damn ignorant," she said.

"But why?" he asked, attempting to fade into the wallpapered background behind the bench where they sat waiting for a table. Through the window, he studied the dirty haze, the tiny building's pebble-dashed exterior, the virtual billboard that scrolled in large, colorful Helvetica script: *you are what your body absorbs!*

"Why?" she said. "Why hand out blessing bags in homeless camps? Why visit former students in county jail? It's my calling, what I do. It's who I am." She glazed over a menu projected from her Smartphone. "I serve others, try to influence their life outcomes and connect them with nature, spirits, and ancestors. It works for some. You could call it *love.* What about you, Ulan? Since you left the camp?"

"Oh," he felt taller but decided to try to hide it, "—a little bit of this, some of that," he said just as Alex buzzed in.

"Whatsup, whatsup my niggas," Alex said as the maître d' appeared, a towering bow-tied humanoid, his smiling orange face looking vaguely like the old school Terminator with synthetic skin plastered over a flat metal skull. It was a newer, efficient, dependable, and practically indestructible bot model.

"This way, please," the maître bot said, its platinum palm up, leading them past the juice bar, past Shimon, a robotic four-armed AI musician playing hypnotic jazz-funk on marimba, past lunching cliques likely from the New Jordan Downs. These gentrified townhouses had replaced WWII public housing where Ulan once lived years back, handing the two diners off to a tuxedoed wait bot.

"They're making these things more human-like daily," Sonora said. "Racism and all."

"Stick with lentils and kale," Alex said to Ulan. "Stay alive, my nigga. We need your shit."

Sonora squinted at Alex, cocking and then shaking her head. She asked the wait bot, "Are you sure your spinach and celery are organic and contain no pesticide residue?"

"Máam, I can assure you that—"

"Do you have any pistachios? What about oranges?"

"No, máam. Pistachios disappeared long ago. When the oranges grew no larger than grapes, we stopped serving them."

"Do you buy from urban farm collectives?"

"Some of—" The wait bot was programmed not to interrupt humans.

Her Amethyst earrings swung back and forth. "Is their soil pesticide-free? How many humans did you replace?"

The wait bot blinked rapidly and emitted a brief scent of burning rubber, to which Sonora wrinkled her nose.

"Don't worry, we gotcha, my nigga," the wait bot said.

A sudden coldness hit his core. "HEY," Ulan said.

"You don't know me like that," Sonora told the wait bot. She gave it a stony stare and pressed her temples with her fingertips. Purse dangling inside her elbow, she crossed herself twice. The rubber smell grew more robust, and the bot's mouth opened, but nothing came out. She snapped her finger next to its fake nose, "I'll stick with avocados, mangos, and broccoli—put red chili peppers in a side bowl, fuckface."

"Defective," Ulan said. "This bitch was probably made in China. Send it back." Ulan considered spraying the bot with bear repellent. "SEND IT BACK," he said.

"I'm sorry," the bot said. "I'll get your order. Would you like some water?" It hurried to the kitchen. Wanting to ensure that no malfeasance would occur, Alex followed it.

Tension released, and Ulan refocused on Sonora. A widower, she said that her methods, readings, spiritual baths, specially devised diets, prayer, and personal ceremony had cured anxiety, addictions, depression, loneliness, and other ailments among her patients. She added more approaches to children that seemed to work and that they enjoyed. "You should come and see," she said.

Ulan saw what he believed was an opportunity. "Yeah, I'd like to get up with you, too," he said. "You're one dope-looking woman." She gave him a sidelong look.

Smitten, Ulan half heard what she said. Over her black gothic off-shoulder tunic was a sheer chiffon, flowing open front patchwork vest with distinctive dark teal netting twinkling with tiny iridescent sequins. Ulan scoped her flowing cropped pants, which gave the illusion of a skirt. Sonora's feet rested in side-zipper soft leather navy anklet booties with stacked three-inch wooden heels when she crossed her legs at her ankles. Her shiny black lipstick allured him, hair straight, raven, with blue streaks, skin tone lightest brown.

"I'm testing this depressed kid who set his house on fire," she said. "What if we taught kids other ways to overcome or at least learn to live with depression?"

Adrenaline spiked in his blood, and he pushed forward his wounded fist full of Affixa™. "Give ém these."

"Hell to the NO. Young people get enough shit from adults as it is," she said, her tone sharp.

Ulan offered a false smile and swallowed hard before he forked salad.

Alex returned to the table edge in time to butt in. "Shit's his golden goose," he said to Sonora. His green and brown striped compound eyes almost seemed to blink when he said to Ulan, "And, again, what about that dream last night? Was it—" he pointed a hand foot to Sonora.

Ulan leaned back, put up his deformed palm, and waved it side to side to signal Alex not to go there.

"I'm not a fan of drones," Sonora said. "I've hated them since Microsoft unleashed Tay—those racist AI chatbots years ago." She pinched the shell to release avocado meat. "Does it go everywhere with you? Do everything?"

Of course, Alex was part of the arrangement with Pharma-Brothers, expected to protect their interest and monitor Ulan's wellbeing.

"Well—uh."

"That's right, honey," Alex's chirpy voice tone deepened. "I practically own him."

"Not true," Ulan said, cutting through tofu fish with a knife, fake meat that had the texture of walleye pollock fish in sandwiches he once ate before overheated seas killed them off.

"That's what I mean, Ulan. Flaming garbage pile in, flaming garbage pile out," she said. "I don't know about you and your friend."

"I do many things without it." He winked at Sonora.

Shimon improvised music in the background, and they ate in silence until the maître d' reappeared. "How is everything?" it said.

Ulan nodded. His mouth was full of kale.

"I see many students with major issues, especially Black

and brown boys that end up in SpED—they act out sometimes, and they're sent to me. Some parents and group homes want extra money for their kids in special education." She mixed broccoli florets with mango slices. "Many parents are depressed, and so are their kids."

"That's why we have Affixa™—," Alex interrupted. "To operate inside the gut-brain axis. That's where your boy here comes in." Alex rubbed their hands together. "He sits on a gold mine."

Ulan's face and neck heated up. "I can get you some cheap," he said, several capsules stuck to his sweaty palm.

"Not cheap enough," she said. "Why should Pharma-Brothers get rich off of people's misery?" Her head skated side to side over her shoulders. "Why should kids need pills to feel normal? Why should anyone? My way is better than yours."

"Normal? No way. I don't think so." He sniffed the air. Psychiatrists diagnosed half the population with depressive disorder and prescribed them Affixa™ to cope. The evidence was irrefutable and good enough for him. It didn't hurt that when demand for Affixa™ increased, so would his bank account as long as he shitted smooth logs. "This *is* the new normal," he said.

"Nah. You can keep your shit. Excuse the pun."

Ulan's heart shrank. Everyone wanted Affixa™ except for Sonora. It had allowed him to come up off the ghetto river embankment and buy new clothes and a 401K. Still, it nagged him that there must be more, something else he wasn't getting on his journey.

"Come by my school tomorrow. I'll show you," she said. Sonora popped a handful of red chili peppers into her mouth, headed for the door, and, as she passed, glared at and then flipped off the maitre d'. Closing her eyes, which seemed to swell, Sonora bared her teeth at the bot just as she had with the feral cat, teeth looking like little picket fences, her eyes turning fire coal red when she reopened them. The maître bot's eyes blinked fast, one lid earlier than the other, followed by the scent of burning rubber. It froze and said, "My nigga, my nigga, my nigga, my nigga, my nigga," as if stuck in a loop.

The wait bot rushed over with a pitcher of cold water when Alex threw up a tiny hand. Ulan nibbled a red chili pepper, and his face nearly exploded. His tongue on fire, Ulan garbled to Alex, "Take care of the bill."

"Showyourite, my nigga," the wait bot said before slouching into extreme catatonia, half-full pitcher in hand.

Retard school? She'd rejected his offers of Affixa™, and he contemplated a rain check on the school visit, but that would mean a missed opportunity to be with Sonora. A little more time with her was better than a lot of office time with Alex.

He pulled out bear repellent and clomped toward the exit.

$$\$\$\$\$\$$$

The morning sky was overcast, and the air was barely breathable before the first bell at General Robert E. Lee Middle School. A sullen group of teachers and staff lined up well ahead of the students, all prime candidates for Affixa™ Ulan judged by their collective countenance.

"Mrs. Larsen is the principal," Sonora said sternly. "I'm not her favorite." A resource officer bot's baton and Ulan' bear repellent kept several stalking animals at bay. An erection pressed upward against his sagging belt as Ulan moved slowly in line behind Sonora toward the amber and green stucco entrance beyond the Rapiscan Backscatter whole body scanner. "Schools and prisons got scanner deals from the TSA years ago," Sonora snorted. "Right after the school bombings."

Ahead of them in the cue were two teachers. Her head

down, shoulders drooped in a gray college sweatshirt, the math teacher pulled from her sizeable brown shoulder bag a double-barreled .45 ACP 1911 pistol, a small clutch, and pepper spray and flung it all into the undersized gray plastic bowl on the metal conveyor that looked like a small children's slide beside the X-ray scanner. *Bbbzzzp!* A low buzz sounded as she passed through.

Ulan smelled hydroponic weed from behind the music teacher who carried a grenade launcher, a 40mm high-tech weapon system that enabled operators to observe and engage targets from around the corner effectively, the round itself exploding just before contact while the shooter remained behind cover. As the line inched forward in the cold air, he clanged it onto the conveyor. Once through, he re-holstered and dropped Visine into his scarlet eyes. Where in hell would he use that?

Ulan strained his neck to peer around to see the screen that another teacher, who checked her watch often, was posted behind to see if he could glimpse Sonora's nude X-ray form. His arousal softened when he couldn't.

"Weeeeeee," Alex said, flying over the equipment.

Another resource officer bot in a dark green uniform with sergeant stripes, a badge, and a gun pulled Ulan aside. "Random check," it said once Ulan passed through the buzzing body scanner. It gouged its wand inside and outside Ulan's thighs, whacked his balls, slapped his stomach, chest, and back and lingered at his butt.

"Whoa, careful now," Alex said.

"What's this?" The officer bot growled at Ulan. "This is a drug-free campus."

Not wanting to give the stupid bot a reason to fuck with him more, Ulan said, "It's my antidepressant. I take them when I start to feel crazy." Ulan snapped his head to the side three times quickly as an example of what crazy looks like. "Besides, it's organic—from the ass of God. I'm one hundred with that."

The bot rubbed its composite forehead and ogled the Affixa™ bottle before it said, "CLEAR."

On playground duty twenty minutes later with Sonora, Ulan monitored students approaching the scanner, tossing away knives, pipes, and drug paraphernalia. One student refused the scanner and created a ruckus. She wore all-black clothing and a pink, spiked Mohawk and said, "I'm a scholar, not a suspect." Retards just as Ulan had expected. Certainly, Sonora could use Affixa™ on them, and since they were there anyway, he might as well hit up a few teachers, too, at three hundred Bitcoin vouchers a pop.

"Step aside, Miss Everleigh," Sergeant Officer Bot said. She resisted, and it grabbed her upper arm and wanded her, reeling her about for several minutes as if she were a ragdoll.

"Let me go, let me go fake assed cop," the girl said. "Fuck you."

It slammed her to the ground, kneeing her in the back until she stopped resisting.

The screening process tested Ulan's dosha; a sour, bitter taste formed in his mouth, and he needed to spit.

Mrs. Larsen's voice boomed over the PA system, "We'll have a surprise *active shooter* drill before lunch today." Even if they were retards, how could kids feel good about being treated like prisoners? Ulan shivered, but not from the chill air.

"Search until you find them," he told Alex. He sent Alex to look for the math and music teachers to whom Ulan would offer Affixa™.

Covering one city block, the two-storied rectangular school was on three sides, surrounded by a black security fence with cold steel bars that towered with an outward curve and terminated with triple-pointed spear tips. Sonora's counseling office was far to the back, functionally nondescript, the last boxy prefab with a transom window next to several dumpsters.

"Whew," Ulan said, having limped his way across the campus. "That was quite a walk to get here."

Standing in the dirt at the bottom of the front-facing steps leading into her office, Sonora said, "Papa Legba, open the way for us to pass." On her knees and with great care, she traced with yellow cornmeal what she said was a *vévé*, a flawless cabalistic geometric diagram, orienting the material such that one would have difficulty stepping over it to enter her office or *oum'phor*, she called it, leaving the entrant little choice but to either step around or through it thereby disrupting the magical astral plane and chief voodoo god attribution, and, upon completing her design, requesting assistance from Legba for earthly problems, *By the power of the Loa LETE-MAGIE, Négre Danhomé, all the vévés, Négre Bhacoulou Thi-Kaka.*

His muscles tensed, and Ulan quickly exhaled through his nose. "You can't be serious," he said. "What's with the mumbo jumbo? Legba? Pssh." A headache came upon him until Sonora batted her long eyelashes, softening Ulan's condemnation. "Well—maybe it's not all mumbo jumbo, actually," he said, stepping back from her design, unable to stop himself.

Several students lined up next to the steps, heads together, speed-talking with one another, jostling for position behind Everleigh, seemingly unencumbered by Sonora's vévé.

"There," Sonora said upon completing her vévé. "That ought to confound the haters for a while." She wiped her palms together, the vévé drawing between them and her oum'phor. "Now we can enter under God's protection," she said.

They took a moment to admire Sonora's creation, Ulan noticing how even prettier Sonora looked when she seemed pleased, him recognizing how she was more than what had met his eye, and starting to comprehend why retarded students might be excited in her presence.

"Stop feeling sorry for yourselves. Go to your classes," a voice behind them said, shattering Ulan's moment of vulnerability. It was Larsen's hologram hovering about seven feet tall in a desert jumpsuit. Her skin was translucent, her eyes large, her forehead small, and her thick ginger hair limped below her shoulders. Alex had never morphed into anything that looked as sinister. She rapped a pair of nun chucks in her palm. Her belittling smile made Ulan's heart beat faster. "Later, I'll roll out basketballs. Some of you can practice your rap game on the digital audio workstation in the safety police office." She squeezed the nun chucks like a dishrag. "I might also have a soccer ball or two."

"I'm a scholar, not a suspect," said Everleigh, still rubbing her shoulder from where she'd been bot handled earlier. She and two boys stood firm as other students dispersed. "I want to see Ms. Hollingsworth," she said. "So do Lil Mac and Fernando." The boy with close-cropped Afro lowered his head; the fat boy turned his body away from Larsen.

Larsen's eyes grew wider and showed much white. Spittle built up in the corners of her virtual mouth. *POP.* She snatched the nun chuck handles apart, stretching the chain.

Everleigh opened the door, and the three children scurried inside Sonora's oum'phor. Larsen eyed Ulan from toe to head and said, "I didn't see you at my check-in desk. Are you a parent?" These words and her scowl put Ulan on edge. He felt his BP elevate and poop coming. "There's something about you I can't put my finger on," she said. "You don't look run-of-the-mill."

What an ugly bitch. Humming, Ulan told himself not to overreact. Sonora stepped around the vévé symbol to his side. He held out his damaged hand to shake, to which Larsen left him hanging. "No, I'm Ulan Mohammed, service rep from PharmaBrothers, to see Ms. Hollingsworth about our product. You might have heard of Affixa™?" His stomach fluttered.

"Affixa™?" Larsen said. "Isn't this great?" The bitch whooped and bounced into a little dance, careful not to cross the cornmeal design. She reached out her hand, and Ulan, adjusting his ARGs for touch, shook it. "Good," she said. "I keep telling this woman that this is an education school—not a hospital." Nun chucks in her armpit, Larsen claps soundless hands. "Her *office*—if you can call it that—looks like a space-ship. Students don't want to leave it," she said.

Just as she did with the feral campsite cat and the Vegan Whole maître bot before, Sonora closed her eyes but quickly reopened them as if she had second thoughts. "I used my money since you won't approve of holistic methods that work," Sonora said. "I'm doing my best with what I've got."

"Like I've told you repeatedly, *Ms. Hollingsworth*—read my lips—get ém in——Affixa™ ém up, do the paperwork—get ém out, is what I say." Larsen squinted at Sonora, scoffed, and sucked her teeth. "Psst. Bach Flower Therapy—pure quackery. Next, you'll want Scientology e-meters."

Ulan stretched his mouth to form a cheeky smile. "We can't have that, can we?" he said. He pulled from his coat pocket the bottle of Affixa™ and shook it. "I'll drop you a free sample on my way out," he told Larsen.

Alex had been hovering all along. "Sheesh," the drone whispered, "What an asshole. But it would be great to get a school account." Alex circled Ulan's head. "The math teacher is in row J38, and she wants a pop. The music teacher wants to know if you have cannabis, too."

Sonora scrunched her pretty face, pointed to the cornmeal design on the ground, and said to Alex, "Only flesh and blood beyond this vévé." Sonora faced Ulan and flexed her fingers.

"Larsen needs help understanding what I am doing in my office, so it must be wrong. She thinks it is Voodoo. I asked her what was wrong with voodoo. My ancestor was the Queen of Voodoo. Madame Laveau. People fear what they do not know. I told my relative that I did hypnotherapy, and she responded that it was *weird*. There is nothing weird about hypnotherapy. Neurolinguistic Programming is a form of hypnotherapy, but it scares people if you call it that. Why? Because they do not understand it."

She guided Ulan around the symbol and pushed open her office door.

"Do you have a toilet inside?" Ulan asked.

$$\$\$\$\$\$\$$$

"It's f-e-a-r-f-u-l, fearful," Fernando said to Lil Mac. "Spelled with an 'e.'" The two boys played EmoScrabble at a game table off to the side, in a small, empty clothes closet now labeled *prayer area*, in the sizeable polygon-shaped room. Sonora explained how the shape was vital because it was based on sacred geometry. She wanted everyone in her office to feel at peace and grounded. Ying and yang, talk therapy, exercise bookcases, tables, or equipment made each of six walls, and in the center was a copper pipe pyramid, large enough for a yoga mat or a couple of children to play under. Following Sonora, Ulan removed his shoes and left them on a rack in the vestibule. Sonora did not welcome anything inside you may have walked on while outside. Something about energy and not letting negativity inside her office. In addition to the Apple computer, her tiny desk was nearly hidden by succulent plants, soothers, colored gels that oozed out and created a calming effect when turned over, and several grey meditative rocks she got from the beach in Oxnard. "They were free and presented themselves on the sand when the tide would leave the beach with the water," she said. Everything in Sonora's office equaled balance, calm, and peacefulness.

"I knew that," Lil Mac said. "I was just testing you."

"Trying to cheat is what you were doing. *Farful's* not even a word."

Curious was the word Fernando rolled when it was his turn to roll the die. The chubby kid used an emotionary to look up the word's meaning and correct spelling. "Give me thirty points for that one," he said. "Two 'u's.'"

"What the hell?" Ulan said, reasonably confirming that these kids were off the chain.

"The game helps them differentiate emotion words and builds their vocabulary," Sonora said. "It's pretty simple, and they love it. I want them also mindful of the sources of sadness, fear, happiness, and joy."

There were benches for seating in the *oum'phor*. A ship model hung from a crossbeam, as did calabashes, baskets, and oriflammes. Looking asleep, Everleigh reclined into a soft leathery chair with what looked like sensors attached to her outer ears and scalp. Five pyramidal orgonite crystals rested on a small table next to her.

"Neurofeedback is training in self-regulation," Sonora said.

"Looks like an EEG or electric chair. Does it hurt?"

"No, silly. She's monitoring her brain activity with a video flying saucer that simulates flight through cave walls in her brain. When the music changes or the saucer stops, that's an opportunity for the brain to adjust, helping to reach her goal, teaching her to improve and balance energy, and stimulating brain receptors for it to grow and change. She is learning how to calm her mind. Like any skill. It takes a while, but over time, her brain will learn. It will change."

"Are you saying a video game will help her improve herself?"

"Yes—with her in control," Sonora added water to the jungle of potted succulents. "NeuroReleasing frees clients from blockages, the garbage they hold on to that must be released. It's like defragging your computer's hard drive. The orgonite pyramids filter toxic energy and convert negative into positive life force energy. They reduce electromagnetic radiation from some of our tools. Bots give off harmful radiation and are not welcome. Mrs. Larsen can come in person, but her hologram can't."

Ulan scanned the room through his ARGs to a table with more plants and geometric rocks, a water wall, a sheep wool floor covering, and five blue bottles. He crossed his arms. "And what about that?" he asked, pointing to the copper pyramid.

"I'm glad you asked. That's a meditation pyramid."

Ulan shuffled over and poked the structure with his pointer finger, recollecting how he'd once scavenged for copper to sell, how in the olden days it was used in home water pipes, how copper mines were now spent. Water was mostly bought in glass bottles by those who could afford it, with plastic containers banned years ago. For some reason, he felt a wisp of connection, like a fleeting inspiration. "Wow," he said.

"We use it to meditate, to balance chakras and energy. Do you meditate?"

Although he'd never meditated, he recalled how his granny would sit in her closet, still and alone, praying for hours. Was she meditating? "Oh, sure," he said if that included time spent every morning massaging his aching leg, struggling to stand, the time before Aiffixa™ he'd spent wondering how he'd make it to the mission for food and water, and the time he now spent on heated toilet seats. "Every day," he said.

"Good. Now give it a try," Sonora said, motioning for him

to sit inside the pyramid on one of the sheepskin rugs. "You probably already know this, but the trick is to sit still for thirty minutes, three or four days a week." She delicately smoothed the rug with her soft hands. "It can help your blood pressure, energy, and pain."

The three students gathered around. "Can you sit still, Mr. Mohammed?" Everleigh asked.

"Don't let thoughts pull you out," Lil Mac said. "No matter how crazy they get. Just watch them."

"Yeah, witness your thought devils," Everleigh said.

"You're way bigger than them," Lil Mac said. "See em' clearly. Kick their asses."

His thoughts scrambled, and his suit coat folded limply over his arm. Ulan moved slightly to the left of the pyramid's base to distance himself from the kid's comments.

"Yeah—no matter what you think about. Get to the stillness," Fernando said. "No llores, senor."

"Come on. You can do it."

He focused on the kids and considered an escape route— retards telling him what to do.

Sonora must've sensed his predicament when she said, "Your mind will object. Your annoying thoughts will resist meditation. A mantra helps. When that happens, I want you to say *Baba Nam Kevalam* until you regain control." Ulan took another step further away from the group. "Say it. Let me hear you say the mantra," Sonora implored him.

Chest tingling, Ulan babbled, "Boom boom, baba boom boom."

"No, no, no," Everleigh said.

"Well, that was stupid to say, wasn't it?" Ulan said, feeling his face warm up from blushing.

In unison, the three students said, "Baba Nam Kevalam, Baba Nam Kevalam, Baba Nam Kevalam."

Ulan twisted up his lips, "Baba Nam Kevalam."

"Your mind is heavily invested in running your life, selling Affixa™, obeying Alex and Rhinehard, and not reading the contract. You are not your mind. Your mind is something you utilize, not the other way around," Sonora said. "Say the mantra when your thoughts intrude."

Fuck it. He could do it if they could. Sonora clasped his damaged hand, and Fernando laid his suit coat on a table next to a projection screen showing Earth from outer space. Ulan removed his ARGs. Everleigh and Lil Mac helped him fold his achy leg into a lotus position, his back relatively straight, gently molding his one good hand and his other crooked fingers such that his index fingers and thumbs touched at the tips, resting on his knees. "It's a mudra," Fernando said as if he was conveying a secret knowledge. "That means a gesture," he said, giggling. "That's worth fifty points," he said.

"It controls energy flow," Lil Mac added.

"You may not like what you begin to think about," Sonora said, patting his shoulder. "Meditation, particularly meditation under pyramids, will bring unprocessed issues to the surface."

"You've got to gut it out," Everleigh said.

"It works best when you close your eyes," Lil Mac said.

Eyes closed, Ulan listened to the waterfall, the soft music from Everleigh's discarded headphones and the silence. After several moments of thinking about Granny, he relaxed somewhat but was tempted to open his eyes and stand when his thought trolls began to appear. *Baba Nam Kevalam*, he whispered. Like a locomotive, they came: his cart retrieval job that he missed, *Baba Nam Kevalam*, his wife who'd abandoned him when he was fired, the home he lost, years living in a tent on the L.A. River embankment to which he never again returned, Tyrone Harris' last breath. *Baba Nam Kevalam, Baba Nam Kevalam.*

He trembled to recall the day he met Rhinehard and Alex, how so desperate for money he'd signed a contract that he hadn't bothered to read that, in effect, keeps him in servitude. There was the poop bag he detested, animals following him, and the bear repellent. *Baba Nam Kevalam, Baba Nam Kevalam, Baba Nam Kevalam.*

He revisited the first time he saw Sonora and came under her spell, a spell he'd never regret, *Baba Nam Kevalam,* and then there were the kids who, contrary to what he wanted to believe, are pretty much that, children transitioning from toy hovercrafts to the real thing, malleable, impressionable, fragile, more intelligent than they've been given credit for. All his thoughts and beliefs had controlled his actions, and he felt so uncomfortable that he wanted to jump up and run.

"Okay, Ulan," Sonora said. A whole hour later, the students had long gone to their classes when he again opened his eyes. The fountain water continued to flow, but the music had stopped. The thought trolls had been derailed and slowed for the moment. He fidgeted with the buttons on his designer shirt, eyes prickling. Sitting still had been tough for him, yet he felt more responsive. He reached out his stitched hand, and Sonora helped him. She passed him a glass of water that he slurped down.

Ulan's mind struggled. "This can't be happening," he said.

"It is, and you did, Ulan," Sonora said. "I'm proud of you. We do yoga too. I'm just saying—"

Ulan tipped his head back for a moment and closed his eyes.

"I appreciate your taking the time to see what we do for yourself, Ulan. Most people discount the young. Non-white students are especially denigrated and prepared for the trash heap." Sonora placed her hand on Ulan's shoulder, which caused his nature to rise. "One more thing. I have a ceremony that will protect you from life's adversities and weaken those attempting to transgress against you," she said.

She flung a purple amethyst embroidered mat to the floor and stuck a gold pin into a wooden side table that it covered. She looped Ulan's gold chain over his head over the pin. She then sprinkled water upon the area of operation in a triangular pattern, saying: *BOLOU, BOYE, BOCICE.* The Earth, as Astral Light, thus nourished, forged the magic chain that will produce the supernatural phenomenon. *Please protect me from the adversity,* she had Ulan say. "Repeat after me:

KY DYO,

ATRGBINIMONSE,

LEGBA,

AGOO DI PHA HWE."

"What is it? What does it mean," Ulan asked, slowly sliding from standing to sitting.

"Magic," Sonora said. "Voodoo magic."

To Ulan, it still sounded like mumbo jumbo. "How does it work?" he said.

"How does Affixa™ work?" she said.

"Voodoo's pseudoscience," he said.

"Yours is drug dealing," she said.

Ulan shrugged his shoulders.

"Everything is spirit. Humans are spirits who inhabit the visible world." He'd never considered himself a drug pusher, much less a *spirit.* "You should visit the encampment with me," she said.

"Uh—you're so much better with the blessings bags," he said, stomach roiling. He searched his coat for the poop bag. "Where's your bathroom?"

Alex caught up with Ulan as he returned across the campus, carrying the poop bag, sweating in the swelter, yet limping noticeably less.

"What took you so damn long?" Alex asked, rubbing its hands together so fast they could catch fire. "I couldn't surveil you in there. What's up with that shit, my nigga?"

Ulan allowed silence to fester between them. Sonora had told him he could master, unravel, and root out annoying thought patterns by seeing them. Finally, he said to Alex, "I'm just tired. Baba Nam Kevalam." Ulan hummed. "Show me to the math and music teachers," he said, and Alex complied.

Between classes, the math teacher sat in the dark classroom. "How many?" Ulan asked her.

"Two," she said.

"Six hundred bitcoins," he said.

And that was that.

Ulan hummed more. How good of a teacher was double-barrel toting Barbarella?

On their way to the next stop, passing Sergeant Bot on hall patrol, Alex said, "That was fucking easy, my nigga. Ca-ching, ca-ching. We can clean up here."

Everleigh sat in the front row of music class; a talking drum planted between her legs. Fernando and Lil Mac were directly behind her. Having gestured Alex and Ulan outside, the music teacher said, "I want three pops of Affixa™ and a pinch of chronic. I have a doctor's prescription for both."

"You don't need that for Affixa™ today," Alex said. "But we don't do chronic, dude."

"HEY, what's that shit?" Sergeant Bot said, appearing out of nowhere. "This campus is drug-free, like I told you niggas before."

The three returned to the classroom to complete their transaction, and the music teacher locked the door behind them.

CRASH, the door busted off its hinges. Sergeant Bot leaped toward Everleigh. "You must be involved," it said.

"I'm a scholar, not a suspect," she said. Once again, it muscled her around like a marionette.

An alarm for the active shooter drill sounded.

"SHOOTER," shouted someone inside the classroom. "It has a gun!" Fernando and Lil Mac jumped up and rushed Sergeant Bot, pinning its legs and arms against the wall, causing it to release Everleigh. The other students all looked stunned and didn't move. The music teacher hid under his desk, Alex buzzed to the ceiling, and Ulan threw his poop bag at the bot. Fists up, he stepped toward it, ready to scuffle. BANG, BANG. Two explosions from the teacher's grenade launcher blew the bot's head and chest apart.

"I'm okay," Everleigh said, dusting off plastic fragments and pointing the way. The other students followed her to safety, to the one bungalow protected by a vévé, Sonora's oum'phor.

"Let's get the fuck up outta here, my nigga," Alex said.

$$$$$$$

Ulan was back on the gold-plated toilet seat, using face recognition to unlock his virtual screen, swiping through it and ordering aloe vera succulents for delivery to Sonora, browsing cyberspace for copper pyramid brands, researching amethyst mats like the one Sonora had moved to perform her Voodoo protection ceremony for him, thinking he'd practice meditating to improve his dosha after the crazy school stuff. Alex alighted on his thigh to plug into Ulan's Gastro-Homie to monitor texture and shit potency.

Ulan pressed a button, and Sonora's plants were on their way to Lee High. His second and third button presses were for a copper pyramid and a TourmaPro mat that, according to his research, offered PEMF therapy to manage his leg pain and fix his injured hand.

A few beats later, his video doorbell showed an Amazon.com drone bot holding a clutch of packages in each of four appendages. Five minutes later, the pyramid was assembled next to his cherry wood-topped desk, towering over his wispy five feet eleven-inch frame, an orgonite orb dangling from the triangle's apex, the amethyst mat spread beneath it.

After a few more minutes, Ulan's legs began to pin and needle on the toilet seat to which he'd returned.

"Something's amiss," Alex said. "The texture's nice and smooth, volume and size hold up, but the chemical composition seems askew." It rubbed its hands together, seemingly nervous. "I'll send the results to the lab for further analysis."

Since he'd visited Sonora's oum'phor, Ulan had noticed his giddier step, more flexibility in his deformed hand, and his calmer mindset when he said the mantra that helped him flush out his thought trolls.

"It's probably nothing," he said to Alex while gazing out of his high-rise window at heavy aerial and road traffic below, vaguely making out the Compton Court through the thick nebulous smog and gray cosmic dust from earth warming and breaches in the magnetosphere, looking next toward the unsheltered encampment along the L.A. River, recollecting that it'd been years since the last substantial rainfall, knowing that if it ever rained enough to flood, thousands parked on the river bed and housed in confluent tunnels would no doubt drown on their way to the Pacific Ocean, knowing too that he had an obligation to return, with Sonora, bringing with him adjuncts to her blessing bags, perhaps tiny wooden houses to replace decrepit cardboard and tent shanties, water, and portable potties, showers, hand-washing stations from Love Beyond Walls, Papa John's, hopefully convincing med bots to transform their Smart Pods into mobile health clinics, him delivering trash cans, dumpsters and scheduling regular pickups, and giving cop bots the option to personally offer homeless people foot washing services and internal and external protection or keep the fuck out. It might only be the tip of the problem-solving iceberg, but it would be something he could do at Sonora's side.

Seated on the amethyst mat under the copper pyramid, Ulan glimpsed cumulus clouds outside, which looked dystopian when combined with everyday grime. He closed his eyes, his index and thumbs meeting and resting on his knees, legs crossed in the lotus position, tuning out piped-in white noise. He chanted *Baba Nam Kevelam* to control his thoughts of Tyrone Harris, of scavenger animals and poop bags, of fucked up principals and teachers armed with an array of weaponry and running schools like prisons. His leg pain decreased, and his thought trolls were nearly eliminated when Rhinehard's scaly voice jarred open his eyes.

"WAKE UP, YOU—you one-check-from-homeless sonofabitch." Rhinehard sat on Ulan's desk, feet dangling off its side, his alligator boot heels alternately kicking and scuffing the fine cherry wood grain, *ka boomft, ka boofmt, ka boomft,* his expensive watch glistening under the late afternoon sun slanting through partially shaded, soundproof, bi-fold windows leading to the balcony, his head down, thumbing through the spiral bound contract from Ulan's inbox.

"It's all over the news," Rhinehard said. "Did you boys have anything to do with the bot killers at Lee High?" Spittle built up in the corners of his mouth. He turned the contract toward Ulan and pointed. "It's right here clear as day—NO SCHOOLS—stay one thousand feet away. Didn't you read it? It's in a book, so maybe you people didn't. Typical."

Alex began to fly erratically. "I tried to tell him," it said.

Ulan hummed the words to the song granny had taught him, remembering as a little boy how his mother stole off all alone, him wondering what his mother was doing, how he found her praying one morning.

"FOOLS—trying to get me sued into bankruptcy." He pointed to another contract clause. "I own your ass, Ulan. I own the shit that comes out of it too. Everything here is mine," he laughed with an edge and gestured around the huge studio apartment. "I should have left your black ass in that homeless camp. I'm confining you to these quarters. If you leave, I'll have you arrested for contract breach." His lips curled, and his face turned red. "Read this shit," he said, flinging the contract to Ulan. "Read it aloud so that I know that you get my drift, NIGGA," he said with an ugly twist to his mouth.

His gut hard, Ulan began to read the contract's words aloud. *The term of the Contract shall commence on July 7, 2037, and end on the Expiration Date decided by Pharma-Brothers Pharmaceutical Company, subject to the other provisions of the Contract. This agreement is between PharmaBrothers and Ulan Mohammed, aka Contractor...*

"I told you not to go. Remember that Ulan? I told you to leave that witch Sonora alone," Alex said. He buzzed near Rhinehard's ear. "There's something else, sir."

Ulan continued to read: *It shall be understood and agreed that any feces quantities listed in the Contract are estimated only and may be increased or decreased per the requirements of PharmaBrothers Pharmaceutical Company...*

As he read, he noticed that the words in the contract had disappeared after reading them. *The Contractor warrants that all feces furnished and all services performed by the Contractor, its agents, and subcontractors shall be free and clear of any defects in quality and quantity...*

Rhinehard's expression turned even more severe and stony. "What is it, traitor?" he said to Alex.

Alex landed on the desk at Rhinehard's side. Rubbing its

hands excitedly, it said, "Lab results show that Ulan' shit is losing affinity."

"Spell that out for me, man."

"It doesn't bind well to receptors like before." Alex gave what almost looked like a smile on its otherwise static face. "It's losing effectiveness."

"No way," Ulan said. Of course, Rhinehard was right about owning everything, which allowed Ulan to save his Bitcoins and keep lots of Affixa™. His purchases, lunch with Sonora, pyramid purchases, and expensive clothes were all expensed to PharmaBrothers. But in Ulan's mind, Rhinehard had *Nigger-Disorder* that was characterized by feelings of entitlement privilege, at odds with reality, an irreconcilable emotional duality with permanent paranoia at its nexus, a mental dissonance like when the founding fathers created beautiful constitutional words such as *all men are created equal* even when they possessed enslaved labor, eventually designing a system to support dysfunction for hundreds of years, a system that helped create demand for drugs like Affixa™. "I'm feeling better than ever," Ulan said.

Once he finished reading, Ulan returned the wordless contract to Rhinehard, who sat entirely still before he uttered, "It can't be possible. I don't understand." He slammed the spiral-bound blank pages to the cherry wood-topped desk, crushing Alex. His contract agreement was void.

Ulan threw up his palms and covered his face when Rhinehard leaned forward and threw the blank contract at him. He was at a crossroads. Like he'd seen Sonora do with the feral cat and the wait bot, he closed his eyes, which swelled like a kitchen sponge, and bared his teeth, eyes burning red when he reopened them. Smelling of burnt rubber, Rhinehard fell into a catatonic state with his arm raised, mouth gaping, eyes bulging, exposed wires popping from his neck where a jugular vein may have been on humans, it repeatedly saying, *my nigga, my nigga, my nigga.*

Ulan settled back onto the TourmaPro mat under the pyramid with white background noise, the orgonite orb spinning at its apex. He closed his eyes, chanting *Baba Nam Kevelam*, forcing Rhinehard, Alex, and the blank contract from his mind, his leg pain decreasing, his index fingers and thumbs meeting, resting on his knees, his damaged hand feeling fully formed. *Baba Nam Kevelam. Baba Nam Kevelam. Baba Nam Kevelam. Sonora, Sonora, Sonora, Sonora, Sonora, Sonora, Sonora, Sonora, Sonora, Sonora, Sonora, Sonora, Sonora, Sonora.* SONORA.

ACKNOWLEDGMENTS

Perceptions Magazine (*Pregnancy Test*)

Stories Through the Ages Baby Boomers Plus 2018 (*Longest Journey*)

Unlikely Stories (*Otis Elevates*)

The Fear of Monkeys (*Job Collateral Lies Dead on Compton Creek*)

Watermelanin Magazine (*Drum Circle*)

Moon Magazine (*Weed Killers*)

Smoky Blue Literary and Arts Magazine (*Leland O. Dunwitty's Square Circle Edumacation*)

The Hamilton Stone Review (*Otis Discovers Mysteree's Secret*)

Tulip Tree Review (*Bruised*)

The Bombay Review (*Dump City*)

Oyster River Pages (*Professor Roach*)

Pennsylvania English (*Vegan Whole*)

Prime Number Magazine Award for Short Fiction finalist (*Don't Worry*)

Green Hills Literary Lantern (*Afixa*™)

Switchgrass Review (Don't Worry: I Got You)

The author expresses his gratitude for the help in creating this book:

UCLA Extension Writer's Program
CSULB Journalism

AC Bilbrew Writers Group
The Saturday Morning Literary Group
2018 PEN America Emerging Voices Fellowship
Tertulia Literary Salon
Writer's Relief

His collection *Crooked Out of Compton* is a semi-finalist for the Chestnutt Review Stubborn Artists Contest and a finalist for the Black Lawrence Press 2020 Big Moose Prize. His short story "Don't Worry" was a finalist in the 2021 Prime Number Magazine Award for Short Fiction. "Bruised" is a Tulip Tree Merit Prize winner.

ABOUT RIZE PRESS

Running Wild Press publishes stories that cross genres with great stories and writing. RIZE publishes great genre stories written by people of color and by authors who identify with other marginalized groups. Our team consists of:

Lisa Diane Kastner, Founder and Executive Editor
Cody Sisco, Acquisitions Editor, RIZE
Benjamin White, Acquisition Editor, Running Wild
Peter A. Wright, Acquisition Editor, Running Wild
Resa Alboher, Editor
Angela Andrews, Editor
Sandra Bush, Editor
Ashley Crantas, Editor
Rebecca Dimyan, Editor
Abigail Efird, Editor
Aimee Hardy, Editor
Henry L. Herz, Editor
Cecilia Kennedy, Editor
Barbara Lockwood, Editor

Scott Schultz, Editor

Evangeline Estropia, Product Manager
Kimberly Ligutan, Product Manager
Lara Macione, Marketing Director
Joelle Mitchell, Licensing and Strategy Lead
Pulp Art Studios, Cover Design
Standout Books, Interior Design
Polgarus Studios, Interior Design

Learn more about us and our stories at www.runningwildpress.com

Loved these stories and want more? Follow us at
www.runningwildpress.com, www.facebook.com/running wildpress,
on Twitter @lisadkastner @RunWildBooks @RIZERWP